THE
MALTA
EXCHANGE

ALSO BY STEVE BERRY

COTTON MALONE NOVELS

The Bishop's Pawn
The Lost Order
The 14th Colony
The Patriot Threat
The Lincoln Myth
The King's Deception
The Jefferson Key
The Emperor's Tomb
The Paris Vendetta
The Charlemagne Pursuit
The Venetian Betrayal
The Alexandria Link
The Templar Legacy

STAND-ALONE NOVELS

The Columbus Affair
The Third Secret
The Romanov Prophecy
The Amber Room

THE
MALTA
EXCHANGE

STEVE
BERRY

MINOTAUR BOOKS
NEW YORK

THE MALTA EXCHANGE. Copyright © 2019 by Steve Berry. All rights reserved. Printed in the United States of America. For information, address St. Martin's Press, 175 Fifth Avenue, New York, N.Y. 10010.

www.minotaurbooks.com

Library of Congress Cataloging-in-Publication Data

Names: Berry, Steve, 1955– author.
Title: The Malta exchange : a novel / Steve Berry.
Description: First edition. | New York : Minotaur Books, 2019.
Identifiers: LCCN 2018050884 | ISBN 9781250140265 (hardcover) |
    ISBN 9781250225658 (international, sold outside the U.S., subject to rights
    availability) | ISBN 9781250232564 (signed edition) | ISBN 9781250140272 (ebook)
Subjects: | GSAFD: Suspense fiction.
Classification: LCC PS3602.E764 M35 2019 | DDC 813/.6—dc23
LC record available at https://lccn.loc.gov/2018050884

First Edition: March 2019

10 9 8 7 6 5 4 3 2 1

For Elizabeth,
My wife,
My always

ACKNOWLEDGMENTS

Again, my sincere thanks to John Sargent, head of Macmillan, and Sally Richardson, who always has nothing but kind words. Then there's Jen Enderlin, who captains St. Martin's, and my publisher at Minotaur, Andrew Martin. Also, a huge debt of gratitude continues for Hector DeJean in Publicity; Jeff Dodes and everyone in Marketing and Sales, especially Paul Hochman; Anne Marie Tallberg, the sage of all things paperback; David Rotstein, who produced the cover; and Mary Beth Roche and her innovative folks in Audio.

As always, a bow to Simon Lipskar, my agent and friend, and to my editor, Kelley Ragland, and her assistant, Maggie Callan, both of whom are wonderful.

A few extra mentions: Meryl Moss and her extraordinary publicity team (especially Deb Zipf and JeriAnn Geller); Jessica Johns and Esther Garver, who continue to keep Steve Berry Enterprises running smoothly; and Rachel Maurizio, guide extraordinaire in Malta.

Ten years ago I dedicated *The Venetian Betrayal* to my new bride, Elizabeth. She was then a novice to writing and publishing, but a fast study, evolving into a first-rate editor with a keen eye for craft and story. She's now half owner (with the incomparable M. J. Rose) of 1001 Dark Nights, a publishing and marketing company focused on the romance genre. She is also executive director of International Thriller Writers, an organization of over four thousand members, 80 percent of whom are working thriller writers.

So this book is for Elizabeth, an extraordinary woman who has not only made my stories better, but made my life better, too.

It is not necessary to believe in God to be a good person.
In a way, the traditional notion of God is outdated.
One can be spiritual, but not religious.

It is not necessary to go to church and give money.
For many, nature can be a church.

Some of the best people in history did not believe in God,
while some of the worst deeds were done in his name.

—POPE FRANCIS I

PROLOGUE

SATURDAY, APRIL 28, 1945
LAKE COMO, ITALY
3:30 P.M.

BENITO AMILCARE ANDREA MUSSOLINI KNEW FATE WAS ABOUT TO
overtake him. He'd known that from the moment, yesterday, when partisans of the 52nd Garibaldi Brigade blocked his route north and halted the
German convoy that had been aiding his escape toward Switzerland. The
column's Wehrmacht commander had made no secret of the fact that he
was tired of fighting and intended on avoiding the advancing American
troops with an uneventful journey back to the Third Reich. Which explained how a downed tree and thirty ragtag partisans captured three
hundred fully armed German regulars.

For twenty-one years he'd ruled Italy, but when the Allies took Sicily,
then invaded the mainland, his fascist associates and King Victor Emmanuel III seized the opportunity to strip him of power. It took Hitler to
rescue him from prison, then install him as head of the Italian Social Republic, headquartered in Milan. Nothing more than a German puppet
regime—a way to maintain the illusion of power. But that was gone now,
too. The Allies had stormed northward taking Milan, which had forced
him to flee farther north to Lake Como and the Swiss border, only a few
kilometers away.

"It is a calm day," Clara said to him.

There'd been countless women in his life. His wife tolerated the mistresses because divorce was not an option. Mainly on religious grounds, but what would being the ex-wife of Il Duce do for her?

Not much.

But of all his dalliances, Claretta Petacci held a special place. Twenty-eight years separated them in age, but somehow she understood him. Never questioning. Never doubting. Always loving. She'd come to Como of her own accord to join him in exile.

But fate was working against them.

The Russians were shelling Berlin, the Brits and Americans racing through Germany unchallenged, the Third Reich in ruins. Hitler cowered in a bunker beneath the rubble of his capital city. The Rome–Berlin Axis had collapsed. The godforsaken war, which should never have been fought in the first place, was drawing to an end.

And they'd lost.

Clara stood at the open window, wrapped in her own thoughts. The view from their lofty perch was of the far-off lake and the mountains on the other side. They'd spent the night in this humble house, their room adorned with a plain bed, a couple of chairs, and a stone floor. No fire burned in the hearth, the only light provided by a bare bulb that shone starkly against the whitewashed walls. His life had been, for a long time, a cascade of luxury and indulgence. So he'd found it ironic that he and Clara—who once sought solace in each other's arms amid the opulence of the Palazzo Venezia—had found themselves in the bed of a peasant's cottage amid the lonely Italian hills.

He stepped over to the window to stand beside her. Dust lay thick on the sill. She held his hand as though he were a child.

"Seven years ago," he said in Italian, "I was an interesting person. Now I am little more than a corpse."

His voice seemed doom-laden and apathetic.

"You're still important," she declared.

He managed a weak smile. "I'm finished. My star has fallen. I have no fight left in me."

Of late he'd stayed more and more angry, belligerent, and uncharacteristically indecisive. Only here and there had his magisterial rage emerged. No one cared anymore what he did, what he thought, or what he said.

Save for Clara.

The cloudy afternoon loomed clammy, the air filled with the sound of distant gunfire. The damn rebels were turning the countryside into a shooting range, flushing out every element of fascism. Below he caught sight of a car winding its way up the narrow road from Azzano. He and Clara had been brought here to the house in the wee hours of the morning. Why? He did not know. But two bearded partisans, wearing peaked caps with a red star and toting machine guns, had stood close guard ever since.

As if they were waiting for something.

"You should not have come," he said to her.

She squeezed his hand. "My place is with you."

He admired her loyalty and wished his Black Shirts possessed just a tiny percentage of it. The drop to the ground from the window was about five meters. But he imagined himself standing much higher, on the balcony at the Palazzo Venezia, in 1936, extolling Italy's grand victory in Abyssinia. Four hundred thousand people had thronged the piazza that day, their reaction wild, ceaseless, and hypnotic. *Duce, Duce, Duce,* they'd screamed, and he'd breathed in the warmth of their mass hysteria.

What a tonic.

But so little of Caesar remained inside him.

He retained his trademark bald head and paunch stomach, but his eyes had yellowed and seemed more and more haunted. He wore his uniform. Black shirt, gray tunic, breeches with red stripes down the sides, jackboots, and a plain gray forage cap. Yesterday, before he'd been taken by the partisans, he'd donned the greatcoat and helmet of a German private in a foolish attempt to hide.

That had been a mistake.

It showed fear.

Some called him a buffoon, others *an adventurer in power politics* or *a gambler in a high stakes game bathed in the past.* Europeans had proclaimed him *the man who made the trains run on time.*

But he was merely Il Duce.

The Leader.

The youngest man ever to rule Italy.

"I await the end of this tragedy," he said. "Strangely detached from everything. I don't feel any more an actor. I'm more the last of the spectators."

Some of that depression he'd felt of late crept back over him and he fought hard to quell its spread.

Now was not the time for self-pity.

The car kept groaning up the steep switchbacks through heavy stands of cedar and fir, its engine growing louder as it approached the house.

He was tired, his face pale, and he needed a shave. He was also unusually untidy, his uniform wrinkled and unkempt. Even worse, he felt at the mercy of events. In a state of panic and flight.

No longer in control.

The car came to a stop below.

A man emerged from the driver's side wearing the pale blue uniform of a Luftwaffe captain, the brown of his collar tabs identifying him as part of the communications corps. Since yesterday only the disheveled, disorganized chaos of the partisans had surrounded him. He'd witnessed their lack of authority at the Dongo city hall, where he'd first been taken, none of his inquisitors really knowing what to do with him. He'd sat in a room thick with talk and nicotine and listened to Milan Radio proclaim an end to fascism, and that every member of the government should be detained.

Imbeciles. All of them.

But they paled in comparison with the Germans.

He'd delayed entering into a pact with Germany for as long as he could. Hitler was a brute, *Mein Kampf* gibberish. He both disliked and distrusted the crazed Austrian. But ultimately public opinion became too strong to ignore and, in 1940, he'd finally succumbed to war.

A horrible error.

To hell with those Aryan bastards. He never wanted to see one of their uniforms again.

Yet here was another.

The uniform entered the house and climbed the stairs to the second floor. He and Clara stayed by the window, but they turned as the bedroom door opened and the uniform entered. He waited for the man to click his heels and offer a salute. But no sign of respect was shown. Instead the newcomer calmly said in Italian, "I wish to speak with you. Alone."

The visitor was a tall, thin man with a long face, large ears, and a sallow complexion. His black hair was slicked back and a clipped mustache brushed a tight-lipped mouth. Mussolini mentally sorted through all of the desperate elements of the situation, looking for options. For the past two decades no one would have dared rebuke him like this. To be feared authority must be absolute, with no boundaries. So his first inclination was to tell this newcomer to get out, but the vacuum of uncertainty that surrounded him overcame his pride.

"Wait outside," he said to Clara.

She hesitated and started to protest but he silenced her with a raise of his hand. She did not object any further and simply nodded, leaving the room.

The uniform closed the door behind her.

"Time is short," the man said. "The Committee of National Liberation and the Volunteer Freedom Corps are coming for you."

Both were trouble, the latter especially since it mainly comprised communists who had long wanted Italy for themselves.

"The decision has been made for you to be shot. I've managed to get ahead of their emissaries, but they are not far behind."

"All thanks to your fellow Germans, who abandoned me."

The man stuffed his right hand into his coat pocket and removed an object.

A ring.

He slipped it onto his left third finger and displayed the face, which contained five rows of letters etched into the dull, pewter surface.

SATOR
AREPO
TENET
OPERA
ROTAS

Now he understood.

This was no ordinary visitor.

He'd dealt with two popes during his time as supreme leader, Pius XI and XII. One was more accommodating than the other, both irritating. Unfortunately, to govern Italy meant having the Catholic Church on your side, which was no small feat. But he'd managed to contain the church, forming an uneasy alliance, one that was also now coming to an end.

"I'm sure this ring is familiar to you," the man said. "It is just like the one you stole from the man you had killed."

More clarity arrived.

After founding a hospital on the frontier of Christendom dedicated to St. John the Baptist in 1070, a small group of Europeans became the Hospitaller Brothers of St. John's of Jerusalem. Their current label, after over 850 years of evolution, was obscenely long.

Sovereign Military Hospitallers Order of St. John of Jerusalem, of Rhodes, and of Malta.

Talk about vanity.

"I speak for His Most Eminent Highness, the prince and grand master himself," the uniform said. "Who asks you once again to relinquish what you possess."

"Are you actually a German officer?" he asked.

The man nodded. "But I was a knight of the order long before there was anything called the Third Reich."

He smiled.

Finally, the shroud had dropped.

This man was nothing more than a spy, which explained why his enemies had allowed this envoy to come.

"You say people are on the way for me. To the partisans I matter not. To the Germans I'm an embarrassment. Only to the communists does my death have value. So tell me, what can *you* offer to deny them their pleasure?"

"Your tricks yesterday failed."

He was sorry to hear that.

He'd first fled Milan to Como, following the narrow, winding road hugging the lakeshore, motoring through dozens of tiny villages hunched beside the still water. Cernobbio, Moltrasio, Tremezzo, Menaggio. Usually it was an easy half-day journey, but it had taken much longer. He'd expected five thousand Black Shirts to be waiting for him. His soldiers. But only twelve had shown. Then a German convoy of thirty-eight lorries and three hundred battle-hardened soldiers appeared, moving north for Austria, so he'd forced his way into the caravan hoping to make it to Chiavenna, where he planned to split off and head toward Switzerland.

But he'd never made it that far.

The bastard Germans sold him out in return for safe passage.

Thankfully, he'd brought along some insurance. Gold and jewels from the Italian treasury, along with stacks of currency and two satchels loaded with important papers, dossiers, and correspondence.

"The partisans have some of your gold," the man said. "But most of it was tossed into the lake by the Germans. Your two briefcases, though, have vanished. Is what I want in one of them?"

"Why would I tell you that?"

"Because I can save your miserable life."

He could not deny that he would like to live. But even more important, "And Clara?"

"I can save her, too."

He stretched his arms behind his back and thrust out his jaw in a familiar and comfortable angle. He then paced the floor, the soles of his boots scuffing off the gritty stone. For the first time in a long while, strength surged through his bones.

"The illustrious order will never perish," he said. *"It is like virtue itself, like faith.* Is that correct?"

"It is. The Comte de Marcellus gave an elegant speech in the French Chamber of Deputies."

"As I recall he was trying to obtain the return of a large tract of land that the Crown had seized from the knights. He failed, but he did manage to obtain a decree of sovereignty. One that made the Hospitallers their own nation within France."

"And we have not perished," the man said.

"Much to my good fortune." He glared at his visitor. "Get me away from these partisans and we can talk about the *Nostra Trinità.*"

The man shook his head. "Perhaps you haven't gleaned the gravity of your situation. You're a doomed man trying to flee for your life with every lire and ounce of gold you could steal." He paused. "Unfortunately, that effort failed. They are coming to kill you. I'm your only hope. You have nothing to bargain with, besides giving me exactly what I want."

"In those two satchels you mentioned, I have correspondence the British will not want public."

The man shrugged. "That's a problem for them."

"Imagine what the knights might do with such incriminating information."

"We have excellent relations with London. I only want the ring and the documents you stole."

"The ring? It's but a chunk of metal."

The uniform held his hand up. "It's much more than that to us."

He shook his head. "You knights are nothing but pariahs. Thrown from Jerusalem, Cyprus, Rhodes, Russia, Malta, now you huddle in two palazzi in Rome clinging to a glory that has long since vanished."

"Then we have something in common."

He grinned. "That we do."

Past the open window he heard the grind of another engine.

His visitor noticed, too.

"They're here," the man said.

A sudden resolve came over him, bolstered by the fact that Holy Roman Emperors, Napoleon, even Hitler himself had all been denied what he'd accomplished.

Defeating the pope.

This man being here was concrete proof of his victory.

"Ask Pius XII what it felt like to kneel before me," he said.

"I doubt that happened."

"Not literally. But figuratively, he knelt. He knew what I could do to his precious church. What I still can do."

Which explained why the Vatican had never outwardly opposed his grab for power. Even after he'd attained total control, the church had continued to stay silent, never once using its massive influence to rally the Italian people into revolt. No king, queen, or emperor had ever been so fortunate.

He pointed at the man's ring. "Like you, I take my strength from Constantine the Great. Only he and I succeeded where all others failed."

The car outside arrived, and he heard doors slam shut as people emerged.

"Tell your grand master that he will regret not saving me," he said.

"You're a fool."

He stiffened his back. "I am Il Duce."

The man in the German uniform seemed unfazed, only shaking his head and saying, "Goodbye, great leader."

And the emissary left.

He continued to stand tall and straight, facing the open doorway. How many times had he sent men to their deaths? Thousands? More like tens of thousands. Now he understood how helpless they felt at the moment of their demise.

Footsteps pounded up the stairs.

A new man entered the room—wiry, black-eyed, black-tempered—holding a machine gun. "I have come to set you free."

He did not believe a word, but played along, "How fortunate."

"We must go. Now."

Clara appeared, entering the room and stepping toward the bed, searching the covers.

"What are you looking for?" the man asked.

"My knickers."

"Never mind them. There's no time. We must go."

Mussolini gently grasped her arm and motioned for them to leave. Was she aware of what was about to happen? He doubted it since, as always, she seemed more concerned with him than herself.

They descended to ground level, left the house, and climbed into the rear seat of a tattered Fiat. A driver was already behind the wheel, and the man with the machine gun did not get in. Instead he stood outside, on the right-hand running board, pointing his weapon inside.

The car ground slowly down the steep road toward the village. Behind, on foot, came the two guards from last night. They all rounded a hairpin turn at a walking pace, but the Fiat picked up speed as it straightened out, the tires hissing on the damp road. The man perched outside ordered the vehicle to stop directly opposite an iron gateway, which formed a recess in the narrow inclined road about five meters wide and two meters deep. The gates blocked a driveway and hung between two large concrete posts, the extending walls about waist-high, curved inward, and topped with bushes.

The man with the machine gun sprang off the running board and opened the car doors. The driver emerged. More orders were yelled and the two other armed men took up positions, one above, the other below on the road. Trees and a sharp bend kept everything out of sight from the houses down in Azzano.

"Get out" came the command.

An agonized look formed on Clara's face, her eyes darting about like a frightened bird's.

Mussolini exited.

She followed.

"Over there," the man said as he waved the muzzle of his gun toward the iron gateway.

Mussolini marched straight to the wall and stood against it. Clara came and stood at his side. He would not make the same mistake as yesterday. He would not be afraid. When they recounted what was about to happen, they would have to lie to make him a coward.

"Benito Mussolini, you are a war criminal. A sentence of death has been proclaimed as justice for the Italian people."

"No. You can't," Clara screamed. "You can't do that."

She hugged his arm.

"Move away from him," the man shouted. "Get away or you will die, too."

She did not flee and the man pressed the trigger.

But nothing happened.

The assailant rattled the bolt and tried to free the jam. Clara screamed and leaped forward grabbing the barrel of the machine gun with both hands.

"You can't kill us like this," she shrieked.

"Bring me your gun," the man hollered.

One of the other two guards ran over and tossed a weapon. Their assassin released his grip on the gun Clara held and caught the offering.

Mussolini realized this was his moment.

Energy filled him.

He made no move to run or defy.

Instead he swept back his jacket with both hands, thrusting his chest forward like the jutting bow of a ship. Past the three men who'd come to murder him he saw the knight in the German uniform walking down the road. Casual. No hurry. Unmolested by the other three. The uniform stopped and stared at the scene. Good. Let him watch.

"Magnus ab integro saeclorum nascitur ordo," Mussolini called out.

He doubted any of these fools spoke Latin.

Only the knight would understand.

The great order of the ages is born afresh.

The machine gun erupted.

Clara was hit first and dropped to the ground. His heart broke to see her die. More rounds came his way. Three thudded into his midsection. Four more found his legs. His knees buckled and he dropped to a sitting position.

His eyes stared across at the knight, and he summoned what little strength was left inside him to say, "This . . . is not . . . over."

Blood spewed out his mouth.

His left shoulder dipped and he slumped to the wet cobbles. He stared up at the cloudy sky, still alive. The smell of cordite hung heavy in the moist air. One of the guards stood over him, the barrel of the weapon aimed down.

He focused on the black dot.

Like a period at the end of a sentence.

The gun fired.

PRESENT DAY

CHAPTER ONE

Tuesday, May 9
Lake Como, Italy
8:40 a.m.

Cotton Malone studied the execution site.

A little after 4:00 p.m., on the afternoon of April 28, 1945, Benito Mussolini and his mistress Claretta Petacci were gunned down just a few feet away from where he stood. In the decades since, the entrance to the Villa Belmonte, beside a narrow road that rose steeply from Azzano about half a mile below, had evolved into a shrine. The iron gate, the low wall, even the clipped hedges were still there, the only change from then being a wooden cross tacked to the stone on one side of the gate that denoted Mussolini's name and date of death. On the other side he saw another addition—a small, glass-fronted wooden box that displayed pictures of Mussolini and Claretta. A huge wreath of fresh flowers hung from the iron fence above the cross. Its banner read EGLI VIVRÀ PER SEMPRE NEL CUORE DEL SUO POPOLO.

He will always live in the hearts of people.

Down in the village he'd been told where to find the spot and that loyalists continued to venerate the site. Which was amazing, considering Mussolini's brutal reputation and the fact that so many decades had passed since his death.

What a quandary Mussolini had faced.

Italy languishing in a state of flux. The Germans fast retreating. Partisans flooding down from the hills. The Allies driving hard from the south, liberating town after town. Only the north, and Switzerland, had offered the possibility of a refuge.

Which never happened.

He stood in the cool of a lovely spring morning.

Yesterday, he'd taken an afternoon flight from Copenhagen to the Milan–Malpensa Airport, then driven a rented Alfa Romeo north to Lake Como. He'd splurged on the sports car, since who didn't like driving a 237-horsepowered engine that could go from zero to sixty in four seconds. He'd visited Como before, staying at the stunning Villa d'Este during an undercover mission years ago for the Magellan Billet. One of the finest hotels in the world. This time the accommodations would not be anywhere near as opulent.

He was on special assignment for British intelligence, working freelance, his target an Italian, a local antiques dealer who'd recently crept onto MI6's radar. Originally his job had been a simple buy and sell. Being in the rare-book business provided him with a certain expertise in negotiating for old and endangered writings. But new information obtained last night had zeroed in on a possible hiding place, so the task had been modified. If the information proved correct, his orders were now to steal the items.

He knew the drill.

Buying involved way too many trails and, until yesterday, had been MI6's only option. But if what they wanted could be appropriated without paying for it, then that was the smart play. Especially considering that what they were after did not belong to the Italian offering it for sale.

He had no illusions.

Twelve years with the Magellan Billet, and a few more after that working freelance for various intelligence agencies, had taught him many lessons. Here he knew he was being paid to handle a job *and* take the fall if anything went wrong. Which was incentive enough not to make any mistakes.

The whole thing, though, seemed intriguing.

In August 1945 Winston Churchill had arrived in Milan under the cover name of Colonel Warden. Supposedly he'd decided to vacation along the shores of Lakes Como, Garda, and Lugano. Not necessarily a bad decision since people had been coming to the crystal Alpine waters for centuries. The use of a code name ensured a measure of privacy, but by then Churchill was no longer Britain's prime minister, having been unceremoniously defeated at the polls.

His first stop was the cemetery in Milan where Mussolini had been hastily buried. He'd stood at the grave, hat in hand, for several minutes. Strange considering the deceased had been a brutal dictator and a war enemy. He'd then traveled north to Como, taking up residence at a lakeside villa. Over the next few weeks the locals spotted him out gardening, fishing, and painting. No one at the time gave it much thought, but decades later historians began to look hard at the journey. Of course, British intelligence had long known what Churchill was after.

Letters.

Between him and Mussolini.

They'd been lost at the time of Mussolini's capture, part of a cache of documents in two satchels that were never seen after April 27, 1945. Rumors were that the local partisans had confiscated them. Some say they were turned over to the communists. Others pointed to the Germans. One line of thought proclaimed that they had been buried in the garden of the villa Churchill had rented.

Nobody knew anything for sure.

But something in August 1945 had warranted the intervention of Winston Churchill himself.

Cotton climbed back into the Alfa Romeo and continued his drive up the steep road. The villa where Mussolini and his mistress had spent their last night still stood somewhere nearby. He'd read the many conflicting accounts of what had happened on that fateful Saturday. Details still eluded historians. In particular, the name of the executioner had been clouded by time. Several ultimately claimed the honor, but no one knew for sure who'd pulled the trigger. Even more mysterious was what had happened to the gold, jewels, currency, and documents Mussolini had intended to take to Switzerland. Most agree that a portion of the wealth had been dumped into the lake, as local fishermen later found gold there after the war. But as with the documents, no meaningful cache had ever come to light. Until two weeks ago, when an email arrived at the British embassy in Rome with an image of a scanned letter.

From Churchill to Mussolini.

More communications followed, along with four more images. No sale price had been arrived at for the five. Instead, Cotton was being paid 50,000 euros for the trip to Como, his negotiating abilities, and the safe return of all five letters.

The villa he was after sat high on a ridge, just off the road that continued on to the Swiss border about six miles away. All around him rose forests where partisans had hidden during the war, waging a relentless guerrilla campaign on both the fascists and the Germans. Their exploits were legendary, capped by the unexpected triumph in capturing Mussolini himself.

For Italy, World War II ended right here.

He found the villa, a modest three-story rectangle, its stone stained with mold and topped by a pitched slate roof set among tall trees. Its many windows caught the full glare of the early-morning sun, the yellow limestone seeming to drain of color as it basked in the bright light. Two white porcelain greyhounds flanked the main entrance. Cypress trees dotted a well-kept yard along with topiary, both of which seemed mandatory for houses around Lake Como.

He parked in front and climbed out to a deep quiet.

The foothills kept rising behind the villa where the road continued its twisted ascent. To the east, through more trees sprouting spring flecks of green, he caught the dark-blue stain of the lake, perhaps half a mile away and a quarter of that below. Boats moved silently back and forth across its mirrored surface. The air was noticeably cooler and, from the nearby garden, he caught a waft of wisteria.

He turned to the front door and came alert.

The thick wooden panel hung partially open.

White gravel crunched beneath his feet as he crossed the drive and stopped short of entering. He gave the door a little push and swung it open, staying on his side of the threshold. No electronic alarms went off inside. Nobody appeared. But he immediately spotted a body sprawled across the terrazzo, facedown, a crimson stain oozing from one side.

He carried no weapon. His intel had said that the house should be empty, its owner away until the late afternoon. MI6 had not only traced the emails it had received but also managed to compose a quick dossier on the potential seller. Nothing about him signaled a threat.

He entered and checked the body for a pulse.

None.

He looked around.

The rooms were pleasant and spacious, the papered walls ornamented with huge oil paintings, dark with age. Smells of musty flowers, candle wax, and tobacco floated in the air. He noticed a large walnut desk, rosewood melodeon, silk brocade sofas and chairs. Intricate inlaid armoires with glass fronts pressed the walls, one after the other, each loaded with objects on display like a museum.

But the place was in a shambles.

Drawers were half opened, tilted at crazy angles, shelves in disarray, a few of the armoires shattered, chairs flung upside down to the floor, some slashed and torn. Even some of the drapes had been pulled from their hangings and lay in crumpled heaps.

Somebody had been looking for something.

Nothing broke the silence save a parrot in a gilded cage that had once stood on a marble pedestal. Now the cage lay on the floor, battered and smashed, the pedestal overturned, the bird uttering loud, excited screeches.

He rolled the body over and noticed two bullet wounds. The victim was in his mid- to late forties, with dark hair and a clean-shaven face. The villa's owner was about the same age, but this corpse did not match the description he'd been given.

Something clattered.

Hard and loud.

From above.

Then heavy footsteps.

Somebody was still here.

The hiding place he sought was located on the third floor, so he headed for the staircase and climbed, passing the second-floor landing. A carpet runner lined the stone risers and cushioned his leather soles, allowing no sound to betray his movement. At the third floor he heard more commotion, like a heavy piece of furniture slamming the floor. Whoever was searching seemed oblivious to any interruption.

He decided on a quick peek to assess things.

He crept ahead.

A narrow green runner ran down the center of the corridor's wood floor. At the far end a half-opened window allowed in the morning sun and a breeze. He came to the room where the noise originated, the same room he'd been directed to find. Whoever had beaten him here was well informed. He stopped at the open doorway and risked a quick glance.

And saw a stout bear.

Several hundred pounds, at least.

The source of the crash was evident from an armoire that lay over-turned. The animal was exploring, swiping odds and ends off the tables, smelling everything as it clattered down. It stood facing away, toward one of the two half-open windows.

He needed to leave.

The bear stopped its foraging and raised its head, sniffing.

Not good.

The animal caught his scent, turned, and faced him, snorting a growl.

He had a split second to make a decision.

Normally you dealt with bears by standing your ground, facing them down. But that advice had clearly been offered by people who'd never been this close to one. Should he head back toward the stairs? Or dart into the room across the hall? One mistake on the way down to the ground floor and the bear would overtake him. He opted for the room across the hall and darted left, entering just as the animal rushed forward in a burst of speed surprising for its size. He slammed the door shut and stood in-side a small bedroom, a huge porcelain stove filling one corner. Two more windows, half open, lined the outer wall, which faced the back of the villa.

He needed a second to think.

But the bear had other ideas.

The door crashed inward.

He rushed to one of the windows and glanced out. The drop was a good thirty feet. That was at least a sprained ankle, maybe a broken bone or worse. The bear hesitated in the doorway, then roared.

Which sealed the deal.

He noticed a ledge just below the window, about eight inches wide. Enough to stand on. Out he went, flattening his hands against the warm stone, his spine pressed to the house. The bear charged the window, poking its head out, swiping a paw armed with sharp claws. He edged his way to the left and maneuvered himself out of range.

He doubted the animal was going to climb out.

But that didn't solve his problem.

What to do next.

CHAPTER TWO

THE KNIGHT LOWERED HIS BINOCULARS.

What a strange sight.

A man standing on a narrow cornice on the third story of a villa, with a bear roaring out a window, clawing at him.

He stood on a promontory about a quarter mile north of the villa, looking down through spring trees. He'd seen the Alfa Romeo driving up the road, a steady, precipitous, corkscrew climb, and took notice when it turned into the villa's drive. When he'd focused the binoculars on the driver who'd emerged he'd immediately noticed that it was the same man from Menaggio, the one asking questions around town yesterday evening. He'd managed, outside a café, a quick snap of a picture from his cell phone, and had been able to learn an identity.

Harold Earl "Cotton" Malone.

Formerly of the United States Justice Department, once attached to a special intelligence unit called the Magellan Billet. A naval commander, pilot, fighter-jet-qualified, with a law degree from Georgetown University. Malone worked at the Judge Advocate General's corps before being reassigned to the Justice Department, where he remained for a dozen years. Not yet fifty years old, he'd retired early and now owned a business. Cotton Malone, Bookseller, Højbro Plads, Copenhagen.

An intriguing change of careers.

Malone possessed a distinguished reputation as a competent intelligence operative, one who still occasionally offered his services out for hire. What he'd not been able to learn was exactly why this American of obvious skills and talent was here, in Italy, asking questions about things that only a few people in the world would know.

He turned from the chaotic scene below and stared at the villa's owner, hunched on the ground, wrists tied behind his back, ankles likewise restrained. A gag prevented the portly Italian from uttering a sound. An associate stood off to one side, keeping a watchful guard.

"You've proven to be quite a problem," he told his prisoner, who watched him with petrified eyes.

He'd arrived at the villa two hours ago. The groundskeeper had appeared without warning and his associate had shot him. He would have preferred no bloodshed, but it had been unavoidable. The villa's owner was already up for the day, dressed, about to leave. The idea had been to catch him before that happened. He'd asked the owner a few obligatory questions, hoping for cooperation, but no answers were forthcoming. Several more attempts at reason also failed, so he and his associate had brought the fat Italian up here, into the woods, still on the villa's grounds, where a measure of privacy among the trees offered an opportunity to make his point clear. As if two bullets into the groundskeeper had not been enough to impress the point.

He stepped over and crouched down, the musk of the cool morning filling his nostrils. "I imagine you now regret making that call to the British embassy in Rome."

A nod of the head.

"You just need to tell me where the letters are that you wanted to sell."

Supposedly, in 1945, after Mussolini was captured, the contents of two satchels found with him had been inventoried by Italian partisans. But no one seriously believed that any list created by them was accurate. He'd read their entries, which documented little to nothing of interest. Most likely that perfunctory effort had all been for show and the valuable stuff had never made it on the list in the first place. Nor had anything on the actual list ever surfaced in the years since.

And this Italian might hold the answer as to why.

"You're going to tell me all about those documents from Mussolini."

Of course the villa owner could not answer and he had no intention of removing the gag.

Not yet, at least.

He motioned and his associate grabbed a coil of rope lying in the leaves. High above stretched several stout limbs. He studied them, finally deciding on one about ten meters off the ground. It took his associate two attempts to toss one end of the coil over the limb. Then he dragged the villa's owner to the rope. He resisted, but with both hands and feet bound the effort proved futile. The Italian wiggled on the ground as his associate tied one end of the rope to the wrist bindings. With both hands his man then grabbed the end of the rope draping down from the limb and tightened the slack enough to tug on the Italian's arms.

Which telegraphed the whole idea.

Once hauled off the ground the man's arms would be extended upward from behind, at an angle that human joints were not meant to experience. The pain would be excruciating, the body's weight eventually dislocating the shoulders.

"You understand what I can do to you?" he asked.

The villa's owner gave a vigorous nod.

He reached beneath his jacket and found his revolver. "I'm going to remove the gag. If you call out, or even raise your voice, I'll shoot you in the face. Is that clear?"

The man nodded.

He freed the gag.

The man sucked in a series of deep, long breaths. He allowed him a moment, then gazed down and said, "The contents of Mussolini's two satchels have long been in dispute. So tell me, how did you come to acquire anything from them?"

The Italian hesitated, so he gestured and his associate tugged on the rope, which began to lift the man's arms up, his body rising from a squat and becoming more deadweight. So the Italian scrambled up to his feet.

"No. No. Stop. Please."

"Answer my question."

"My grandfather was there. In Dongo, when they found Il Duce. He helped sort out the papers from the satchels, and he kept some of them."

"Why?"

"He thought one day they could be sold."

"What did he do with them?"

"Nothing. He just kept them. My father had them next, then they came to me."

"How many documents do you have?"

"Fifty-five pages. All inside one of the original satchels, which he kept, too."

He fished his left hand into his pant pocket and removed the ring. "And did your grandfather find this, too?"

The Italian nodded.

It had galled him to see it in the villa, displayed inside one of the armoires as some curiosity.

He'd promptly liberated the sacred object.

"Do you have any idea what this is?" he asked, holding the ring's pewter face up for the man to see.

SATOR
AREPO
TENET
OPERA
ROTAS

No reply.

"Do these five words mean anything to you? Does the ring mean anything to you?"

He motioned for the rope to be tugged a couple of times.

"I have no idea," the man cried out, getting the message. "Only that it bears the Maltese cross inside. My grandfather told me it came from one of the satchels. That's why I have it. A memento."

Only a few people in the world knew the ring's true significance, and clearly this greedy soul was one of them.

A background check had revealed that this man had lived above Lake Como all of his life in a villa that his family had owned since the 17th century. It wasn't anything extravagant, similar to hundreds of others surrounding the lake. His prisoner dealt in antiques, usually buying from cash-strapped estates, but was not above stealing. No surprise that he was in possession of missing World War II documents.

He gestured and his associate tightened the rope more. The arms were about at their natural limit before the onslaught of excruciating pain, the man's feet still planted on the ground.

"A memento of what?" he asked, motioning with the ring.

"Il Duce. He had it with him. It bears the cross inside, but I don't know what it means."

"You never tried to find out."

A shake of the head. "Never."

He wondered whether to believe him.

"There are so many who still worship Mussolini," the owner said. "I know people who think he was a great man. My hope was that, one day, people like that would pay for mementos."

The Italian's breath was short, his voice fast and weak.

"And what do *you* think of the former great leader?"

"I care nothing for politics. None of that matters to me."

He pointed a finger. "I suppose only money is your god."

No reply.

"The British have no intention of buying your documents," he said. "It was foolish of you to contact them. They have a man, right now, inside your villa, surely there to steal them."

Fortunately, at the moment that operative was detained by some of the local wildlife.

"Where have you hidden the satchel containing those fifty-five pages of documents, including the letters you wanted to sell?"

"In the villa. On the third floor."

Finally, some cooperation.

He listened as the Italian described the hiding place.

"Ingenious," he said, when the explanation ended. "Is everything there?"

The man nodded. "All I have."

He wondered if Malone knew that information, too.

He gestured and his man relaxed the pressure on the rope, which allowed the arms to drop down.

The villa's owner sighed from relief.

"Why did you not display the letters?" he asked. "As you did the ring."

"My father told me that it might be risky. He said we should hold on to them quietly, until others were willing to pay."

"So why sell now?"

"I need money. I read an article in a magazine about Churchill and Mussolini that speculated about the letters. I decided, why speculate. I have them. So I called the British."

"What was to be your price?"

"Five million euros."

For the love of money is a root of all kinds of evils. It is through this craving that some have wandered away from the faith and pierced themselves with many pangs.

The Bible was right.

He hated greed.

Enough.

This endeavor had run its course.

He raised his arm and shot the owner in the head.

A sound suppressor at the end of the barrel made sure the round drew no attention. Just a pop that could not be heard beyond a few meters. This fool should have realized that the only bargaining chip he had was the hiding place. But fear stymied reason, and people always thought they could talk their way out of things.

"Do it," he said to his associate.

The body was hauled up, the dead man's arms wrenched hard backward. He heard a crack as the shoulders separated. Then the rope was tied around the trunk, the corpse dangling awkwardly in the air, as a reminder, just as had been done centuries ago.

Deuteronomy was right.

Vengeance is mine, and retribution. In due time their foot will slip. For the day of their calamity is near, and the impending things are hastening upon them.

He grabbed the binoculars and stepped back to where he could again see the villa below. The only disturbance came from the morning breeze hissing through the conifers, tugging at his clothes. His second problem was still perched on the third-floor ledge.

The bear was not in sight.

He lowered the binoculars.

That animal was about to be the least of Harold Earl "Cotton" Malone's concerns.

CHAPTER THREE

COTTON STOOD ROCK-STILL ON THE LEDGE. THE BEAR HAD disappeared back inside the villa, but he could hear the animal rustling around. There was a second open window, beyond the one from which he'd escaped, that offered an opportunity to flee his perch and go back inside. But that would mean passing by the bear's window, which did not seem like a good idea.

He strained his weight back on the balls of his feet, hands pressed tight to the wall, trying not to lose his balance. To his left, the tip of a gabled roof from a first-floor offshoot rose to a pitch. The jump down was about eight feet. He could make that. Since it seemed the only course available he sidestepped his way across the cornice, reaching a clawing hand around the corner and making the turn, keeping his body flat against the exterior wall.

He sucked in a few deep breaths.

Good thing Cassiopeia wasn't here. She hated heights as much as he hated enclosed spaces. He used thoughts of her to take his mind off his current predicament. He missed her. Their relationship was in a good place. They'd finally made peace with all of their demons. She was in France, working on her 13th-century castle reconstruction. They were scheduled to get together next week for a few days of fun in Nice. In the meantime he'd agreed to this supposed cakewalk of a job—an easy 50,000 euros—that had turned into anything but.

He stopped his creep along the edge above the gable.

The one thing he could not do was land directly on the ridge.

That would be life changing.

He jumped, angling for one of the sides, and his feet found hard slate. He had only a moment to secure a grip before he rebounded and slid off. His fingernails tore against the warm stone, then his hands caught on the ridge where he held on tight.

Releasing his grip, he scuttled down the slope of the slate toward guttering, his legs extended, using the soles of his shoes as brakes until he found the copper. The gutters squeaked in protest and shifted from his weight, but held. He lowered himself over the edge, clinging to it, wincing at every groan of protest the metal supports uttered. From there he dropped to the ground, landing in the grass near a copse of shrubbery.

Unfortunately, he had to go back inside the villa.

He could wait until the bear moved on, but that could take a while. The owner might return and find the body. The police would then be called and this would become a crime scene, preventing any attempt at finding those letters.

Now was the time, bear or no bear.

But he wasn't going to be foolish.

He hustled around to the front door. Earlier, he'd noticed a gun case in the ground-floor salon. He reentered the villa and heard the bear foraging upstairs. He found the case, which was locked. Eight rifles stood at attention inside. He grabbed a nearby chair and shattered the glass, removing one of the single-barreled shotguns. In a cabinet beneath he located shells. He slid five inside, then pumped the weapon, chambering a round, readying himself for the climb to the third floor. He didn't want to kill the animal but would if necessary.

He climbed the stairs again to the third-floor landing.

The bear remained in the bedroom from which he'd escaped out to the ledge. Judging by the noise, the animal was continuing to wreak havoc on the décor. He approached the open door. The bear's attention was elsewhere, which allowed him to scoot past to the other side, near the open window at the end of the hall. He was cornered, but it seemed the only way to herd the animal toward the stairway and down to the front door, which he'd left wide open.

A quick count to three and he stepped back into the doorway, firing a blast of the shotgun into the far wall. The bear jumped with a start, then roared in fright. Cotton fled back toward the open window in the hall, pumping another round into the chamber. The bear rushed from the bedroom, tossed a quick glance his way, then turned and loped down the third-floor hall in the opposite direction. To make sure the animal kept going, he fired again into the ceiling. Wood splinters and plaster dust showered down.

The bear disappeared onto the stairs.

He followed to the second-floor landing and watched as the animal rushed out the front door.

That worked.

But at a cost of noise that somebody might have noticed.

THE KNIGHT HEARD TWO GUN BLASTS.

The villa's owner had told him that what he sought waited inside a small study on the third floor. He'd watched as Malone had worked his way off the ledge, found solid ground, then reentered the house. The two gunshots were surely Malone's, so he had to assume his adversary was now armed.

At least the bear was gone.

The animal had fled the villa, running as fast as its bulk would allow into the trees beyond.

He was pleased. This might be the place.

Everything pointed in the right direction.

In his escape attempt Mussolini had taken many documents north with him, presumably those of the greatest importance, papers that could be used for political advantage. He'd been seeking refuge in a neutral country, one that had worked hard to stay out of the war. Hitler had wanted to invade Switzerland, but Mussolini had taken the credit for stopping him. Il Duce had been betting that Swiss authorities would be grateful enough to grant him political sanctuary. Historians all agreed that he probably brought with him written proof of his efforts to save the Swiss from the Germans. But apparently he'd also brought his legendary correspondence with Churchill, which had drawn the current interest of the British.

His hope?

Maybe, just maybe, there might also be something else within the villa owner's cache. Something special. What he'd sought for a long time. The appearance of the ring had encouraged him. This could, indeed, be the right place.

Was it there?

Only one way to find out.

COTTON SET THE SHOTGUN DOWN AND LIFTED ONE CORNER OF THE Turkish rug that covered the third-floor study. He examined the wooden floor planks, each pitted and weathered, and at first glance nothing seemed unusual.

Everything nailed in place.

He dropped to his knees and began to softly tap the surface, searching for the hiding place that he'd been told was there. Finally he detected a hollowness. He kept tapping, defining the outline of a square-shaped cavity. To get it open he'd brought along a hefty pocketknife he'd bought yesterday on his way north from the airport.

He opened the blade.

It took a few minutes but he managed to free a panel composed of fused planks. From the lack of dirt and grit in the joints it seemed that it had recently been removed, then replaced. Below the floor he discovered a small cavity that contained a tattered satchel, made of elephant skin, he'd been told, with a broken clasp bound by a sash cord.

He lifted it out.

Etched into the side was a perched eagle, wings extended, clutching a bundle of sticks with an ax.

It was an ancient symbol from imperial Rome, reflecting power over life and death. Nineteenth- and early-20th-century Italian political organizations had routinely adopted it as their emblem. Eventually it appeared on the flag of the National Fascist Party, which took its name from the *fasces* symbol.

He opened the satchel.

Inside was a well-preserved treasure trove of documents sealed within a thick fold of oilskin. He was fluent in Italian, and several other languages, one of the benefits of having an eidetic memory, so he took a quick inventory, flicking through the brittle sheets. Most dealt with the war, partisan activities, and military reports. There were a few typed letters from Hitler, originals, with Italian translations pinned to them, and some carbons sent to Germany. A few had postscripts and marginal notations in longhand. At the bottom of the stack lay a sheaf of prewar letters between Mussolini and Churchill.

More than five, though.

Eleven total.

Seemed the seller was holding a few in reserve.

Jackpot.

He replaced the documents and closed the satchel. All had remained quiet inside the villa. The bear was long gone. He should follow suit. He left the study, turning toward the staircase, passing several of the open third-floor doors. His orders called for him to drive to Milan and promptly turn over whatever he obtained.

Suddenly he was struck hard from behind.

His body jerked forward, as though hit by an explosion at his right ear. Trails of light arced before him. His legs caved. He quickly realized there'd been no explosion, only a blow to the back of his head. He tried to rebound, but collapsed, consciousness drifting in and out.

He hit the floor hard against his right shoulder.

Then all daylight vanished.

CHAPTER FOUR

Malta
9:50 A.M.

Luke Daniels loved the sea, which was strange for an ex–Army Ranger. Most of his service to the country had occurred on dry land. But ever since leaving the military and joining the Magellan Billet, he'd found himself on water more often than not. He'd first met Cotton Malone in the cold chop of the Øresund off Denmark, and only recently he'd completed risky assignments in the Indian Ocean and Java Sea. Now he was bobbing along off the north coast of Malta, sitting in the bow of a twenty-five-foot, deep V-hull, his short hair and open shirt damp with salt spray. He'd found an advertisement yesterday for a local water sports business, one of a zillion vendors that ran out of the many seaside resorts, each catering to the thousands of tourists who came here year-round.

Up, up in the air. Imagine a parachute glide using our special parasailing boat. Our guests take off from the boat and soar to 250 feet over the sea with breathtaking views of the island. At the end of this unforgettable experience, they land back safely on the boat. You can live this flying adventure alone or with a friend. You can glide either in the morning, or take off in the afternoon, to enjoy the famous sunsets of Malta. An unforgettable experience not to be missed. Try it with your friends. Flying duration is ten minutes.

He'd opted to omit anyone else and booked the entire boat for the morning, paying a premium since he wanted to be airborne longer than ten minutes and at a specific spot above the island at a specific time.

"Get ready," the helmsman called out. "We're almost there."

He was hunting for a big fish, but not the kind that occupied the blue waters around him. Instead he was tailing His Eminence, Kastor Cardinal Gallo, one of the current 231 princes of the Roman Catholic Church.

He'd been given the pertinent vitals.

Gallo had been born and raised on Malta, his father a commercial fisherman, his mother a schoolteacher. He left the island before the age of twenty and attended seminary in Ireland, but completed his studies at the Pontifical Gregorian University in Rome. John Paul II ordained him to the priesthood inside St. Peter's Basilica. He then served various parishes around the world, but ended up back in Rome studying canon law and earning a doctorate. Benedict XVI elevated him to the cardinalate, appointing him prefect of the Apostolic Signatura, the court of last appeal to any ecclesiastical judgment. There he'd stayed through the last two pontificates until his outspokenness got him into trouble and he was demoted. Now he carried only the title of patron of the Sovereign Military Order of Malta, a largely ceremonial post usually given to a cardinal near death or out of favor. At the relatively vibrant age of fifty-six, Gallo seemed firmly implanted into the latter category.

The boat slowed to a cruise.

Luke climbed from the bow, past the tanned driver, and hopped up on the stern platform, sitting on a low bench. A second crewman handed him a skimpy nylon harness, which he stepped into. As a Ranger he'd leaped from airplanes at all altitudes, several times into combat situations, twice into open ocean. Heights were not a problem, but the thought of dangling from a parachute at the end of three hundred feet of tow rope, held aloft only by narrow webs of nylon, bothered him. Like he always said, if flying was so safe, why'd they call the airport a terminal?

He slipped on the contraption.

The attendant checked the harness, tugging at places to make sure all was secure and tightening the straps around his chest. Stainless-steel D-clips were snapped onto metal rings, mating him to the chute.

"Sit back. Try not to hang," the guy yelled. "Don't hold on to anything and enjoy the ride."

He gave a thumbs-up.

The boat's engine revved.

The bow rose to a throbbing pulse, dividing the water with a milky-white wake. The brightly colored canopy above him, flapping in the stiff wind, caught air. Suspension lines drew taut. The tips of his tennis shoes swung freely as he rose from the stern. A thick nylon line unraveled from a hydraulic spool as he kept climbing.

Slow and steady.

He grabbed his bearings, about a quarter mile off the north shore.

Malta sat in the center of a narrow channel, 60 miles from Sicily, less than 200 miles north of Africa, an island in the Mediterranean of a mere 120 square miles, rising no more than eight hundred feet at its highest point. The Romans called it Melita, meaning "honey," after the rich local variety. Location had forged its history. The Phoenicians, Carthaginians, Greeks, Romans, Byzantines, Arabs, Normans, Swabians, Angevins, Aragonese, Hospitallers, French, and British all had claimed it at one time or another. Now it was an independent democratic republic, a member of the United Nations, the European Union, and the British Commonwealth. A barren rock devoid of water, arid in summer, drenched in winter, constantly raided through the centuries by one invader after another. The south shore loomed impregnable, mainly towering serrated cliffs, streaky hills, and jagged ridges, impossible to breach. But here, on the north shore, long bays jutted inland like fjords, creating marvelous harbors.

At the hotel last night he'd read a short history from one of the tourist books in the room. Since ancient times the native Maltese had always lived away from the coast to avoid weather, pirates, and slavers. The Sovereign Knights of Rhodes, though, had been a sea power. Once they arrived in the 16th century and became the Knights of Malta, to combat the threat of invasion and secure their hold on the island, they ringed the coast with watchtowers, built of local orange-brown limestone, positioned apart at strategic distances so they could signal one another in succession. Some were small, others mini fortresses. The one he was staring at now from three hundred feet above the towboat had been erected in 1658, still solid and serviceable.

Madliena Tower.

He'd learned about it yesterday during a quick on-site visit, including that it had served as an artillery battery during World War II. He'd climbed its spiral staircase to a parapet and stared out at the sea to exactly where he was now. Like its siblings, Madliena occupied a bare rocky promontory. Zero cover. Wide open. Making any type of meaningful surveillance from land impossible.

So he'd improvised.

He checked his watch.

10:00 A.M.

Shortly Cardinal Gallo should be standing on the parapet of the Madliena Tower.

Which in and of itself raised questions.

The pope had died thirteen days ago. The Apostolic Constitution mandated that the body must be buried within four to six days. Then a nine-day mourning period, the *novemdiales,* occurred. A conclave was required to be convened fifteen days after the date of death. But with less than a day left until it began, Cardinal Gallo had suddenly fled Rome for Malta. That act had caught the attention of Washington and Luke had been dispatched to monitor Gallo's activities. Why? That was above his pay grade.

He'd just been told to get there and watch.

He was now high enough that all sound had vanished. A warm, stiff wind played across his face. Foamed breakers smashed against the rocky shoreline. He was no longer a Magellan Billet rookie, or a Frat Boy as Cotton Malone liked to call him. More an experienced operative. His boss, Stephanie Nelle, seemed to have developed confidence in him. Even his relationship with his uncle, former president and now U.S. senator Danny Daniels, had evolved into a good place. He'd found a home at the Justice Department and intended on hanging around.

Time to earn his keep, though.

He reached back and freed the Velcro on the pocket to his shorts, removing the high-tech receiver. It had been waiting for him at his hotel yesterday when he'd arrived on the island. He took the advice of the guy below and sat back in the harness, stuffing fobs into both ears. He switched on the device and aimed its laser at the tower, about a quarter mile away. He stared down at the shoreline and was pleased to see that his target had arrived.

And he could hear every word.

CHAPTER FIVE

KASTOR CARDINAL GALLO STOOD ATOP THE MADLIENA TOWER AND soaked in the sun. The chilly northeast winds common to January and February were gone, replaced by a southern sirocco that had blown in from Africa, the dry, hot air ridding the island of its spring humidity. Today's weather was what his mother liked to label *healthy*, and he recalled as a child looking forward to the sirocco's periodic arrival.

He savored the earthy, decadent smell of the steamy land, accented by a hint of salt blowing in from the sea. He was annoyed to be out of Rome, the intrigue prior to a conclave a necessary evil that had to be endured. What one of his professors once said? *Suspicion can rot the mind.* True. But there was no better way to ease the anxiety of paranoia than to be present and alert. This time there seemed more of a pre-scramble than usual.

Canon law expressly forbid campaigning for the papacy, but no one paid that prohibition much attention. Kastor had participated in two conclaves since his elevation to cardinal. At neither had he been a serious contender. The first one because of his relative youth and inexperience, the next thanks to his outspokenness. His only vote at either had come from himself, made on the first ballot when it seemed a tradition to recognize those who would never be pope.

Four hundred years ago a knight adorned in a red cape with a white cross would have manned this tower, on the lookout for both friends and foes. He'd not chosen this spot for the meeting, somebody else had made the selection. But he appreciated the symbolism.

Friends and foes.

He had his share of both.

The upcoming conclave could be his last. Cardinals over the age of eighty were forbidden to vote. And though he was two dozen years away from that prohibition, depending on who was selected, the next papacy could be a long one. So if anything was going to happen his way, the coming few days could be his best shot.

A man clambered up from the stairway to the sunny parapet. He was swarthy, beak-nosed, with an unreadable expression. His face, neck, and hands cast the texture of desert sand, burned brown from the sun. Definitely Indian, but whether Hindu, Muslim, or Christian remained to be seen. He wore dark-green fatigues, a black pullover shirt, and boots. His hair, black, wild, and unruly, sprang from a high skull in uneven tufts that tousled in the wind. A piratical gold earring glinted in the sunlight.

"I'm honored to make your acquaintance," the man said in perfect Malti, which he'd not heard in a while.

A callused hand was offered to shake, which he accepted.

Kastor had come dressed not as a cardinal, resplendent in a black simar with scarlet piping, his chest wrapped in a scarlet sash, as he was accustomed to wearing in public. Today he wore street clothes, an ordinary man out to enjoy the sights. Thankfully, the parapet was empty, save for the two of them.

"What's your name?" he asked the man, keeping to Malti.

"How about *kardinali?*"

The reply rubbed him wrong. But since he knew nothing about this envoy he decided to keep the irritation to himself. Still, he felt compelled to point out, "I was under the impression I was the only bearer of a red hat here."

The man grinned, smug and self-contained. A finger was pointed his way. Long, with a slight upturn past the middle joint. "Quite right, Eminence. It's only that you're not dressed like a cardinal. Not even a ring to kiss. But I understand the need for discretion. You are, after all, a person of, shall we say, infamous notoriety."

Like he needed reminding.

Four years ago the now dead pope had decided the job of prefect of the Apostolic Signatura demanded a more moderate personality, somebody less outspoken, more complacent, a man who could *inspire trust not controversy.* True, he'd been warned about his public comments. And equally true, he'd ignored the advice. So his firing had not been a shock. But what happened afterward had given him pause. He'd been publicly chastised by colleagues and privately commanded to obey the Holy Father, ordered by the curia to keep his opinions to himself. He hated that bunch of bishops and bureaucrats, ingrates who administered the church as eunuchs had once run the Chinese court, attenuated to every subtlety, immune to all decency and emotion. They were supposedly concerned with the essence of Catholicism, practicing an obedience to superiors and a reverence for tradition.

Sadly for them, they were anything but.

Something he'd heard once had been driven home during the ordeal.

War doesn't determine who's right, only who's left.

And that had not been him.

For the first time in his professional life he'd felt like a pawn, powerless to either stop or change what was happening. Just a muted observer. What had the Vatican secretary of state told him?

If a man knows to do right and doeth it not, to him it is sin.

Jesus to the Pharisees.

But they'd seriously underestimated the indignation that their petty rationalizations could not extinguish. Thank heaven his reputation as a man who breathed the Catholic past had remained intact.

His beliefs had never been in doubt.

He strongly opposed the radical feminism of the church, which was why he'd publicly criticized a recent papal decision to allow altar girls. Marriage, to him, was only between a man and a woman, and homosexuality should never be tolerated. Abortion was nothing more than murder, no matter the circumstances. Embryonic stem-cell research seemed a heretical abomination. Euthanasia and assisted suicide repulsed him. Never should divorced and remarried Catholics be allowed to receive communion.

And Islam.

Nothing good would ever come from placating that plague on faith.

Thankfully, he was not alone in his orthodoxy. For him, and many others within the church, there was only black and white, the pope's job to steer toward the white. Of late, though, popes liked to proclaim nothing but gray. They avoided the extremes, craving the middle, wanting more to be loved and admired than feared.

Big mistake.

But he'd made his share of bad moves, too.

And paid a heavy price.

He'd been stripped of his office. Ostracized. Proclaimed *a threat to all the faithful in every parish of every country.* He became radioactive, the other cardinals withdrawing—even the damn hired help had avoided him. He'd gone into free fall, relegated to doing little to nothing these past four years, except wait.

The injustice only fueled his indignation.

But watching the church prostrate itself before the masses had sickened him most of all.

Then fate finally shone down.

Thirteen days ago a blood vessel in the pope's brain burst, bringing instant death. The pontificate had been meant to be one of average length, five to ten years at best. The pope had just started his fifth year. His plan had been to use the remaining time to quietly compel the support needed for the next conclave. Cardinals were, by nature, pliable. Negotiable. They also gathered in flocks. But it took a careful mixture of persuasion and intimidation to coalesce them into doing anything meaningful. Thankfully, he'd already amassed an impressive collection of damning information on many of the so-called princes of the church. Lots of juicy secrets.

But he needed more.

"What is your given name," he asked the man facing him, keeping his voice low.

"Arani Chatterjee."

He nodded, then stared out at the great sparkling plain of the Mediterranean, admiring the arc of a flawless azure sky. A tempest of swells rolled and tumbled, as they had all his life. He counted four parasailers enjoying the day.

"Men have searched a long time for what I seek," he said to Chatterjee.

"The *Nostra Trinità* has proven elusive, as it was meant to be."

This man was informed. "What do you know of it?"

"A great deal. The Turks tried to find it. Holy Roman emperors tried and failed. Napoleon came with an army, occupied the island, stripped the churches bare, but didn't find it, either."

"And Mussolini?"

Chatterjee inclined his head. "Now that is the question we are here to answer."

Kastor had no choice but to tolerate this man's brashness. But who was he to judge. He, too, had exhibited that quality on more than one occasion to more than one superior.

Pope Francis had been the worst.

They'd never seen eye-to-eye. How could they? The crazed Argentine was far more concerned with people worshiping him than protecting the faith. *It is not necessary to believe in God to be a good person.* What a ludicrous statement to be made by the Vicar of Christ. *The traditional notion of God is outdated.* How did Francis think a billion faithful would react to such nonsense? *It is not necessary to go to church and give money.* Really? Talk about naïveté. *For many, nature can be a church.* Pure garbage. *Some of the best people in history did not believe in God, while some of the worst deeds were done in his name.*

On that alone Francis had been right.

"Thankfully," Chatterjee said, "you have me to aid your quest. I've been working on this for some time."

News to him. "What have you learned?"

His visitor stepped close to the parapets. "Before we discuss that, there's a matter we have to deal with." Chatterjee pointed out to the water. "You see the black-and-red boat."

He watched as the designated towboat pitched through the water, keeping a single parasailer aloft in the hot sirocco, which continued to sough, rising in strength and hissing across the tower.

Chatterjee waved his arms in the air.

"What are you doing?" he asked.

"Solving that problem."

CHAPTER SIX

Luke heard the words *solving that problem* and saw one of the men on the Madliena Tower waving his arms.

Crap.

He'd been made.

He glanced down three hundred feet at the towboat and saw the attendant who'd helped him into the harness wielding a machete.

Ah, come on.

"To the man out there hanging in the air," a voice in English said in his ear. "If you can hear me, raise your arm."

He decided to not be any more predictable than he'd apparently already been and did nothing.

"Really?" the voice said in his ear. "I know you can hear me."

What the hell. He raised his arm.

"Much better. Technology is such a marvel. Of course, I doubt you speak Malti, which is why I chose it up to now. I don't appreciate you listening in on my private conversation."

The voice carried—a British accent.

How had he been found out? Good question. He'd been abruptly rerouted from another assignment and told to fly directly to Malta, with intel on a meeting at the Madliena Tower at 1:00 P.M. today. He'd arrived yesterday, checked into a hotel, then immediately reconnoitered the locale and, while there, noticed parasailers offshore. So he'd quietly hired the boat for the next afternoon, but somewhere along the way there'd been a leak.

Big time.

"You'll not be making any reports back to your superiors," the voice said in his ear. "I'm told you're with American intelligence. This really doesn't concern the United States in any way."

I'm told? By who?

But this wasn't a two-way conversation.

"Here's an interesting piece of local folklore," the voice said. "The Maltese paint their boats in bright colors to ward off bad spirits and coax good luck. Sadly for you, the one headed your way will offer neither."

He stared out over the water and spotted a boat, striped in bright bands of blue and yellow, racing straight for his position. He saw two men, one piloting, the other shouldering a rifle, their attention directly ahead.

At the Madliena Tower he caught another wave of arms.

The man below on the towboat stepped onto the stern platform and started hacking at the braided nylon hoist rope. Each thrust was accompanied by a troublesome vibration that reached all the way up the line. The man then stopped chopping and started sawing.

The towrope snapped.

His forward acceleration stopped and for an instant he was suspended high in the air, floating, at the mercy of the strong southern winds. The new boat with the two men swept in closer as the towboat sped away. Other boats had moved off with their parasailers.

He started to descend.

Faster than normal. No surprise. These chutes were super lightweight, loaded with venting meant for staying up, not landing soft.

The Med was approaching fast.

He wasn't wearing boots, nor were his ankles taped for a hard landing. He wore only shorts and a shirt with tennis shoes, all bought this morning at a Valletta store. He'd brought along only a few euros, the laser ear, and keys to his rental car.

The water was less than fifty feet away.

Time to be a Ranger again.

He worked the harness, releasing the buckles, one hand over his head gripped to the steel riser that supported his weight on the chute. Once in the water he'd have to free himself fast, then deal with the newcomers.

He hit hard and submerged, shaking off the cold water, wiggling from the harness, then clawing upward. He broke the surface and saw that the boat with the two men had drawn close. He was a quarter mile offshore and the currents were working against him. No way he could swim to land. He saw the man with the rifle level the weapon, aiming his way. He sucked a deep breath, tucked and rolled, then powered himself deep.

Bullets swished downward, slowed by the dense water.

He stopped sinking and settled, maintaining depth, staring back up to the surface. He could not hold his breath forever. And what was the old saying? *A good offense is the best defense.*

He kicked hard and made a free ascent, swimming beneath the dark outline of the boat. The angle of the bullets still trying to find their way through the water indicated on which side the men thought he would surface. He kept his eyes on the keel, staying close to the swaying hulk. The outboard rested in idle, the boat drifting along with the current. If they decided to power up and speed off he could be in real trouble from a spinning prop.

He surfaced and sucked a quiet breath, waiting until his side of the boat rocked down, then he planted his palms and used the sway back up from the swells to flip out of the water.

His body felt primed, coiled, his brain calm and controlled. He had only an instant of surprise, which he used to his advantage, pivoting off the gunnel and kicking the pilot in the chest, sending the man over the side.

The guy with the rifle swung around.

Luke lunged forward and, with a solid right, caught the guy hard in the jaw, then pounced and wrenched the weapon away, slamming the rifle butt up under the shooter's chin.

Something cracked and the man slumped to the gunnel.

He shoved the body into the water.

That was easy.

Now he had the high ground.

He stared across at the Madliena Tower. Gallo and the other man were still there, watching. He laid the rifle down and pushed the throttle forward. The engine roared to life. He swung the boat around toward shore and heard a shot.

Behind him.

He turned.

Another boat was racing his way.

Single occupant wearing a ball cap, steering the craft and firing a handgun. He had the rifle, but he could not pilot the boat and fire too. He started to zigzag across the water, making himself a more difficult target.

Two more shots came his way.

He veered south toward Valletta. The other boat turned, too, angling toward him in a wide arc, closing the gap.

In a few seconds they were parallel.

He released his grip on the wheel and grabbed the rifle with both hands.

His pursuer drew closer.

He turned, ready to plant his feet and fire quick enough that his unmanned rudder would stay on course.

But the driver held no gun.

Instead the other boat suddenly slowed to a stop and the driver's hands were raised in the air, as if surrendering. He regripped the wheel and worked the throttle, swinging around toward the other craft. He eased up close and lifted the rifle with one hand, finger on the trigger, while he worked the wheel and throttle with the other.

His pursuer removed the cap and long blond hair draped out.

"Who are you?" he called out.

"Laura Price."

"And the reason you're shooting at me?"

"Just trying to get your attention."

Both of their boats bobbed in the choppy water.

"It worked."

"If I'd wanted to take you down, I would have."

He smiled. "You always so confident?"

"I'm here to help."

"You're going to have to do better than that."

"Mind if I get my cell phone?"

He shrugged. "Go ahead."

He trained the rifle on her as she searched for something in a pocket. Her hand came back into view holding a flip phone. He hadn't seen one of those in a while. She tossed the unit across the water at him, which he caught.

"Push 2," she called out.

He kept the rifle trained on her. With his other hand he pressed the button and lifted the unit to his ear, his eyes never leaving Laura Price.

Two rings.

The call was answered.

"This is Stephanie Nelle."

CHAPTER SEVEN

Lake Como

Pain cleaved Cotton's head in half, starting at the nape of his neck and lancing forward to the back of his eyes. But he fought through the fog, grabbed hold of his senses, and saw a man running down the third-floor corridor, turning for the staircase.

He rose to his feet and rushed after him.

The guy had a head start and was already turning for the second floor. He decided to make up some ground and pivoted off the heavy stone railing, launching himself over the side and across the open space between the risers, catching his attacker in a flying tackle. Thankfully the other guy took the brunt of the impact and they rolled down to the next landing. The satchel flew from the man's grasp, over the railing, careening to the foyer below. Cotton broke free, came to his feet, and threw a punch to the face. His assailant lunged and they fell onto the balustrade with its thick array of stone spindles. The landing itself was more a narrow corridor leading from one side of the house to the other, its exterior wall broken by two windows, both closed.

He pushed away and made a quick appraisal of his problem.

Stocky, fair-haired, dressed in jeans and a pullover knit shirt.

The guy rushed forward, avoiding another punch, wrapping his arms across Cotton's chest in a tight embrace. Together they staggered back and crashed into one of the windows. The glass shattered from the impact and he tried to rebound, but the man kept pushing him closer to the shattered window. He kicked backward and caught the man just above the ankle with the heel of his shoe. A grunt of pain and the pressure around his chest slackened. He drove an elbow into the midsection and managed to reverse positions, thrusting one of his attacker's hands through the shattered window, raking the arm from side to side across ridges of broken glass. The man bellowed in agony and tried to withdraw, but Cotton shoved all of his weight forward, slashing the arm from elbow to wrist.

Another scream of pain and his adversary held up the torn arm, gaping at the ripped flesh that hung loosely like red ribbons.

Blood poured out.

The man retreated toward the stairs and the outer railing, trying to get away.

A bang startled him.

The man jerked from an impact, as if in a spasm. Blood spewed from an exit wound as a bullet ripped through the chest.

Another bang.

More spasms.

He realized what was happening. Somebody was shooting from below. A third bullet pitched the guy forward, then he fell, straight as a falling tree, smacking the floor face-first, fighting for breath, groaning in pain. Cotton dropped down below the railing and risked a peek through the spindles. No one was below. The rifle he had used with the bear still lay upstairs in the third-floor hall.

He heard another shot from beyond the front door.

His attacker was no longer moving or moaning. He rose and hustled down the stairs and out the front door. Black spots still danced before his eyes from the blow to his neck. Thankfully, adrenaline surged through him and helped with the vertigo. Outside he continued to see no one. The grounds rose steadily in three directions up toward the forested highlands. He heard the distant, muted churn of an engine coughing to life, the sound magnified by the silence.

But from where?

Echoes made it difficult to pinpoint.

He stared up toward the trees but saw no vehicle. Luckily there was only one road leading up from the lake. He might be able to cut off whoever had been here.

He turned for the Alfa Romeo.

And stopped.

The right front tire was flat.

Now he knew what the fourth shot had been for.

He wasn't going anywhere. Not quickly, at least. Somebody had come here ahead of him, prepared, obviously in the know.

Another buyer?

Possibly.

He headed back inside the villa and climbed to the second floor. He checked the body for a pulse and found none. He riffled through the dead man's pockets and discovered no ID or wallet. Perhaps MI6 could provide an identification.

He noticed something on one finger.

A ring.

Pewter.

Old looking.

With letters etched onto its face.

He slipped it off and examined it closer. Nothing else appeared on its exterior, but inside he saw a tiny image.

The four distinctive arrow points, joined at the center, a dead giveaway.

An eight-pointed Maltese cross.

He pocketed the ring.

Then he recalled the satchel that had gone over the railing. He descended to the ground floor and searched for where it should be lying.

Nothing.

Apparently the shooter had retrieved it.

Wonderful.

The Brits were going to love this.

CHAPTER EIGHT

MALTA

LUKE'S ATTENTION ALTERNATED BETWEEN THE PHONE AND THE woman in the boat across the water, one arm keeping the rifle trained. He was having trouble hearing over the hum of the outboard, so he cut the engine.

"Who is she?" he asked Stephanie.

"She wanted me to bring her on, noting you might need help. I asked how she knew anything about anything, but she offered nothing. I told her you could handle it without her help."

"Any reason you didn't pass that intel on to me?"

"Her call just came about an hour ago. I tried to reach you, but you didn't answer."

He'd left his phone in the rental car.

"I answered this call because it's the same number from earlier," she said.

He was drifting away from the other boat and watched as Laura Price maneuvered herself back near him. He lowered the rifle, deciding she was no longer a direct threat. But that didn't mean she wasn't trouble.

"Tell me about her," he said.

"What makes you think I know anything?"

"We wouldn't still be talking if you didn't."

He'd worked with Stephanie long enough to know that she never left anything to chance. She ran the Magellan Billet with military efficiency, accepting nothing less than perfection from her agents. Thanks to her personal relationship with his uncle, former president Danny Daniels, Luke liked to think that he enjoyed a closer connection with his boss, though he knew she would never show favoritism. Stephanie expected her people to do their jobs. Period. Who you were mattered not. Mistakes were barely tolerated. Results. That's what she wanted. And she'd diverted him here to get results.

But he'd messed up.

Bad.

"She works for the Malta Security Service," Stephanie said.

"This little island has an intelligence agency?"

"Part of the Armed Forces of Malta. It's not big, but it does exist. She worked at the CIA for a few years. They remember her at Langley. Seems she doesn't follow orders well. An adrenaline junkie. A loose cannon, but generally one that fires in the right direction."

"That sounds like me."

"My thoughts exactly."

"Any idea why the Maltese are involved in this?"

"Not a clue. But she's apparently been on you the whole time."

Which he'd missed.

Another mistake.

He stared across the water at his stalker. She was blond and striking with high cheekbones and a pretty mouth. Straight, squared-off bangs highlighted a narrow brow. She wore jeans, belted at the waist, with an open-collared shirt that revealed deeply tanned arms. A looker. No question. And she seemed in terrific shape, muscle-hardened in a way he liked. Obviously, she knew how to drive a boat, shoot a gun, and try to make herself useful. Combined with the balls of an alley cat he could see how she might be regarded as a loose cannon.

"What do you want me to do?" he asked.

"I don't like pushy people or liars. Get rid of her."

He smiled to himself. "It'd be my pleasure."

"Tell me what happened with Gallo."

"A slight problem. But I'll fix it."

"Do that."

And the call ended.

He continued to speak into the phone, pretending the conversation was ongoing, but assessing the situation. He still held the rifle. Laura Price lingered about twenty feet off his port side. He simulated ending the call and motioned with the phone that he needed to return it to her. If he kept it cool he may just be able to catch her off guard. Things were bad with the cardinal, but he'd find that trail again. Crap happened. The trick was not to let it stink everything up.

The rifle was pointed down toward the deck.

He motioned with the phone and she worked the boat closer. He tossed it over. She caught the unit and he used that moment to level the weapon and fire three rounds into her engine.

She lunged to the deck.

The outboard erupted in sparks and smoke.

He chuckled.

Those three hundred horses were now useless.

He turned the key and brought his own boat to life, spinning the wheel, engaging the throttle, throwing out a wake as he motored away that soaked the other boat. A glance back and he saw Price rebound to her feet, but he was already too far away for any meaningful shot from her on a pitching deck.

He threw her a wave, hoping never to see her again.

Time to find Gallo and get back on track.

He glanced toward shore and the Madliena Tower. The cardinal and the other man were gone. He worked the wheel and avoided some of the larger chops, paralleling the coast, cruising east toward Valletta where his rental car awaited. Vibrations from the engine rattled up through the deck and energized him.

No one was following.

Clearly, Laura Price would have to find a lift back to shore.

But those were the breaks.

He tried to fool himself into thinking that he understood women. But truth be told, he didn't. He liked to toss out a devil-may-care attitude and make the ladies think he was some kind of bad boy they could tame. That worked in his favor more times than not, but there was always the occasional disaster.

Actually he was a mama's boy, calling that saint of a woman every Sunday, no matter where he might be in the world. She knew that he was an intelligence agent. Stephanie had allowed him to reveal that to her and she'd loved it. Of her four children—whom they named Matthew, Mark, Luke, and John—he was the wild child. The others had respectable jobs, families, homes, mortgages. He alone remained single, traveling the world, doing what the Magellan Billet needed done.

He'd yet to find that perfect combination of lover, companion, confidante, and partner. Maybe one day. Women seemed to marry a man expecting him to change, but he doesn't. Men marry a woman expecting that she won't change, but she does. That was a problem. What had one potential bride told him? *Husbands are like cars. They're all good the first year.*

Lots of truth to that one.

Career, achievement, independence, and travel were tops on his list at the moment. Marriage and children not so much. Danny Daniels being his uncle may have cracked open a few doors that might have otherwise been closed, but those doors stayed open thanks to him being damn good at what he did. Of course, the past half hour had not been his finest moment.

He kept the boat headed south, recalling more of what he'd read last night.

After the Great Siege of 1565, when the Turks tried to forcibly take Malta, Grand Master Jean Parisot de Valette decided to build a fortified town on a barren limestone peninsula on the north coast. It would be Europe's first planned city since Roman times, laid out on a grid, with a moat on its southern side and bastion walls all around. Harbors shielded to the east and west, providing ideal anchorages. For a seafaring power like the Knights of Malta, the location proved a perfect headquarters, and they eventually adapted the island into an impregnable naval base.

Two miles long and a mile wide, Valletta's cluster of tightly packed buildings had long housed the knights and everything needed to support them. The city remained the sole witness to four centuries of hard work and magnificence. Its churches, shops, residences, palazzi, storehouses, forts, and the grand master's palace had somehow survived, even after Hitler relentlessly bombed every square inch during World War II.

Its buildings stood in straight lines, purposefully packed close to shade the streets from the intense Mediterranean sun and to allow a sea breeze to pass through unimpeded. All told, about two thousand structures of noble elegance had been built within five years. But it took another twenty-five years after to perfect it. Little had changed since the 17th century. Luke particularly liked what de Valette had said about his creation.

Built by gentlemen for gentlemen.

The white battlements of Fort St. Elmo came into view, standing point guard at the end of the towering peninsula, commanding a stunning view of the open sea. He imagined its cannon blasting out into the harbor, repelling the advancing Turks. The whole Great Siege seemed the stuff of Hollywood. Suleiman the Magnificent—what a name—sent 40,000 warriors and over 200 ships to take Malta for Islam. De Valette commanded 500 knights, 1,100 soldiers, and 6,000 local militia. Despite pleas, no Christian king lifted a finger to help, as they were too busy killing one another.

So de Valette stood alone.

The invasion came furious and bloody, all happening during a miserably hot summer. Fort St. Elmo held out a month before finally yielding. But a lack of supplies, little fresh water, and dysentery ravaged the Turks. Terror ran rampant on both sides. Dead knights were mutilated, their headless bodies floated across the harbor on crosses to the occupied forts on the other side. Grand Master de Valette's reply was to decapitate Turkish prisoners and fire their heads back as cannonballs.

Talk about tit-for-tat.

Finally, in September 1565, reinforcements arrived from Sicily and the Turks retreated. If things had turned out differently, Muslim shipping would have ruled the Mediterranean from a Maltese base and all of Europe would have been at risk.

But the knights saved Christendom.

He angled the boat past Fort St. Elmo and headed into the Grand Harbor, still girdled by forts and watchtowers. Waving flags cast a colorful welcome along the bastions and across the harbor in the Three Cities. A cruise ship nestled close to one of the long wharves, its passengers flooding onto the docks. Another was anchored offshore. He angled toward the marina. The towboat from earlier was nowhere to be seen. The boat's engine lost its steady thumping beat and slowed, ready to reenter the pro-tected haven crowded with yachts swinging peacefully at anchor.

His car waited in a small lot a few blocks away.

He eased the boat close to the dock, killing the engine and tying it off to a couple of empty cleats.

He hopped off, leaving the rifle in the boat, and trotted ashore.

Two men cut him off.

CHAPTER NINE

Lake Como

THE KNIGHT LEFT THE VILLA AND FOUND THE HIGHWAY THAT LED back down toward the lake. The elephant-skin satchel lay on the passenger seat next to him. He'd retrieved it while the fight had ensued on the second floor. Malone had apparently found what the villa's owner had confessed was there. Even its contents were exactly as reported.

Thank goodness he'd moved fast.

He'd instructed his associate only to incapacitate Malone, then retrieve the satchel. A simple task. He needed the American alive. Apparently, though, something had gone wrong. What he could not allow was for his associate to be taken prisoner. So he'd handled that problem, retrieved the satchel, and made sure Malone had no way to give chase. The idea had been only to turn the trail ice-cold and send the ex-agent back to the Brits empty-handed. That had now been accomplished, but at a higher cost than expected.

He found the highway that snaked around the jagged shoreline and turned north. Four kilometers later he cruised into Menaggio. Façades of colorful stucco buildings lined its quaint streets. The morning sun bore down, painting the building exteriors in contrasting shades of golden tan. Craggy mountains and wisps of fog swept across a semi-circle of spring foliage that rose up sharply behind the steeply pitched roofs. He parked just beyond the Piazza Garibaldi, taking the satchel and walking slow, head down, casual, drawing no attention, using his ears rather than his eyes to keep watch around him.

He entered the hotel and climbed the wooden stairs to his room. Inside, he spread out the satchel's contents on a table. Amazing how it had stayed secreted since 1945. A quick perusal of the pages revealed carbon copies, originals, and handwritten notes. Mainly reports and assessments, some orders to the military. But the correspondence between Churchill and Mussolini was the jackpot. He scanned the eleven letters, easy for him as he was fluent in both German and Italian. One in particular, an original in English from Churchill to Il Duce, made him smile.

I write to implore you that we should thus discard the feelings of irritation that might arise by our turpitude, the persistently perfidious opportunism with which successive governments of ours have tried to falsify our relationship. Of late, circumstances in this world have obliged us to conduct business together, and we can scarcely conduct business in a spirit of moral indignation. Instead, we must be wary and precise and somewhat trusting in each other. I fear that in spite of the insistent temptation it will profit us little to be disagreeable. So let us properly address what might be enough to prevent you from entering into any long term military relationship with the abhorrent German Chancellor.

How long have you wanted to bring Malta within the Italian sphere? You have repeatedly proclaimed that the Maltese are part of the Italian race, that even their speech is a derivative of the Italian dialect. Your rhetoric has been clear that Malta historically was, and should be now, part of a greater Italy. What if such a thing were possible? What if you alone could achieve what countless Italian leaders before you failed to accomplish?

Having thus acquired this card in your hand as a mark of friendship, a possible surrender of this certain and valuable island, we would accept as a *quid pro quo* that Italy remain neutral in the coming conflict. No political or military agreement would be made with the Germans. No assistance would be offered to the German cause. We recognize that this course might cause difficulties between Italy and Germany. Hitler would never tolerate an open Italian alliance with Great Britain. So, in order to allow your neutrality to manifest itself in a way that cannot be denied, we would not publicly acknowledge Italy as an ally in the current struggle. Nor, though, would we treat you as an enemy. Instead, for us, you would become a nation with a 'belligerent status' toward the United Kingdom. Not friend, nor foe, just one to be wary about. This would provide you with credible deniability towards the Germans that you have agreed to no terms with us, as that is not the case. But such status would ensure Italy a place at the peace table after the Germans are defeated, and defeated they shall be. There, the Italian territorial claims to Malta can be discussed and finally arranged.

The letter went on to extol other virtues in defying Hitler and secretly climbing into bed with England.

It was signed in heavy black ink.

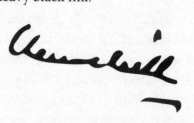

Churchill.

He noted the date.

May 18, 1940.

Churchill had just become prime minister. Apparently, the British Bulldog had wasted no time trying to make a deal, desperately wanting to keep Italy from formally entering the war on Hitler's side. The letter had been sent in response to one from Mussolini that had come a few days prior, a carbon of which was in the satchel.

I have been proclaiming for several years that Italy should have uncontested access to the world's oceans and shipping lanes. That is vital for our national sovereignty. The freedom of a country is proportional to the strength of its navy. We are now, and have been for a long time, a prisoner in the Mediterranean. Hitler is convinced that, to break British control, your bases on Cyprus, Gibraltar, Malta, and Egypt must be neutralized. Italy will never be an independent nation so long as she has Corsica and Malta as the bars of her Mediterranean prison and Gibraltar and Suez as the walls. Hitler's foreign policy takes for granted that Britain and France would someday need to be faced down. He has pointed out to me that, through armed conquest, Italian North Africa and Italian East Africa, now separated by the Anglo-Egyptian Sudan, could be linked. Even better, the Mediterranean prison would be destroyed. As you surely realize, at that point Italy would be able to march either to the Indian Ocean through the Sudan and Abyssinia, or to the Atlantic by way of French North Africa. That is meaningful to me. What Hitler offers is an alliance to make that possible. What do you offer, Prime Minister?

Churchill dangled Malta.

But cleverly, only after the war had been won, where it would be quietly ceded away. Which obviously had not been enough to entice Mussolini.

The knight knew his military history.

The British had been concerned about whether Malta could be properly defended. It was not the 16th century. Modern weapons were nothing like those the Turks had utilized in trying to breach the island's defenses. Bombers and ships with high-caliber cannons could wreak havoc. It would take a lot of men and weapons to hold the island.

Perhaps it was not worth it.

It had been the French, in May 1940, while their country was being invaded, who suggested that Mussolini might be appeased by handing over Malta. That way Italy would stay out of the war, allowing the Allies to focus on France. But Churchill convinced the War Cabinet that no such territorial concessions should be made, though others had favored a deal.

Now he knew why.

Churchill knew the offer would have been in vain.

On June 10, 1940, Italy declared war on Britain, then promptly the next day attacked Malta, laying siege. Rommel warned that *without Malta the Axis will end by losing control of North Africa.*

So their attacks were relentless.

Ultimately, Hitler dropped more bombs on Malta than on London. For five years most Maltese lived underground, utilizing the tunnels left over from the knights as air raid shelters, storerooms, and water reservoirs.

They took a pounding.

Over thirty thousand buildings were destroyed.

People nearly starved as food convoy after convoy fell to U-boats. A battleship, two aircraft carriers, thirty-eight submarines, and five Allied cruisers were sunk in its defense. Over a thousand Maltese died. Many more were injured. Churchill told the world that *the eyes of the whole British Empire are watching Malta in her struggle day by day.*

And they held the island.

After the war, the king granted the entire population the George's Cross. No wonder Churchill had wanted to make sure those letters never saw the light of day. Imagine what the British people would have thought of their revered leader had they known he'd been willing to cede that precious ground away.

Excitement surged through him.

He'd found most of what he'd been looking for.

But the one thing he'd been hoping to locate was not here. Had Malone removed it? Possible. But not likely.

No matter.

The Brits would be in contact. Of that he was sure.

He stared out the window and watched people move along the broad sweep of the piazza. He caressed the pewter ring that adorned his right hand, silently reading its five words.

Sator. Arepo. Tenet. Opera. Rotas.

Time for them to once again lead the way.

CHAPTER TEN

Malta

Kastor had listened as Chatterjee spoke to the parasailer. He then watched as the unidentified man hit the water and eventually overpowered two men in a boat. Then another boat had given chase, firing shots as the parasailer sped away, confronting him farther down the coast. The last thing he saw was the parasailer heading off toward Valletta.

Alone.

"What was that about?" he asked Arani.

"People are interested in what you're doing, Eminence."

News to him. "What people?"

No reply.

So he asked, "Who was that parasailer?"

"An American agent, sent here to spy on you. We learned of his involvement yesterday. Thankfully I was able to get ahead of him and paid off that parasailing crew. Those other two men should have dealt with him but, as you saw, he escaped."

"Who was the woman in the other boat?"

"A good question. I have to make a call."

Chatterjee retreated to the far side of the parapet and used a cell phone.

He'd not liked any of what he'd just heard and resented being treated like an inferior. And who was the *we*, as in *we learned*.

He stared back out to the sea.

The north shore had always been different to him. He and his brother had been born on the south side of the island, on a plot of land overlooking another swath of the Mediterranean. The old farmhouse had been built of the local coralline limestone, an interesting compound that emerged from the ground soft and damp but eventually, after age and sun, turned hard and white.

Like himself. Pliable as a child.

Unbending in adulthood.

His father had fished the Med all of his life, back when it was still possible to make a living. Both of his parents had been good people, neither one of them going out of their way ever to make an enemy. Sadly, they died in a car crash when he was twelve. It happened in April, just after the alfalfa had bloomed, blanketing the ground in color and the air with an aromatic scent.

To this day he hated spring.

With no family willing to take them, he and his brother had been sent to St. Augustus orphanage, on the east side of the island, a dreary, unimpressive place run by the Ursuline Sisters. There he grew to know the church. Its stability. Rules. History. Along with the many opportunities it presented. And where some at the orphanage rebelled, he'd come to appreciate the nuns' insistence on discipline. Those cold, bland women were, if nothing else, consistent. They made their point only once and you were expected to obey. Three years ago he'd forgotten a few of the lessons those unbending women had taught him and overplayed his hand, allowing the pope to cut his legs out from under him.

A stupid, stupid error.

He'd held a position of great power and influence. Prefect of the Apostolic Signatura. In charge of the highest judicial authority of the Catholic Church. When it came to ecclesiastical matters only the pope's word ranked higher. That position had also made him privy to a wealth of confidential information on laymen, priests, bishops, and cardinals. He'd amassed a treasure trove of confidential files. The plan had been to eventually use that knowledge to privately elevate his stature within the College of Cardinals. And if played right, he might be able to adapt his colleagues' gratitude into a serious run at the papacy.

Any Catholic male who reached the age of reason, not a heretic, not in schism, and not notorious thanks to simony, could be elected pope. But in reality, only cardinals had a chance. The last non-cardinal elected was in 1379. Without question, certain cardinals were more likely than others to be chosen. The fancy word was *papabile*. Able to be pope. That used to mean Italian. Not anymore, thanks to a succession of foreign popes. Still, there was no way ever to know who would emerge as a favorite. What was the saying? *He who enters the conclave as pope, comes out a cardinal.* History had proven that nine times out of ten a non-favorite won. Which made sense. Every so-called favorite had his own carefully crafted support group. Many of those formed shortly before or during a conclave, and rarely did one group ever sway another to accept *their* candidate. Which meant the man finally elected was never everyone's favorite. Instead, he was just a compromise that two-thirds of the cardinals could agree upon.

Which was fine.

He wasn't interested in being anyone's favorite.

Contra mundum.

Against the world.

His motto.

Chatterjee returned after ending his call. "I'll deal with our American spy in the boat."

"In what way?"

The man chuckled. "Do you really want to know? Just accept that I'm here, at your service, Eminence."

He felt another rush of anger at the patronizing tone. But the past few years, if nothing else, had taught him some measure of patience.

"And the woman?" he asked.

"I'm working on that, too."

"Are you Hindu?"

"I'm an atheist."

He needed to calm himself and expunge the growing rancor simmering inside him. This conversation was going nowhere. But he needed to know, "What are your qualifications to deal with my current needs?"

Chatterjee stared him down. "I can fight, shoot, and don't mind killing someone if the need arises."

"Are we going to war?"

"You tell me, Eminence. As you pointed out, people have been searching for the *Nostra Trinità* a long time."

"And what do you know about it?"

"Quite a bit. I hold a doctorate in medieval history from the University of York. My dissertation was on Jerusalem between the times of the Jews, Muslims, and Christians, from the 1st to 5th centuries, with an emphasis on European brotherhoods and their effect on intersect occupation. The Sovereign Military Hospitallers Order of St. John of Jerusalem, of Rhodes, and of Malta being one of those. I'm also quite good at scouring and stealing from archives, libraries, and newspaper morgues. I have few to no morals, and will do whatever is necessary to get the job done. I wrote a book on the Hospitallers. Didn't sell all that well, but it did draw the attention of certain people likewise interested in the knights."

"Can you name a few names?"

Chatterjee chuckled. "Never kiss and tell. First rule of my business."

He could see that this man masked a tough and sinewy intelligence beneath an overabundance of carefully cultivated rudeness. Ordinarily, he would not waste time with such arrogance. But nothing about this situation was ordinary.

He bought a few moments to think by watching the swift passage of a gull, its wings set, as it rode the thermals and glided out to sea. What it must feel like to be that unencumbered. Finally he turned toward Chatterjee and said, "You realize that the conclave begins in a little over twenty-four hours. There is no time for nonsense."

"How about I whet your appetite with something I'm sure you don't know. A good-faith offering, if you will."

He'd been told to come here and *all would be explained.*

So he had to trust that this was not a waste of time.

"I'm listening."

CHAPTER
ELEVEN

June 1798

Napoleon Bonaparte ignored the screams that echoed through the long corridors and admired the palace. For the past 225 years grand masters had dwelled within these walls, roaming the broad marble passageways, admiring the picture galleries, feasting in the great banqueting hall. There was even an observatory in the tower above. The building stretched long, like the Louvre, spanning two floors, its walls double-layered and filled with rubble like a fortress, a full one hundred meters of its elegant façade facing the Piazza dei Cavalieri, the Square of the Knights.

Sacred ground, he'd been told.

No Maltese had ever been allowed in the square, or the palace, without a permit. He'd already decided to curry favor with the locals by abolishing that law and renaming the plaza the Square of Liberty.

A good move.

The conqueror's prerogative.

He was thrilled. Everything had gone perfectly.

He'd sailed from France a month ago with hundreds of ships and 7,000 troops, all headed for the taking of Egypt. On the way he'd decided to seize Malta, arriving at Valletta three days ago. Standing on the deck of his flagship in the harbor he'd been impressed with the embattlements, the town itself sweeping down by terraces from the summit, the honey-colored buildings stacked one above the other, appearing as if chiseled from a single stone. He'd been informed that the numerous domes and towers would cast an exotic effect, and he'd seen for himself the truth of that observation.

What had the knights called it?

Civitates Humillima.

Most humble city.

Not since the Turks in 1565 had so many sails appeared off the Maltese coast. Back then the knights had been ready to defend to the death what they considered to be their island. This time the invader had caught them unprepared. Thankfully, his spies had proven their worth, identifying only 332 knights, 50 of whom were too old to fight, all undersupplied and poorly led. The fortress cannon had not been fired in a century, the powder rotten, the shot defective. Then, when the French knights, numbering nearly 200 of the 332, refused to fight, it all ended after two days with a total surrender, the grand master signing away the island and every vestige of sovereignty.

He stared again at the palace walls.

Little remained of its great heritage. It was more a melancholy air of desertion that emanated from its echoing walls and empty vestibules. What had happened to all those grand masters? Those select few who'd once teetered on the verge of absolutism. They lived as kings, wearing crowns, receiving ambassadors, and sending envoys to foreign courts. They kept a covey of chaplains and physicians, scores of servants, gamekeepers, falconers, drummers, trumpeters, valets, grooms, pages, wigmakers, clock winders, even rat catchers. Unlimited funds had been at their disposal. Popes and emperors catered to their wishes.

But no more.

Once the threat from Eastern infidels waned, the knights lost their purpose. They resorted to drinking and dueling among themselves, their former discipline disintegrating into chaos. The German and Italian langues were gone. Most of the others were near collapse. A once grand institution had become little more than a place to support, in idleness, the younger men of certain privileged families. Even worse, revolutions across Europe, especially the one in France, led to their lands being seized, enough that, by one count he'd seen, the knights' revenues had been depleted by nearly two-thirds.

Now all they had belonged to France.

He heard footsteps and turned. One of his aides-de-camp marched down *the wide corridor, the click of his boots resonating off the marble walls. Napoleon knew what the man wanted.*

They were ready for him in the Hall of the Supreme Council.

He nodded and led the way through the maze, the towering walls bare, all of the tapestries and paintings commandeered by his soldiers now stored on his flagship along with the other booty. His men had ravaged both Valletta and the rest of the island collecting armor, silver surgical instruments, ivory chess sets, furniture, chests of coin, and bars of gold. Even the treasured Sword and Dagger of de Valette, presented to that long-dead grand master by the king of Spain for his valor during the Great Siege, had been taken.

He had it all.

The L' Orient *packed with spoils.*

But he'd not found what he'd really come for.

The one thing that might prove more valuable than all of that gold and silver.

He entered the grand hall. At its far end, nearly thirty meters away, on a raised dais, surmounted by a crimson velvet canopy ringed with gold fringe, stood the throne of the grand master. This was where the supreme council and chapter general had gathered for centuries, the center of the knights' power. On the surrounding walls were twelve magnificent friezes that depicted the Great Siege. A memorial to a noble and hallowed time. A way to ensure the memory of that greatest moment never faded.

He could appreciate such propaganda.

The hall was empty save for a single trestle table at its center. One man sat before it, tied to a wooden chair, hands flat out in front of him, palms down, a nail piercing the center of each keeping them in place. The pitiful soul wore bedclothes, obviously seized by his soldiers while sleeping. The prisoner moaned, his head flopping down on the table, spittle dripping off his chin, blood oozing from the wounds. Napoleon stepped close and found it hard to take a satisfying breath thanks to the stench from bowels and bladder having relieved themselves.

"You are causing yourself so much pain, and for nothing," he said. "Your leader has abandoned you."

All true.

Ferdinand von Hompesch, the grand master, had handed over Malta without a fight, freely opening Valletta's gates. It helped that the knights swore an obligation not to take up arms against fellow Christians.

"Your grand master took the Arm and Hand of St. John and the icon of Our Lady of Philermo and sailed away."

He saw terror grow in the man's eyes as he realized his dire predicament.

"Before Hompesch left, though, I removed the ring from the hand of St. John." He displayed it on his finger. "A lovely jewel, which I will keep." He shrugged. "What good is it to a dead saint?"

No reply. But he didn't expect one.

"Your grand master left you here to face me. Alone."

"I . . . have told you . . . nothing. I will tell . . . you . . . nothing."

He motioned and his aide brought over a ceramic bowl, setting it on the table. The tortured Hospitaller looked up and seemed to recognize the bunches of plants that lay within.

"From the Rock of the General," he said. "I was told about its healing properties, so I had some of it retrieved for you."

Just off the coast of Gozo, north of Malta, rose a small limestone islet. Breakers had for eons chafed foam onto its gray, barren sides. Atop that rock grew a scrubby plant, unknown anywhere else in the world. He'd heard the tales of its styptic qualities, how it could stanch bleeding when packed on a wound. Fifty years ago a grand master had declared the islet off limits, posting guards, keeping the plant solely for the knights. Three years' confinement as an oarsman on a galley was the penalty for any violation. He planned to end that self-serving prohibition, after hoarding an ample amount.

"Can you smell it?" he asked.

The odor was sharp, pungent, mixing unpleasantly with the putrid waft of the tortured man's waste. He wanted to remove a handkerchief and shield his nose, but knew better. Generals in chief never flinched.

"Tell me what I want to know and the plant can soothe your wounds," he said.

No reply.

"You have kept your oath and not revealed a thing. I must admit, that is most admirable. But your life as a Knight of Malta is over. The order itself is over. There is no need to keep your promise any longer. Ease your suffering and tell me where I can find the Nostra Trinità."

The man's eyes grew wide with the mention.

"How . . . do you know . . . of that?"

"Its existence is no secret within the church, to certain cardinals. They told me about it, or at least what they knew. I'm intrigued and curious, so forget your promise and tell me where it is hidden."

The knight shook his head. "Promises are all . . . we have left."

The man's head collapsed back to the table.

He could only imagine the agony the nails were inflicting. He stepped closer and noticed the pewter ring on the right hand.

And the letters.

He reached down and slid the trinket off.

The man raised his head at the violation. "That is . . . not . . . yours."

He stared deep into the man's pained eyes. "I was told of this ring, too. The sign of Constantine. The symbol of your Secreti. *A long-honored brotherhood." He allowed his praise to hang in the air, then made his point. "I have come for Constantine's Gift. Make no mistake, dear knight, your life depends on whether I obtain it."*

Kastor stared at Chatterjee. "How do you know all that?"

"As I said, Eminence, I have been working on this for some time."

So had he, scouring the Vatican Library. As prefect of the Apostolic Signatura he'd had access to even the closed portions, the so-called secret archives, labeled that only because they required papal permission to utilize. He'd used his time wisely among those stacks, learning all he could about the *Nostra Trinità.*

Our Trinity.

"Napoleon came to Malta searching for the Hospitallers' precious possession," Chatterjee said. "That knight with his hands nailed to the table never revealed a thing. I read about his heroism in old records. The ones that lie in attics, or in basements, forgotten by time, nobody really knowing if they are truth or fiction. In the end Napoleon skewered the man through the chest, covering the floor in the Hall of the Supreme Council with as much blood as the heart could pump before he died."

"Which means he didn't learn a thing."

"Did I say that?"

Now he was intrigued.

"Are you saying we can find it?"

Chatterjee grinned. "We need to leave."

"Where are we going?"

"Someone wants to speak with you."

"I thought *you* were the person I was supposed to see."

"I never said that, Eminence. You simply assumed."

Yes, he had.

"A piece of advice," Chatterjee said. "Assume nothing. That course will serve you well in the hours ahead."

CHAPTER TWELVE

Cotton entered the Four Seasons in Milan. He'd driven the thirty miles south from Como in a little over an hour.

The time was approaching 1:00 P.M.

His mind still reeled at the loss of the documents.

Failure was not his style.

Before flying from Denmark yesterday he'd engaged in a little research. The general consensus seemed to be that any letters between Churchill and Mussolini would have involved an attempt by Churchill to either prevent or sever Italy's alliance with Germany. Once he'd conquered Ethiopia in 1936, Mussolini had openly wanted to rekindle a friendship with Britain. He personally disliked Hitler and did not want to see Europe fall under Germany's influence. But the British thought appeasing Hitler, and opposing Mussolini, was the better course, so they'd rebuffed his advances. Not until 1938 had Britain finally capitulated. But by then it was too late. Italy had already shifted toward Hitler.

Historical speculation on what might have been written between Churchill and Mussolini ran rampant. Unfortunately he hadn't been able to read any of the letters inside the satchel. He'd planned on doing that once he returned to his hotel in Menaggio, even though the Brits had emphatically told him not to be so curious.

But what did they say about the best-laid plans?

He'd been able to change the tire, using the small spare the rental came equipped with, and he'd made it south without incident. The man who'd hired him waited in a sunny, elegant dining room that overlooked an inner courtyard. His name was Sir James Grant, presently of MI6, Great Britain's famed foreign intelligence service. He hadn't met or heard of Grant before yesterday, an urbane and elegant gentleman in his mid-fifties, with dark eyes that cast an expressionless quality typical of professional spies. He noticed that Grant wore the same three-button dark-blue suit with a vest from yesterday. Cotton had called ahead to say that he was on the way with an interesting story, specifically alerting his employer to the two bodies in the villa.

The hotel was impressive, a former convent located in the heart of Milan's fashionable shopping district. Apparently British intelligence's per diem for fieldwork was much more generous than the Justice Department's. He stepped into the dining room, sat at the table, and explained more of what had happened.

Grant laughed at the bear. "That's a new one. I've been at this for twenty years and never had an agent encounter that before."

"Was the satchel real elephant skin?" he asked.

"It's said Mussolini shot the animal himself. How many pages would you estimate were inside?"

"Fifty or so. But only eleven letters. I'm sorry about losing them. Whoever was there wanted that satchel."

"After you called earlier, I sent a man north to investigate. He found the body inside, as you described, and it seems to be the villa's groundskeeper. We also found the dead man upstairs. Shot twice with one arm shredded. Quite horrible, my man said. Then he located the owner, hanging from a tree in the woods north of the villa." Grant paused. "His arms had been pulled up behind his back, his shoulders separated, a bullet to the head."

Cotton sat back in the chair. "Have you identified the dead guy who attacked me?"

"Not yet. His fingerprints are not in any database. Which is unusual, to say the least. But we'll learn who he is." Grant motioned at a plate of pastries on the table. "Please. Help yourself. I ordered those in case you were hungry."

He caught the diversion, a way to move things off to another subject. Stephanie Nelle was known to use the same tactic. But since he was hungry, he helped himself to a couple of croissants. A waiter sauntered over and he ordered a glass of orange juice.

"Fresh-squeezed?" he asked the waiter.

"But of course."

He smiled. Perfect. Thanks to his mother, who'd discouraged him from both, he'd never acquired a taste for alcohol or coffee. But fresh-squeezed juice? Especially from those tart and tangy Spanish oranges?

That was the best.

The ring rested in his pocket. He decided to do a little hedging of his own and keep that tidbit to himself while he determined what this cagey Brit knew that he didn't. But he did decide to share a little. "There were eleven letters between Churchill and Mussolini. Five were being sold to you. Maybe the other six had been offered to another buyer. He wanted five million euros from you. More, probably, from the other guy. So you both decided it was cheaper to steal them."

"I agree, we were being played. I should not be surprised. The seller's reputation does precede him."

He enjoyed another of the pastries and pointed at the plate. "Those are good."

"Do you know the story of the croissant?"

More hedging.

He played along and shook his head.

"In 1686 a baker was supposedly working through the night while the Turks lay siege to Budapest. He heard rumblings underground, beneath his store, and alerted officials. They discovered a Turkish attempt to tunnel under the city walls. Of course, the tunnel was promptly destroyed. As a reward, the baker asked only that he been given the sole right to bake crescent-shaped rolls commemorating the incident, the crescent being the symbol of Islam. Bread the masses could eat, devouring their enemy. And the *croissant,* which is French for 'crescent,' was born."

Cotton buttered a fourth pastry.

"During the recent Syrian civil war," Grant said, "Islamic fundamentalists banned Muslims from eating croissants. They cited the tale I just told you to support their action. They wanted no part of anything that celebrated a Muslim defeat."

"You know that story from Budapest is bullshit."

Grant chuckled. "No doubt. A total fiction. But it sounds delightful. Just like the story that Winston Churchill wanted to sell out Great Britain during World War II. Sounds good. Plays good. But it's not real, either."

"Then why were you willing to pay a fortune for those letters?"

"The Churchill family is tired of hearing lies. Our hope was that this would put the matter to rest."

He pondered on that one a moment, considering what Matthew said in the Bible about naïveté. *Behold, I am sending you out as sheep in the midst of wolves, so be wise as serpents and innocent as doves.* Proverbs seemed instructive, too. *The simple inherit folly, but the prudent are crowned with knowledge.*

Damn straight.

"Those lies about Churchill are over seventy years old," he noted.

The waiter returned with his juice and he enjoyed a few sips.

Smooth and sweet.

"Definitely fresh-squeezed."

"It's the Four Seasons," Grant said. "What did you expect?"

The waiter left.

"I expect the gentleman who hired me to be honest. Three men are dead. Your letters are gone. Yet you haven't shown the slightest concern. Which means either, one, the letters are irrelevant. Two, there was something else you were after. Or three, both. I choose three. What's your vote?"

No reply.

Time to play his hold card.

He found the ring in his pocket and laid it on the table. Grant stared a moment, before lifting it and closely examining the letters.

SATOR
AREPO
TENET
OPERA
ROTAS

Cotton leaned in. "That came off the dead guy in the villa who attacked me."

"Which you failed to mention, until this moment."

He reached for a fifth croissant. "Yeah, I noticed that, too."

"You took it off the corpse?" Grant asked.

"It's my nature to be curious."

Grant smiled. "I'm sure you've seen that the words can be read the same in every direction. Up. Down. Left. Right. It's a palindrome. *Sator. Arepo. Tenet. Opera. Rotas.*"

"You know what it means? My Latin is a little rusty."

"In its purest form, *sator* is 'farmer, planter, originator.' *Arepo?* Unknown. There is no such Latin word. *Tenet* means 'hold, keep, preserve.' *Opera* is 'work, effort, deed.' *Rotas?* 'Wheels.'"

He assembled the meaning.

The farmer Arepo works wheels.

"It makes no sense," he said.

"The full meaning of these words has been a matter of debate for centuries. No one has ever ascertained an accurate meaning. What we do know is that this palindrome once served as the personal mark of Constantine the Great."

He'd recalled something similar from a few years ago.

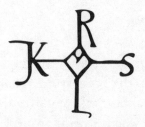

The monogram of Charlemagne. A sign of royal identity, usually formed around combining initials. When Charlemagne was crowned Holy Roman Emperor, the pope bestowed on him a one-word name.

Carolus.

Charles the Great.

So a monogram had been designed around that label.

The one on the ring seemed far more complex, and came four hundred years before Charlemagne.

"What do you know of Constantine?" Grant asked.

His eidetic memory recalled some details. Constantine ruled the Roman Empire in the 4th century, defeating all challengers, uniting the throne under one ruler. He founded a new capital on the Bosphorus, where Europe met Asia, which became Constantinople, a city set apart from Rome, ushering in the Byzantine culture. He was also the only Roman ruler to ever have *the Great* attached after his name.

He pointed at the ring. "There's etching inside."

Grant looked. "The eight-pointed Maltese cross."

"Can we get some bacon?" He was more hungry than he thought.

"Anything you like," Grant said.

He needed time to think, so more food might do the trick. "Bacon and eggs would be terrific. The eggs over hard. I hate runny."

"I couldn't agree more. Though, being an Englishman, that's probably an odd preference."

Grant motioned for the waiter and placed the order, then turned back and stared at him across the table. "Have we both hedged enough?"

He agreed, time to drop the act. "You paid me an obscene fee, then sent me in there blind just to see what would happen."

"And if that were true?"

"If I were still a Justice Department agent, I'd probably beat the living crap out of you."

"And in your retirement?"

"It's still up in the air."

He allowed his words to settle in, staring out through the wall of glass to the hotel's cloisterlike courtyard. Then he faced the Brit. "I'm going to eat my free breakfast, take my fifty thousand euros, and head home. As we like to say where I come from, I don't have a dog in this fight."

"What do you know of the Knights Hospitallers? Or, as they are called today, the Knights of Malta?"

"Not a whole lot."

"Thankfully, I do."

* * *

Sometime around 1070 a small group of merchants from Amalfi founded the Hospice of St. John the Almoner near the Church of the Holy Sepulcher in Jerusalem. They were Good Samaritans, stretcher bearers for pilgrims who'd survived the arduous journey to the Holy Land. Eventually they constructed hospitals across all of the land conquered by the Crusaders. In 1113 Pope Paschall II bestowed upon them papal legitimacy, their trademark habit a black surcoat with a cowl, an eight-pointed cross in white linen affixed to the left breast. By 1150 they had grown into soldier-monks, knights errant of the cross, becoming the Order of the Hospital of St. John of Jerusalem.

Their first duty always remained caring for the sick, but their second was *tuition fifei*. *Defense of the faith.* Interested parents would place their son's name forward at birth and pay a large fee. Acceptance came at age eighteen. To be eligible then the young man had to be strong, well built, and fit enough to endure the life of a soldier.

And the pedigree had to be perfect.

In the beginning, an applicant had only to be legitimately born into a noble family. By the 14th century that evolved into both parents having to be of noble, land-owning gentry. A hundred years later applicants had to prove nobility in the male line back four generations. Eventually, by the 16th century, all four grandparents were required to be of noble stock. Passage money, what it took to support a knight for a year in the Holy Land, became the final initiation fee. Once anointed, each knight endured a year's training, then swore to have faith, repent his sins, and live in humility, being merciful, sincere, wholehearted, and brave enough to endure persecution.

With the fall of the Holy Land in 1291, the age of the warrior-monk ended. The Knights Templar never grasped that change and faded in 1307. The Hospitallers adapted, keeping their primary mission charity but evolving from a land-based cavalry force to a sea power, conquering and taking Rhodes in 1310. They then became the Order of the Knights of Rhodes and acquired a new purpose.

Keeping both the Ottomans and the corsairs at bay.

After Constantinople fell in 1453, Rhodes became the last outpost of Christianity in the East. The knights acted as a buffer between the Latin-Christian Western world and the Eastern infidels. Their fighting ships and galleys dominated the Mediterranean, their white cross on a red matte striking fear into their enemies.

Members organized themselves into eight langues, *one for Provence, Auvergne, France, Italy, Castile, England, Germany, and Aragon, which represented the major political divisions of the time. Those were further subdivided into bailiwicks and commanderies. The* langues *headquartered in* auberges, *where members lived and ate communally. Traditional national rivalries never faded, though, and led to regimental conflicts between the* langues, *but enforced discipline and a strong hand eventually forged the* langues *into a tight, cohesive fighting force.*

In 1522 the Turks finally succeeded in retaking Rhodes.

The knights loaded their ships and left, drifting for seven years. In 1530 Charles V of Spain granted them Malta, and its twelve thousand inhabitants, in exchange for a single falcon, payable yearly to the viceroy of Sicily on All Saints' Day.

The island had not been much of a prize. Just a chunk of limestone seven leagues long and four wide. Its stony soil was unfit for growing much other than cotton, figs, melons, and other fruits. Honey was its major export and main claim to fame. Just a few springs near the center was all the running water. Rain was the main supply. Wood was so scarce the locals used sun-dried cow dung for cooking. The south coast claimed no harbors, coves, or bays, the shore tall and rocky. The north coast was the opposite, with plenty of anchorage, including two fine harbors suitable for any fleet. Which was perfect, since the knights were a seafaring power. But the gift of an island was not merely gratuitous. Charles intended for them to employ their forces and arms against the perfidious enemies of the Holy Faith.

Which they did.

Becoming the Sovereign and Military Order of the Knights of Malta, exempt from civil duties and taxes, bowing to no authority save the pope.

There they stayed until 1798.

"Now they are Sovereign Military Hospitallers Order of St. John of Jerusalem, of Rhodes, and of Malta," Grant said. "The world's oldest surviving chivalric order. Headquartered in Rome. The eight-pointed cross of St. John remains their emblem. Four barbed arrowheads, joined at the center, each point representing the eight beatitudes, the four arms symbolizing prudence, temperance, fortitude, and justice. Its whiteness is a reminder of purity."

The waiter brought Cotton's bacon and eggs. He pointed at the ring, which Grant still held. "Is that connected to the Hospitallers?"

"I believe it is."

He ate his late breakfast, noticing the eggs had been fried perfectly. "So the dead guy could be a knight?"

"That's my assumption." Grant sipped his coffee. "You may not believe this, but I was genuinely hoping this was only about the letters. A part of me wanted it to be that simple. But in this business nothing is ever simple." Grant paused. "The Hospitallers possess the largest, most extensive collection of Mussolini's writings and personal belongings in the world. They've been secretly acquiring it for decades. A bit of an odd obsession, wouldn't you say? But they refuse to confirm or deny anything. As they like to say, what they may or may not own is a private matter."

"Like that stops MI6." But he did connect the dots. "You think the Hospitallers were the ones after the Churchill letters?"

Grant reached into his inside jacket pocket and removed a cell phone. He punched the screen, then handed it over. On it, Cotton saw a man hanging from a rope, arms yanked up from behind, his neck angled over in death.

He handed the phone back. "The villa owner?"

Grant nodded. "When the Crusaders invaded the Holy Land, they became a brutal lot. They were fighting an enemy like none they had ever seen. The Arabs were tough, relentless, and unmerciful. To show their adversary that they could be equal to the task, they devised new means of torture and punishment." Grant gestured with the phone. "One of those involved hanging their prisoners in this particular way. It became a trademark. So yes, I think the Knights of Malta are involved."

Cotton kept enjoying his breakfast, waiting for the pitch.

"We need someone, other than us, to look into this," Grant said. "That's why I hired one of the best intelligence operatives in the world."

He grinned. "Now you're blowing smoke up my ass."

"Just being honest. You do realize that there are people at MI6 who still hold a grudge your way."

He knew what Grant was referring to. An incident that involved his son, Gary, and a former head of British intelligence. "I did what I had to do."

"Which is exactly why I want you on this. I have a situation here, Cotton. One that may be wider than I first thought. I need your help. I'll double your fee."

Music to his ears and, luckily, he had a few days free. But he wanted to know more. "What do you want me to do?"

"Make contact with the Knights of Malta." Grant laid the ring on the table. "Start with inquiring about why the dead man in that villa was wearing this. Then find out anything you can on their Mussolini collection. And I'm not particular on how you accomplish that objective."

Which meant the local criminal codes did not have to be observed. But he had to ask, "Is that all I get from you? Pretty damn vague."

"I would ask that you allow me the luxury of withholding further facts until I'm sure of a few matters. There is a possibility this might be nothing at all. That we are on the wrong trail."

"Looking for what?"

Grant did not reply.

He shrugged. "Okay. For a hundred thousand euros, I can be a good bird dog. I'll sniff around and see where it leads."

"Excellent. Hopefully, I'll have some clarity shortly that I can share."

"Can I at least know what you're waiting for?"

"A situation on Malta to resolve itself."

CHAPTER THIRTEEN

KASTOR EMERGED FROM THE CAR.

He'd ridden from the Madliena Tower with Chatterjee, following the north coast highway to the town of St. Paul's Bay. It began as a sleepy fishing village, the adjacent shoreline one of the easier points on the island from which to gain land. Now it was a popular tourist spot, its unstylish concrete buildings overflowing with an overpriced array of restaurants, cafés, and boutiques, the mass-market hotels and nondescript apartments packed with people year-round.

He caught sight of one of the coastal towers, high above, standing guard from its lofty perch. Another grand master creation, this one in 1610 by Wigancourt, who built six facing the sea. He knew about the famed Frenchman. A knight his entire adult life, including during the Great Siege, he was popular with the Maltese, which was rare for grand masters. The viaduct he completed delivered water to Valletta until the 20th century.

Out in the calm bay boats lay at anchor, so many that their bulk formed a carpet on the water. Beyond them, he spotted the small island where the faithful believed that Paul himself first came ashore. What a tale. In A.D. 60 275 prisoners were being ferried toward Rome to be tried, Paul included. Their ship was ruined in a dreadful storm, drifting two weeks before breaking up just off the coast. Despite not knowing how to swim, miraculously all of the prisoners made it to shore. The Bible itself recounted the event, noting that *later we learned that the island was named Malta. The people who lived there showed us great kindness and they made a fire and called us all to warm ourselves.* As the story went, while Paul was ashore a poisonous snake bit him but he survived, which the locals took as a sign that he was no ordinary man.

No. That he was not.

More a brilliant rebel.

Like himself.

Kastor stood before a formidable church, one of 360 that dotted the island, this one a high building of burnt ocher, with a graceful spire and a beautiful cupola, vivid against the drabness of the shady street. Not much had changed in thirty years. As a young priest, serving his first parish, he'd said mass here many times. He noticed that the same two clocks remained in the tower. One real, the other a trompe l'oeil, installed by overly superstitious locals to supposedly confuse the devil when he came to collect souls.

He and Chatterjee entered through the front doors. Inside was the same low roof supported by arches, with little pomp or circumstance, shadows still the only adornment. A solitary figure stood beside the front pew.

"Come in, my friend. Please. We have much to discuss."

A tall, stout, older man, with a noticeable midsection, paraded down the center aisle. He was robust, with a thick patch of pale-white hair and features framed by a pair of wispy white sideburns. Few angles defined the round face, the skin streaked by veins of yellow and purple, perhaps the lasting effects from years of smoking.

Danjel Spagna.

The few times Kastor had seen him at the Vatican, Spagna had worn the black cassock, purple skullcap, and silver pectoral cross of an archbishop. Today he was dressed casually, nothing reflecting any ecclesiastical status.

He'd never actually met Spagna, only heard the tales.

The press called it all the Vatican, but the Holy See was not the Vatican City State. The latter came into existence as sovereign territory only in 1929 because of the Lateran Treaty. It consisted of chapels, halls, galleries, gardens, offices, apartments, and museums. The Holy See, the episcopal

seat of Rome and the pope, dated back to Christ, and was an ind
dent sovereign entity that did not end at the death of a pontiff. The
See acted and spoke for the whole church, currently maintaining di
matic relations with 180 nations. Ambassadors were officially accred
not to the Vatican City State, but to the Holy See. The pope was its
challenged head, but it was administered by the curia, with the secret.
of state acting like a prime minister, a buffer between the over two tho
sand employees and the pope. The old joke came from John XXIII. Wh
asked how many people worked at the Vatican, he quipped *about half of ther*

As in any other nation, security had always been a concern.

The most secret agency within the Holy See had existed since th
16th century, created specifically by Pius V to end the life of the Protestant Elizabeth I and support her cousin, the Catholic Mary, Queen of
Scots, for the English throne. Though it failed in that mission, ever since
it had served popes through schisms, revolutions, dictators, persecutions,
attacks, world wars, even assassination attempts. First called the Supreme
Congregation for the Holy Inquisition of Heretical Error, then the much
shorter Holy Alliance. In the 20th century it was changed to the Entity.

Its motto?

With the Cross and the Sword.

Never once had the Holy See acknowledged the Entity's existence, but
those in the know regarded it as the oldest and one of the best intelligence
agencies in the world. A model of secrecy and efficiency. Respected. Feared.
Overseen for the past thirty-six years by Archbishop Danjel Spagna.

The pope's spymaster.

A Belgian, Spagna first came to the attention of John Paul II when, as
a young priest, he learned that the Vatican might be bugged. Eight listening devices were found inside the Apostolic Palace, all of Soviet origin. The
world was never told, but a grateful pope elevated Spagna to monsignor
and assigned him to the Entity. There he became the Pole's personal envoy, a conduit between Rome and Warsaw, making many clandestine vis-
its to Eastern Europe. Some said he was the one who secretly worked
with the Americans to help bring down the Soviet Union, ferrying information to and from Washington. But again, nothing was ever confirmed
or denied. After the Soviet Union fell, Spagna was elevated to archbishop
and given full operational control of the Entity. A cardinal served as its

titular head, but Spagna ran things on a daily basis. No publicity had ever surrounded him. No scandal. No controversy. Only the strongest had run with John Paul II, and Spagna may have been the toughest of them all. He'd even acquired a label.

Domino Suo.

Lord's Own.

"What do you want with me?" Kastor asked. "I worked in the Vatican a long time, and never once did we speak."

"Don't be offended," Spagna said, his aging eyes the color of lead. "I only speak to a red vulture when absolutely necessary. They don't care for me, and I don't care for them. You, though, I have studied in detail." Spagna's lips twitched into an ironic smile. "You were born and raised on this barren rock of an island. A true Maltese. There aren't many of those left in this world. You said mass right in this church, as a young priest, back when you were fresh and new—and silent."

Kastor caught the jab.

"You have superb academic credentials from the finest institutions. A credit to a superior intelligence. You're handsome, photogenic, and articulate. Together those are rare qualities among the red vultures. In many ways you are almost too good to be true. That raised warning flags with me. So I took the time to look deeper." Spagna pointed. "That's where you really learn about someone."

He agreed.

"I spoke with one of the nuns who raised you. She's an old woman now, living out her retirement in Portugal, but she remembers you from the orphanage. Amazing how some things can stick in the mind." Spagna pointed again. "You stuck in hers. She told me a story about the festival of Our Lady of the Lily. Every town on this island holds at least one big festival each year. Quite the celebrations, I'm told. Seems like a lovely tradition. You were thirteen at the time, I believe. That nun watched as you stole three *pasti* from one of the street vendors. The owner never saw what you did. But she did. *Halliel ftit,* she called you. Little thief."

He said nothing.

"She told me how you took those pastries, went off, and devoured them like a rat. Amazingly, all of the nuns at the orphanage knew you liked to steal. Did you know that?"

No, he didn't.

"Some of them wanted to punish you. But the mother superior forbid it."

He was surprised at the show of generosity. He remembered that cranky old woman as a cold bitch.

"The old nun told me the mother superior wanted to see how far you'd go," Spagna said. "And you showed her. You stole trinkets, clothes, books, money, and never once did you show an ounce of remorse. The old nun said that the mother superior wanted you to destroy yourself. To be caught, chastised, shamed, ridiculed. She wanted you to mete out your own punishment. Yet that never happened. Instead, you left the orphanage and went off to become a priest. The mother superior thought perhaps God himself had decided to intervene, so she let you go and never said a word. Now here you are, poised to steal the papacy."

This man's interest in him was frightening. So for once he decided to keep his mouth shut and see where this led.

"That mother superior was right," Spagna noted. "You are, indeed, your own worst enemy. As an adult you managed to do what you failed to achieve as a child. You meted out your own punishment. To your credit, you achieved a position only a few of the red vultures have ever attained. Prefect of the Apostolic Signatura. That's a lofty post. Enabling, in so many ways. But your mouth. That foul, vile mouth of yours got you fired. For some odd reason you thought people cared what you had to say."

"Maybe I cared."

Spagna laughed. "That was never in doubt. I'm sure you cared a great deal. Which, dear Kastor Gallo, is another of your problems."

"Eminence. That is my title, *Archbishop*."

The older man flicked a hand, as if swiping the rebuff away. "You are a fool. Nothing more. Nothing less. Just a plain, ordinary fool."

He'd not risked this journey from Rome to be chastised by a subordinate. But he was damn curious as to what was going on. He'd been told to come to Malta immediately and meet with someone at the Madliena Tower. Since the person who'd sent the message was trustworthy and understood what was at stake, he'd not questioned the request. But never had he thought the Lord's Own would be the person he'd be seeing.

"Say what you have to say," he said.

"I want to find the *Nostra Trinità*. You've searched a long time. Now I want to join with you. I know things you don't."

He did not doubt that observation and was surprised by the request. This man had kept the Vatican's secrets for decades. Too long, if the murmurs he'd heard within the curia were to be believed.

"Why do you want it?" he asked.

"It's the church's ultimate secret. The one that has eluded us. Every organization has secrets. Ours is seventeen hundred years old. Before I die, or am fired like you, I want this secret secured."

He decided to be clear. "I want to use it to become pope."

Spagna nodded. "I know. You want to be pope. I want you to be pope."

Had he heard correctly? "Why?"

"Is that important? Just be grateful that I do."

Not good enough. "Why help me?"

"Because you actually have a chance at winning."

Really? "How? As you've just noted, I'm a thief and a fool."

"Both attributes are common to the red vultures, so neither is a liability. I also know for a fact that your ultra-orthodox views are shared by a great many. I'm assuming that, as prefect of the Apostolic Signatura, you amassed the necessary damning information on your colleagues."

He had, so he nodded.

"I thought as much. I'm privy to some of the same information."

That didn't surprise him.

"John Paul II wanted the world to think him a reformer, but he was a real hard-liner. There was nothing progressive about that Pole," Spagna said. "The Soviets tried to kill him, but he survived and stayed the course, held the line, and brought Moscow to its knees. I liked him. He loved to say one thing publicly, then privately do another. He was really good at that, and I learned from him. The church was stronger then. We were feared. We were also much more effective on the world stage. We destroyed the Iron Curtain and crushed the Soviet Union. We were a power. Not anymore. We've waned to nothing. And though I do consider you a fool, you'll be my fool, Kastor."

He didn't like the sound of that. "I doubt it."

"Don't be so hasty. I have something you don't."

He was listening.

"The leverage to bring the undecided cardinals over to your side. Enough to garner the magic two-thirds vote."

"The *Nostra Trinità* can do that."

"Maybe. But it's a bit of an unknown. And that's all contingent on you finding it. I can provide something more tangible. More recent. Something you can use either in addition to, or in lieu of, what you're after."

He liked what he was hearing.

Still—

"What do *you* want?"

"That blood vessel bursting in the pope's brain offers us both an opportunity," Spagna said.

Not an answer.

He needed to make a phone call. He'd apparently been kept in the dark about a great many things. Why? He wasn't sure. Having Spagna as an ally could indeed change everything. In some ways they were alike. Both pariahs. Everyone avoided the Entity, except the pope and the Secretariat of State, which had no choice but to work with it.

"What does it feel like to be alone?" he asked Spagna.

"You tell me."

"I'm not. I have friends. Supporters. As you said, there are many who agree with me. You have no one."

"He has me," Chatterjee said.

"And what is your job?" Kastor asked.

"I assist the archbishop, from time to time, on matters with which I have some expertise."

He recalled their talk at the tower. "Like scouring and stealing from archives, libraries, and newspaper morgues, doing whatever is necessary to get the job done?"

"Absolutely."

"Then we're lucky to have you. What about that parasailer? The Americans knew what you were doing."

"No, Kastor," Spagna said. "They knew what *you* were doing. Which is why I'm here."

Troubling to hear for a second time.

"The Entity itself is somewhat in crisis," Spagna said. "Many of my own people think it's time I step aside. I have subordinates who want my job.

The red vulture who's in charge despises me. But the dead pope liked me, so there was nothing anyone could do. That may not be the case after the coming conclave, depending on who becomes pope. I don't want to step aside. I don't want to be *forced* to step aside."

He stared at the bearlike man, a bit shambled in street clothes but definitely comfortable with his power.

"Your problem," Spagna said, "is that you've always wanted things too fast. Since childhood the concept of patience has been foreign to you. That's why you find yourself with the dubious title of patron of the Sovereign Military Order of Malta and not prefect of the Apostolic Signatura. Seven cardinals have held that patron post over the past sixty years. Seven losers. Now you're the eighth. I was surprised, after your firing, when you requested such an innocuous job, which the pope gladly granted. But that was precisely where you wanted to be. That's when I first became interested in what you were doing. But as always, you were impatient. You wreaked havoc inside the Hospitallers. They're now in a state of civil war, fighting among themselves, unsure what's happening to them. All thanks to you."

"Which gives me a great freedom of movement. I started that chaos. I control it. So I also know how to avoid it."

Spagna chuckled. "And there it is. The liar and the thief showing himself in all his glory. That's why you'll make a great pope. At least for me, you will. I can work with you, Kastor, like I did with the Pole. We'll understand each other. I saved your hide a little while ago with that American parasailer, as a show of my good faith."

"And what if I don't want your help?"

"Then I'll take my chances with another candidate. One who will appreciate the kind of assistance I can offer."

He got the message. "I'm listening."

Spagna retreated to the front pew and reached down, lifting up a thin sheaf of papers, bound together in a binder. The older man approached and offered them. The top sheet, visible through the clear plastic, was blank.

"I gave it no title. Perhaps you could offer one. After you've read it."

He accepted the binder and started to open to the next page.

"Wait," Spagna said.

He looked up, unaccustomed to being ordered.

"I offer this as a second show of my good faith," the spymaster said. "By reading it, though, you agree to work with me, on my terms. If you're not inclined to do that, hand it back and we will not speak again."

Choice time.

He had few allies in the world. As a kid he'd been closer to his brother than any other person. And for good reason. They'd shared a womb, born identical twins, Pollux the older by a little over a minute. As kids it had been difficult for anyone to tell them apart. That similarity had carried over into adulthood, though they both now tried hard to distinguish themselves. His brown hair was short and tight to the scalp, while Pollux's hung below the ears. He stayed clean-shaven. His brother had always sported the remnants of a monk's beard. Though their height, size, shape, and facial features remained mirror images, he wore glasses for nearsightedness and the scarlet of a cardinal, while Pollux retained perfect vision and had never favored the priesthood. Their father had named them for the constellation Gemini, Latin for "twins," and its two brightest stars, Castor and Pollux. As a fisherman, the stars had been important to their father. But that man was gone, and this was his decision alone. What was the old cliché?

Never look a gift horse in the mouth?

"I'll keep it."

Spagna smiled. "We'll be in touch before nightfall."

"How will you know where to find me?"

Spagna smirked.

"Please, Kastor. Asking ridiculous questions only shows your ignorance."

CHAPTER
FOURTEEN

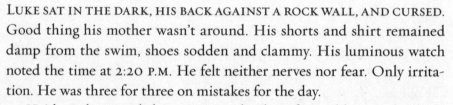

LUKE SAT IN THE DARK, HIS BACK AGAINST A ROCK WALL, AND CURSED.
Good thing his mother wasn't around. His shorts and shirt remained
damp from the swim, shoes sodden and clammy. His luminous watch
noted the time at 2:20 P.M. He felt neither nerves nor fear. Only irritation. He was three for three on mistakes for the day.

He'd tried to avoid the two men who'd confronted him at the dock,
dodging and weaving through Valletta's unbroken cordon of waterfront
streets. But they eventually cornered him. An arm had snapped closed
across his throat, another hand clamped on his mouth, and then the arm
across his windpipe tightened until his vision had flashed with lights.

What happened after that was sketchy.

He vaguely recalled being carried into a building, down a flight of stairs,
into coolness, then lowered into the ground and dropped onto soft earth.
When he came around absolute blackness had enveloped him, so thick that
he couldn't see his hand in front of his face. He'd used his fingers to examine the rough-hewn walls of his prison, which was circular and measured about five paces across. Reaching up, he'd determined the hole was
wider at the bottom, the sides tapering inward as they rose. A clever way
to prevent any attempt to climb out since you'd fall long before making it
even halfway up.

The air hung humid and stale, as if it had been breathed to exhaustion.

Sweat coursed down the small of his back. His mouth felt pasty. What he'd give for a bottled water. As screwups went, this day ranked high on the list.

What would Malone say?

Good going, Frat Boy.

Hard to live up to a legend. And that perfectly described Cotton Malone. But if you were going to strive to be the best, then you had to know the best. Pappy might be retired and selling books in Denmark, but he remained if not at, then certainly near, the top of his game. Of course, he'd never tell Malone that. He'd worked with him twice and both times he'd learned things. The goal? Work hard another decade and new agents might talk about him the way the current ones spoke of Malone. That was possible. Why not? Everybody needed goals. And time was indeed the best teacher.

Trouble was, eventually it killed all of its students.

He wondered where Pappy was now. Probably at his shop in Copenhagen, doing whatever booksellers do.

What a day.

He reached down and played with a handful of the parched sand that formed the pit's floor. How long had this hole been in the ground? How many others had rotted away here? He figured he was somewhere beneath Valletta, as he vaguely recalled not being carried all that far. But where? Who the hell knew?

A sound disturbed the silence.

Like a door opening above.

Shafts of light appeared across the top of the pit.

He was now able to see that he'd been right. The hole was bell-shaped. About ten feet deep. Tapering upward to an opening about four feet wide.

He looked up and saw Laura Price.

Which caught him off guard. He'd been wondering who the two guys worked for. His best guess had been the guy on the tower with the cardinal.

A rope fell from above, which she used to climb down. The moment her feet hit the earthen floor, he clipped her legs out from under her and she dropped to the soft sandy floor.

He came to his feet and stood over her.

She shook her head. "Feel better after that cheap shot?"

"Where am I?"

"Inside a piece of history. You should feel honored. The Knights of Malta once dug these prisons all over the island. They're called *guvas*. Means 'birdcage.' Bad little knights were thrown in and left for days, or weeks, at a time. A few even forever. The only *guva* most people think still exists is beneath Fort St. Angelo, not far from here. But there's another, right here. As you can see, there's no way out except by ladder or rope."

She stood, wearing a look of unpredictability, her blond hair loosely gathered by a leather thong. Everything about her breathed freedom. He watched as she brushed the dirt from her clothes and examined the walls.

"Did you notice this?" she asked, pointing at the rock.

He stepped over and, in the dim light, spotted carved letters.

AD MELIORES.

"Toward better things," she said, translating. "Obviously, a plea from a former occupant."

He noticed more carvings. Names. Dates. Coats of arms.

"All they could do," she said, "was carve away and hope someone above showed mercy. This place is really old. Probably late 16th or early 17th century."

He couldn't care less about the history lesson. "Why am I here?"

"You stuck your nose where it didn't belong."

"I was doing my job."

Since this pain in the ass knew who he worked for there was no need to be coy. And besides, his main source of exercise was pushing his luck.

"Do you have any idea what you're into?" she asked.

"Why don't you enlighten me?"

Her right arm whirled through the blackness, her fist heading up for his jaw. But his guard was up and he was ready. His left hand stopped the potential blow with a quick grab of her wrist.

"Not bad," she said.

"I try."

"After you shot my engine up, to get here I had to steal a boat from a guy who came by."

He grinned. What was it about the badass girls that attracted him?

"Do you have any idea what's happening tomorrow?" she asked.

Because he talked with a Tennessee mountain accent, had never attended college, and showed little to no interest in current affairs, people always thought him uninformed. Truth be told he read several newspapers each day, online of course, and devoured the daily security updates all Magellan Billet agents received. Once assigned to Malta, he'd read everything he could on Kastor Cardinal Gallo and what was about to happen at the Vatican.

"A conclave," he told her.

"And this is going to be one for the record books. Mind letting go of my arm?"

He did.

"I bet that jaw of yours has had quite a few fists pounded into it."

She was working him and he knew it. But what the hell? He liked it. "It takes a beating but keeps on ticking."

"I bet it does. Like I said, this conclave will be a mess. There's no front-runner. No solid contender. No favorite. One hundred and fifteen cardinals will be inside the Sistine voting. Who will they select as pope?" She shrugged. "I have no idea. Neither do they, by the way. That's what happens when a pope dies suddenly. But I do know who some people don't want. Kastor Cardinal Gallo."

Interesting. "What people?"

"That's only for me to know."

"Have you been following me since yesterday?"

She nodded. "I assume that when Stephanie Nelle was telling you to get rid of me, she also told you who I work for."

"Why does an island this small need an intelligence agency?"

"We sit on the southernmost border of the EU. We're the front line between Europe and Africa. Get something onto this rock and you can easily get into the EU. That's why we need an intelligence agency."

"Why didn't you just identify yourself to Stephanie to start with?"

"We were hoping to keep this contained."

"Who is *we*?"

"My boss. He gave me an order. I do what he tells me."

"How did you know I was headed into trouble?"

"Same answer. My boss told me. The man on the Madliena Tower, with Gallo, sometimes works with Vatican intelligence. We've seen him before. He piqued our interest and led me to you."

He'd caught the magic words. *Vatican intelligence.* "The Entity is working with Cardinal Gallo?"

"It's a possibility."

Not a complete answer, and he could see that she was acquiring a case of lockjaw, a familiar malady with field operatives since the idea was to always get far more than you ever gave. "Any reason why you didn't help me out *before* that idiot cut the towline?"

"And miss all the fun of watching you at work? That was worth the price of admission. But I did tell your boss you were in trouble."

He shrugged. "What else could a guy ask for?"

"And so we're clear, if you hadn't shot up my engine, I would have saved you the trouble of being down here. As it was, all I had to work with was my phone."

"Which I so conveniently returned."

"Yes, you did. We need to leave."

"We?"

"I prefer to work alone, but I've been told you're now on the team whether I like it or not."

"What are we going to do?"

"Deal with Cardinal Gallo."

CHAPTER FIFTEEN

KASTOR WALKED PAST THE RECTORY OUTSIDE THE CATHEDRAL. As the legend went, the Apostle Paul had been a guest of the local governor, a man named Publius. After curing the governor's father of fever and flux, Paul converted Publius to Christianity. He then designated the governor's house as Malta's first church and the Roman its bishop. Ever since, a church had occupied the same spot within Mdina's fortified walls, eventually becoming a cathedral in the 12th century and still serving as the seat for the Archdiocese of Malta.

Mdina sat nearly in the center of the island, surrounded by thick bastions, one of the world's few remaining walled cities. It served as the island's capital until the 16th century, when the knights arrived and built Valletta. Chatterjee had returned him to the Madliena Tower, where he'd found his rental car then driven alone to Mdina. The fact that Danjel Spagna was here, watching his every move, bothered him. As did the fact that the Americans were also watching.

Chatterjee had assured him they were dealing with the parasailer. He'd noticed there'd been no mention of the woman in the boat, but he assumed that problem was being handled, too. If it was anyone else besides the Entity he'd be concerned, but Spagna was renowned for his ability to get things done. The man had served five popes, surviving each successive purge when the old was swept away and the new welcomed. While that was thought somewhat therapeutic for the curia, it could be a bad idea for the intelligence business. Continuity was the name of that game. The Entity worked thanks to Spagna's institutional memory and his steady hand. The fact that the spymaster wanted to make him pope was both gratifying and frightening.

He needed all the help he could get.

He carried with him the thin plastic binder Spagna had offered. He'd resisted the urge to read the pages quickly, intent on finding a quiet place for a thorough review, practicing some of that patience Spagna had so unceremoniously advised.

He avoided the cathedral's rectory and kept walking through the walled town, savoring the waft of Mdina's sun-warmed stone. He could hear the voices of history, all the way back to antiquity, demanding to be remembered. Occasionally he caught sight of the soft-footed cats, most tawny orange and sullen black, that still prowled every nook and cranny, as they had during his childhood.

Malta's oldest families still lived among Mdina's aristocratic aloofness. For centuries the locals called it the Silent City, since the only sounds within the walls were footsteps. But it was here that the revolt against the French invaders began in 1800. Napoleon had looted every church, defiled every sanctuary, cleaned out every *auberge*. The little general then sailed off to Egypt, leaving a garrison of a thousand regulars to maintain order. The Maltese, though at first glad the knights were gone, quickly grew to hate the French even more. The final insult came here, when the invaders held an auction to sell off the contents of Mdina's Carmelite church. A riot erupted and the French commander was murdered. Church bells rang coast-to-coast, calling the people to arms. Within ninety days the entire garrison fled the island.

The lesson?

Never underestimate the Maltese.

He followed the labyrinth of angled streets, so narrow that you could reach out from the upper floors of one house and touch the one opposite. Wrought-iron grilles protected many of the windows, remnants from a time when those dwellings had to fend for themselves. He passed a flock of tourists, enjoying the sites, taking refuge from the sun within the cool cavern of passageways. He also caught the cross-currents of voices.

The Maltese were a proud lot. Always had been. They worked hard, longing mainly to get married, have children, and enjoy life. The church had once dominated everything, but not so much anymore. Malta had gone international, joining the EU, breaking further from Great Britain and its older generations. Divorce had even been legalized by a national referendum. Four hundred and fifty thousand people now lived on the island. And true, the locals could be petty toward one another, prone to jealousy, even quick to pick a fight—what was the saying? *A crossed Maltese stays cross*—but even with all its faults, Malta, and its people, were his home.

He found his favorite restaurant, tucked away in a quiet corner against the bastion walls. Two vaulted stone chambers from the 17th century served as the dining room, but his chosen spot was outside in an enclosed courtyard adorned with greenery and a tinkling fountain. It had been a few years since he'd last visited.

He ordered his favorite dish, rabbit stew, then laid the plastic binder on the table. There were maybe twenty typewritten pages inside. He glanced around. The courtyard was empty, no one enjoying a late lunch, or early supper, depending on your point of view. The waiter brought him a glass of red wine, Italian, as he'd never cared for Maltese grapes. He waited until the young man stepped back inside before opening the binder and reading.

Two years ago the Holy Father directed that I conduct a confidential assessment and, if possible, an audit of certain departments within the Holy See. Prior to becoming pope, while he was a cardinal, the Holy Father had served within a variety of departments and was concerned about what he termed "systematic waste, fraud, and abuse." I was requested to conduct a thorough but wholly secret investigation, drawing no attention to my efforts. After twenty months of clandestine study I can now provide the following summary:

(1) There is little to no transparency in any of the bookkeeping maintained within the Holy See. In fact, it is common practice for departments to maintain two sets of records. One that could be shown to anyone who might request information, the other detailing the actual income, costs, and expenditures. This practice is well

known to the cardinals currently overseeing those departments, as it is done under their direct supervision and many of them personally retain the more accurate, second set of books;

(2) Contracts for services by the Holy See to outside third-party providers (which total in the tens of millions of euros annually) are routinely secured without competitive bidding and without regard to cost. Corruption is rampant relative to the awarding of these contracts. Bribery and kickbacks are common. Many times as much as 200 percent over the current market value is paid by the Holy See for these goods and services, all linked to corruption;

(3) There is an ongoing and systematic theft of tax-free souvenirs from the Vatican's retail shops. This merchandise is being stolen by the pallet load, then secretly sold to outside vendors at vastly reduced prices. The moneys generated from these thefts are currently secretly being shared by at least three cardinals;

(4) One particular outside, third-party transaction is noteworthy. It involves a deal made with an American corporation allowing that company's cigarettes to be sold in Vatican stores, but only thanks to a secret fee paid to at least two cardinals. Part of that deal also allows several other cardinals to benefit from extreme discounts on at least two hundred packs of cigarettes, collectively, purchased by them each month, for their own use;

(5) An Italian charitable foundation for a local pediatric hospital recently (and secretly) paid €200,000 to renovate a cardinal's Rome apartment;

(6) The Vatican pension fund currently has a nearly €800 million deficit and is teetering on bankruptcy, though current public financial records show a balance sheet far to the contrary;

(7) There is no detailed inventory of the nearly 5000 buildings owned within Rome by the Holy See. Current balance sheets list the

total worth of the Holy See's real estate holdings within France, England, Switzerland, and Italy at €400 million. The best guess of the actual worth for these properties is over €3 billion. The best explanation for this odd discrepancy downward is that the curia sees public relations advantages in downplaying the actual net worth of the church;

(8) Retirement packages to at least three dozen cardinals are highly exorbitant, far beyond anything considered reasonable;

(9) The granting of free or low-rent apartments to cardinals currently serving within the curia is common. Rents in prime Rome locations are at times as much as 100 percent below market value. One example: a one-hundred-square-meter apartment near St. Peter's Basilica is currently being rented to one cardinal for €20.67 a month. If market rates were applied to all of the Holy See's rental apartments, somewhere around €20 million would be generated in revenue each year, as opposed to the less than €6 million currently being realized. The same discrepancy is present regarding the Holy See's commercial real estate, where many of the current leases are far below market value and could generate somewhere near €30 million more per year.

He could hardly believe his eyes.

It was incredible, made even more so since the information came from within the Vatican itself. Gathered by the Entity.

Straight from the curia.

The word *curia* meant "court," but in the sense of a royal court, not a court of law. Its principal departments consisted of the Secretariat of State, nine congregations, three tribunals, five councils, and eleven offices and commissions. Together they were the administrative apparatus of the Holy See, its civil service, acting in the pope's name, with his authority, providing a central, governing organization. Without it, the church could not function. Popes loved to both complain about, and tinker with, the curia.

But rarely had it changed.

It was presently controlled by the Apostolic Constitution *Pastor bonus,* issued by John Paul II in 1988, later revised by Francis I.

The waiter arrived with his rabbit stew in a thick-sided crockery bowl, leaving it, along with a basket of warm bread and another glass of wine. He took a moment and enjoyed the stew's aroma, remembering the way his mother would make the same dish. She'd spend Friday evenings searching for the best rabbit, killing it herself, then dressing and chopping the carcass, marinating the meat with red wine. He and his brother would watch the preparations with fascination, standing on their tiptoes, peering over the counter.

And the sounds.

They'd stayed in his psyche.

The basso tick of a clock hanging on the kitchen wall. The deep bongs of distant church bells. The water boiling. The snap of bone.

Saturday morning the house would wake to the smell of garlic as the stew simmered. He knew all of her ingredients by heart. Tomato passata, olive oil, sugar, bay leaves, carrots, potatoes, peas.

A wondrous mix.

He enjoyed a spoonful of what sat before him.

Not bad.

The restaurant prepared an admirable stew, but it was nothing like what his mother had created.

He missed those weekends.

Before the orphanage. Where there'd been no stew.

No mother.

Spagna was right. He had become a thief and a liar. Why didn't the mother superior do something? Why had she allowed it to happen? He didn't for a moment believe God had intervened, sending him off to the seminary and a new life. Faith was not something he'd ever totally embraced. Odd for a cardinal. But he could not help it. Fate was more his style. His life had been a series of fateful events, each one sending him along a seemingly predetermined path to this moment. Had he messed up with the last pope? Absolutely. But what did he have to feel bad about? According to what he'd just read, the Holy See seemed riddled with thieves and liars, too.

He kept eating.

The Roman Catholic Church carried the distinction of being the oldest continuous human institution in the world. It could deal with just about anything except the unexpected—and a pope dying in an instant certainly fit into that category.

Popes came in cycles of young and old.

A young Pius XII, then an old John XXIII. A vibrant Paul VI, followed by the frail John Paul I. The lion John Paul II, succeeded by the elder placeholder Benedict XVI. The pattern stretched back centuries, rarely varying. The last Vicar of Christ, now lying in the crypt beneath St. Peter's, had been older. His reign had been intended to be short, about a decade, giving other challengers the time to amass support. The longest-serving pope remained the first. Peter. Some said thirty-four, others thirty-seven years. Nobody really knew. So if history were to be trusted, the next pope would be younger, lingering longer, potentially having a greater impact.

He liked that he would not have to disrupt the natural cycle.

He finished the stew and the waiter returned to carry away the dishes. He asked for more wine, which was poured. The young man had no idea who he was serving. He liked how he could move about the world with anonymity. Few outside of the Vatican knew or cared that he existed. And who was he anyway? Just a priest from a rock in the Mediterranean who'd risen to great stature, only to have it all stripped away. Thankfully, they could not take his red hat. Nor the friends he'd made. Men who remained in positions of power and influence and who would shortly be looking for a leader.

There'd been Greek, Syrian, African, Spanish, French, German, and Dutch popes. One Englishman, a single Pole, two laymen, and a ton of Italians. All were either nobles, former slaves, peasants, or aristocracy. Never, though, had there been a Portuguese, Irish, Scandinavian, Slovak, Slovenian, Bohemian, Hungarian, or American pope.

Nor a Maltese.

Thankfully, that blood vessel suddenly rupturing would limit the cardinals' time for scheming. And make no mistake, cardinals schemed. The whole idea of sealing them away had been to limit the opportunities for bribery and shorten the time for deal making. The Latin root of the word *conclave* meant "a room that can be locked up."

That meant few cardinals would be prepared for the coming battle. Thankfully, it appeared he would not be one of those.

He glanced down at the plastic binder.

Thank God one truth remained inviolate.

Powerful men wanted only one thing.

To keep their power.

CHAPTER
SIXTEEN

COTTON TOOK A SUITE AT ROME'S HOTEL D'INGHILTERRA, ON THE top floor with a balcony that ran the length of the building, spring geraniums bursting from its planters. He was being paid top dollar, so, as with the Alfa Romeo, he decided to splurge. He sat on the bed and stared out the terrace doors. Golden blocks of sunshine washed in through the clear glass. Beyond the railing stretched the city's trademarked irregularly shaped roofs, with their gnarled pipe vents and ceramic-crowned chimneys, satellite dishes the only nod to the 21st century.

He'd flown south with Sir James Grant in a private jet, the trip a quick seventy minutes, during which he'd learned little more about what was happening. Their talks had been about books and world affairs. Along the way he'd confirmed a transfer of one hundred thousand euros into his Danish account. Not that the Brits didn't have credit with him. It was just always better to be paid in advance.

He needed a shower and a change of clothes, so he took advantage of the hotel's amenities, the spacious bathroom an amalgam of shiny marble and mirrors. He'd chosen the Inghilterra not only for its reputation but also for its location. It sat only a short distance away from the Via Condotti, the most popular shopping street in Rome, an endless panorama of high-end clothes, leather, silver, glass, jewelry, and stationery. Also on the Via Condotti, at number 68, sat the Palazzo di Malta.

In 1798, when the Hospitallers were tossed from Malta by Napoleon, they wandered the world searching for a home. Finally in 1834 they found one in Rome. Two villas, one here, the other—Villa del Priorato di Malta—a few miles away atop Aventine Hill. About an acre and a half of territory between the two, both independent, holding allegiance to no one, a Roman Catholic country unto itself, making up the smallest sovereign nation in the world.

On the flight south he'd also made use of the onboard WiFi, learning as much as possible about the Hospitallers. Incredibly, they still existed, over nine hundred years after their founding. They were governed by a chapter general of the membership that met once every five years to choose a sovereign council of six members and six high officers who administered things on an everyday basis. The grand master supervised it all, elected for life, holding the rank of cardinal but with no conclave vote for pope. No longer warrior-monks, today they were a quiet, pious, humanitarian organization supporting international health care, operating war zone refugee camps, caring for South American slum children, treating leprosy in Africa and Asia, managing first-aid clinics in the Middle East, running blood banks, ambulance services, soup kitchens, and field hospitals worldwide. Their help was extended to all, regardless of race, creed, or religion. Membership, though, came by invitation only, with a current roster of over thirteen thousand men and women divided into two classes of knights and dames. Protestants, Jews, Muslims, and divorced people were not allowed. More than 40 percent of the members were connected in some way with Europe's oldest Catholic families. Over one hundred thousand people worked for the organization, 80 percent of those volunteers.

Fifty-five members, though, were special.

Knights of Justice.

Professed men who took religious vows of poverty, chastity, and obedience, they were the last remnants of the former Hospitallers. They were also its ruling class, holding all of the important positions of power.

The order itself was impressive.

One hundred and four countries maintained formal diplomatic relations, including an exchange of embassies. It possessed its own constitution and actively operated within fifty-four nations, having the ability to transport medicine and supplies around the world without customs inspections or political interference. It even possessed observer status in the United Nations, issuing its own passports, license plates, stamps, and coins. Not a country, as there were no citizens or borders to defend, more a sovereign entity, all of its efforts focused on helping the sick and protecting its name and heritage, which members defended zealously.

But the knights were troubled.

Big time.

He'd read several news accounts from *L'Osservatore Romano* about recent internal strife. Major stuff. The now deceased pope had even been drawn into a civil war within the knights' hierarchy that involved a cardinal, Kastor Gallo, and the grand master, a Frenchman. Gallo served as the Vatican envoy to the knights, a largely ceremonial post with supposedly little to no influence, there *to promote the spiritual interests of the Order, its members, and its relations with the Holy See.* But Gallo had interjected himself into the order's internal affairs. The dispute centered on an obscure Hospitaller program that had distributed condoms in certain parts of the world to help with the combat of sexually transmitted diseases and AIDS. Problem was, that conflicted with clear Vatican policy forbidding the use of contraception. Gallo used that error to drive a wedge between the grand master and the pope, forcing the former's resignation. That led to conflict among the professed knights, compelling the fifty-six to choose sides. They'd split almost fifty–fifty over the issue. Half supporting their grand master, the other half disagreeing. The pope had tried to counter the chaos, ordering a reversal of the grand master's resignation, but that effort failed. And though fighting among themselves, the knights had collectively resented both the pope's and Gallo's interference. One article from a few months back made the point crystal clear.

> The Holy See has a unique relationship with the knights in that the pope appoints a cardinal patron to promote amicable relations between the Order and the Vatican. Cardinal Gallo was chosen for that position, after the pope removed him as head of the Vatican's supreme court. But Gallo and the pope have never been friends. In fact, Gallo has emerged as one of the pope's top critics and the Knights of Malta have now found themselves in the middle of that

dispute. In an extraordinary rebuke of both Gallo and the pontiff, the Hospitallers said that the replacement of its grand master was an "act of internal governmental administration of the Sovereign Order of Malta and consequently falls solely within its competence. The Holy See, or any representative thereof, has no say in such matters."

The whole thing seemed a nasty business.

But he assumed that boys would be boys, politics the same everywhere.

According to other newspaper reports, there'd recently been a wholesale purge within the knights, with many of the highest-ranking officers replaced and the entire organization still reeling from the turmoil. Everyone seemed to be awaiting the next pope for guidance, as the current Vicar of Christ had died before the dust had fully settled. What remained unclear, at least to Cotton, was how a squabble within a modern-day charitable organization, albeit one nine hundred years old, had become a security concern of the United Kingdom.

Cotton entered the Palazzo di Malta, a tall archway opening from the street and draining into an enclosed courtyard lined with parked cars, mainly black Mercedes coupes, each with a similar license plate.

SMOM, followed by a single number.

Sovereign Military Order of Malta.

A giant eight-pointed, white Maltese cross adorned the dark cobbles. The buildings around him rose three stories, all of the windows shuttered and closed. James Grant had told him that this was the Hospitallers' main administrative headquarters—its magisterial palace, the seat of the grand master and where the sovereign council convened.

Waiting for him was a man, looking prim in a three-buttoned, dark suit. Cotton had worn only a pale-blue button-down with the sleeves rolled up, khaki trousers, and loafers. Seriously underdressed. But at least he was showered and shaved. Grant had called ahead and secured the necessary clearances to allow him into the courtyard. He was right on time and a little surprised at the lack of security, but the whole place was the definition of low-key. Only a small plaque on the wooden gates at the archway denoted who occupied the building.

He approached the man in the suit. "I'm Cotton Malone. I have an appointment."

The man bowed his head in a timid indication of welcome. "I was sent to meet you."

He wondered about the courtesy. "Is that customary?"

"Only for visitors that MI6 asks us to accommodate, on short notice."

He caught the unshielded wave of irritation that floated across the words. "Are you aware of why I'm here?"

"Definitely. May I see it?"

He fished the ring from his pocket and displayed it.

"Quite a special piece of jewelry," the man said.

"Care to offer more?"

Both arms were withdrawn from behind the man's back to display his right hand. On one finger he saw an identical ring with the same palindrome of five words.

"It's a badge," the man said. "From another time. A responsibility that is no longer relevant."

"And yet I retrieved this one and you're still wearing one. Two in a single day—from something, as you say, that is no longer relevant."

No reply.

"Are you a knight?" he asked.

"I am."

"Professed?"

The guy nodded. "You're familiar with us?"

"Actually, I knew little to nothing about you until a couple of hours ago. And I still know zero about this ring."

He displayed it again for the man to see.

"Where exactly did you get it?" the man asked.

He'd come here for answers, and to receive, sometimes you gotta give. "Off a dead man."

"Did he have a name?"

"MI6 is working on supplying one. He carried no identification." He found his cell phone and showed a head shot of the corpse that Grant had sent. "One of yours?"

"I'll find out. Can you provide me with this photo?"

"Absolutely. Do I get to speak with the grand master?"

"We don't have one at present. Only a lieutenant ad interim. A temporary replacement. We're awaiting the conclave and a new pope before choosing a permanent leader."

He'd read earlier that grand masters were elected by the professed knights, in secret. But before they assumed office, the election had to be communicated in writing to the pope. That, of course, presupposed that a pope existed.

"Do I get to speak with the lieutenant ad interim?" he asked.

The man nodded. "He's waiting for you." Then he motioned at the stone stairway to their right. "Follow me, please."

Twelve years he worked for the Magellan Billet. Stephanie Nelle had recruited him straight out of the navy and he'd come with little to no training, learning everything on the job. Along the way he'd acquired a set of instincts that kept him alive and allowed him to quit on his own terms, retiring early, able to buy a bookshop in Denmark, fulfilling a lifelong dream. One of those instincts had flared earlier in Milan when James Grant so easily agreed to double his fee. Another arose when the money was promptly paid. Now a third festered with the bad vibes he was receiving from this emissary. Luckily, this was not his first briar patch, and he knew how to walk among thorns.

He approached the stairs, his host two steps beyond.

"By the way," he said, "what's your position with the knights?"

"I have several titles, one of which involves providing security for the organization. I help make sure everyone and everything stays safe."

The words were delivered with a confidence that came from being dressed in a shirt and tie. But they made sense. He assumed an outfit as large as the Hospitallers had a need for security.

They climbed the stairs.

He heard the distinctive thump of rotors beating through air.

A helicopter. Close by and coming closer.

"What's that?" he asked.

"Your transportation."

CHAPTER
SEVENTEEN

LUKE CLIMBED OUT OF THE *GUVA*.

Laura followed him, also using the rope. He caught her ease of technique and the fact that she barely needed a second breath from the effort. His original assessment seemed correct. She was in terrific shape.

He saw he was standing in an underground chamber, the walls more rough stone, the floor dank earth. Bright bulbs enclosed within metal cages lined the low ceiling and hurt his eyes. A door led out to a lit passageway beyond.

"These tunnels are from the knights," she said. "They burrowed like groundhogs under the city. They were mainly for water delivery and sanitation. But they also served as a way to move men and weapons around unnoticed. Miles of them still exist. During World War II the Maltese hid from the German bombers down here. Some are cleared and easy to get to. Others, not so much. This complex, and the *guva*, are known only to the government."

She started for the exit. The tunnel beyond seemed to go on forever. He didn't move. She stopped and turned back toward him, noticing his hesitation.

"You know what I want," he said to her.

She stood her ground. "I wouldn't press things. I'm not happy about having a partner. This does not involve the Americans in any way."

"Except for the fact that I'm now in on this."

"Only because Stephanie Nelle sent you here. Now my boss says you're to stay in."

"From what I hear, you don't take orders all that well."

"I do my job."

Something wasn't making sense. "Why did you call Stephanie in the first place?"

"To tell her that you were an idiot. Vatican intelligence made you the minute you hit this island."

"Why didn't you just say that to her?"

She shrugged. "I can take a hint. She clearly did not want my help. So I didn't offer anything."

"Did the Entity know I was coming here?"

"If it'll make you feel better, yes, they did."

She had an intensity in her eyes, a shade of brown that came close to blackness. She also had a wonderful square jaw that suggested tenacity.

Which he liked.

"Look," she said. "Contrary to what the faithful think, a conclave is not run by the Holy Spirit. Nothing from heaven comes down and inspires those old men on how to vote. The church was created by men and is run by men. It's men who will elect the pope. That means things can go wrong. Our focus is Kastor Gallo, the *kappillan* from Malta."

He smirked. "I don't speak Maltese spy language."

"A priest, who went on to become a bishop, a cardinal, then a total pain in the ass. He's caused a lot of problems, made a lot of enemies. Now he's making a play for the papacy."

"Who wants to stop him?"

"Hell if I know. It only matters to me because my boss says it does. Our problem is that Kastor Gallo is a lot of things, but he's not stupid. Unfortunately, you are. And thanks to you, he now knows he's being watched."

She was right. He'd definitely screwed things up by being made, and she was obviously pissed. He would be, too, if the roles were reversed. So he decided to lighten things up. "It's not all that bad. Who knows, you might learn something from this joint operation."

She shook her head. "Like how to be caught listening in on a conversation?"

"You don't back off, do you?"

"No, I don't. I have a job to do, and the clock is ticking. Right now we have to get ahead of Gallo." She shook her head. "I was supposed to observe and report. Simple and easy. But now, thanks to your interference, we have to change things up. I have less than one day left to deliver. And unlike you, I always deliver."

Her voice came low and throaty and strangely erotic. But it also held an odd quality, like she was trying to earn the trust of a small dog only to strangle it once she held it in her arms.

No matter.

He decided to quit pushing.

"For the record," he said, "there are a zillion people out there on the streets of Valletta. I had no way of knowing the Entity was on me."

"Your problem is you don't know the players. A little local knowledge goes a long way. I'm assuming that's why they now want us together."

"All you had to do was say that to Stephanie in the first place."

She tossed him a grin. "Okay. I'll give you that one. But I was hoping to leave you out there on the water."

Finally. The truth.

Which made sense.

He glanced around. "How do we get out of here?"

"Down that tunnel is a staircase up."

"Then what?"

"We have an appointment to keep."

CHAPTER EIGHTEEN

KASTOR CONTINUED TO READ.

Spagna had apparently been thorough with his investigation, especially with regard to the tradition known as Peter's Pence.

The alms of St. Peter were donations made directly to Rome, rather than to local parishes. It started back in the 9th century when the English king Alfred collected a pence from landowners as financial support for the pope. The practice eventually spread across Europe before fading with the Reformation. Pius IX, in 1871, brought it back but changed its purpose. No longer was the money solely for the pope's exclusive use—now it was spent to help the poor worldwide. The collection was taken each year, in all churches, on the feast of Saints Peter and Paul. Nobody outside the curia really knew exactly how much was acquired annually.

Except Spagna.

There is a serious and continual problem with the Peter's Pence collections. Currently, the annual total is between €200 and €250 million. Last year, the Holy Father called on each Catholic to be a witness of charity. He encouraged them to "open your eyes and see the misery of the world, the wounds of our brothers and sisters who are denied their dignity, and let us recognize that we are compelled to heed their cry for help." According to the Vatican's own website, the Peter's Pence collection "unites us in solidarity to the Holy See and its works of charity to those in need. Your generosity allows the pope to respond to our suffering brothers and sisters." Nothing could be further from the truth. Over the course of the past five years, 78% of what was collected through Peter's Pence has been used to fund budgetary deficits within the Holy See. These deficits were the direct result of the waste, fraud, and abuse, as is detailed in this summary report. A select group of cardinals are privy to both the false advertising and the misappropriation of Peter's Pence. No less than four cardinals are involved in the deception.

He could barely contain himself.

So many of the pompous, arrogant red vultures, as Spagna called the cardinals, had reveled in his demise. Yet apparently some of them were guilty of the most heinous of crimes. What many had suspected for decades, himself included, now seemed confirmed.

Corruption ran rampant in the curia.

In fact, it appeared to be institutionalized.

Worse yet, the ones in charge seemed intent on both covering it up and keeping it going.

Contrary to what people thought, the pope's word was not absolute when it came to running the church. The curia had existed for over a thousand years, and during that time it had perfected the art of survival. The system was so entrenched, so convoluted, that no one had ever successfully mounted any meaningful reform. Popes of late had tried, John Paul I and Francis I the most notable. Both failed. And one, Benedict XVI, resigned in frustration over making changes, as they would have entailed firing many of his longtime friends. Tales of internal investigations and secret audits had long run rampant. Francis had even empowered two so-called independent commissions to both investigate the abuses and recommend changes, but nothing ever materialized.

Which, again, was no surprise.

The curia were experts in procrastination and misdirection. Magicians extraordinaire. As Spagna had just confirmed, two sets of records and fanciful accounting were commonplace. So adept were they, even pressure from the pope himself could be deflected. Why? Because in the end, a pope needed the curia. It took people to run a multibillion-euro enterprise and, as wasteful as it may be, the curia kept the Holy See going. Similar to the Allies after World War II who held their noses and made use of ex-Nazis all across Germany. Not the best choice, just the only choice.

He needed to finish the final few pages.

So he turned his attention back to the summary.

> There is an incident that illustrates precisely the level and extent of the current abuses. One cardinal, the beneficiary of a free apartment located close to Vatican City, wanted to expand his living space. When his neighbor, an elderly priest granted a rent subsidy for health reasons, was hospitalized, the cardinal commissioned renovations and broke through a wall between the two apartments, appropriating additional living space, even to the extent of retaining the elderly priest's furniture. Once discharged from the hospital, the priest discovered the intrusion. But there was nothing he could do. No one within the Holy See would challenge the cardinal. The priest died a short time later (which is why the incident remained quiet) and that cardinal still has possession of his enlarged, rent-free apartment.

He rattled through his brain trying to put a name to the anonymous cardinal. He knew of several who lived in and around the Vatican. No matter who it might be, he was going to enjoy destroying that man.

> Another curious anomaly has been discovered. John Paul I died in September 1978, after only thirty-three days as pope. But there exists within the Vatican bank an account bearing his name that currently has €110,000 on deposit. Even more curious, there has been continuous activity within that account to this day. One cardinal's name is associated with that activity. There are at least eight other accounts associated with deceased persons where unexplained financial activity is occurring. The best explanation points to institutionalized theft and embezzlement.
>
> Then there is the process of sainthood where corruption appears to have risen to its greatest heights. The process of sainthood has

been steeped in secrecy for centuries. To open a case for beatification a fee of €50,000 is currently charged. On top of that another €15,000 is required to offset "operating costs." These moneys go not only to the Holy See, but to pay the unreasonably high fees charged by expert theologians, doctors, and bishops who examine the proposed saint's cause. To that are added the costs for researchers, the drafting of the candidate's résumé, and the work of the postulator who champions the candidate's nomination. The average cost per sainthood candidate is nearly €500,000. But that is not all. At each point along the process there are festivities where prelates are invited to speak of the future saint's acts and miracles. Gifts are routinely provided to those prelates, which is in addition to the above-detailed expenses. In the end, the total cost to become a saint ranges somewhere between €600,000 and €750,000.

To illustrate the extent of this massive revenue stream, under John Paul II, 1,338 anointed blessed and 482 saints were named. The amount of moneys generated from these 1,820 accounts topped €1 billion. Incredibly, in 1983, John Paul II ordered that all of those moneys were to be managed, not by the Church but by the individual postulators, who were instructed to keep "regularly updated ledgers" on every single potential saint, detailing where all moneys collected were spent. But no oversight on these outsiders was ordered. No audits were ever performed. The postulators operated outside the Holy See with a free hand, one that still exists today. Needless to say, their misuse of over a billion euros exceeds the scope of this summary. But I am privy to their corruption and embezzlement, which is massive, all occurring under the watchful eye of at least six current cardinals, who have also secretly shared in those proceeds.

He stopped reading, astonished by the hypocrisy. What arrogant, pompous, lying thieves. Never once had he stolen from the church. No gratuities. No free trips. No special gifts, as he knew some of the cardinals called that patronage. Nothing. Odd, since Spagna was right. In his youth he'd been vastly different. Stealing had been common. But the older he became, the less physical things mattered. He was after something far more alluring. More satisfying.

Absolute power.

The café's courtyard remained empty. The time was approaching 4:00 P.M. He nursed a third glass of wine, his thoughts a whirlwind of confusion. He had no doubt that every allegation Spagna had made could be proven. The Entity would know how to follow money trails, how to sniff out dummy accounts and fraud, how to break through walls of secrecy and learn who was controlling what and how much.

Everything he'd read was true.

That was the whole point of passing it on. As was the lack of names. Not a single offender had been identified. This had been designed to merely whet his appetite.

And it succeeded.

Movement to his right caught his attention.

From the shadows he saw Arani Chatterjee, who entered the courtyard and calmly walked over and sat at the table uninvited.

"I see I was easy to find."

"Your love of this place is noted in our files." Chatterjee pointed. "Did you read it?"

He nodded. "Does he have the proof?"

"Oh, yes." Chatterjee reached into his pocket and produced a flash drive. "It's all on here. Audio recordings, documents, records scans, bank statements, surveillance reports. Every detail on every allegation, along with the name of every offender. Quite a list of bishops, monsignors, and cardinals, I'm told, most of whom should go to jail. Thankfully for them, the Holy See has no prisons."

He could only imagine that list of names. It had to include the heads of the Institute of Religious Works, a fancy label for the Vatican Bank, which controlled all of the church's financial assets. Also the *Amministrazione del Patrimonio della sede Apostolica,* which maintained the real estate holdings. The Governorate, which managed the museums and all of the for-profit commercial activities like the retail shops and stores. Along with the Prefecture for the Economic Affairs of the Holy See that oversaw every Vatican office. Those were the big four, and the cardinals currently managing them came from around the world. Chile, Honduras, the United States, India, Germany, the Congo, Australia. Not a one of them had ever lifted a finger to help him.

They would all go down.

But only after they voted for his papacy.

Every damn one of them would write his name on their ballot.

"What does Revelation warn?" Chatterjee asked. "That a corrupt church sits on the city of seven hills?"

Which is what Rome had long been called.

"And its corruption will grow and finally be destroyed," Chatterjee added, repocketing the flash drive.

All well and good, but, "I need to know what Spagna wants in return for this—invaluable—help."

"Right now? Simply that you find the *Nostra Trinità*. As he told you, he wants that secured. He understands that you want to use it to make you pope. If the legends are to be believed, it might have a certain value. But seventeen hundred years have passed since its creation. What you just read, though, is more immediate and has a far greater value. So he wants a trade. Let him have the Trinity, and you get all that,"—Chatterjee pointed at the pages—"plus the flash drive."

"Will he destroy the *Nostra Trinità*?"

"Absolutely."

He didn't necessarily disagree with that course. That had been his intention, too. Once he achieved the papacy, the last thing he'd want was for anything to cast doubt.

"Also," Chatterjee said, "after an appropriate time, no more than ninety days beyond your coronation, you will make the archbishop a cardinal. He wants to die with a red hat on his head."

"He doesn't seem to like the 'red vultures.'"

"He despises them. But he still wants to be one."

"He's a bit old."

"You will likewise appoint him head of the Entity, dismissing the current cardinal who oversees that department. He's no friend of the archbishop's and, by the way, no friend of yours, either."

"Making Spagna a cardinal will raise a lot of questions."

"So? Only a pope chooses a cardinal and that is not subject to question or review. It's solely your decision. And no secret appointments. This one is all public."

It was almost like this demon was reading his mind. Popes had the power to name cardinals *in pectore,* in the breast, with only the pope knowing of the appointment, *in his heart.* But *in pectore* cardinals could only function after the appointment became public. In modern times it had been used to protect an appointee from hostile political situations in places like China, Ukraine, Latvia, and Russia. Once the pope made the appointment public, the secret cardinal would then assume his duties and be ranked within the cardinalate back to the time of his selection. However, if a pope died before revealing the *in pectore* cardinal, the appointment died, too.

"John Paul II gave Archbishop Spagna an *in pectore* appointment, but died before revealing it," Chatterjee said. "Not this time. He wants the red hat and the investiture ceremony. He wants all of the red vultures to be there and watch as he joins their ranks. The one thing you and he agree on is a mutual hatred of the curia."

For so long the taste of failure had lingered in his mouth. Becoming pope would, in one stroke, regain everything he'd lost. He'd once said that the church's greatest sin of modern times was an unwillingness to become involved.

The sin of omission.

Popes had grown soft, their voices devoid of thunder.

He would change that.

He'd originally thought that what he sought might be the best weapon to use in the coming conclave to sway votes. Now it seemed only a means to a better end. And he had no problem with any of Spagna's demands.

But there were two things.

First—

"As head of the Entity, Spagna will do whatever I need done. No questions. No debate. Just do it."

"Of course, that goes without saying."

And second—

"What happened with the woman in the boat and the American parasailer?"

Chatterjee nodded. *"Alea jacta est."*

He grinned at the irony.

The die is cast.

CHAPTER
NINETEEN

COTTON FELT THE SWOOP AS THE HELICOPTER BEGAN TO DESCEND toward the Italian countryside. His greeter had led him to the top of the Palazzo di Malta, where a black-and-white AgustaWestland AW139 bearing civilian markings had landed on a small pad. He'd been under the mistaken impression that the interim grand master would be at the palazzo. Instead he'd been informed that the lieutenant ad interim waited at Villa Pagana, a seaside residence in Rapallo, about 250 miles to the north.

Evening was approaching, the late-afternoon sun hanging solemn in the western sky. Being transported a long way from Rome only raised more red flags in his already suspicious mind. True, the pessimist might be right in the long run, but he'd come to know that the optimist had a better time along the way. So he decided to keep an open mind.

He stared down at Rapallo, which looked like a typical seaside Italian town. An amphitheater of hills faced the sea supporting a jumble of white-washed houses with red-tile roofs that funneled downward to a stark stretch of sandy beach. A promenade lined the shore, flanked by a small castle. Boats and yachts rolled at anchor in the blue waters of the Ligurian Sea.

The chopper came in low over the shoreline and flew inland, angling toward one of the villas, an impressive three-story battlement of ocher stone, set among a thick stand of maritime pines dominating a rocky promontory. A red flag with a white Maltese cross flew above its parapets.

"The villa was built in the 1600s," his escort told him. "But it has only been the summer residence of the grand masters since the 1950s."

They sat in a comfortable rear compartment, free of vibration, with black leather seats and enough insulation that their voices could be heard over the rotors.

He glanced out the window and noticed the manicured grounds, dotted with cacti, palm trees, and a carpet of flowers. At the promontory's tip he spotted a ruined fortification. A small grassy clearing not far from the house seemed to serve as a landing pad, and the pilot eased the helicopter down to a gentle stop.

A black Mercedes coupe waited beyond the wash of the blades, and he followed his host to the car. In the backseat, across from him, sat a broad-shouldered man with neatly combed dark hair. He was clean-featured with a hard, lanky build. He sat straight with a military bearing, his jaw stretched forward, the face as bland as milk. As with his escort from Rome, this one wore a three-buttoned dark suit and striped tie, a pale-blue handkerchief providing a discreet contrast of color at the top of the breast pocket.

"I'm Pollux Gallo, the lieutenant ad interim."

No hand was extended to shake, but his host did offer a slight smile of welcome.

"Cotton Malone. Sir James Grant sent me."

The car drove across the grass and found a paved drive, heading away from the villa.

"Where are we going?"

"To obtain the answers you seek."

He'd immediately noticed the ring on Gallo's right hand. He found the one he'd taken from the dead man in his pocket.

"I was briefed by the British on what happened to you earlier today," Gallo said. "They told me about that ring. I believe I can shed some light on the matter."

"Were you shown a photo of the dead man?"

Gallo nodded. "He's not one of us. But we've seen these copied rings before. There are jewelry stores across France and Italy that sell them. The palindrome is called a Sator Square, after the first word in the line of five. It has existed for a long time, with Roman origins."

"Why is a Maltese cross inside?"

Gallo shrugged. "A good question."

"I bet the one on your finger has a cross inside it, too. My guess is those copycats don't have that addition."

Finally a slight rise of the eyebrows signaling irritation. Good. This guy needed to know that he wasn't dealing with an amateur.

He'd always hated funerals and only attended them when absolutely necessary. His first had been as a teenager, when his grandfather died. His own father disappeared when he was ten, lost at sea in a navy submarine. As a teenager, he and his mother moved back to Georgia and lived on the family's onion farm. He and his grandfather grew close, and eventually seeing the old man in that coffin had hurt more than he'd ever imagined. He also remembered the funeral director. A dour man, not much different in looks and bearing from the statue sitting across from him, uttering predictable words.

So he told himself to stay alert.

"In 1957," Gallo said, his voice lowered, "a trial occurred in Padua, Italy, where some of the partisans involved in the 1945 disappearance of Mussolini's gold were prosecuted. Rumors had been rampant for years of how the gold might have been kept by the locals. Twelve years of investigation led to thirty-five defendants being charged with theft. Three hundred witnesses were subpoenaed. The trial was expected to last eight months, but was abruptly halted by the presiding judge after only twenty-six witnesses testified. It never reconvened and no further official inquiry was ever made into the gold's disappearance. The presiding judge at that trial resigned his post in 1958. Interestingly, afterward he lived a posh life in a villa. That judge's grandson was the man killed this morning. The owner of the villa by Lake Como."

"Obviously, the judge was paid off."

"I have no idea. I can only tell you what happened. We know that, on April 25, 1945, Allied forces were less than fifty miles from Milan. Mussolini called an emergency meeting of his cabinet and told them he was fleeing north to Switzerland. He then ordered what was left of the Italian treasury brought to the cabinet meeting. It consisted of gold ingots, currency, and the Italian crown jewels. He distributed the cash and jewels among his ministers and ordered them to leave the city with their caches. He kept the gold, some of the currency, and a few of the jewels. The best estimate is that about a hundred million U.S. dollars' worth, in 1945 values, came north with him. Most of the currency would be worthless today. But the gold and jewels are another matter. Surely worth over a billion euros in today's value."

That was indeed an impressive treasure.

"Which answers your question," Gallo said. "The Italian justice system leaves a lot to be desired. Corruption is common. There is little doubt that judge was bribed. But again, we'll never know the truth, as the matter was not investigated. But part of that 1957 trial record consists of depositions detailing the inventory of two elephant-skin satchels, which were taken from Mussolini when he was captured. Both had the party's symbol etched on the outside. An eagle clutching a fasces."

One of which he'd held in his hands earlier.

"Both of those satchels disappeared," Gallo said. "They have not been seen since 1945. By 1960 nearly everyone associated with what had been found with Mussolini had either died or disappeared. Ever since, men have searched. Now, today, you apparently found one of the satchels."

They were following a two-lane switchback road that descended from the promontory. The man who'd brought him from Rome sat in the front passenger seat, a third man in another dark suit driving. Neither had spoken, or even acknowledged that there was someone else in the car.

"What do you know about the letters between Mussolini and Churchill?" he asked Gallo.

"I'm familiar with the speculation. The British have long believed Mussolini brought some, or all, of his correspondence with Churchill north during his escape attempt. That is a possibility. There was an emissary of ours present both in Dongo and at the villa where Mussolini and his mistress were kept the night before they died. Mussolini spoke of documents he had that the British might find embarrassing. He even offered them in return for safe passage out of Italy. But he did not elaborate on what those were and, by the time he spoke of them, they were no longer in his possession. The partisans had them in Dongo."

"Why was an emissary of the Hospitallers talking to Mussolini?"

"We wanted something he stole from us returned. We hoped he'd brought it north, too."

Cotton motioned with the ring. "Something like this?"

Gallo nodded. "One of these rings was involved. Taken from a professed knight whom Mussolini had ordered killed. We definitely wanted it returned."

He waited for more, but nothing was offered. So he tried something easier. "I need to know more about this ring."

"It represents a sect that once existed within our ranks called the *Secreti*. They date back to the Crusades and our time in Jerusalem, and they were a part of us in Rhodes and Malta. Only the highest-ranking knights were invited to join, their numbers small. For a long time not even the grand masters were privy to their activities. That was because grand masters only lived a few years, or even a few months. Many of them inept and corrupt. The *Secreti* lasted longer and kept true to their vows. They became a law unto themselves, trusting no one, using their own methods, their own rules, their own justice to keep the order's secrets safe. The only thing those men trusted was God. For all intents and purposes, though, they ended when Napoleon claimed Malta. The knights dispersed across the globe, our secrets going with them. They were formally disbanded just after World War II."

"Yet you, the guy in the front seat, and the dead man back at Como are all still wearing the ring."

Gallo smiled. The effort seemed almost painful. "Merely ceremonial, Mr. Malone. A hark back to another time. We Hospitallers are appreciative of the past. We like to recall it. And to answer your question from earlier, there is a Maltese cross etched inside my ring. But the *Secreti* no longer exist. Our rings are mere copies, made by a Roman jeweler. I can provide his name and address, if you like."

It all sounded so innocent, so correct, but nothing about this man rang right. Particularly annoying was the lowered voice, which seemed a means of ascendancy, a way to shrink others down and control the conversation.

"You're in temporary charge of the Hospitallers?" he asked.

Gallo nodded. "I was selected to fill the position after the grand master was forced to resign. We planned on making a permanent choice two weeks ago, but the pope's death changed that. We will convene after the conclave and select a new leader."

He was curious, "Your last name. Gallo. Any relation to Cardinal Gallo?"

"He is my brother."

Now that was convenient. From the media accounts he'd read the cardinal had wreaked havoc within the Hospitallers, essentially masterminding the grand master's ouster. Then his brother emerged as the temporary man in charge? What were the odds on that one? He also recalled what James Grant had wanted him to explore.

"I'm told that the knights have a fascination with Mussolini?"

Gallo gave a slight shake of his head. "Not a fascination. More a historical interest. But that is a private matter, one we don't discuss outside our ranks."

Exactly what James Grant had warned they would say.

His host shifted slightly in the leather seat. Enough that Cotton caught a glimpse of what he thought might be a shoulder holster beneath the suit jacket.

Intriguing.

Why did a professed man of God carry a weapon? True, Hospitallers were once warrior-monks, defending the honor of Christ and the church.

But not anymore.

They were now climbing a ridge on a second switchback road. The Ligurian Sea stretched toward the western horizon, looking pale and weary in the faint red glow of the setting sun. The lights of Portofino could be seen in the distance. Ahead, he spotted an irregular group of buildings, perched on a precipitous neck of stone, facing the water. They had a fortresslike character from the crenellated walls to the distinctive towers, and seemed more hacked by the wind and rain from the rock than human-made.

"We're headed for that monastery?" he asked Gallo.

"It was once a holy place. But we acquired the site about sixty years ago."

The car kept climbing.

"When we were forced from Malta by Napoleon," Gallo said, "we took some of our archives with us. They were stored in various places around Europe, sometimes not all that carefully. Finally we obtained this site, refurbished the old buildings, and consolidated everything. There is a small repository still on Malta, but the majority of our records and artifacts are kept here."

The car turned onto a short drive, then passed through an open gate into an enclosed courtyard. Floodlights lit the cobbles to reveal another huge white Maltese cross etched into their surface.

The Mercedes stopped.

"You should feel privileged," Gallo said.

"How so?"

"Few outside the knights are ever allowed here."

But he was not comforted by the honor.

THE KNIGHT LOWERED THE BINOCULARS.

His view of the old monastery, now an archival repository for the Knights of Malta, was unobstructed from his dark perch. He'd watched from the trees as the car entered the lit courtyard and Cotton Malone emerged.

He'd traveled south from Como at a leisurely pace with the elephant-skin satchel and its contents safe within his car. Before leaving Menaggio, he'd read all eleven letters between Churchill and Mussolini, learning enough of the details that he could now speak intelligently about them.

And he had.

Talking to the British by phone, informing them as to what he possessed, what he wanted, and learning what they desired in return.

Which had surprised him.

But it had been doable.

He glanced at his watch.

Time to go.

He had a meeting.

CHAPTER
TWENTY

5:40 P.M.

LUKE STEPPED OUT OF THE BUILDING ONTO ONE OF VALLETTA'S QUI-
eter side streets. Actually, more an alley between two walls of stone. He
saw traffic moving along perpendicular at either end. He'd followed Laura
Price up from the tunnels into a basement full of wooden crates. Mostly
wine. From the looks of things, it was some sort of storage room. She
seemed to know her way around the nooks and crannies.

The evening was still warm from the sweltering day. They headed to
one end of the alley. When he caught sight of the harbor he realized he
was not far from his car. He'd always been blessed with a keen sense of direction. Numbers and names were tough to recall. Faces not much better.
But where he'd been? That stuck with him.

"I need my phone," he told her. "It's in my car."

"Can't it wait?"

"No. It can't."

He led the way.

"Cardinal Gallo is currently in Mdina," she told him. "That's about
twelve kilometers from here. The man who was on the Madliena Tower,
Arani Chatterjee, is there in Mdina with him."

Good. He owed that SOB.

"Chatterjee likes to call himself an archaeologist, and he has credentials, but he's really just a grave robber, a dealer in stolen antiquities."

They kept walking.

People filled the sidewalks, most dressed in T-shirts, shorts, and sandals. A brisk breeze swept in from the sea like an invisible river.

One question bothered him. "Why is everyone in such a panic over this conclave?"

"Picking a pope is a big deal."

"Really? I hadn't realized."

She caught his sarcasm.

"That's not the only thing in play," she said. "Gallo came here to meet with an archbishop named Danjel Spagna."

That name he knew. "He manages the Entity. I assume that's unusual."

"To say the least."

He loved a good book and spent much of his mandatory downtime reading. History was a favorite subject. He especially enjoyed books that dealt with the intelligence business. The exploits of the Entity were legendary, dating back centuries. It had been involved in one way or another with Britain's Elizabeth I, France's St. Bartholomew's Eve Massacre, the Spanish Armada, the assassinations of a Dutch prince and a French king, the attempted assassination of a Portuguese ruler, the War of Spanish Succession, the French Revolution, Napoleon's rise and fall, Cuba's war against Spain, several South American secessions, the fall of Kaiser Wilhelm during World War I, Hitler in World War II, and communism in the 1980s.

An amazing résumé.

He recalled what Simon Wiesenthal, the famed Nazi hunter, once said. *The best and most effective espionage service in the world belongs to the Vatican.*

Now here he was, at odds with it.

Ahead, he spotted the small parking lot where he'd started this morning. He hurried over and found his phone inside the rental, along with his Beretta, which he tucked at the base of his spine beneath his shirt.

"You do know that it's illegal to carry a weapon on this island without a special permit, which they rarely grant," she said.

"It's also illegal to assault and kidnap somebody. But that didn't stop you."

"I had no choice."

Maybe. But he was still pissed about it.

"Don't let the local police see that gun. Agent or no agent, they'll arrest you, and I don't have time to get you out."

"Not a problem."

"We need to head toward central downtown."

He wondered if Stephanie Nelle had really approved this joint operation. His last instructions had been to get rid of Laura Price. He should call in, but he decided to give this little venture a bit more time and see where things led before bothering the boss.

A few minutes' walk and they found themselves on busy Republic Street, which ran from the southern city gate, past Freedom Square, to bastions at the water's edge. An impenetrable mass of people had taken possession of it, many surely from the cruise ships he'd seen earlier. Cars were obviously not allowed. The steady breeze sponged away what would surely be the cloying, musty smell of crowded humanity. The shops and eateries, lined one after the other like rabbit hutches, were all doing a brisk business. The co-cathedral and grand master's palace were closed, but the cobbled squares radiating from both were choked with visitors. Valletta seemed to be living up to its reputation as a popular tourist destination.

"Where are we going?" he asked.

But she did not answer him.

Instead they plunged into the chaos.

Among the crowd he spotted three uniformed police on Segways, one of whose gazes lingered a bit longer in their direction than it should. He might have dismissed it as paranoia, but that same officer found a handheld radio and started speaking into it. His gaze raked more of the faces around him and he spied another uniformed officer, on foot, who also stared their way just long enough to grab his attention.

"You catching this?" he said to her.

"I count four. They're definitely watching."

He liked that she was alert, aware of what was around her.

He surveyed the crowd again, his professional curiosity at its max. The nearest threat was fifty feet away, but the cops were situated in every direction, blocking the alleys radiating off Republic Street.

"I'll identify myself and deal with them," she said.

Seemed like the right course. One good guy to another. Surely she was known to the locals. There might be some animosity between law enforcement agencies, like back home, but in the end everyone tried to get along. What bothered him was that none of the police had approached. Instead they'd assumed a perimeter, held their positions, and used their radios.

Calling who?

"Stay here," she said.

Thirty yards away a blue-and-white police car turned out of one of the alleys, lights flashing, and inched its way through the pedestrian-only crowd toward the square that fronted the co-cathedral. From its front passenger side a man emerged. Tall, older, heavily built, with a mat of silver-white hair and white sideburns, dressed casually. He paused to look around and sniff the air, as if he knew someone was watching. He then found a cigar from his back pocket, snipped the end with a gold-colored guillotine, and lit the tip as he continued to survey the scene.

"Get out of here," she said, under her breath.

"You know that guy."

"That's Danjel Spagna. Get out of here."

Not his style to cut and run.

The officers were converging, all four closing the circle, coming straight for them.

Spagna blew a cloud of bluish smoke to the sky, then pointed with the cigar and called out, "Ms. Price. I need you and Mr. Daniels to come with me."

"I vote no," Luke said.

"Ditto."

"Two each?" he whispered.

"Absolutely."

He whirled and pounced on the officer closest, kicking him off the Segway. A second cop rushed forward, but Luke was a step ahead, planting his shoulder into the man's chest with a quick charge that lifted the guy off his feet, flinging him backward and down hard to the cobbles. Turning, he saw that Laura was not having the same success. One of her two targets had tackled her to the ground and the other, whom initially she'd managed to take down, had rebounded. Now they were subduing her. He could intervene, but it would only be another few moments before all four cops were up and in the mix and who knew how many more would arrive.

She'd been right.

One of them had to get out of here.

And he was elected.

He dissolved into the sea of people that had parted when the confrontation started, tucking his head and elbowing his way forward, layering bodies between him and trouble. He heard shouts behind him and managed a quick peek over his shoulder, seeing Laura being yanked to her feet and led toward the man she'd identified as Spagna. He escaped the crowd at its outer fringes and made his way down one of the alleys. No one was in pursuit. He ducked into a recessed doorway and found his cell phone, connecting to Stephanie's direct line. She answered and he filled her in on all that had happened, including the latest dilemma.

"Things have changed, Luke. I need you to work with Ms. Price."

"So you okayed this partnership?"

"I went along with it. Temporarily."

"Ordinarily I'd be a good little soldier and do exactly as you say. But I need to know what the hell is going on. I'm flying blind here."

"All I can say is that Danjel Spagna being there, in Valletta, is proof enough that something big is brewing. Earlier I thought Ms. Price just an irritant. Now we need her help. She has institutional knowledge that can speed things up for us."

Stephanie's tone was slow and even, just like in every crisis. That's what made her so good. She never lost her cool.

But he was beginning to lose his. "Spagna has her."

"You're a smart guy. Change that."

He started to toss her a wisecrack but he knew what she wanted to hear. "I'll make it happen."

"Good. I have a two-front war at the moment, and the other end is in big trouble."

The last thing he ever wanted was to add to her problems.

His job was to solve things.

"It's Cotton, Luke. He's walked into a hornet's nest."

CHAPTER
TWENTY-ONE

ITALY

COTTON CROSSED THE PAVED COURTYARD, FOLLOWING POLLUX Gallo into the monastery's refectory, a spacious room of plastered limestone blocks and a tile floor littered with workstations.

"We spent a lot of money refurbishing this complex," Gallo said. "It was nearly falling in on itself. Now it is the Conservatory of Library and Archives. A state-of-the-art facility."

And unknown to the world, Cotton silently added. But he assumed a lot about the Knights of Malta would fit into that category.

His original greeter from Rome had accompanied them inside, the driver remaining with the car. Waiting in the refectory were two brown-robed monks. Both were young and short-haired, with a no-nonsense glint in their eyes. Not exactly the religious type. They stood quiet and attentive.

"I thought this was no longer a monastery," he said.

"It's not, but these brothers are part of a contingent that maintains the archive."

Gallo motioned ahead and they left through a plank door in the far side, entering a lit cloister that led past former monk cells on one side and a garden on the other. Each of the cells was identified by a number and letter, the old wooden doors replaced with metal panels and keypad locks.

"Each room contains a different segment of our archives," Gallo said.

"We have everything cataloged and electronically indexed for easy reference. The rooms are also climate-controlled."

They rounded a corner and, on the far side of the cloister, entered a room through another metal door, this one open, taller and wider than the others. The space beyond was more like a hall, what had surely once been the chapter house. Wooden benches, where the monks had congregated, still lined the now painted stone walls. He noticed the irregular shape and the two central columns that supported arched ribs for the vaults, dividing the floor and ceiling into three bays. He also felt the change in temperature and humidity, both lower, which signaled sophisticated climate control. Wisely, a fire-suppression sprinkler system dotted the ceiling, exposed metal pipes connecting each faucet. Lighting spilled out from hanging opaque, glass balls that tossed off a warm glow. Stout oak tables stood in rows across the tile floor. On them sat manuscripts, ecclesiastical plates, pectorals, reliquaries, and crosses. His trained bibliophile eye focused on the manuscripts, where he spied chrysobulls, sigillia, and documents bearing holy seals. Glass domes protected each from any casual touch.

"We have around fifteen thousand manuscripts stored in the facility," Gallo said. "Most are originals and first editions. There are rare Bibles, the classics, scientific texts, dictionaries. We have a little of everything, but we've been collecting for nine centuries. This room houses a few of the items we occasionally allow visitors to see."

"Potential contributors?"

Gallo nodded. "It takes over two hundred million euros to keep the order solvent each year. Most comes from governments, the United Nations, and the EU. But we also depend on the generosity of private donors. So yes, this collection can sometimes be helpful in spurring their interest."

The two robed brothers at first waited outside but eventually followed them into the chapter house. His escort from Rome had lingered back in the refectory. He knew Gallo was probably armed, and on the walk over he'd noticed the distinctive bulge of a weapon holstered at the base of the spine beneath each of the two robes as well.

Nothing but trouble surrounded him.

Which seemed the story of his life.

"Why don't we dispense with coy," Gallo said. His host stood with the straight back of self-discipline. "The British have long wanted to see inside this archive. They've covertly tried several times. Now they've finally succeeded."

"With your permission, of course. You know full well I'm here on their behalf. And we didn't ask for this tour."

"They called and demanded to speak to me. They insinuated that my fellow knights were somehow involved with what happened to you earlier today at Lake Como. Murder. Theft. Burglary. I told Sir James Grant that he was mistaken."

But that was a lie. Too much here just didn't add up. Or more correctly, it added up to something that wasn't good. Here he was again among that great, swirling maelstrom of possibilities where his life hung in the balance. Parts of him detested and parts of him craved the conflict. For a dozen years he'd lived with that threat every day. Move. Countermove. All part of the game. But he'd retired out early in order to quit playing.

Yeah, right.

He stepped close to one of the tables and examined through a glass dome what was noted as a 13th-century gospel with an exquisite wooden cover and Moroccan leather binding. He guessed it had to be worth several hundred thousand dollars. He kept his eyes down on the artifact but began to ready himself. As a Magellan Billet agent, most of his mistakes had come when there was too much time to think. Act. React. Counteract. Doesn't matter. Just do something.

"Where are they?" he asked, continuing to focus on the old gospel, its cover darkened with age and infested with a fine spiderweb of cracks like an unrestored Rembrandt.

Gallo seemed to know exactly what he meant and motioned. One of the robes walked to the far side of the next row of tables and lifted the elephant-skin satchel from the floor. He gave it a quick glance, then returned to perusing the objects on the table before him, inching ever closer to the second robed monk.

"Who shot the guy in the villa?" he asked Gallo.

"Why does it matter? That man failed to do his job."

He faced his adversary. "Which wasn't to kill me or be captured. No. You wanted the British to know you were there."

"I did, but thankfully the ring led you straight here."

"Along with you hanging a guy by his arms pulled up behind his back."

"Which once sent fear down the spines of Saracens in the Holy Land."

That was a bold admission, which meant Gallo thought himself in control of the situation.

He returned to perusing the objects on the table. "These manuscripts are impressive."

"As a bookseller, I thought you might appreciate our collection."

"I do. Why are the Churchill–Mussolini letters so important to you?"

"They are a means to an end."

Only two things made sense. Either James Grant had no idea what was going on and he'd sent someone to find out. Or he had every idea and he'd sent that same someone so they would not come back.

He chose option two.

Which made his next course clear.

His target was now about four feet away, and the blankness of the young, robed man's gaze seemed almost like a warning. He stopped and admired another of the exquisite manuscripts under glass. He almost hated what he was about to do.

But what choice did he have.

Gallo's gun beneath his suit jacket was in easier reach than the ones the brown robes toted. He'd need a few seconds so, on the pretense of admiring the manuscript before him, he suddenly grabbed the heavy glass cover and hurled it toward Gallo. His left hand flew up in a back fist to the face of the brother standing beside him, followed by an elbow to the kidneys.

The guy went reeling.

He used that moment to part the robe and grab the man's weapon. He then kneed the guy in the face, sending him downward. The glass cover had hit Gallo, but he managed to deflect it away where it shattered across the hard floor. The other brother was reaching back for his gun.

So was Gallo.

He sent two bullets their way.

Both men disappeared beneath the tables.

He readjusted his aim and fired into the lighted glass fixtures hanging above him, exploding two of them in a burst of sparks and smoke. Gallo was rising back up, so he fired that way again, the round ricocheting off the top of the table. He exploded another fixture, which added more sparks and smoke.

Would it be enough?

An alarm sounded and the sprinklers erupted, called to action by the possibility of a fire. He upended the table before him, depositing the artifacts it displayed onto the wet floor, their glass domes bursting to shards. He left the thick oak top lying perpendicular to the floor, using it as a shield to block Gallo and the other robe from firing beneath the tables. He could now use that protected route to make his way toward the exit. Dropping down, he rolled across the tile, alternating between patches of dry and wet as he passed more tables and the aisles in between. Gallo would surely figure it out and change positions, but it would take a few seconds.

He had to make the most of the time he'd bought.

Three shots came his way, but the downed table continued to run interference. He scrambled up on all fours and hurried past the last row. Before coming to his feet he carefully peered over the top and saw Gallo and the other robe standing, guns ready, waiting for him to emerge.

Water continued to rain down.

The klaxon still sounded.

Shots came his way.

He decided to keep doing the unexpected and fired twice, once each into the clear domes on the tables where the two men stood. Glass exploded, shards spreading outward like seeds cast from a hand. Gallo and his acolyte reared back to avoid the projectiles. He used that moment to flee the chapter house, back into the cloister. He could retrace the route toward the refectory, but that was a long, open run and he wouldn't make it far without drawing fire. Neither could he escape left or right—the cloister would only become a shooting gallery. But a set of double plank doors about twenty feet away might offer refuge.

He raced toward them and the iron lock clicked open on the first try. He shoved the leaden oak door inward, then closed it gently, hoping his pursuers wouldn't notice.

There was no lock on the inside.

More incandescent fixtures lantern-lit a chapel, the interior spacious, an impressive gilded altar and sculpted statues casting ghostly images through the dim light. No one was in sight.

The fire alarm stopped.

He searched the darkness toward the altar and spotted stairs to the right. A pallid glow strained from below. He headed for them and descended into a crypt, a cold cloud of worry filling him. Was he simply heading down into a dead end? An iron gate opened into an ample, three-naved wide space. The ceiling was low-vaulted, a small rectangular altar niche to his right. Three medieval stone sarcophagi topped with immense slabs of carved granite lined the center. The only break in the darkness came from a tiny yellow light near the altar that illuminated a few square feet. The rest of the space remained in shadows, the air stale and fetid and noticeably chilly.

He heard the oak door opening above.

His eyes, alert and watchful, shot to the top of the low vault not two feet from the crown of his head.

Footsteps bounded across the marble floor.

He crept across the crypt into a far nave. His mind filled with anticipation, which he tried to suppress with a wave of self-control. He'd fired a lot of rounds in the chapter house, so he checked the gun's magazine.

Empty.

Great.

He needed something to defend himself with, so he searched the darkness. In a small apse about twenty feet away he spotted an iron candelabrum. He hustled over. The ornament stood about five feet tall, a solitary wax candle, about four inches thick, rising from the center. He grabbed the stem and noticed its weight. Solid. He brought both the candelabrum and candle with him as he assumed a position behind another of the pillars.

Someone started down the steps to the crypt.

He peered around the edge, past the tombs, through the blackness. The tiny altar light offered little assistance. His emotions alternated between fear and excitement, his body alive with a strange kind of energy, an unexplained power that had always clarified his thoughts. In the archway, at the base of the stairs, stood the outline of one of the robed brothers.

The silhouette crept in, gun leading the way.

He tightened his grip on the iron stem and cocked his arms back. He knew he had to draw the guy closer, so he ground the sole of his right shoe into the grit on the floor. A quick glance around the pillar confirmed that the man was now moving toward him. Shadows bobbed, swelled, then lessened on the ceiling. His muscles tensed. He silently counted to five, clenched his teeth, then lunged, swinging the candelabrum. He caught the guy square in the chest, sending the shadow back onto one of the Romanesque tombs. He tossed the iron aside and swung his fist hard to the face. The gun left the man's grip and rattled across the mosaics.

His pursuer shot up and pounced.

But he was ready.

A second facial punch and another to the midsection sent the man teetering. He then tripped the guy's feet out from under him, which allowed the head to pop the flagstones hard.

The man's body went still.

He searched the floor for the gun, finding it and curving his fingers around the butt just as another set of footsteps bounded down and into the crypt.

Two shots came in his direction.

Dust snowed down from the vault as bullets found stone. He sought cover behind the pillar, peered around the edge, and fired once. The bullet ricocheted off the far wall, a signal that he was armed and ready.

It seemed to get attention.

"There's no way out."

Gallo's voice, lashing across the chamber with an icy menace, from a position behind the farthest tomb.

Between him and the only exit was an armed man bent on killing him. But Gallo was pinned, too. No way for him to get back to the stairs without being shot, either. He needed to draw Gallo out, cause a mistake.

He glanced around and spotted the thick candle on the floor.

He reached down and took hold of it, then focused across the dim nave, determining that there was enough darkness for the candle to be mistaken for something else. So he arced the wax cylinder across the open space between the pillars, flipping it end over end, hoping the diversion would draw fire.

And it did.

As the candle passed midway, Gallo stepped out and fired.

Cotton leveled the pistol and pulled the trigger twice, both rounds finding Gallo's chest.

The man staggered back but did not fall. Gallo swung his weapon around, leveling the aim, and started firing. Cotton dove behind the pillar as bullets pinged off stone in all directions. He stayed close to the gritty floor, as there was a real danger of being hit by a ricochet.

The firing stopped.

He gave it a few more seconds, then came to his feet.

A quick glance toward the other side of the crypt and he saw no Gallo.

He heard the door above open.

Clearly he'd caught the guy solid with both rounds, which meant body armor beneath that tailored suit.

These knights came prepared.

He raced for the stairs and headed back to ground level. The chapel was empty. The oak door at the far end hung three-quarters closed. He approached and stared out into the cloister, catching a fleeting glance of Pollux Gallo on the opposite side, reentering the refectory. He headed after him but, by the time he arrived, Gallo was ninety seconds ahead and the refectory was empty.

A car cranked outside.

He bolted for the exterior door and opened it to see the Mercedes fleeing the courtyard through the main gate.

Gallo was gone.

CHAPTER TWENTY-TWO

THE KNIGHT ABANDONED HIS PERCH OVER THE MONASTERY AS Malone entered the refectory. He climbed into his car and drove away, heading inland along the Italian coast.

The pope dying so suddenly had changed everything. He'd always thought there'd be more time to prepare. But that was not the case. Everything was happening fast. Luckily, Danjel Spagna had entered the picture. Usually, the archbishop lurked only in the shadows, never surfacing, working through minions. But not here. Obviously, the Lord's Own wanted something, too. His presence both simplified and complicated things. But it was just one more challenge that would have to be met.

He kept driving, heading away from the archive.

The die was now cast. There was no turning back. Only going forward remained a viable option. The next forty-eight hours would determine everyone's future. As much planning as possible had been imparted.

Now he just needed a little luck.

He checked his watch.

7:40 P.M.

He'd spent the past few years preparing for this moment. So much reading. Studying. Analyzing. And it all came down to the one man who'd stared down the Roman Catholic Church and won.

Benito Amilcare Andrea Mussolini.

To his good fortune, Mussolini rose to power as the church's influence within Italy had begun to wane. No longer was it a political powerhouse. Pius XI wanted a reinvigoration and Mussolini wanted his rule legitimized by what had always been the most influential institution in Italy. To appease the pope and show the people his supposed graciousness, Il Duce negotiated the 1929 Lateran Treaty that finally recognized the full sovereignty of the Holy See over Vatican City.

Italians were thrilled with the concession.

So was Mussolini.

For the next nine years he enjoyed almost no interference from the Vatican, killing and torturing whomever he wanted. Even Catholics were harassed. Churches vandalized. Violence against clerics became commonplace.

He had free rein.

Finally, in 1939, Pius XI decided to make a public denunciation. A virulent speech was written, printed, ready to be delivered and distributed to the world.

Then Pius died.

All printed copies of the speech were seized and ordered destroyed by the Vatican secretary of state. No one ever heard or read a word of that papal repudiation. As was noted at the time, *not a comma* remained.

Three weeks later the man who accomplished that suppression became Pius XII. The new pope was suave, emollient, and devious. He immediately returned to the previously charted course of political appeasement, one that never directly confronted either Italy or Germany.

And the knight knew why.

The *Nostra Trinità*.

Which, by then, Mussolini either had in his possession, or knew where to find.

A fact that Pius XII well knew.

He was now beyond Rapallo along the coast.

Everything had led to this moment. He would now either succeed or die in the process. No third option existed. Not with the evils he was contemplating.

He stared out the windshield. A car waited ahead, its headlights off, a man standing outside in the blackness. He stopped his own vehicle, climbed out, and walked the ten meters over to where Sir James Grant waited alone. Somewhere, not far off, he heard the pound of surf on rock.

"Is Malone dead?" Grant asked.

"It's being handled right now. I saw its beginning myself."

"All this goes for naught if Malone leaves that archive unscathed."

He actually didn't give a damn about any threat Cotton Malone represented to Grant. He'd told his people to deal with it but, if problems arose, to withdraw and not take foolish risks. Malone was not his problem.

To this point he'd led what could only be described as a sedentary life, his battles nearly all intellectual and emotional. He'd patiently watched as others rose and fell in stature. He'd learned how desire could sometimes water down determination and that realization, more than anything else, explained his current irrevocable course. It had started this morning and continued when he spoke, by phone, with James Grant a few hours later. He'd made a bold move to secure the Churchill letters from that villa, then left three calling cards. The owner hanging by his arms. The ring on the dead knight's hand. And Cotton Malone still breathing. All three messages had been received, and Grant had made contact.

Now it was time to make a deal.

"I want those letters," Grant said. "Now."

"And you know what I want."

He'd never realized until recently that the British held the key. It had been Danjel Spagna who'd passed that piece of vital information along a few weeks ago, when he'd first approached the Lord's Own for help.

"I know what you want," Grant said. "You've been searching for it since Napoleon took Malta. I know the story of the knight captured in Valletta during Napoleon's invasion. They took him to the grand master's palace and nailed his hands to a table."

"And the little general in chief skewered him. That man was *Secreti*. He wore the ring. He also kept the secret."

That knight's bravery had long been revered. With French troops bearing down on Valletta and the island doomed, he had been the one who oversaw the protection of the knights' most precious objects. Books, records, and artifacts were trekked to the south shore and hastily shipped away. Some made it to Europe, some didn't. A decision, though, was made to leave the most precious possession on the island.

The *Nostra Trinità*.

That doomed knight, foreseeing his own demise, had supposedly made sure the French would never locate the Trinity. But if the stories were to be believed, he'd also left a way for the right people to refind it.

"MI6 has long known about what Mussolini may have found," Grant said. "He was intent on your *Nostra Trinità*."

"I want what he found."

"And you'll have it," Grant said, "when I get those letters."

He pointed the remote toward his car and clicked the button. The interior lit up and the elephant-skin satchel could be seen propped on the passenger seat. "That's everything Malone acquired. Everything the villa owner was trying to sell. There are eleven letters inside."

"Did you read them?"

"Of course. They definitely change history."

"I wish you hadn't done that."

He shrugged. "I could not care less about British pride or the reputation of Winston Churchill. Now tell me what I want to know."

He listened as Grant explained all of what British intelligence had discovered in the 1930s. What had been hinted at in the phone call earlier.

He was amazed. "Are you certain of this?"

Grant shrugged. "As certain as decades-old information can be."

He got the message. A risk existed. Nothing new about that. A fact Grant should have realized, too.

"Is that all?" he asked.

Grant nodded.

"Then the letters are yours."

The Brit started to walk toward the car for the satchel. The knight reached beneath his jacket and found the gun. With it in hand, he stepped close and fired one round into the back of James Grant's skull.

The shot cracked across the night.

The Brit collapsed to the ground.

One reason he'd chosen this spot for their meeting was the privacy it offered. Few people frequented this area after dark. He replaced the gun in its holster and hoisted Grant's body over his shoulder. The man was surprisingly stout for an old codger. The other reason was its proximity to the sea. He walked through the dark toward the cliff and tossed Grant over the side. The car would be found tomorrow, but the body would take longer, if it ever was found. The tides here were swift and notorious.

He stared out at the black water.

What did Ecclesiastes say?

Cast the bread upon the waters, for thou shalt find it after many days.

He hoped not.

CHAPTER
TWENTY-THREE

LUKE WONDERED WHY COTTON MALONE WAS INVOLVED WITH ANY of this, but knew better than to ask Stephanie questions. None of that mattered to his situation. He was apparently one segment of a larger mission. Nothing unusual there. The job was to get his part right. To that end Stephanie had given him a directive relative to Laura Price and she expected it to be done. So that's exactly what was going to happen.

He made his way back toward Republic Street, which remained congested, the crowd still focused on the commotion. Dusk had passed toward darkness, the streets and squares all amber-lit. He kept to the alley and was able to see Laura, her arms being held by policemen, talking to the big man she'd identified as Spagna. The conversation did not seem amicable. Spagna continued to puff on the cigar. The local cops seemed to be taking their orders from him. Only two of the four were still there, while a fifth, the driver of the car that had brought Spagna, stood off to the side.

He liked the odds.

The head of Vatican intelligence had apparently come in search of both him and Laura. The big guy had specifically called out *Mr. Daniels.* So Spagna was privy to solid information. And what had spooked Stephanie? Her attitude had shifted 180 degrees. A lot was happening fast. But he was accustomed to the speed lane. In fact, he preferred it.

He watched as Laura was stuffed into the rear seat of the blue-and-white police car, its lights still flashing. Spagna hesitated outside the vehicle, speaking to one of the uniformed officers. The other uniform, the driver, climbed in behind the wheel. Finally, Spagna opened the passenger-side door and pointed with the cigar, barking something out to another policeman before folding himself inside.

They were apparently leaving.

But the going would be slow, considering the snaking current of pedestrians that choked the streets in both directions. They'd have to inch their way for a bit, until finding one of the alleys. He had his gun and could shoot his way in and out. But that could turn messy in an infinite number of ways.

Better to innovate.

He'd already noticed that the piazza near the cathedral and the grand master's palace was dotted with vendor carts. Some selling food and drink, others arts and crafts. He counted ten. The police car had begun its departure, keeping the lights flashing and tossing out short bursts of its siren to clear a path through the crowd.

He fled the alley and sprinted into the melee, maneuvering his way toward one of the carts, this one hawking color prints of Valletta and Malta. It was wooden, its heft supported by four large, spoked wheels. He noticed that two bricks were wedged under a couple of those wheels, one front, the other back, to keep it in place. He kept a sharp eye out for any more police, but saw none in uniform. Of course, that didn't mean they weren't around.

Not to mention cameras.

Surely this hot spot was under constant video surveillance.

He told himself to hurry. Get it done. Indecision was what usually got you. He'd learned that early on from Malone. Be right. Be wrong. Doesn't matter. Just don't hesitate.

He crossed Republic and entered the piazza, hurrying toward its far end where the police car had stopped, the siren still bursting off and on. He came to the cart with the artwork, its owner talking with potential customers. Other folks admired the prints hanging from its display. He kicked one of the bricks aside, then swung around to the rear and grabbed the stout, wooden handles. The owner and the customers were momentarily caught off guard and he used that instant to shove the heavy bulk forward.

He kept pushing, increasing speed and momentum, the wheels rattling across the old rutted cobbles, crashing the cart into the side of the police car, making sure he kept it nestled tight to the front passenger-side door.

The collision grabbed everyone's attention.

He realized there'd be a moment of confusion inside the car, but the driver would emerge quickly.

And sure enough, he did, opening his door.

Luke leaped onto the hood and pivoted across, planting both feet in the guy's face, driving the cop backward then down. He landed on the hood and dropped to his feet ready to deal with the driver, but the cop was out cold. He reached back and found his Beretta, aiming it inside the vehicle.

"Let's go," he said to Laura.

He opened the rear door from the outside, keeping his gun trained on the Vatican spymaster.

"You live up to your advance billing," Spagna said. "I was told you were one of Stephanie's tough young bucks."

"I get the job done."

"Only because I let you."

Laura stood beside him.

He couldn't resist. "What does that mean?"

"We don't have time for you two to spar," she said. "Come on."

And she motioned to Spagna, who climbed across the front seat and out the driver's side, minus the cigar.

That was a shocker.

"I assume you know what you're doing," Luke asked her.

"I always do."

The three of them pushed through the gawkers and headed for another of the alleys. No other police were in sight. A low, muted rumble of thunder shook the evening air.

"Mr. Daniels, I saw you watching and assumed you'd make a move," Spagna said, as they hustled. "Tell him, Laura."

He glanced her way.

"Before they put me in the back of that car, Spagna told me to be ready to go. He said you'd come."

"I was the one who alerted the Maltese to both of you," Spagna said.

"I used the attack on the water from earlier as the pretense. I wanted local resources to find you, but now we need to be alone."

"That conversation I witnessed between the two of you didn't look all that friendly," he said.

"I tell my people," Spagna said, "that sometimes an actor has to play, in a single room, what the script describes as forty rooms. He must make the audience believe all forty exist. To do that, he must change reality. That's what a good spy does, too. Change reality. Ms. Price is a good spy."

"Whose side are you on?" Luke asked Spagna.

"Always, my church. My job is to protect it."

"And what about you?" he said to Laura.

He didn't like being played. Not ever.

She stared him down. "The only side that matters. My own."

They kept moving.

He tried to calm down and be the eyes and ears Stephanie needed on the ground. They were now sufficiently far from Republic Street that they could slow their pace. They stopped at the end of an alley, where it intersected with another busy thoroughfare littered with cars. The shops here were all closed for the night. Fewer people on the sidewalks, too.

"It's nice to make your acquaintance, Mr. Daniels," Spagna said, offering a hand.

Play the part. Be the gentleman.

He offered his hand in return.

"You both should be honored. I don't usually work the field."

"Why are you now?" Luke asked.

Spagna extended his arms in a mock embrace. "Because everything is happening here, on this ancient island. And being at the center of the storm is always the best place to be."

This guy had style, he'd give him that.

"By the way, Mr. Daniels, do you have a cell phone?"

He nodded and found the unit. Spagna took it from him and tossed it into the street, where an oncoming car crushed the case.

Malone's voice rushed through his head.

Dumb-ass mistake, Frat Boy.

You think?

"We don't need to be tracked. I know the Magellan Billet's standard issue contains constant GPS."

"Aren't you a wealth of inside information," Luke noted. "I bet you'd be hell playing Spy Jeopardy."

"You can keep your Beretta," Spagna said, pointing to his exposed shirttail. "Call it a show of my good faith."

Comforting. But not enough to alleviate his suspicions.

"Tell him what you told me," Laura said to Spagna.

"I know what Cardinal Gallo is after."

"That's all great. But I need to check in with Stephanie Nelle," Luke pointed out. "She gives me my orders."

More thunder growled in the distance, signaling storms were coming.

"You can contact her," Spagna said. "Later. I'll make sure that happens. Right now she has her hands full trying to save a former agent named Cotton Malone."

CHAPTER TWENTY-FOUR

COTTON WALKED BACK THROUGH THE REFECTORY, PAST THE EMPTY workstations, and reentered the cloister. Pollux Gallo was gone, but it remained unclear if he'd fled alone. The two brown-robed brothers from the chapter house might still be somewhere on the premises.

He headed back their way with the gun ready.

His clothes were wet from the dousing of the sprinklers, and at the chapter house door he heard the faucets still spewing. He'd regretted the destruction to the manuscripts. All no doubt irreplaceable. But Gallo had brought him here to die. He'd had no choice.

The sprinklers shut off.

He came alert, wondering if that was automatic or by human hand. He peered inside. The tables with their glass domes dripped with water, the floor soaked and puddled. He slipped inside and made a quick run down the end aisle, looking for the guy he'd first taken down, but nobody was there. He fled the chapter house and headed back to the crypt and found the same thing. The robed brother he'd taken down there was also gone. Where were they? And why had Gallo not kept up the attack?

He needed to check the rest of the monastery. Grant had specifically wanted to know about anything on Mussolini. He decided that, so long as he was here, he'd see if there was anything to find.

He left the crypt and returned to the cloister, checking the metal doors, one after another, that lined its inner wall. All of them were closed and protected by electronic locks that required a code from a keypad. At a point diagonally opposite to the chapter house he stopped and stared out through the arches into the darkened courtyard. Lights lit the cloistered corridors on both the ground and second floors. Across, on the far side, he noticed a half-open door on the second level. He was still cautious about the two brothers who had vanished, so he made his way to the nearest staircase and hustled up, keeping a watch in all directions.

The second floor seemed as quiet as the one below.

He approached the half-open door, the room beyond lit with bright fluorescent bulbs. The space was small, maybe thirty feet square, with dark-stained timbers overhead. The stone walls were lined with shelves and cabinets, the center containing another of the stout oak tables, this one devoid of any displays.

He stepped inside and surveyed the shelves.

Many were filled with books, all on Mussolini, in various languages. His trained eye noticed the bindings. Some were cloth, others leather, most wrapped with paper covers protected by Mylar. Several hundred at least. He noticed no overhead sprinklers here. Which made sense. Green metal cabinets, lined in rows, flanked the walls. He opened one to find folios of documents bearing dates starting in 1928 and continuing to 1943. Many of the brittle and fragile typewritten pages inside reminded him of what he'd seen in the elephant-skin satchel. He scanned a few and realized this was the Mussolini archive.

To his right he saw another of the metal cabinets, its doors not fully closed. He stepped across and opened them, revealing four shelves of identical thin, leather-bound volumes. He noticed dates on the spines. All mid- to late 1942. Here and there a book was missing, perhaps nine gone. He slid one of the volumes free. The pages were filled with a heavy, masculine script in black ink. He read some of the Italian, each entry headlined with a specific date, as in a diary.

His gaze raked the room at the shelves and he began to notice gaps where more books had once stood. He wondered if this room had been picked over, the important stuff removed.

He heard a noise beyond the exit doors, out in the cloister.

A scuttle of footsteps.

Perhaps his two problems had finally materialized.

He hustled across and assumed a position to the left of the door, between two of the metal cabinets, his spine flat to the stone wall. He kept the gun at his side, finger on the trigger, ready, raising it as the noise drew closer. Maybe they intended on charging in with a frontal assault.

He waited.

Someone entered the archive.

He aimed his gun.

"I was looking for you," Stephanie Nelle said calmly.

He lowered the weapon. "What in the hell are you doing here?"

"That was actually going to be my question to you."

"I'm here because I got greedy and thought I could make an easy hundred thousand euros. I've been playing 'the bait' all day, and I almost got eaten. Why are you here? And heads up, there are still a couple of threats hanging around."

She waved off his concern. "I doubt they're still here."

"What brings you into the field?"

"There's a problem developing in Rome with the conclave set to start tomorrow. It's a big mess, Cotton, and the Entity is involved."

Those folks he knew all too well, including their head, Danjel Spagna.

"The Lord's Own?" he asked, adding a smile.

She nodded. "He's on Malta. He and I go way back, to my time years ago at the State Department."

He knew what she was referring to.

"Luke is on Malta, too," she said.

"How is Frat Boy doing? Last time I saw him, he was in a hospital bed."

"He recovered. But he has his hands full at the moment. And what's happening there relates directly to what's happening here. I came to enlist your help."

He'd heard that tone before and knew what it meant.

Shut up and listen.

"Grant sent you here for Gallo to kill you."

"I already figured that out."

"Grant is also going to trade for the Churchill letters, the ones that were taken from you this morning. I'm not sure where or how, but that's his plan."

He'd known at the breakfast table in Milan that Grant was holding back. He should have said no thanks and headed back to Copenhagen. But he'd kept going. Why? For the money. What else? And that wasn't like him. But a hundred thousand euros would go a long way to handle the overhead at his bookshop. And the bills had to be paid.

"Who's Grant going to trade with for the letters?" he asked. "And what does he have to offer?"

Behind Stephanie, in the doorway, a man appeared. A new face. Tall, broad-shouldered, thick brown hair falling to his ears, a monk's beard dusting his chin and jaw.

"Cotton," Stephanie said. "This is Pollux Gallo. The lieutenant ad interim of the Knights of Malta. I think he can answer both of your questions."

CHAPTER TWENTY-FIVE

Kastor rode with Chatterjee.

A torrent of rain glistened beyond the car windows with each stab and flash of blue-white lightning. The steady slapping of the wipers worked to dull his senses.

They'd left Mdina in Chatterjee's vehicle, heading toward Marsaskala, an ancient town nestled close to a sheltered bay on the eastern shore. A familiar place, with buildings that stretched on both sides of the water with a promenade that offered views of low shelving rocks, colorful fishing boats, and the old saltpans. He knew its name derived partly from *marsa,* Arabic for "bay," and *skala,* Italian for *sqalli,* meaning "Sicilian." In years past, Sicilian fishermen often sought harbor there, as it was less than a hundred kilometers south of their home. Summer was its busy time. Many Maltese families owned vacation homes there, its array of bars and restaurants catering to a seasonal crowd.

As a boy he'd come here often to swim, drying off on the warm rocks after a dousing in the cold Mediterranean. Back then the journey took a while, as the roadways were nothing like today. Few outside of Valletta were paved and none led anywhere except to dead ends, mostly at the water's edge. All that changed in the 1970s when tourism exploded. Despite the modernization, though, history still tugged at every glance around the island. The knights' presence remained strong, more, he knew, for the tourists than for any genuine love.

The Maltese and the Hospitallers never got along. They'd been resented from the start as foreigners who'd been given *their* land by another foreigner. The knights had not helped matters by bringing nearly continuous war to the island, their occupation deemed a constant threat to the Arab world. Even worse, they treated the local population more as tenement workers and soldiers in need than fellow citizens.

The knights never understood how to rule a place so small as Malta. People living so close to one another for so long had learned to appreciate the needs and desires of their neighbors. It was a kind, cooperative society, which the knights governed with heartless tyranny. By 1798 the Maltese were fed up and the French had been welcomed as liberators, with Napoleon lauded as their champion. Few on Malta had been sad to see the knights tossed out. But that joy had quickly been replaced with loathing, and the same mistake was not made twice. The French were vanquished within two years. Eventually, with the defeat of Napoleon in 1814, the British gained the island and maintained control until 1964.

September 21.

Independence Day.

That old nun from the orphanage had been wrong about the festival of Our Lady of the Lily and the three stolen *pasti*. All that had happened at an Independence Day celebration. He'd not corrected Spagna, but he remembered every detail. What had she called him?

Halliel ftit. Little thief?

His cell phone vibrated in his pocket. He removed the unit, noted the caller, and answered.

About time.

"I have good news," the voice said in his ear. "I now know where Mussolini hid what he found."

He closed his eyes in relief. "Tell me."

"The British have had the information all along. I was able to use the Churchill letters to obtain what we need from James Grant."

"Where is it hidden?"

"I can't say on an open cell line."

"Can you get it?"

"It might be a challenge, but it's obtainable."

"And the man you just mentioned?"

"No longer a factor."

He, too, was being careful with his words, but he was able to say, "I'm with a man named Chatterjee. He works with a friend from Rome. We have a problem. There's an American and a Maltese agent watching me."

"Has the friend you mentioned made contact with you?"

"A bit of a surprise. But yes. You could have warned me."

"It's better this way. He's the best in the world, and now he's on your side."

"Which came as news to me."

"But welcomed, I'm sure. I arranged it, so please take advantage of the situation. Only a few more hours remain. Stay anonymous and above the fray. Let your new friend handle the dirty work."

He did not need to be reminded. He'd begged for a fight with the last pope and had been given one. Unfortunately—though he foolishly thought otherwise at the time—that war had been over before it even started.

This one would be fought far differently.

He felt safe to say, "I've been supplied with some new information, the kind that will be powerful and persuasive. It involves a great deal of personal scandal. More than enough to get what we want."

"I'll be anxious to hear more about that."

"Is there a reason you withheld the identity of our new friend? He was never mentioned when you told me to come here."

"I apologize. It was a condition of his involvement. But take heart. In just a few days you will be his superior."

He loved the sound of that.

"Find whatever there is to be found," he said into the phone. "And quickly."

"I intend to do just that. One thing. Where is this new powerful and persuasive information you just mentioned?"

He glanced across the car. "Chatterjee has it."

A pause, then the voice said, "Take care."

He ended the call.

They motored out of Marsaskala and headed toward St. Thomas Bay, the snug anchorage protected by steep cliffs on three sides. A jumble of lit buildings lined the narrow lane on both sides.

"Where are we going?" he asked, glad that Chatterjee knew better than to inquire about the phone conversation.

"To speak with someone who knows things."

He was annoyed by the secretive reply. He should be in Rome. Cardinals were surely arriving by the hour, being assigned their rooms in the Domus Sanctae Marthae, readying themselves to be sealed away in conclave.

Yet he was here, in the rain.

"When do I get that flash drive in your pocket?"

Chatterjee chuckled. "The archbishop wants this hunt to play itself out first."

He was finding it hard to disguise his mounting frustrations. "Is finding the *Nostra Trinità* a condition for that to happen?"

"Not at all. If this effort fails, then it fails. But the archbishop doesn't see the need, at the moment, to hand over the details of the curia's corruption. You'll have the flash drive before you enter the conclave."

Then he saw the point, his thoughts borne along on a surge of revelation. "He thinks I'll use it beforehand. He wants all of the blackmail to happen inside the conclave, where no one can speak of it once things are over."

"A wise precaution, don't you think. Though he has full confidence in your ability to persuade the right cardinals to support your candidacy, if something goes wrong at least it will remain a private matter, the cardinals bound by their oath to secrecy."

"And I take all the blame."

"There's an element of risk in everything we do."

"Except for your boss."

"Quite the contrary. The archbishop has taken a huge risk backing you."

But he wondered about that observation. Spagna had not survived for as long as he had by taking *huge* risks.

He resented Spagna's invasion into his life. Sometimes, in the morning, while shaving, he caught the mirrored reflection of a man he might not ever have recognized but for the fact he'd created him. Crafted as carefully as a sculptor working a slab of stone. As with everyone, though, scars existed, the stigmata of a troubled past, and even he'd thought himself finished, his mistakes leading toward a lonely failure. But now it seemed he might have a second chance.

"Might I ask a question?" Chatterjee said.

Why not? "Go ahead."

"What name do you plan to take as pope?"

An odd question, but one he had definitely considered.

He actually admired the full title. His Holiness, Bishop of Rome, Vicar of Jesus Christ, Successor of the Prince of the Apostles, Supreme Pontiff of the Universal Church, Primate of Italy, Archbishop and Metropolitan of the Roman Province, Sovereign of the Vatican City State, Servant of the servants of God.

But that was a bit much, even to him.

The early bishops of Rome had all used their baptismal names after election. Then, in the mid-6th century, Mercurius wisely decided that a pope should not bear the name of a pagan Roman god. Mercury. So he adopted the label John II in honor of his predecessor who had been venerated as a martyr. Later on, when clerics from the north, beyond the Alps, rose to the papacy, they replaced their foreign names with more traditional ones. The last pope to use his baptismal name was Marcellus II in 1555.

Which he would emulate.

"I'll be Kastor I."

Chatterjee chuckled.

"What's so funny?"

"Spagna knows you all too well. The password for the flash drive is KASTOR I."

CHAPTER
TWENTY-SIX

COTTON STARED AT THE MAN WHO CALLED HIMSELF POLLUX GALLO. "The guy who just tried to kill me used that name, too."

"I know, and I apologize," Gallo said. "But I have a serious situation simmering within the ranks of the Hospitallers. The man you were dealing with was an imposter."

Obviously. "Who was he?"

"A knight, as were the others with him. Every organization has its share of fanatics. We are no exception."

That subject required more delving, but first he wanted to hear more from Stephanie.

"Cotton, I had no idea you were involved with any of this until a few hours ago," she said. "I've been working this situation for over a week, but I just learned about the Brits."

"What situation?"

"I'm not exactly sure. Things have been fluid, to say the least. I understand you've been dealing with James Grant, and Grant has been dealing with the Entity."

Back when he was active with the Magellan Billet he'd worked several times with Danjel Spagna's people. Most of the Western world's spy agencies did the same. The Vatican was an intelligence gold mine. Every day ecclesiastical, political, and economic information poured in from thousands of priests, bishops, laypeople, and nuncios. An amazing array of eyes and ears in nearly every country in the world. No one else possessed that kind of surveillance network.

"Of course," Stephanie said, "working with the Entity is not a one-way street. Information has to be traded. I've learned that a week ago, James Grant shared the fact that the Churchill letters had surfaced. He'd tracked the potential seller, then inquired if the Vatican had any information on that seller. Anything that might corroborate the letters' authenticity. Smartly, he didn't want to waste time dealing with a fraud. He spoke with Spagna personally."

He asked, "What did Grant learn?"

"Supposedly, Spagna was no help. Yet the Lord's Own is now on Malta, wreaking havoc, and Grant is here in Italy searching for those letters. Hopefully Luke has things under control there, though he's had some issues today."

He smiled at her performance assessment. "He'll get the job done."

"I'm sure he will. But like you, he's working blind."

Gallo said, "This is a difficult situation for me, Mr. Malone. My twin brother, Cardinal Gallo, is deeply involved with all of this. I'm afraid he's drawn himself into another difficult situation."

"I read about him and what's happening within your organization. You said twin. Identical?"

Gallo nodded.

Unfortunately, in the articles he'd read there'd been no photograph of Cardinal Gallo. Which would have been helpful in ferreting out the imposter he'd just encountered.

"Who just tried to kill me?" he asked.

"A group within our ranks known as the *Secreti*."

He noticed no ring on the man's fingers, and no evidence that he may have worn one in the past. "The imposter told me about them and said they no longer existed."

"And until a few hours ago I would have agreed with him. But that's not the case. They do exist, in some new form. It's my belief they're the ones who attacked you in the villa and killed three men, including one of their own."

"To keep me from taking him?"

Gallo said, "That seems logical. You have to understand, thanks to my brother, the Knights of Malta are currently in a state of fracture, polarized to the extreme. It's a civil war. One side is loyal to the order, the other is in open rebellion. You met some of the rebels tonight."

"Where were you when those rebels were trying to kill me?"

"In Rome. I only learned of the situation, and that you were at the Villa Malta, after you were airborne. I've been in contact with Ms. Nelle for the past few days, working with her. When I mentioned the situation and your name, we came north as fast as possible."

He had no reason to doubt this man, particularly with Stephanie involved.

"The *Secreti* want the Churchill letters," Gallo said, "so they can make a deal with the British. Supposedly, the British have information that the *Secreti* want."

"Like what?" he asked.

Gallo hesitated, but a nod from Stephanie seemed to answer his reluctance to speak.

"Tell him," she said.

"The Knights Hospitallers are unique among the warrior-monks," Gallo said. "The Templars are gone. The Teutonics barely exist. But the Hospitallers remain strong. We are a viable, worldwide charitable organization. Some of that survival is thanks to our adaptability, perpetually making ourselves useful. Some of it is due to perseverance, some to luck. But some is attributable to what we once knew. It involves something called the *Nostra Trinità*. Our Trinity."

"Sounds ancestral," Cotton noted.

"It is. In fact, it goes to our core. At first it was the *Nostra Due*. The Holy Duo. Two documents the knights had always held dear from our earliest existence. The *Pie Postulatio Voluntatis,* the Most Pious Request, from 1113, that recognized our existence and confirmed our independence and sovereignty. The second is the *Ad Providam,* from 1312, where Pope Clement V handed over all of the Templars' property to us in perpetuity. The Templars had been dissolved five years earlier and the *Ad Providam* gave us nearly everything they owned. There are signed originals of both of those documents in the Vatican, so there is little doubt of their existence. But we always kept our own originals."

"Why?" Stephanie asked.

"They are the sole evidence of our legitimacy, our independence. Both those principles have been called into question many times in the past, and it was always those two papal decrees that ended any debate."

"And the third part, which made it a trinity?" Cotton asked.

"It came to us later, in the Middle Ages, and is much more mysterious. No one alive today, to my knowledge, has ever seen it. It's called the *Constitutum Constantini.* Constantine's Gift. It's what Napoleon and Mussolini sought, and it's also what my brother is after. All three documents were kept together and guarded for centuries by the *Secreti,* whose members pledged an oath to protect them. And they did, until 1798, when all three documents disappeared and have not been seen since. To bind them together in solidarity, the *Secreti* wore a ring with a palindrome that dates back to Constantine the Great."

He explained to Stephanie about the ring and the five lines that could be read the same in every direction.

SATOR
AREPO
TENET
OPERA
ROTAS

"The Latin has been interpreted many different ways," Gallo said. "One variation is something like 'the sower, with his eye on the plow, holds its wheels with care.' Which is nonsense, as are all of the other interpretations."

Including Grant's from earlier.

"The real message is hidden." Gallo reached inside his jacket pocket and removed a pen and small notebook. He drew a cross of squares and inserted letters, adding four other boxes outside the cross.

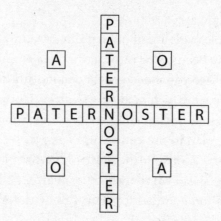

"Taken together, the letters of the five words are an anagram. The key is the N at the middle. All of the letters in the palindrome are paired except the central N, which stands alone. By repositioning the letters around the central N, a cross can be made that reads *Pater Noster,* in both directions. Latin for 'Our Father,' and the first two words of the Lord's Prayer. The remaining four letters, which are two A's and two O's, are a reference to Alpha and Omega. The beginning and end. Symbols of eternity, from the Book of Revelation. For Christians in the 4th century that meant the omnipresence of God."

"Who would have thought?" Cotton said. "That can't be a coincidence."

"It's not. Early Christians shared the five-worded palindrome as a way to identify themselves with one another. Constantine himself sanctioned its use. The *Secreti* eventually adopted it as their symbol."

"What does any of this have to do with the coming conclave?" Stephanie asked.

Cotton was wondering the same thing.

"Perhaps everything," Gallo said. "There's a relevance today to Constantine's Gift that my brother has somehow garnered. With Archbishop Spagna's help, I'm sure. As I've already told Ms. Nelle, Kastor wants to be pope."

That was new to the mix, and he filed further inquiry away for later. Right now he wanted more information about the third part of that trinity.

"Here's what I do know," Gallo said. "Constantine sanctioned Christianity over paganism. By then, it was no longer some small regional movement. A sizable percentage of the entire population was Christian. So he made it the official state religion, with himself in charge. The *Constitutum Constantini* has something to do with that move. What? I truly don't know."

"No one in the organization has a clue what the document says?" Stephanie asked.

Gallo shook his head. "My brother discovered in the Vatican archives that it has something to do with the early church. Its structure and organization. What that might be? I don't know. What I do know is that popes have long feared its surfacing, preferring that the document stay hidden. The Hospitallers accommodated that request and kept it hidden."

"Using that to their advantage," Cotton added.

"That's true. It's why we survived and the other orders perished."

He could tell Gallo was hedging. So he said, "Now's not the time to be coy."

The admonishment brought a curious stare, then a nod.

"You're correct. This is not the time. We did use what we knew to our advantage." Gallo paused. "Within five hundred years of Constantine's death, the church became the most powerful political force in Europe. Not until the 16th century and Martin Luther did anyone successfully challenge its authority. Then along came Napoleon. In his world there was room for only one omnipotent ruler with the ear of God. Himself. He wanted the church gone. He wanted his own *new docile religion,* to use his words. So he abolished both the Inquisition and the Index of Prohibited Books and established a new Catholic creed, even a new Christian calendar. Year One started in 1792, and he identified Paris as the *holy city,* with Rome as its subsidiary. He wanted a new world religion, like Constantine wanted with Christianity, and, like Constantine, he wanted himself as head. But first he had to destroy the Roman Catholic Church."

Cotton was familiar with some of what he was hearing, particularly the use of religion as a political tool. But other parts were new to him.

So he kept listening.

"Napoleon invaded Italy and defeated the papal army," Gallo said. "He then marched on Rome and entered unopposed, plundering the Vatican. In 1798 he proclaimed Rome a republic and demanded the pope renounce his temporal authority. Pius VI refused, so he took the pope prisoner, where he died in captivity seven months later. A new pope tried to make peace, but failed, and Napoleon invaded Italy again and took that pope prisoner, too. He was only released when the British ended Napoleon's rule in 1814. Then something extraordinary happened. After Napoleon was exiled to St. Helena, the pope wrote letters urging leniency. Can you imagine? After all Napoleon had done—held him prisoner, stripped him of everything—he still wanted mercy extended."

"Could simply have been the Christian thing to do," Cotton noted.

"Perhaps. But we'll never know. Napoleon died in 1821, still a prisoner. The pope in 1823. It has always been our belief that the Holy See thought Napoleon possessed Constantine's Gift and, for whatever reason, it was dangerous enough for them to placate him."

"Did Napoleon have it?" Stephanie asked.

Gallo shook his head. "But he ran a good bluff, using the two opportunities when he'd plundered the Vatican to his advantage. He likewise looted Malta."

Cotton was curious. "Did the church know that the Trinity had been lost when Napoleon invaded Malta?"

Gallo nodded. "Absolutely. But no one at the time had any idea where it had been hidden. We know now that the man who hid it away was executed, never revealing what he knew."

"And now your brother is after it," Stephanie asked. "Spagna too?"

"That's my assessment."

"You still have not explained why the *Secreti* just tried to kill me."

"That's simple," Gallo said. "The British asked for that to happen."

Stephanie nodded. "He's right. James Grant is running rogue."

No real surprise.

"And Mussolini?" he said. "How does he figure into all this?"

Gallo faced him. "That's precisely why my brother and Archbishop Spagna have teamed together."

CHAPTER
TWENTY-SEVEN

LUKE REFLECTED ON HOW FAST THINGS CHANGED.

He'd gone from hanging in the air to drenched in the Mediterranean, then thrown into a dungeon, attacked by the police, and now he was inside an apartment located in the heart of Valletta, led there by the head of Vatican intelligence and accompanied by an agent for Maltese security. He wasn't sure who, if anyone, he should listen to, much less trust. Laura Price had gone from telling him to get as far away as he could to seemingly now working with the enemy.

"We're near the old Inquisitor's Palace," Spagna said. "What a job that must have been. Appointed by the pope, sent here to eliminate heresy and all things contrary to the Catholic faith. His word was absolute. That's a position I would have relished."

Luke surveyed the tiny apartment. Only three rooms, brightened by cheerful curtains, the furniture all a bit too large. No photos, candy dishes, or knickknacks. Nothing personal. No one lived here, at least not on a long-term basis. He'd been in enough safe houses so far during his time with the Magellan Billet to know the look.

"This place one of yours?"

Spagna nodded. "Our people use it."

When they'd arrived he'd noticed an oddity out front, engraved into the eroding stone lintel above a set of shuttered windows. An eye sandwiched between two axes. Spagna had explained that it noted who'd lived in the building long ago.

The executioner.

No coincidence that the holder of that unenviable office lived near the Inquisitor's Palace.

Luke heard a vibration and watched as Spagna found a phone in his pocket, stepping outside to take the call.

"You want to tell me what's happening here," he asked Laura.

"Spagna told me that he was aware of Cardinal Gallo's presence on the island and that he had the situation under control."

"And you bought that?"

"He called my boss once we were in the car and I was ordered to cooperate. I'm betting your boss is going to tell you the same thing."

Except that his phone had been conveniently destroyed, making that difficult to determine. "You still have your phone?"

She shook her head. "Spagna took it."

No surprise.

"So we're isolated, with the pope's spy out there controlling the information flow. This is not good. On many levels."

He stepped over to the windows, parted the curtains, and glanced down at the deserted street two floors below.

Spagna returned and closed the door behind him. "First, let's be clear. Either of you can leave anytime you want."

"Then why corral us?" Luke asked.

"As you saw, the locals have a different opinion of you."

"Thanks to you."

Spagna nodded. "Sadly for you, that's true. I would prefer not to involve any of my assets. I have a chaotic situation at the moment that is extremely time-sensitive, and most of my people are readying the Vatican for a conclave."

Luke asked, "What's happening with Cotton Malone?"

"That was the subject of the call I just received. It seems Mr. Malone has extricated himself from danger. Your Ms. Nelle is with him now, as is the temporary head of the Hospitallers."

He was definitely being sucked into something bigger. That was obvious. And he had to keep going, no matter the risks. Some would call that foolish. He called it doing his job.

"My man Chatterjee has been with Cardinal Gallo for the past two hours," Spagna said. "I wanted the cardinal contained to give us time to deal with a more pressing problem."

Luke could hardly wait to hear.

"Listen up, this is your intel briefing. Books and movies love to show Christians being fed to lions. A little ridiculous, if you ask me. Yes, persecutions happened. No question. But seventeen hundred years ago Christians were finally in the right place, at the right time. Still, they had a problem. Their new religion had fractured into a hundred pieces, so many versions of Christianity, each fighting with the other. Constantine the Great saw the political potential of that new religion, but only if those factions could be united. So he called the Council of Nicaea and summoned bishops from all over the empire."

Luke had heard those words—*Council of Nicaea*—before, but knew little to nothing about their importance.

"The bishops came to Asia Minor," Spagna said. "Nobody really knows how many. Maybe three hundred. Some say more. It was the first great Christian council and they were deeply divided over Christ's divinity. One group said the Son had been begotten from the Father with no separate beginning. The other argued the Son had been created from nothing with his own beginning. Sounds silly to us. Who cares? He was Christ, for Christ's sake. But it was a big deal to them. And during the summer of 325, those bishops debated that point into the ground. Constantine himself presided over the sessions. In the end they came to a consensus, with the emperor's approval, that the Son came from the Father, equal to the Father. They created a creed that said that, and all but two bishops agreed. Those two were excommunicated and banished. They then decided the rest of what true Christians should believe. Things like when Easter would be celebrated, how priests would act, how the church would be organized. Everything contrary to that was deemed heretical, unworthy of belief. And so began the Catholic Church, as we know it today."

"And this has what to do with what's happening now?" Laura asked.

Luke was beginning to like her directness.

"It has everything to do with now," Spagna said. "Once the council ended, Constantine invited all of the bishops to his palace for a grand banquet. Officially, the dinner was to celebrate his twentieth anniversary as emperor. But it became much more. From the precious few accounts that have survived, we know the bishops left that night with gifts for themselves and money for their churches. But they also executed a document. Signed by all, including the emperor himself. That document has a name. The *Constitutum Constantini.* Constantine's Gift. It stayed with the emperor until his death in 337. Eventually it came into the pope's possession, but he lost it. Then during the Middle Ages the Knights of Rhodes, who eventually became the Knights of Malta, obtained it. It became one of three documents they venerated and protected. Their *Nostra Trinità.* Our Trinity. Napoleon invaded Malta looking for it, but never found a thing. It all seemed forgotten, until the 1930s, when Mussolini searched again."

"Why would any of that matter now?" Luke asked. "It's so old."

"I assure you, the *Constitutum Constantini* still matters. Perhaps today more than ever. Cardinal Gallo understands its significance. I understand its significance. That's why we have to find it first."

"*We?*" Laura asked.

"I have assurances from both of your superiors that you're mine for the next few days."

"I think I'll wait on that one until I hear it from my boss," Luke said.

Spagna frowned. "Are you always so difficult?"

"Just to people I don't like."

"We just met, Mr. Daniels. How could you possibly know if you like me or not?"

"My mama used to say that she *didn't need to wallow with the pigs to know it stunk in the pen.*"

Spagna smiled. "Sounds like an intelligent woman."

"The smartest I've ever known. I'd say it stinks here, too."

"Regardless of your personal feelings," Spagna said, "we have a job to do. But first, some things have to play out in Italy."

Luke shook his head. More gobbledygook. "I'm assuming you don't plan to explain yourself."

Spagna smiled, pointed a finger, and said, "That's where you're wrong."

CHAPTER TWENTY-EIGHT

COTTON WAITED FOR AN ANSWER TO HIS QUESTION OF HOW Mussolini factored into the situation.

"You must understand," Gallo said, "that my brother and I, though identical twins, are vastly different people. I chose a military career, then one of charitable service with the knights. He chose a purely religious path. And where ambition is not out of the question in my world, it can be fatal in his. I have no interest in the conclave, no interest in who is pope. But there are others who do. My brother sits at the top of that list, followed closely by Archbishop Spagna."

"The Entity is trying to influence the conclave?" Stephanie asked.

"They have on many occasions before. Why would this time be different?"

"Answer my question," Cotton said. "All this information here on Mussolini. Why do you have it? It can't just be historic curiosity."

"Far from that." Gallo motioned to the room. "This collection is a vast research project that has taken us decades. Let me tell you something only those within the ranks of the professed knights know. The order owns two properties inside Rome. The Palazzo di Malta, from where you departed, and the Villa del Priorato di Malta. There's a story about when Mussolini visited the Priorato."

* * *

Il Duce admired the grand priory, lit to the night in all its glory. The build-ing sat on Aventine Hill, one of Rome's famous seven, overlooking the Tiber—once a Benedictine monastery, then a Templar stronghold, now belonging to the Hospitallers. Their jurisdictional claim was marked by a red flag with a white, eight-pointed cross bristling in the warm night air.

The day had been glorious. He'd just returned from an operatic spec-tacle staged in honor of a state visit by the German chancellor, Adolf Hitler. Held at the Foro Mussolini, literally his forum, inside the Stadio del Cipressi, where tens of thousands had heeded the call to attend. Everything had been carefully rehearsed, including the triumphant conclusion of the program where hundreds of torch-bearing youths had formed a huge swastika, yell-ing Heil Hitler *in the flickering flames. Hitler had been impressed. So much that the chancellor had proclaimed* the Roman state resurrected, from remote tradition, to new life.

High praise.

With Hitler down for the night, he'd decided to head back into Rome and handle another matter that required his personal attention. So he'd appeared unannounced at the Villa del Priorato di Malta.

The grand master stood beside him.

Ludovico Chigi della Rovere-Albani.

The seventy-sixth man to hold the position. An Italian at least. Born to a noble family with a lineage back to the 15th century. He'd been elected head of the Knights of Malta in 1931 and, for the past seven years, he'd kept a low profile.

But not quite low enough.

"I'm aware that you've been thwarting my efforts with the pope," he told Chigi. "Going behind me, undermining negotiations."

"I only do as the Holy Father asks of me."

"Really? Would you kill, if the Holy Father asked that of you?"

"That would never happen."

"Don't be so sure. Your illustrious order slaughtered thousands of people for centuries. All for popes. What makes you so different now?"

"Both we and the world have changed."

"And the Secreti? Have they changed?"

The older man's face remained stoic. He'd hoped to catch this man off guard, but the ruse had not worked. They stood in the parterre garden among sculpted shrubbery and tall cypress trees.

"I have the Nostra Trinità," he proclaimed.

"You have nothing."

"Don't be so sure. Your knights did not remain silent."

"Yet you killed them anyway."

"I killed no one."

"Which you say as though you truly believe."

He pointed beyond the garden, to the main gate. "Is it true what they say?"

"Have a look for yourself."

He paraded toward the tall stone screen. Beneath an arch-headed central portone two iron doors stood closed. In one was the Il Buco Della Serratura. Such a long name for something so simple.

The keyhole.

His spies had reported what could be seen through the opening. He approached the door, bent down, and peered through. In the distance, at the end of a garden allée, framed in clipped cypresses, he saw the lit copper-green dome of St. Peter's Basilica. He smiled at the intriguing symbolism and faced the grand master. "Is it an accident or by design that the Hospitallers have the center of Roman Catholicism directly in their keyhole?"

"That's not for me to say. But we have guarded the church for a long time."

"Extracting much in return for the service."

"We are good, loyal, and faithful. Unlike you."

"I am your leader."

"That's not true. Where we stand does not belong to Italy. This is a separate nation. I am leader here."

"It would take my Black Shirts only a few minutes to subdue all of you. Then I could burn this separate nation to the ground. I could then take the Palazzo di Malta and do the same. Don't tempt me."

Chigi shrugged, as if unconcerned. "Do what you must. We've been homeless before and survived."

Time to get to the point of the visit. "Tell Pius to leave me alone. Do that, *and the* Constitutum Constantini *stays with me. I've even done him a favor and sealed it away where no one can get to it. His precious faith will not be threatened. You see, O exalted one, king of your own country, I am now guardian of the church. Not you. Me. And the church will do as I say."*

"That encounter happened in May 1938, and the keyhole is still there," Gallo said. "People line up every day to peek through it at the dome of St. Peter's, over two miles away."

"How do you know about what Mussolini said that night?" Stephanie asked.

Good question. He, too, was skeptical.

"We worked with American and British intelligence during the war," Gallo said. "Our nation status gave us a diplomatic presence worldwide. We provided medical services in every combat theater, but we also passed on information about the Axis to the Allies. And we were a conduit to both of the Pius popes. In the course of that, we learned that Mussolini had blackmailed the Holy See into complacency, convincing the Vatican that he possessed Our Trinity. Both popes demanded proof from us that we still possessed the Trinity. Of course, we could not supply it. So they capitulated and stayed silent about all of the fascist atrocities. Pius XI had planned to break that silence, but died before that happened. Pius XII chose to maintain that silence. Historians have argued for decades why the Vatican did not do more to stop the evil in Italy and Germany. The answer was simple. The church was threatened by something important enough to command its attention."

"Did Mussolini have the *Nostra Trinità*?" Stephanie asked.

Gallo shook his head. "We have no idea. Il Duce killed three knights, one a *Secreti,* to obtain whatever he found. That we know for a fact. So we've spent the past seven decades gathering all we could." He motioned to the room. "This is the result of those efforts. Mr. Malone, you asked how Mussolini is important here. This is how."

"Is the church currently aware of any of this?" Stephanie asked.

"Archbishop Spagna certainly is. Perhaps a few cardinals know of the *Constitutum Constantini.* Within the order a handful know the history, I being one of those. But this certainly is not a subject of common knowledge. The pope dying so sudden has apparently aroused the ambitions of the archbishop, the *Secreti,* and my brother. All three want to take advantage of the situation."

"Aren't you the lieutenant ad interim, thanks to your brother," Cotton asked again.

"I agreed to serve as a way to try to heal the rifts within our ranks. But the petty infighting and ridiculous egos of the most senior of our officers has taxed my patience. Even so, my allegiance is to my brothers. And only to them."

"Over your own brother?"

"Even over my own brother." Gallo hesitated, then said, "I foolishly thought I was the only one who could keep Kastor in check. I know him. Perhaps even better than he knows himself. I apologize again for what's happened to you, Mr. Malone. I'm trying hard to rectify the situation."

He decided to cut the guy a little slack. "My apologies, too. I'm just trying to understand the lay of the land."

"I appreciate that. So what I'm about to tell you has remained within our ranks, as a cherished secret, for a long time. But I need your help, so I'm going to break protocol and tell you both a secret."

CHAPTER
TWENTY-NINE

L‍UKE LISTENED TO S‍PAGNA AS HE EXPLAINED.

"In the early 1930s Mussolini wanted to show the world that Rome had returned to all of its imperial glory. So he started a massive urban redevelopment project. Neighborhoods were razed, buildings leveled, grand boulevards cleared and paved. People come to Rome today from all over the world and marvel at the architecture. What they don't realize is that most of it bears the imprint not only of emperors and popes, but also of a cruel fascist."

He and Laura listened as Spagna told them how Mussolini had wanted to attract a World's Fair and even the Olympics. To do that he appropriated a tract of swampy land north of the city, adjacent to the Tiber, and constructed a grand complex.

The Foro Mussolini.

"Like the Forum Caesaris and the Forum Augusti. But in the ancient world those were places of commerce and religious worship. This one dealt only with sports, games, and politics. There were gyms, running tracks, swimming pools, and a garish twenty-thousand-seat travertine stadium, ringed by sixty marble statues of nude males wielding clubs, swords, and slings. It became a Black Shirt playground, home to the Fascist Academy of Physical Education, used for training and competitions. Mussolini himself worked out there regularly, and even more incredible, the place still stands."

That surprised Luke.

"The complex is used for international competitions," Spagna said. "The buildings house the Italian National Olympic Committee, a television station, a museum, a fencing academy, even a high-tech courthouse where terrorists and Mafioso were tried. The site has adapted, but there's one part that has remained exactly the same."

He waited.

"The obelisk."

COTTON HAD NEVER HEARD OF THE FORO MUSSOLINI AND THE obelisk that Pollux Gallo had just described.

But he was intrigued.

"The obelisk is fifty-five feet tall," Gallo said. "The largest single piece of marble ever quarried at Carrara. A perfect slab, free of cracks and imperfections, topped with a tip of gilded bronze. On it is inscribed MUS-SOLINI DUX."

He silently translated.

Mussolini leader.

"It was dedicated on November 4, 1932, to great pomp. Behind it stretches a huge piazza, paved with mosaics of muscled athletes, eagles, and odes to Il Duce. It's all so repulsive, so grandiose. Like the man himself. But the obelisk is one of the last remaining monuments that still bears Mussolini's name."

Cotton knew the significance of obelisks, symbols of imperial power for centuries. Egyptians, Romans, emperors, and popes all used them. A natural that the fascists would turn to one.

"But it's what lies inside the obelisk," Gallo said. "That's our real secret."

LUKE HAD TO ADMIT, THE WHOLE THING SOUNDED FASCINATING. But he had to keep telling himself to not get caught up with the story and pay close attention to Spagna. This man had an unknown agenda.

"By any standard, the forum and the obelisk were grand gestures,"

Spagna said. "But Mussolini went one better. He commissioned a codex to be written by an Italian classical scholar. A fanciful account on the rise of fascism, its supposed achievements, and its place in history. One thousand two hundred and twenty words of pure propaganda, which, on October 27, 1932, he sealed inside the base of the obelisk."

Spagna explained how objects were routinely placed inside monuments, first done as an offering, a superstition. Eventually the practice of foundation deposits was used to carry forward the memory of the builder or the people who produced the structure. Mussolini particularly enjoyed the custom, filming the ceremonies for the newsreels. He would sign a dedication document with great flourish, seal it within a metal tube, then cement it himself inside the *prima pietra,* the first stone.

"The story goes," Spagna said, "that in order to free the codex and read its grand fascist message, the obelisk would have to come down. For future generations to know the greatness of Mussolini, his monument would have to fall. Ironic, wouldn't you say?"

"Is that obelisk still standing?" Laura asked.

Spagna nodded. "In all its glory."

"And why is that important now?" Luke asked.

"The British learned that Mussolini sealed something else inside that obelisk, along with the codex, something that has become quite important of late."

Spagna reached into his pocket for an object.

And tossed it over.

COTTON FOCUSED ON WHAT POLLUX GALLO WAS SAYING.

"In the 1930s Mussolini managed to infiltrate our ranks," Gallo said. "He did that, at first, simply to know what we were doing, just as he did with the church. We watched him, too. From those efforts Mussolini came to learn some of our most precious secrets, and one in particular. How to find the *Nostra Trinità.* Supposedly a map was created. A way to locate the hiding place. We've searched since 1798 for that map, but it was Mussolini who may have succeeded in finding it."

LUKE EXAMINED WHAT SPAGNA HAD THROWN HIS WAY.

A coin.

No. More a medal.

Its obverse featured Mussolini in profile, his head sheathed in a lion skin. The reverse showed an obelisk and bore a legend.

FORO MVSSOLINI A.X.

"What does it mean?" he asked Spagna.

"By wearing the lion skin, he linked himself to Hercules and the first of his twelve labors, the killing of the Nemean lion. Mussolini was obsessed with mythology." Spagna pointed. "The obelisk on that medal is the same one at the foro, with the same inscription. Then there's one other piece of information. At the base of the obelisk is a stone that has ANNO X carved into it. That coin you're holding was found in Mussolini's pocket the day he was killed. One of the *Secreti* was there and retrieved it before they took the great leader and his mistress back to Milan and hung their corpses upside down for all to see."

Luke motioned. "Mussolini created this medal?"

Spagna nodded. "It was specially commissioned for the dedication of the Foro Mussolini. Several were placed inside the obelisk with the codex. Those were made of gold. The one you're holding is bronze. Made just for Il Duce, and it being in his pocket was significant. As was what Mussolini called out just before they shot him at Lake Como. *Magnus ab integro saeclorum nascitur ordo.* The great order of the ages is born afresh. Meaningless at the time. But not when you consider the text of the codex that Mussolini commissioned. The one inside the obelisk. It has an epigraph at its beginning. A quote from Virgil's Eclogues 4.5. *The great order of the ages is born afresh.*"

"That's too many coincidences to be a coincidence," Laura said.

"You're correct," Spagna said. "Which means what we need is waiting inside that obelisk, and it's up to Mr. Malone to find it."

COTTON WAITED FOR GALLO TO FINISH.

"We've suspected for some time that the obelisk served as Mussolini's hiding place for what he might have located. Probably behind a stone at the base, marked ANNO X. The time has come to see if that's true. And quickly."

He caught the urgent tone. "You think the men who just tried to kill me are headed that way?"

"I do."

Which might explain the fake Gallo's hasty retreat. He checked his watch. "They have less than an hour's head start. It's a long drive back to Rome."

"Three hours," Stephanie said.

"I can get us there faster," Gallo noted. "We have the helicopter, which is still at the villa."

Cotton glanced at Stephanie, who seemed to be reading his mind.

"I get it," she said. "This is the time for you to bow out. I wouldn't blame you. As you say, you don't have a dog in this fight."

That was right. He'd been hired for a job, which he'd extended, but it was over. He should find a hotel, go to sleep, then head for the nearest airport in the morning and fly back to Copenhagen. After all, he was retired from the intelligence business. But he wasn't dead. Not yet, anyway. And he was curious. What had the Knights of Malta guarded? The *Nostra Trinità*? The *Constitutum Constantini*? Which both Napoleon and Mussolini had been after? Perhaps waiting at the base of an obelisk in Rome? There since 1932? Which might affect the coming conclave and the election of a pope? That was a lot of fascinating questions. He wasn't due in Nice to meet Cassiopeia for a few days. So why not? He'd come this far.

"I'll stay in," he said.

She smiled. "The chopper will be here in fifteen minutes."

"Kind of sure of yourself, weren't you?"

"I was hoping. It'll get us to Rome a good hour before anyone else. I appreciate this, Cotton."

A man entered the archive and approached, whispering into Gallo's ear, who nodded as the messenger withdrew.

"I've learned some additional information that's disturbing," Gallo said. "I'm told men are on Malta, there to kill my brother."

CHAPTER THIRTY

KASTOR ENTERED THE SHOP.

The door jingled as he and Chatterjee stepped inside, the dim space lit only by a couple of overhead bulbs. He took in the stale air with a hint of sea damp, along with the well-trundled floor, the cobwebbed corners, and the fascinating wares.

Clocks.

Most of their wooden cases were in various stages of construction. Some were being carved, others painted, a couple more half gilded. He tried to remember if he'd seen this shop as a child, but he could not remember ever visiting this side of St. Thomas Bay. He recalled that among the many summer homes ringing the bay there'd always been an array of eclectic shops and entrepreneurs. One, a potter who'd turned out dishes, bowls, and vases on a spinning wheel, came to mind.

But no one who crafted the famous *tal-lira* clocks.

He knew them well.

Dating back to the 17th century, they were unique to Malta and found all across the island. One had hung in the orphanage. His job one summer had been to wind its inner mechanism. Always two doors, one glassed on the outside, the other inside supporting the face and a small aperture revealing the pendulum. Traditionally, none had ever been produced on a mass level, each made individually.

Like here.

An old dog, worn and scraggy, appeared from behind the counter. It shuffled a few steps, then lay down. A wall shielded the front from the rear of the building, broken by an open doorway. A man emerged through a threadbare curtain. Aged, coarse-featured, silver beard, deep-set eyes peering out from behind thick spectacles.

"You don't look like a cardinal," the old man said.

He wanted to come back with a barbed comment but resisted the temptation. "Is this your shop?"

The man nodded. "My family has been making clocks for three hundred years. Sadly, though, I'll be the last. My two children have no interest in continuing the tradition."

"And you are?"

"Nick Tawil."

He faced Chatterjee. "Why are we here?"

"This man knows a lot about the *Nostra Trinità*. It has been his life's obsession."

"Is that true?" he asked Tawil.

"Guilty as charged."

A sharp flash lit the shop windows, followed by a clap of thunder. Rain continued to splatter the panes. He needed a moment to digest things. So he perused the clocks under construction. "How many do you make a year?"

"Seven, sometimes eight."

"What do you charge? Five, six thousand euros?"

"More like seven."

"That's a good living."

He recalled the clock that had hung in his parents' house. Not all that impressive, but it had kept impeccable time. He noticed gilding being applied to one of the frames. "Twenty-four-carat?"

"What else."

The finish looked a little dull, but he realized that the final product would eventually be buffed to a shine.

He turned back toward Tawil. "What is it you supposedly know?"

"I've been searching for the knights' Trinity a long time. My father searched. My grandfather searched."

"Are you a knight?"

Tawil shook his head. "I'm not Catholic."

His suspicious nature took hold and he glanced toward Chatterjee. "How do you know this clockmaker?"

"We've been friends a long time."

"That we have," Tawil added, walking over and crouching down near the dog, stroking the animal's dark coat. "There's a place not far away from here. An ancient graveyard beside the sea that has been there a long time. It's where the knight Napoleon killed in the grand master's palace, with his palms nailed to a table, is buried."

Now he knew where Chatterjee had learned the story.

"My grandfather told me that the map to the *Nostra Trinità* had been buried with him."

"How would he know that?'

"I have no idea. But my grandfather was no fool."

"Was the map buried there?"

Tawil shrugged. "We'll never know. In the early 1930s the grave was violated. My grandfather and several other men tried to stop the robbers. But they were killed, and the robbers got away. So no one knows what, if anything, was found."

He heard the pain in the man's voice.

"My grandfather spent much of his life trying to find the *Nostra Trinità*. He learned a great deal. I have all of his books and papers."

Which he'd like to examine. But first, "I want to see that grave."

"In the rain?" Tawil asked.

"Why not? I'm already wet."

The clockmaker chuckled. "Good point."

Headlights brushed through the store, sweeping inward from the street side windows. He came alert. Car doors slammed. He stepped to the window and spied out into the darkness. Chatterjee stood beside him. Two forms walked to the black shadow of the car he and Chatterjee had arrived in. A flash of light broke the darkness and the vehicle seemed to bulge from within, everything erupting outward, the roof flying off into the rain, followed by a blast of heat and light that tossed the hulk off the ground as it exploded.

His body froze in terror.

He'd never seen such a thing before.

The car smashed downward onto splayed wheels, a mass of gasoline-fed flames and smoke mushrooming upward. In the glow he saw the two men turn toward the shop and aim automatic rifles.

Chatterjee's sinewy arm yanked him toward the floor.

Tawil still stood near the dog.

"Get down," Chatterjee yelled.

A torrent of gunfire ripped into the shop.

Windows shattered from the onslaught.

Bullets found flesh with a sickening thud. Tawil groaned in pain and his body crumpled sideways to the floor, muscle spasms jerking from the wounds. The dog sprang up in fright and threw out a shrill bark before bolting toward the back of the shop. The storm outside could now be clearly heard. Rain and wind funneled through the destroyed windows and gave off a wet, eerie moan of longing. More rounds found their way inside, searching for targets.

"Crawl past the counter," Chatterjee said.

"What about the old man?"

"He's not my problem. You are."

Chatterjee reached back and found a gun he'd apparently been concealing. He gestured with the weapon. "Get going. I'm right behind you."

He stayed low and made his way to the other side of the counter and through the thin curtain. Chatterjee returned fire, sending two shots out into the dark, then belly-crawling his way through the curtain.

"That should at least slow them down, knowing we're armed. Let's go."

"And the clockmaker?"

"He's dead."

What was happening? Who was after him?

"How did these people know we were here?" he asked. "Where did they come from?"

"Eminence, this is not the time for analysis."

He caught no measure of respect with the use of his title.

Chatterjee stood. He did, too. They were in a dilapidated back room littered with mounds of debris. Darkness loomed, except for the weak light of a freestanding lamp in one corner. A stairway led up. Two windows opened to the outside, both covered in thin cheesecloth. No rear door.

Chatterjee stepped to one of the windows, stared out, then yanked the cloth coverings aside.

"Look out there."

He came close and saw it. A dock. With a small boat bobbing at one side.

"That's our ticket out of here," Chatterjee said.

The storm was still raging, more rain than wind, thank God. The Med could be unforgiving in rough weather. For centuries the sea itself had been the island's primary means of defense. The coastal currents were murderous, as was the rocky southern shoreline looming with deep gorges and bold headlands.

But all of that seemed far preferable to here.

The shop's front door banged open.

"We need to leave," he said.

But their path out was blocked by a filigreed iron grille. Chatterjee heaved at the inner wooden sash, which slid up with a protest, then he braced his feet against the wall and grabbed the iron with both hands. The grille gave a little from the tugs. He grabbed on, too, and together they forced the wet wood, crumbled with age, to release the screws, freeing the grille.

Chatterjee tossed the iron aside.

He clambered out over the sill. Chatterjee followed. The rain continued to fall with a monotonous determination out of a black sky. A path led from the shop to the dock. He was careful with his wild scramble across the wet rocks, his soles slipping with every step. He stole a few glances back over his shoulder at the threat behind. A sickening feeling of fear clawed at his stomach.

"Keep moving," Chatterjee said.

They reached the dock and he saw that the boat was a typical *dghajsa*. Small. Sturdy. High stem and stern. They were mainly used as water taxis around the Grand Harbor and the other bays. More like a gondola, not meant for the open sea. Usually propelled by oars, this one came equipped with an outboard engine. He could see Chatterjee was likewise concerned.

But they had no choice.

"Get in," Chatterjee said.

They hopped into the boat and he released the mooring lines. The choppy sea and wind pushed them quickly away from the dock. Chatter-jee yanked on the outboard's starting cord and the engine revved to life.

They sped off into the night.

CHAPTER THIRTY-ONE

Cotton sat in the helicopter, heading south to Rome, Pollux Gallo and Stephanie flying with him. At first Stephanie had wanted to remain behind to coordinate what he was doing with Luke's activities on Malta. Gallo had offered her the Villa Pagana in Rapallo as her headquarters, and she'd nearly accepted his generosity, but in the end she opted to come along instead, wanting to be back in Rome.

"I know you must find this confusing," Gallo said to him. "Brother against brother. And twin brothers at that."

"Have you always been estranged?"

"Just the opposite, in fact. Our parents were killed when we were children, so we only had each other. We were raised in an orphanage, the nuns a poor substitute, but they did the best they could. Kastor and I clung to each other. But as we grew older, we drifted apart. Our personalities changed. Though we look alike, we don't think alike. By the time we were twenty, he was off to seminary and I was in the army."

"You said back at the archive that your brother wants to be pope. You know that for sure?"

"Without question. He told me so himself. He views this conclave as a gift from God, an unexpected opportunity that he must use to full advantage."

"You spoke on the subject?"

Gallo nodded. "We had a heated discussion. One of many of late."

"Is Archbishop Spagna his ally?" Stephanie asked.

"That's what I've learned. Kastor traveled to Malta yesterday specifically to meet with Spagna."

"And you know this how?" Cotton asked.

"Just like Spagna, we have spies, too."

He did not doubt that observation and he was still troubled by the comment made at the archive, which had yet to be explained. "Why do you think your brother's life is in danger?"

"We have people on Malta, inside Fort St. Angelo. Several knights are permanently stationed there. They've been watching my brother's activities and report he might be in danger."

"From who?" Stephanie asked.

"The *Secreti*. They're on the island. We know that for sure."

Cotton glanced across at Stephanie. "Nothing from Luke?"

She shook her head. "Silence. The GPS signal from his phone has also stopped. He's working with a Maltese security agent named Laura Price. They're both now with Spagna. The head of Maltese security tells me the situation is under control, so I have to trust Luke can handle himself."

"He can."

The chopper kept knifing through the night air. He glanced out the windows and spotted a dark rural landscape, broken occasionally by the lights of a village or a farmhouse. They were not yet to Rome, still north in Tuscany, he estimated.

"I see now," Gallo said, "that my brother's interest in the knights was totally self-serving, as is usual for him. He used his position to learn our secrets. To use them for his own advantage. Hopefully, we'll be able to prevent any further harm and end his bid for the papacy before he ever begins."

A canvas sack rested on the cabin floor. Gallo pointed toward it and said, "I brought what we'll need. I'm guessing the legend is not true and there's no need to destroy the whole obelisk to get to the codex, or whatever else Mussolini may have left inside. We've long thought a marked stone at the base could provide access to the repository."

"Planning on blowing it open?" Stephanie asked.

Gallo chuckled. "I'm hoping a sledgehammer will do the trick. But there are a great many in Italy who would not be sad to see that obelisk fall. The government has tried several times to raze it."

Yet it still stood. Like the flowers at the site where Mussolini had been shot.

"Why would the *Secreti* want your brother dead?" Cotton asked.

"He's antagonized half of the knights into enemies."

"But they're not the kind who normally kill people."

"The *Secreti* are fanatics, which makes them unpredictable and dangerous. They apparently view Kastor as a threat to the order. Their entire purpose is to eliminate threats. So the last thing they would want is for Kastor to become pope."

"And they'll kill to stop that?" Stephanie asked.

"I'm not sure what they'll do. All I know is that they are on Malta."

He felt the chopper start to descend and begin a wide turn. Outside the windows he saw they'd arrived on the outskirts of Rome. He caught sight of the forum, its two stadiums, running tracks, tennis courts, and other buildings, partially lit to the night, and the obelisk, rising at the entrance before an imposing avenue that stretched to a far piazza.

He checked his watch.

Nearly midnight.

It had been a long day.

THE KNIGHT STARED AT THE LIT OBELISK, ABLE TO SEE IN THE DIM wash of light the enormous inscription etched into its side.

MUSSOLINI DUX.

Finally. The truth may be told.

Was the map there? Or maybe the *Nostra Trinità* itself?

Waiting patiently?

Within the order a precious few were privy to the most confidential of information. Thankfully, he was one of those. He knew the story of Mussolini's visit to the Villa del Priorato di Malta and what he told Grand Master Rovere-Albani. *I've even done him a favor and sealed it away where no one can get to it.* If Mussolini truly found the Trinity, this could be his hiding place.

At least that's what James Grant had told him. Now it was time to determine if the information he'd risked everything to obtain was true.

Finally, the Brits were out of the way.

Only the Americans remained.

But he'd handle them.

CHAPTER THIRTY-TWO

KASTOR HUNCHED IN THE LOW-RIDING *DGHAJSA* AS CHATTERJEE headed them out of the bay and toward open sea. He didn't necessarily agree with the wisdom of that move in the storm but decided not to argue. The idea was surely to get as far away from the men with guns as possible. To a place where they could come ashore in seclusion and safety.

The Mediterranean's great plain loomed dark. Giant thunderheads banked overhead, bolts of lightning cracking inside the clouds, charging them with a white glow. Waves clawed over the side as they rose and fell into the troughs. On the distant horizon he saw more flickering of thunderclouds.

He knew the coastal geography.

South Malta was littered with towering cliffs, some dropping over 250 meters. They were now out of St. Thomas Bay heading toward Delimara Point. He could see the lighthouse beacon through the storm. Though invisible in the night, he knew that Fort Delimara loomed ahead, built by the British in the 19th century. Mostly underground, its armaments and casements were set in the cliffs near the point. It had been a derelict during his childhood and, to his knowledge, remained so today. So no refuge could be sought there.

The rain continued to squall.

Chatterjee angled the motor a quarter to starboard, on a path to cut across Marsaxlokk Bay. The bow heaved against the waves. High on emotion and lack of sleep, Kastor felt riddled with anxiety. He turned back toward Chatterjee and, in the distance, spotted the fast-approaching profile of a powerboat, running lights winking green and red.

"That could be trouble," he called out, pointing, his words thrown back in his face by the wind.

Chatterjee turned around and saw their pursuer, too. "These people came prepared."

Which made him wonder again who his enemy might be. "Why do they want me dead?"

"You think too highly of yourself, Eminence."

Then it hit him.

"They're after you?"

"I would say so."

They passed the southern tip of the bay. The famed cart ruts were nearby, at the Dingli Cliffs. Pairs of grooves cut into the rocky ground back in the Bronze Age that crisscrossed one another, a remnant of the past that he recalled from childhood. No one really knew how they originated. Sledges? Wheels? Slides? Hard to say. A mystery. One the nuns could never explain.

Like right now.

This was madness.

Out on the sea during a raging storm in a *dghajsa* propelled by a mere few horsepower, while a powerboat carrying who-knew-what bore down on them.

He grabbed his bearings.

Then he remembered the caves.

The south shore was littered with them, their names reflective of their history. Cat's. Reflection. Circle. Elephant. Honeymoon. The Ghar Hasan was perhaps the most famous. Supposedly the Saracen Hasan took refuge there with a young maiden he abducted. He recalled a footpath that led to stone steps heading down a limestone cliff. Inside were a series of passages, none of them hospitable, but Hasan had supposedly occupied one of them. That cave was too high from the water to be of any help. But the grottoes that existed below could provide a place to hide. The Blue Grotto was the most famous. He racked his brain and thought back. His gaze raked the darkened shoreline, periodically illuminated by lightning. The prop continued to bite the water. Their pursuer was coming ever closer, but still loomed a couple of kilometers away.

He pointed to the right. "Head toward shore."

"You're thinking the grottoes," Chatterjee asked.

"It's the only shelter we've got. If we hurry, we might be able to disappear into one without being seen. But you're going to have to get close for us to be able to see."

He checked his watch, the hands illuminated in the darkness.

12:20 A.M.

Another day had begun.

Which brought the conclave ever closer, now less than twelve hours away.

This was way beyond anything he'd ever experienced. Granted, he'd defied the Holy See with his outspoken dissension, but that was vastly different from men trying to kill him. Genuine fear surged through him, an unusual feeling. Never once had he feared the pope or the curia. Regret? Definitely, he'd felt that. Nobody liked to lose.

But this was nothing like that.

His eyes focused through the night, searching for an opening in the towering cliffs. Lightning continued to flash at regular intervals, offering a few precious seconds of clarity.

"There," he yelled, pointing ahead. "A grotto. I saw it."

"I did, too," Chatterjee said.

They rounded another point, the bow headed toward a small bay, homing in on the spot he'd seen in the last flash. Ill-tempered squalls kept scuffing the wavetops white. Another lightning bolt exploded overhead and he saw they were headed for an arch in the limestone wall, the entrance formed by a craggy arc of rain-sheered rock, a curtain of rivulets pouring down to the sea.

The powerboat was momentarily out of sight, which allowed them time to find the dark chasm in the cliff wall. Chatterjee navigated to the archway and they passed beneath the waterfall that spilled down across the opening. Kastor's clothes were soaked, the *dghajsa* puddled with water. Now, though, they were sheltered by a roof of stone, the grotto beyond calm to the night. During the day, combined with sunlight and the surrounding chain of rock, the water would reflect the phosphorescent colors of the submerged flora forming shades of blue and green. Tonight there was only black.

"There's a ledge," he called out, seeing its outline in the blackness.

Chatterjee eased to it. "Get out."

He stared back at the Indian.

"Get out," Chatterjee said again. "Stay out of sight. I'll divert them."

"Let's stay together."

For some reason he did not want to be alone.

"You're going to be pope. I'm hired help. Now get the hell out of this boat and let me do my job."

He hopped onto the limestone, the ledge perched just above the surface. He heard the *dghajsa*'s outboard rev and the craft sped away, deeper into the grotto, toward the exit on the far side. From beyond the entrance he heard the roar of the powerboat, drawing closer, its engine a steady drone above the wind and rain. Chatterjee slipped back out into the storm.

Then a new sound invaded the monotony.

Rat, tat, tat.

Gunfire.

More fear swept through him. He'd never felt more helpless. A need to withdraw came over him. He stared into the blackness and saw an even darker splotch. A cave? He carefully inched his way across the rough rock, slippery with seawater, and saw he was half right. Not a cave, more a tunnel. He knew most of them came to a dead end. He headed inside. This one drained into a small chamber hewn from the rock.

More gunfire could be heard.

He recalled the caves he'd explored as a child, most decorated with stalactites and splash deposits. Sometimes even crude paintings from antiquity. Hard to know if this one came with any of that. He sat on the wet limestone, breathing evenly, gathering his strength. He dared not give way to panic and forced his mind to behave.

What a predicament for a prince of the church.

He backed himself against the wall, his head pounding like a piston.

Once again he felt like Paul, who also supposedly found refuge in a Maltese cave. Paul was not one of the original twelve, but an apostle nonetheless. A servant of Christ who experienced a sudden, startling revelation that set him apart from others. He gained a reputation for bucking the law. His fate was sealed by writing letters to the Romans, Galatians, and Corinthians. He recalled the words from Acts about the viper on Malta. How the locals said, *No doubt this man is a murderer, whom, though he has escaped the sea, yet justice does not allow to live.* But Paul shook off the bite of the viper and *they were expecting that he would swell up or suddenly fall down dead. But after they had looked for a long time and saw no harm come to him, they changed their minds and said that he was a god.*

He'd planned to also shake off the viper, suffer no harm, and be regarded as a god. Like Paul, though, it seemed he might meet a horrible fate. No one really knew how or when Paul died. But every account that had survived described a violent demise in one form or another. Decapitation. Crucifixion. Stabbing. Strangulation.

Would his fate be similar?

There'd not been any more shots for a few minutes.

A good sign?

Had Chatterjee led them away?

From the tunnel's entrance, back into the grotto, he heard the hum of an engine. Low, steady. His gaze locked on the blackness.

A new surge of fear swept through him.

Footsteps approached. Coming his way across the hard stone through the tunnel. He dared not say a word. Then a form appeared in the chamber. No details. No face. Just a man.

"Eminence."

Chatterjee's voice.

Thank God.

"Are they gone?" he asked, hoping.

Chatterjee stepped farther inside. Another form appeared behind him, the outline of a gun in the man's right hand.

"No," Chatterjee said. "And I was caught."

He did not know what to say.

The form behind him stood still.

He wanted to stand but his muscles had frozen. Two bangs echoed off the stone walls, which hurt his ears. Chatterjee pitched forward and fell hard to the ground, not moving. He stared at the dark form in astonishment. Would it all end here? Alone? Inside a cliff. With no meaning or purpose? All that he'd endured would come to nothing?

He finally gave in to his calling and closed his eyes, saying a prayer, hoping God, if he existed, was indeed merciful.

Nothing happened.

He opened his eyes.

The sound of footsteps moved away.

CHAPTER THIRTY-THREE

LUKE FINISHED OFF ANOTHER OF THE RING-SHAPED LOAVES FILLED with cheese and meat. Laura called them *ftira*, something of a cross between a calzone and a sandwich. What he particularly liked was the thin slices of potato that adorned the outer crust. Unusual. But tasty. He washed the late supper down with a Kinnie, reminiscent of a Coke with less sugar. A beer would have been preferable, but none had been offered. He'd been grateful for the meal. He was hungry, and every growing boy needed three squares a day. Or at least that's what his mother always said.

Laura had eaten a little before an older, dark-haired man with a pouch around his waist appeared. She introduced him as Kevin Hahn, her boss, head of Maltese security. She then left with Spagna and Hahn. He'd wondered about all the chumminess that excluded him, but decided not to allow his feelings to be hurt, using the time to think.

A couple of newspapers were lying on the kitchen table. The *Malta Independent.* He noticed a front-page headline dated a few days ago—ALL IS READY FOR THE CONCLAVE—and scanned the article.

VATICAN CITY—Cardinals are filing into Rome for preliminary meetings to ponder who among them might be best to lead the church. Invitations to attend went out to all cardinal-electors under the age of 80 the day after the pope died. They arrive by private car, taxi, and mini bus at the gates of the Vatican for gatherings known as general congregations, closed-door meetings in which they will get to know each other and decide who will next lead 1.2 billion Catholics.

"We need a man of governance, by that I mean a man who is intimately connected with the people he chooses to help him govern the church," Cardinal Tim Hutchinson, the former archbishop of Westminster in London, said.

The voting-cardinals, numbering about 150, have been holding two meetings a day. One of their purposes is to select the conclave officers and review all of the rules. They also talk of the Holy See, the curia, and the expectations of a new pope. These preliminary sessions provide the cardinals a chance to size up potential candidates by watching them closely in the debates and checking discreetly with other cardinals about their qualifications or any skeletons in their closets. All necessary as these men come from all over the world and are rarely together.

"We've had meetings all this week to get to know each other better and consider the situations that we face," Hutchinson said.

He added that he could not say, at this stage, who the favorites might be. Cardinals never reveal publicly who they prefer but they do occasionally drop hints in interviews by discussing their view of the ideal candidate. The most frequently mentioned quality is an ability to communicate the Catholic faith convincingly. But the suddenness of the pope's death means that no front-runner currently stands out.

The Sistine Chapel itself is being prepared. The chimney is installed, leading down to the stove where the ballots will be burned after each vote. White smoke signals success. Black smoke failure. The color of each is ensured by a chemical pack added to the flames.

A further mix of high-tech gadgetry and Old World tradition will ensure secrecy, including a scrambling device that will block any attempt to phone or text the outside world. Bug sweepers will also guarantee the chapel is secure from unwanted eavesdroppers. Jamming will be used both inside the Sistine and at the nearby guesthouse at Santa Marta where the cardinals will sleep during the conclave. Computers will also be banned, so email and Twitter are firmly out of bounds.

But it's not all down to high-tech gadgets.

A number of traditions will be strictly followed to ensure that the ballot is secret . . .

Luke recalled what Spagna had said about his people and conclave preparations. The Entity would possess all of the necessary expertise to ensure that secrecy was maintained. And who better than the Lord's Own to protect the faithful.

The door opened and Spagna returned.

Alone.

Now his feelings were hurt.

"Where's Laura?" he asked.

"She'll be back shortly."

"Is she in trouble with the boss?"

"I imagine that's a situation you are quite familiar with."

He grinned. "I've had my share of trouble."

"I bet you have. When she gets back, I'll need you both to take care of a situation that has arisen."

The rain had eased but was still drizzling down.

"I'm trying to find my man who has Cardinal Gallo contained," Spagna said. "But I'm having trouble making contact. He was headed toward St. Thomas Bay, to a local clockmaker's shop. I need you both to go there and see what's happening."

"You think there's a problem?"

"I have one of those bad feelings."

He'd heard that before from Stephanie, and though he'd learned to trust her instincts, this guy was a stranger.

"I have to check in with my boss," Luke made clear. "And that's not a request. If you have a problem with that, then I'm out of here."

"Your supervisor is on a helicopter headed toward Rome, unavailable at the moment. Cotton Malone and the temporary head of the Knights of Malta are with her. You should know that the temporary head is the twin brother of Cardinal Gallo."

"Aren't you a wealth of information," he noted.

"That's my job and, you're right, I lied earlier. I don't have Stephanie Nelle's okay to use your services. But I'll obtain it the moment it's possible. I do have permission to use Ms. Price, though. So for the moment, it's your call to stay or go. Make up your mind."

"Why aren't you working the conclave?"

"My people are preparing things as we speak."

"And here you are. On a treasure hunt. Makes a fellow wonder."

"Ever heard of multitasking?"

Luke rose from the table and tossed away the paper remnants from his supper into a trash can.

"There's a car downstairs, parked across the street. A green Toyota. Here are the keys." Spagna laid them on the table, along with a cell phone. "The directions to where you need to go are loaded on the map app. If you're in, head there when Ms. Price returns. If not, give both to her. She'll handle it. Either the both of you or her alone, find Gallo and my man and don't let them out of your sight. Call me when you have them. My number is also loaded in the phone as number 1 on speed dial."

Spagna left the apartment.

Bossy guy.

He had no choice. Which Spagna well knew. He had to stay. But now he had a cell phone. So he grabbed the unit and punched in the Magellan Billet emergency contact number. The phone did not connect. Instead, a message displayed that read INTERNATIONAL SERVICE NOT AVAILABLE.

He smiled.

Spagna was no fool.

He decided a trip to the head was in order. No telling when there'd be another chance. He laid his Beretta on the table, stepped into the bathroom, used the facilities, then washed his face and hands. Drying them with some paper towels, he walked back toward the trash bin in the outer room and tossed the paper away.

The door banged open, bursting from its jamb.

Which startled him.

Two men rushed inside.

Nothing in their look or manner signaled friend.

No way to reach the gun, so he spun on his right heel and jammed an elbow down then up into the nearest threat. His assailant crumpled from the blow, dazed. He lunged, gritted his teeth, and kicked again. The second man flew back against the wall, rattling the hanging pictures. He advanced to finish the second guy off and momentarily forgot about the first man. A blow to his spine came hard and unexpected.

Followed by another.

Electric pain resonated down his back. His legs went limp, the pain overtaking the adrenaline, compounding his uneasiness. But he was well trained, well conditioned, a combat veteran who'd fought hand-to-hand in close quarters. He knew how to block pain from his mind and fight while hurt.

He spun around.

A fist smashed into his face.

If not for the tingling in his spine he could have counteracted, but he was too dazed to respond. The image before him, a man standing firm and ready, twirled.

So did the room.

Another fist smashed into his jaw.

He staggered back.

A third fist slammed into his midsection and the wind left him. Breath strangled in his lungs. A final blow, an ax-handle combination of both arms with hands intertwined, came down across his neck.

He crumpled to the floor and vaguely heard one of the men standing over him, panting hard, say, "Grab him."

He tried to react, but couldn't.

The fog in his brain prevented his muscles from responding. His arms and legs were gripped hard. He tried to resist, but his muscles seemed paralyzed.

"Throw him through the window," one of the men said.

CHAPTER THIRTY-FOUR

COTTON HOPPED FROM THE HELICOPTER. THEY'D LANDED RIGHT IN the middle of the Stadio di Marmi, the Stadium of Marble, on a carpet of thin green grass. Benches for twenty thousand encircled them, just beyond a six-lane running track. The shadowy outline of colossal statues ringed the stadium's upper edge, like something out of ancient Greece or Rome.

The rotors wound down as they made their way for the exit. Gallo carried the heavy duffel bag, he and Stephanie following. The pilot waited with the chopper. This part of north Rome seemed wholly deserted at such an early-morning hour, the entire Foro Mussolini, or Foro Italico as it was now called, quiet.

They exited through a ramp up, the stadium itself sunk in the ancient way with the top row of seats at ground level. Gallo led them toward a fountain adorned with a massive marble ball that spun on a bed of pressurized water. To their left stretched a wide paved expanse.

"The Piazzale dell'Impero. The Empire Way," Gallo said. "A testament to fascist propaganda. One of the few left in the world. My brother would fully appreciate its audacity."

Amber lights lit the way, both sides lined with stout blocks of white marble. The avenue itself was all mosaic tiles forming maps, fasces, and sports images along with prophetic slogans. As they walked Cotton read a few. DVCE. Leader. DVCE A NOI. Leader with us. MOLTI NEMICI MOLTO

ONORE. Much enemy, much honor. DVCE LA NOSTRA GIOVINEZZA A VOI
DEDICHIAMO. Duce, we give you our youth.

Audacity was right.

"This place was part training ground, part metaphor," Gallo said.
"Mussolini hoped that sport and physical strength would secure Italy's
place in the world. Entangling athletic and martial glory was central to
fascism. My brother likes metaphors, too. He thinks reminding everyone
of the Catholic past will somehow secure the future. As with the fascists,
intertwining fear with ignorance is key to what my brother has in mind
for the church."

"You two certainly disagree," Stephanie said.

"He's my identical twin, there's a bond between us, and I do love him.
But thankfully, I've always been able to separate those emotions from how
I feel about him as a cardinal of the church."

He knew little about Brother Gallo and nothing at all about Cardinal
Gallo. But these two men definitely had issues.

"Anything from Luke?" he asked Stephanie.

She shook her head. "Nothing."

At the far end of the avenue stood the obelisk. No lights directly illuminated the white marble, which seemed fitting. It existed, but no effort
was made to overly glorify its existence. Lights ringed a perimeter twenty
feet away, angled up to the stars. Its style was likewise nontraditional, a series of irregular-shaped stepped stones rising upward to a tall, central pillar.

"They cut it from a single block," Gallo said. "Then encased it in wood
and iron and floated all three hundred tons by the sea and the Tiber to
here. It took three years to carve and stand upright. All thirty-six meters.
Every step was documented and reported by the fascist press, extolled for
the masses to worship and appreciate."

Interesting how dictators required shows of greatness as a way to prove
they were entitled to power. Democratically elected leaders never had such
a need since the people themselves vested them with power, and no one
expected perfection. In fact, failure could be another stepping-stone to
greatness. Dictators never accepted failure. They preferred to have their
mistakes forgotten, overshadowed with spectacle.

They approached the obelisk.

Gallo pointed upward. "Notice the letters in the inscription."

He studied them in the dim wash of light. All uppercase, arranged vertically, MVSSOLINI on the spire, DVX beneath, each one over a yard high.

"They are incised rather than sculpted," Gallo said, "to prevent abrasion or removal. Il Duce thought ahead. He made them too large and too deep to ever be removed."

Ironic, Cotton thought. Similar to memories of fascism itself, which still seemed to linger in the 21st century.

They circled the monument.

Its marble was devoid of any other markings save the words OPERA BALILLA ANNO X carved into a tall panel at the base.

"The fascist youth organization Opera Nazionale Balilla immortalized itself, too," Gallo said. "Youth Organization Balilla. Tenth anniversary. The obelisk was dedicated on November 4, 1932, the tenth anniversary of the march on Rome and the start of the fascist regime."

"It's amazing the thing is still here," Stephanie said. "Every relic related to Hitler has been excised. Mussolini, though, seems different."

"Somebody tried to blow it up in 1941, but barely did any damage. People have suggested razing it for decades. But the Italians have never needed to delete their history." Gallo motioned at the obelisk. "Even if it's sometimes overdramatic. To them, destroying a monument like this is only a sign of weakness, of fear, not strength."

He continued to study the towering structure.

"We know Mussolini placed his codex inside," Gallo said. "Newspaper accounts from the time make no mistake of that fact. But no one knows where he placed the codex. It was done in a private ceremony, and no accounts have survived. As you can see, there's only one stone outside the central pillar with markings on it. The best guess is that the codex is behind it. What do you think? That marble has to be five centimeters thick."

"At least."

And the panel that bore the words OPERA BALILLA ANNO X measured about eight by four feet. A stout, solid stone rectangle built to last. And it had. For eighty years. He knew what Gallo wanted, so he climbed up on the four-foot-tall raised base and examined the large incised X—part of ANNO X—which had been intended as a reference to ten years of fascist rule. "How about X marks the spot?"

"Seems as good a place as any," Stephanie said.

Gallo unzipped the duffel bag and removed two sledgehammers and a flashlight. Cotton accepted one of the sledgehammers, and Gallo climbed up with the other.

Stephanie held the flashlight from below.

He nearly smiled at the irony. How many times had he damaged a World Heritage Site. Too many times to count, all just unfortunate occurrences. Now here he was about to intentionally deface a part of history.

He gripped the sledgehammer and swung.

The business end smacked the x hard. Gallo followed with a blow of his own. But the marble held firm.

They repeated the blows.

"Did you feel that," Gallo asked. "There's a little give. It could be hollow behind."

He agreed.

Stephanie aimed the flashlight at the x. Fissures had begun to spiderweb in all directions. Cotton glanced around and still saw no one. He wondered about security cameras. There had to be some. Yet no one had come to the obelisk's defense.

They resumed the assault.

A few blows later the marble gave way.

He and Gallo stepped back as chunks fell, creating a cloud of white dust. As they'd suspected, a small hollow niche loomed behind the outer wall. He laid the sledgehammer down and waited for the dust to settle. Stephanie handed him the flashlight.

He saw a metal tube, about two feet long and six inches wide, lying inside, a fasces etched into its dull exterior. Gallo reached in and removed the container, bringing it out to the base's edge.

"How do we open it?" Stephanie asked.

"They made them of lead and soldered the ends," Gallo said. "We should be able to break the joint. The idea was to be able to retrieve what they'd sealed away. I brought a rubber mallet, there in the bag."

"You know a lot about these things," Cotton noted.

"We've studied Mussolini and the fascists for a long time. We're hoping what we've been searching for is inside this repository."

She handed up the mallet. Gallo gently worked one end of the sealed tube, cracking his way around the soldered joint.

"They used a soft material and a light solder on purpose," Gallo said. "But keeping it airtight was essential."

The end cap gave way and Cotton shone the flashlight inside to see something rolled up.

Gallo slid it free.

Not paper. Stiff. Thicker.

Parchment.

Gallo unrolled the sheet, which measured about eighteen inches wide and two feet long. Black ink filled one side of the handwritten page. At the top were the words CODEX FORI MUSSOLINI. But what caught their collective attention was what had fallen free as Gallo unraveled the document.

Another sheet.

Thinner.

Browner.

More fragile.

Paper.

CHAPTER THIRTY-FIVE

LUKE HUNG IN THE AIR, HELD ALOFT AT HIS HANDS AND CALVES BY the two assailants. His head drooped down, still spinning. They were moving him toward one of the windows, intent on tossing him through the glass. In the open doorway behind him he saw the upside-down image of Laura rushing inside, pouncing on the man to his right, who released his hold and turned his attention toward her. He decided not to look a gift horse in the mouth and grabbed his wits, wiggling free from the other man's grasp, dropping to the floor and clipping the legs out from under his attacker. He rolled and wrapped his right arm around the man's throat and clamped hard, cutting off air and sending the guy into unconsciousness. Laura had already taken down her target, who lay still on the floor.

"Any idea who these idiots are?" he asked, breathing hard.

"Not a clue. But they came straight here, to an Entity safe house, which means they know Spagna's business."

"Where is the Lord's Own?"

"At another house, not far from here. He and my boss took me there when we left earlier."

That subject begged further investigation but, for the moment, he let it go and quickly searched both men. No ID. No weapons.

Forget them. Focus.

"Get a sheet off the bed," he said. "We'll rip it into strips and tie these bastards up for later."

He stepped to the table and grabbed the cell phone, car keys, and his gun.

They had to find Spagna.

He and Laura hustled west toward the piazza where everything had started, the sounds of cars fading as buildings began to soundproof the pedestrian-only zone. He kept a lookout behind them but noticed no one following. The only noise came from the occasional chatter of people and the whistle from a breeze.

Wispy high-level clouds veiled and unveiled a luminous moon, the storm having passed, the buildings and streets being strobed like a light turned on and off in a dark room. Floodlights encased the co-cathedral, bathing the ancient stone in a warm chalk-white glow. The building squatted like a massive four-legged creature, the bell towers ears, transepts paws, silently studying its territory. He followed Laura deeper into the old city. Past the cathedral zone the sidewalks became deserted. Streetlights periodically cast a lambent glow into a raisin-black night. Cars hunched close to the curb on both sides of every route, a few decorated with yellow summons, revealing the length of their illegal stay. Protective shutters were drawn tight on most of the apartment windows, only cracks of light indicating people inside. As he looked ahead, fifty yards, a new sound broke the silence.

One of the third-floor windows exploded.

A body flew out headfirst, flipped in midair, then slammed onto the hood of a parked car.

He raced forward.

Laura followed.

He instantly recognized the face.

Laura grabbed at the bloody shirt. "Spagna." Her voice carried a plea for a response. "Spagna."

He tried for a pulse. Faint. Blood poured from slashes across the face. The archbishop's nose bled profusely. But amazingly, he opened his eyes.

"Can you hear me?" Luke asked.

No response.

He saw panic in Laura's face. A first.

Spagna's bloody right hand jerked up and grabbed her arm. "Do . . . what I . . . told you. Both . . . of you."

A soft pop came from above and something whizzed close to Luke's right cheek. Spagna's chest exploded. Another swoosh and the skull ripped apart right before his eyes, blood and sinew splattering on him and Laura.

He whirled around and looked up.

In the shattered window three floors above, two men stood, guns pointed. Obviously, their first priority had been to finish what they'd started. In the instant it took them to re-aim their weapons at two unexpected intruders, he leaped at Laura, shoving her behind a car. They slammed onto the damp pavement, she on the bottom, he shielding her on top.

More soft pops echoed.

Bullets rained down.

One struck the hood next to Spagna's body, another shattered the windshield. Thankfully, the row of parked cars provided an ideal angle of protection, the third floor seemingly one story short of being high enough to shoot over them.

"We need to get out of here," she said.

"We can take these guys."

"Gallo is the priority now. That's what Spagna meant. We have to get to Gallo. Come on, and stay down."

She followed his lead, crouching low, using the cars as a shield while working down the street. More bullets tried to find a way through metal and glass. Fifty yards away he glanced back. The faces had disappeared from the window. Two forms suddenly popped out the building's front entrance. He and Laura took off running, turning at the first corner. He figured they had half a football field's lead. So he started making turns, trying to find a way out of the labyrinth of alleys.

They found a main boulevard.

He gulped in the humid air and looked around. The pavement was well lit and lined with more parked cars. Their pursuers were approaching, confirmed by the sound of running steps, coming closer.

Enough running. "Let's take these bastards out."

She didn't argue. He gripped his Beretta and they assumed a position on either side of the alley's end. But the footsteps could no longer be heard. They waited, but no one came.

What the hell?

Laura seemed surprised, too.

"In just a short time there are going to be a lot of police around here," she said.

He still had the car keys and phone with directions on it Spagna had supplied.

"Let's go find Cardinal Gallo."

CHAPTER THIRTY-SIX

COTTON REACHED DOWN AND LIFTED THE SINGLE SHEET THAT HAD fallen free. He was careful with his grip at the edges, mindful of how to handle something so rare, which was, after all, his main business.

He unrolled and studied the page.

Six lines. Typewritten.

He translated the German in his head and read it out for Stephanie, in English.

> Deliver the contents personally into the hands of von Hompesch. This must be done at once and with all possible discretion. Where oil meets stone, death is the end of a dark prison. Pride crowned, another shielded. Three blushes bloomed to ranks and file. H Z P D R S Q X

"What does it mean?" she asked.

"Let's leave here, before we're found out," Gallo said. "I can explain some of it along the way."

Good advice.

They both hopped down and replaced the tools in the duffel bag. Gallo re-rolled the parchment and the single page, slipping them back into the metal tube. Cotton carried the tube as they retraced their steps down the avenue toward the stadium.

"The knight who wrote those words served Grand Master Ferdinand von Hompesch, on Malta, as the prior of *la nostra ronti maggiore della sacra religione,*" Gallo said.

"Our major church of the sacred religion," Cotton translated for Stephanie.

"The conventional church of the knights," Gallo said. "The co-cathedral in Valletta. We've long thought the secret lay there, simply because of the connection of its prior to von Hompesch."

"There has to be more than that," Stephanie asked.

They kept walking.

"There is."

He listened as Gallo told them about a man tortured by Napoleon during his invasion of Malta. A man whose hands had been nailed to a table and still refused to tell the French invaders a thing.

"Legend says that the dead man left a way to find the *Nostra Trinità.* He was the prior of the cathedral and part of the *Secreti.* After Napoleon slaughtered him, he was buried along the east shore of Malta in a church cemetery. He lay there in quiet repose until his grave was violated in the 1930s."

"By Mussolini?" Cotton asked.

Gallo nodded. "And he clearly found something that commanded two popes' attention. Enough that he was able to compel them to stay out of his politics. We've always thought something significant came from that grave."

"Was it the message we just read?" Stephanie asked.

"It has to be. And there's one other thing." Gallo stopped, laying the heavy duffel bag down. "Mussolini killed three of our brothers to obtain what we just read. Those men, like that long-ago prior of the cathedral, died fulfilling their oaths. What we always believed, and now know to be true, is that Mussolini ultimately found nothing. He lied to the Vatican. A good one, for sure, but a lie nonetheless."

"How can you be so sure?" Stephanie asked.

"That's easy," Cotton said. "If he'd found the ultimate prize, it would have been inside that obelisk, instead of just clues as to where it might be."

Gallo nodded. "He also apparently altered the original message, since there were no typewriters on Malta in 1798. The original would have been handwritten. Let's hope he transcribed it correctly. It's now incumbent on us to find what he could not locate and return it to our custody."

He could hear the pain in Gallo's voice. Surely membership in any long-standing secret brotherhood involved a healthy dose of male bonding. But a society with overt religious overtones and ancient historical purposes added entirely different dimensions. Eighty-plus years had passed since those three brothers had died, yet the wound seemed fresh as yesterday to Pollux Gallo.

"We need to go to Malta," Gallo said.

"Why do you say that?" Cotton asked.

"It was in the words we just read. *Where oil meets stone.* What we seek is there."

THE KNIGHT HAD WATCHED WHAT WAS HAPPENING AT THE OBELISK with both fascination and worry. The *Codex Fori Mussolini* seemed to be exactly where the newspaper accounts from the 1930s had suggested.

An excellent turn of events.

It would be an easy matter to assume control of the situation and deal with the Americans here and now, as he'd done at the villa by Lake Como. He had the resources available. Just a simple gesture would call them to action. But that did not seem like the smart play.

Not yet, anyway.

Nothing had ever been gained through impetuousness. Rash thinking always resulted in unsatisfying results. He'd come this far thanks to smart choices and smart moves, timed perfectly. No sense stopping now. His grand plan contained many moving parts. So much had to go right, and at precisely the right time. The original path he'd mapped toward success now seemed obsolete. Too many new and unpredictable players had entered the field. Which seemed troublesome, but it also oozed with opportunity.

He'd been able to listen to the conversation at the obelisk. The information on the sheet that had fallen free of the codex had to be what

Mussolini stole, then hid away. The British were convinced of that fact, that's what James Grant had said, and now it seemed they may have been correct.

Better to let this play out.

And take advantage of his good fortune.

CHAPTER THIRTY-SEVEN

KASTOR HAD NOT MOVED.

Nor had Chatterjee, who lay a few meters away.

Once the black form had left the cavern, no one else had approached through the tunnel. After a motor revved, then faded, not a sound had betrayed the night beside the slosh of the sea from the grotto. He'd never seen anyone shot before. But tonight he'd borne witness to two lives ending that way.

Tiredness and a sense of hopelessness crept over him. He was shaking, fear seeping from every pore like a wounded animal. Probably shock setting in. Lying still, he tried to repair himself. But that self-awareness did little to alleviate a bleak despair. Which made him feel ashamed.

Thankfully, no one was here to see his weakness.

And he could not show even a trace of that in the days ahead.

The church was wounded and in turmoil. China and Russia were drifting from its orbit. Europeans were avoiding mass. In Central and South America its once strong moral hold had become frail. And America. The worst of all. Deviant priests and indifferent bishops had inflicted immeasurable damage. People were leaving the church in droves. Few studied for the priesthood anymore. Even fewer Catholics cared. Traditionalists had drawn many of the older faithful away, while the young were simply disenchanted with religion in general. An educated laity seemed no longer willing to blindly memorize catechism and ignore the dreaded question, why.

The time had come for a man of action. One who knew the church's laws and legacy, one who respected tradition and believed that the essence of truth lay within the Vatican, no reaching out required. The Roman Catholic Church was the greatest dynasty in human history. But malleable popes and a gluttony of poor thinking had led it astray.

That had to end.

He was about to challenge the College of Cardinals. Not all of them. Only a select few. The ones who could wield influence and bring the rest around where he could achieve the votes needed to win the papacy. He'd thought the *Constitutum Constantini* might be enough to accomplish that goal, but Spagna had unexpectedly offered something better.

And it was all on the flash drive Chatterjee had shown him.

He grabbed hold of his emotions and crawled across the rough stone, hoping it was still there. Chatterjee had fallen on his left side, so he rolled the body over and searched the pockets, finding the drive.

Thank God.

His salvation.

Provided it was real.

Too bad about Chatterjee. The man had tried to help, though he'd wondered what that help would ultimately cost from Spagna. It could not be as simple as Chatterjee had explained. Keep his job? A cardinal's hat? There had to be more at stake than that.

And there was.

Killers.

Men who shot other men in cold blood with no compulsion. Who were they? Why had they not shot him? If there was any semblance of faith left in his bones, he should come to his knees and pray to God for both thanks and guidance. But he'd long ago lost any belief that there actually existed a merciful omnipotent being who watched over the earth with the benevolence of a loving father. That was a myth, part of religion, which had been created by man, organized by man, and existed for over two thousand years thanks to man.

Spagna had been right about one thing. The pressure had to be applied once the cardinals were locked away inside the Sistine Chapel, where no one could seek help from the outside.

But first things first. Get out of here.

He came to his feet and felt his way through the black tunnel, back to the grotto. The *dghajsa* was tied to a rock, seemingly waiting for him. He wondered if it was a trap, a way to get him back out on the water. But he discounted that as justified paranoia. If they, whoever *they* were, had wanted him dead, they would have shot him with Chatterjee.

He hopped in the boat and untied the line.

Three pulls and the outboard cranked.

The last time he'd piloted a boat had been as a child, with his father. He maneuvered out of the grotto and into the bay beyond. The storm had abated, the rain slackened to sprinkles, the wind subsided. He swung the bow around and headed out toward the open Med. No other vessels were in sight. The question was where to go. He could turn and parallel the south coast, perhaps docking at the popular Blue Grotto, which wasn't all that far away. There he could make his way up to a road and find his way back to Valletta, leaving the island as fast as he could. Or he could retrace his route to the clockmaker's house. Surely the police were there by now, considering a car had exploded. He could seek their protection, invoking his status as a cardinal. Insist on being taken to Rome. But that could mean publicity, and he could ill afford anything negative at the moment.

Only a few more hours remain. Stay anonymous and above the fray. Let your new friend handle the dirty work.

The advice he'd been given just a short while ago on the phone.

Still, the clockmaker's house seemed the safest route.

He turned the tiller east.

LUKE DROVE THE VOLVO COUPE AND FOLLOWED THE DIRECTIONS provided on the cell phone. It helped that Laura knew the island and recalled a series of shops near St. Thomas Bay, just beyond the village of Marsaskala, one of them a longtime clockmaker. Neither of them had spoken of Spagna, their focus centered on getting out of Valletta.

"How deep is your boss involved in this?" he asked.

"He told me to work with Spagna. For once I decided not to argue and to do as I was told."

"Where did this conversation take place?"

"In the apartment Spagna was tossed from."

"You were gone awhile."

She was being stingy with the information and the tone of his question signaled irritation.

"Look," she said. "They didn't tell me their life story. Spagna said he needed us both to help him out. His more immediate concern was that he was having trouble making contact with Chatterjee. He wanted the two of us to check it out. He told me that he left a car, the keys, a cell phone, and directions with you. If you were there, then both of us should head out. If you were gone, then you'd decided to opt out and I was to do it on my own."

Exactly what the archbishop had told him, too.

"I headed back and found you were having a party without me."

"I appreciate you crashin' it. Any idea who those people were?"

She shook her head. "Probably with the same ones who found Spagna. They knew both locations."

"The Entity has a helluva leak."

"To say the least. But right now we need to find Cardinal Gallo."

The farther from Valletta they drove, the less it rained. She'd used the cell phone to confirm her own navigation, but she easily led them to the correct site. Ahead, he caught the strobe of blue lights off into the night before he saw the police and emergency vehicles.

"That's not good," he said. Then he spotted the burned-out hulk of a car illuminated by headlights and added, "Neither is that."

Apparently Spagna's fears were justified.

"Pull off somewhere," Laura said. "We don't need to be seen."

He veered from the road and into the first drive he saw.

They both exited the car.

KASTOR RETRACED THE PATH ACROSS THE WATER HE AND CHATTER-jee had taken earlier. He was still shaken by everything that had happened. He felt out of control, in a spiral someone else had created and manipulated. People were dying around him with no explanation. Yet he was buoyed by the hope that the flash drive in his pocket might offer salvation. Even better, he would not have to deal with Danjel Spagna on terms of the other man's making.

He had leverage to use on the Lord's Own.

The sea had calmed, but the water remained stirred from the storm. The *dghajsa*'s outboard worked hard, and he struggled to keep the bow pointed toward shore. The feisty little boats could be finicky. They were built for durability, not ease or comfort. He rounded a dark point jutting from the shore and reentered the bay behind the clockmaker's shop.

He hoped his assessment would prove correct.

And that the trouble from earlier was long gone.

LUKE APPROACHED THE CLOCKMAKER'S SHOP.

He and Laura had crossed the road and made their way toward it from behind the scattered houses in the space between the buildings and the bay. They'd climbed a couple of fences, but nothing had impeded them except a few dogs who showed little interest. Back home in Tennessee he would have already been revealed by a pack of inquisitive, noisy hounds.

No police patrolled the rear of the clockmaker's shop. He examined the building and noticed the cracked stone, chipped paint on the windows, and vines creeping up one side. He spotted no back door, but one of the windows hung open with its iron grille gone. They rushed over and climbed into some sort of storage room. A doorway on the far side opened to what was surely the street side where all of the activity was still happening. Lights burned beyond a thin curtain. He signaled for quiet and they approached the barrier. Peering past the jamb he saw that the shop was empty, all of the windows shattered, fresh bloodstains on the wood floor. Outside, near the burned-out vehicle, stood four policemen.

"Somebody was shot," Laura whispered.

"Not to mention the extra-crispy car."

No body was evident. It must have been removed already.

Was it Gallo?

"I assume you know where the morgue is?" he asked.

She nodded.

Making contact with the locals could be problematic, especially after what had happened earlier when Spagna first appeared.

"You know what we have to do," he said.

She nodded her assent.

They retreated to the window and climbed out into the humid night. Before they could turn and head toward the car, an engine out on the water grew louder. He focused on a dock that jutted into the bay, lit by a small incandescent fixture. One of the colorful local boats appeared from the night and eased to a stop.

"You see that," he said to Laura, pointing.

Kastor Cardinal Gallo.

He shook his head. "Finally. A break."

CHAPTER
THIRTY-EIGHT

COTTON DOZED IN AND OUT, TRYING TO CATCH A QUICK NAP AS THE Department of Justice jet lifted off from Rome's Fiumicino–Leonardo da Vinci airport. He, Stephanie, and Gallo had used the helicopter for a short hop west from the obelisk and found the DOJ jet waiting, the same one that had brought Stephanie across the Atlantic. Only he and Gallo were making the ninety-minute flight south to Malta. Stephanie had been flown on to Rome in the chopper, deposited back at the Palazzo di Malta downtown, exactly where Cotton had started a few hours ago. She'd received a phone call on the trip to the airport and said that there were matters requiring her personal attention. She offered no details and, knowing better, he hadn't asked. Disturbingly, James Grant had dropped off the radar. London had no idea of his whereabouts, and the contact number Cotton possessed went to voice mail. Stephanie had told him she would monitor that situation from the U.S. embassy and asked to be kept informed as to what happened once they were on the ground.

Gallo himself had developed a case of lockjaw, sitting in his seat with his eyes closed, apparently trying to grab a little rest, too.

Actually, that was fine.

He needed time to think.

Where oil meets stone, death is the end of a dark prison. Pride crowned, another shielded. Three blushes bloomed to ranks and file.

What an odd assortment of phrases. Not random, for sure. But not coherent, either.

Then there were the letters.

H Z P D R S Q X

"What did you mean that the message points to Malta," he asked Gallo. "*Where oil meets stone.* You knew exactly what that meant."

Gallo roused from his rest, looking annoyed.

"The first part simply requests that it be delivered to von Hempesch. Clearly, the cathedral's prior created the message for his grand master. He also created it before being captured by Napoleon. Every piece of evidence indicates that only the prior was involved in the hiding. There is no record of him leaving the island in the forty-eight hours between the time Napoleon arrived and the prior died. It's doubtful he involved others, so whatever he hid away has to be on Malta. Then there is Mattia Preti. What do you know of him?"

"Never heard of him."

"He was like so many others who came to Malta in the 17th century. Men looking for a purpose, a place where they could live a full life and excel. He was an Italian artist who stayed the rest of his life, ultimately transforming the cathedral in Valletta into a wonder. The barrel vault of the church became his masterpiece. It took him six years to complete. When finished it depicted eighteen episodes from the life of St. John the Baptist. Normally murals like those were done with watercolors. But Preti broke with tradition and applied oil paint directly to stone."

He saw the connection. *Where oil meets stone.* "So everything points to the cathedral on Malta."

Gallo nodded. "It seems that way, and it makes sense. The French appeared in 1798 with no warning. The fight for the island took little more than a day before a full surrender. Sadly, only a small part of our treasures and records made it out of the city. Most were seized by the French during their plunder, lost forever when the ship where they had been stored on sank in Egypt."

Gallo went silent for a moment, then continued.

"It was a sad era in our existence. By the time Napoleon arrived the knights had lost all sense of purpose. The Protestant Reformation had reduced our ranks. Then, during the 16th and 17th centuries, revenues from European sponsors dwindled to nothing. Malta itself was a barren island with little to no export potential. To raise money we started policing the Mediterranean, protecting Christian ships from Ottoman corsairs. We became so good at it we evolved into privateers, capturing and looting Muslim ships, becoming corsairs ourselves. We made a lot of money from that but, as you might expect, such lawlessness leads to a moral decline, one that began to seep through the entire order. Eventually, we thought ourselves above kings and queens, exempt from the law, which made us even more enemies. So no one cared when the French took Malta and vanquished us." Gallo paused a moment. "By the mid-18th century we rediscovered our original purpose—aiding the sick. Thankfully, that tortured prior never faltered in his duty and denied Napoleon the *Nostra Trinità*. Our Trinity stayed hidden, and now we know that even Mussolini failed to find it."

Cotton pointed at the metal tube lying on another of the seats. "How can you be sure that the message is the same one from that prior? As you noted before, Mussolini prepared that typed sheet."

"We can't. But finding it is consistent with what I told you about Mussolini and his statements to our grand master in 1936 at their one and only meeting. He said he altered the memory to preserve it. Then he hid it where no one could get it. We have to believe that he changed nothing. Why would he? He might have had to really find it himself one day."

"It's interesting that Mussolini didn't go after it."

"He didn't have to. All he had to do was convince the pope that he could."

"But by hiding the message away, it's almost like he was placating the pope."

"He was. Definitely. For all his bravado, Mussolini was intimidated by popes. He pursued a policy of wooing both Piuses, and to a degree it worked."

"I wonder what it takes to blackmail a pope?"

Gallo stirred in his seat. "I've asked myself that for years. Of the three parts of the *Nostra Trinità*, only the *Constitutum Constantini* could pose a threat. The other two are known documents, with copies in the Vatican. But that Gift of Constantine has to be unique. We've always believed that Mussolini used the threat of its public release as private blackmail. But did he really? We'll never know. What we do know is that neither Pius XI nor Pius XII ever openly defied the fascist government."

"Still, the church has been around for two thousand years. There's not much that could strike a deep blow. It would have to be something that goes to its core. Cutting its legs right out from under it."

Gallo nodded. "Even more important, it has to be something that would have resonated in the 1930s and 1940s. Something that still carried a virulent punch, one the church thought it couldn't endure. That was a difficult time. The world was disintegrating into war. People were focused on merely surviving. Religion was not an important aspect of their lives. We've long speculated on what that document might have contained, but that's all it is, speculation."

"How long had you possessed it?"

"The best we can determine is it came to us sometime in the 13th century. How? We have no idea. That's been lost to time. But we know that it stayed with us until 1798."

"No one ever read it? No oral tradition is associated with it?"

"Not that has survived. It was closely held by the *Secreti*. Now, at least, we have clues as to where it might be."

"There's still the matter of the *Secreti*," Cotton pointed out.

"I realize that, and we should stay alert. They'll be aware of the cathedral's importance, too. And I assume they'll know that I've come to Malta. We cannot underestimate their reach."

He agreed with that assessment. "What about your brother?"

Though Stephanie had said precious little before leaving for Rome, she had revealed that Archbishop Danjel Spagna had been killed, along with another Entity field operative. Cardinal Gallo, while initially missing, had been located by Luke, who had the situation on the ground under control.

"My brother and I will speak," Gallo said, the voice trailing off. "He's caused so much turmoil. It will take a long time to repair that damage."

Cotton was an only child. His father died when he was ten, lost in a navy submarine disaster, so he'd come to rely on his mother. A good woman. She still lived in middle Georgia, running the onion farm her family had owned for generations. She, too, had been an only child, so there were no more Malones. Not by blood, at least. His own son, Gary, an only child, was his in every way save for genes, the result of an affair his ex-wife had seventeen years ago. They'd all laid those demons to rest, part of the past, but he'd be a liar if he said that the prospect of the Malone bloodline ending didn't bother him.

"My brother and I shared a womb," Gallo said. "We're identical physically, though I've tried hard to alter my look so as not to be so readily identified with him. But mentally we are night and day. I've always strived to live a different life, to stay out of the spotlight, away from trouble. To make myself useful and not a nuisance. As I told you, I didn't ask for my current position. I took it out of necessity to try to minimize an already bad situation. Once there's a new pope, the brothers will meet and a new grand master will be chosen."

"You?"

Gallo shook his head. "That job will belong to someone else. I made that clear when I accepted this temporary post."

"I still don't see your brother's purpose in disrupting the Hospitallers. He seemed to go out of his way to create trouble."

"He thrives in conflict. He's after the *Nostra Trinità,* somehow thinking it will make him pope."

"Will it?"

"I can't see how, but he's convinced—as he always seems to be."

Gallo closed his eyes again and tilted his head back on the seat. The jet's windows were dark to the outside, the cabin lights dim. The drone of the engines cast a monotonous tone that seemed to only add weight to his own eyelids.

They'd be on the ground in a little over an hour.

Some rest would be good.

But answers would be better.

CHAPTER
THIRTY-NINE

LUKE STOOD ON THE TARMAC STARING UP INTO THE NIGHT SKY. Laura was inside the small terminal building with Cardinal Gallo. They'd driven the short distance from St. Thomas Bay to Malta's main airport. Gallo had not resisted coming with them, and Luke could understand why after listening to what had happened out on the water. He'd finally connected with Stephanie by phone and learned what had happened in Italy. Laura had called in to her boss, and people had been dispatched to the grotto Gallo had described in search of Chatterjee's body. Now Cotton Malone and the cardinal's twin brother were on final approach, about to land.

Thank goodness Stephanie had stayed behind. He didn't really want to face her right now. He hadn't handled things like they'd needed to be handled. A simple recon assignment had turned into anything but, and now Pappy himself was on the way to save the day. He shouldn't feel that way about Malone. He liked the man. More than that, he respected him. But Malone was retired and this was *his* assignment. He'd been the one to screw up and it was up to him to fix it, no help from an ex-agent-turned-bookseller required.

But that wasn't his call.

Stephanie had already told him to follow Malone's lead and all would be explained. Great. He could hardly wait.

The time was approaching 2:00 A.M. and the international airport's main terminal loomed quiet. No rumble of engines disturbed the night. He was standing near a building used by private planes, many of them parked off to his right. One multimillion-dollar jet after another. Flashing lights from the north grew brighter, and he watched as they dropped down for a landing and another pricey jet taxied his way. The words DE-PARTMENT OF JUSTICE on the side identified its owner. The engines wound down and two men emerged from the open cabin door. Malone first, then another, whom he assumed was Pollux Gallo. Same height and shape as the cardinal, only different hair and a beard. He caught the facial resemblance as they drew close. Malone shook hands, then introduced him.

"Luke is active duty, Magellan Billet," Malone explained to Pollux Gallo. "He's the senior man on this job."

"That's not what I was told," Luke pointed out.

"And what did I tell you about working the field?"

He smiled, recalling the advice from their first encounter together. *You can do anything you want, as long as the job gets done.*

"Forget what Stephanie said. This is not my show," Malone said. "I'm backup. Where's the cardinal?"

That vote of confidence felt good. Another reason it was hard not to like Malone. He was a straight shooter, all the way. Luke pointed to the right and they headed inside the concrete-block building. He watched as the brothers greeted each other with the warmth of two alligators. No handshake. No hug. Not even a smile. Hard for him to understand that estrangement given how close he was to his three siblings.

"Are you pleased with yourself," Pollux Gallo asked, the tone not congenial.

"This is not the time," the cardinal said.

"It's never the time with you. People are dying, Kastor, because of your reckless actions."

"I require no lecture from you. I need to be back in Rome."

"Not until this is done," Luke said. "I've been fully briefed on everything from Italy, and my orders are to see this through before any of you leave this island."

COTTON LIKED THE NEW AND IMPROVED LUKE DANIELS.

Tough, confident, in charge.

Not the same cocky former Ranger who'd dropped out of the sky into the cold Øresund not all that long ago. Stephanie's report that things had not gone well here mattered little. Rarely did anything go as planned in the field. Getting knocked down was a constant occupational hazard. The trick was in knowing how to get back up and keep going. Some learned how, others not so much. Good to see Luke had fallen into the former category.

The two Gallos were a study in stark contrast. Pollux's face stayed as somber as a funeral director, while Kastor's flashed bright and alert. Their personalities seemed night and day. Interesting how identical twins could be so different. Apparently, environment really did affect genes.

Laura Price had stayed curiously quiet, watching the unfolding confrontation with clear interest. He knew nothing about her, which lumped her into the same category as both Gallos. Three unknowns usually added up to trouble, so he told himself to stay ready. He'd meant what he said. This was Luke's show, but he'd agreed to see it through as a favor to Stephanie. He'd always found it hard to tell her no. Besides, he'd been paid in full by the British and he owed them their money's worth.

"I just received a call from the people who went to find Arani Chatterjee's body," Laura finally said, "in the grotto the cardinal described. It wasn't there."

Cardinal Gallo seemed shocked. "He was dead. I checked myself. I saw him shot. Are you sure your people found the right spot? There are a lot of caves along the south shore."

"They were in the right place. But there was no body. And the two men Luke and I left tied up in the safe house are gone, too."

Cotton smiled. "Lots of stuff disappearing around here."

"We can't worry about any of that right now," Luke said.

He agreed and pointed at the metal tube they'd brought off the plane. "Show him."

Pollux slid the parchment and the typed page free and displayed both to his brother. The cardinal seemed uninterested in Mussolini's fascist manifesto. Instead he focused on the clues.

"I assume you read German," Cotton asked.

"I do, and this is gibberish."

"Which was surely the whole idea," Pollux said. "You would have to be privy to information that only a few people on earth would know to solve that riddle. Luckily, I'm one of those."

Cotton caught the unsaid words.

The cardinal was not.

"We have to go to the co-cathedral," Pollux said.

"I should return to Rome," the cardinal said. "This doesn't require me any longer."

"Except that you're the cause of it all," Pollux blurted out, in the first sign of any emotion. "You wanted the *Nostra Trinità*. Unfortunately, you're not going to get it. But we are going to finish this, brother. Finish what *you* started, so the Trinity can be restored to the knights, where it belongs." Gallo paused. "Then you and I are going to have a talk. In private."

Cardinal Gallo stayed silent.

"All this sibling rivalry is fascinating," Laura said. "But there are still threats on this island, and plenty of unknowns. Particularly with cars blowing up and bodies disappearing."

Cotton saw that Luke caught the wry grin on his face, which telegraphed exactly what needed to be made clear.

"Not a problem," Luke said. "We can handle it."

CHAPTER FORTY

KASTOR HAD ALWAYS ADMIRED THE CHURCH OF ST. JOHN THE BAPtist. Solid, austere, its thick walls conveying an unmistakable message of power and strength. Two large towers with octagonal spires flanked either side of its main entrance, each housing bells. Nearly every church on the island mimicked its shape and style, which was not unintentional.

The knights had been smart with its location, choosing a high spot in the center of their new city and erecting a landmark that could be seen from nearly anywhere on, or off, the island. Its austere façade faced west, the altar east, as was traditional in the 16th century. Its sober and robust exterior shielded an amazing expression of baroque art inside, all dedicated to the knights' patron saint, John the Baptist. Everything about it was tied to the Order, but Napoleon had left a mark, too. As soon as the French stole the island, the bishop of Malta made a request. He wanted the church for his diocese and saw the invasion as an opportunity to wrest it away from the knights. So Napoleon handed it over and decreed that it would be forever called the Co-Cathedral of St. John the Baptist, available to all.

And the name had stuck.

He remained unsure what to make of the new additions to the team. But what choice did he have? Spagna and Chatterjee were both dead. Thankfully, the flash drive remained safe in his pocket. He'd not said a word about it and did not intend to. That prize was his alone. And what had happened to Chatterjee's body? Did the man who'd killed him return and ferry it away?

If so, why?

They rounded the cathedral's exterior and found a small square that spread out from a side entrance. The cobbles remained damp from the rain. A few people lingered in the square despite the late hour. On the ride from the airport Pollux had worked the phone, speaking with the cathedral's operating foundation, letting them know he was on the way. Though the Hospitallers no longer actually owned the church, they retained great influence over its use. It actually wasn't much of a church anymore. More a tourist attraction. Forty years ago things had been different. Fewer visitors to the island then. The world had yet to discover Malta. He recalled visiting with his parents several times, then many more once at the orphanage. Everything here was familiar territory. So why did he feel so out of place?

The wooden doors creaked opened and a middle-aged man in jeans introduced himself as the curator. He was pale-skinned, with an owlish face adorned by thick-rimmed glasses. His hair was tousled, his eyes tired, probably the effects of being woken from a sound sleep.

Pollux stepped up and assumed the lead. "I appreciate you being here at this late hour. It's important we be inside the church for a little while. Undisturbed."

The curator nodded.

It was odd to see his brother in a position of authority. Always it had been Pollux following *his* lead. But he told himself that Pollux was temporary head of the knights thanks to him. Whatever power his brother possessed came from him. He found it unsettling to take a backseat, though it seemed the wisest course. Nothing would be gained by a confrontation. Besides, he was curious about what they might find. Still, the clock was ticking down, the conclave set to begin in less than ten hours. Every cardinal who planned to be inside the Sistine Chapel voting had to be at the Domus Sanctae Marthae by 10:00 A.M. After that, there was no admittance.

He followed the entourage inside to a wide rectangular nave, flanked by two narrow aisles, topped by a ribbed barrel vault. The aisles were further divided into a series of impressive side chapels. The air was noticeably cooler. Lavish stone carvings, gilding, and marble ornamentation sheathed every square centimeter of wall, floor, and ceiling. Nothing had been omitted. Elaborate baroque motifs burst forth in profiles of foliage, flowers, angels, and triumphal symbols of all shapes and kinds. He knew that none of them had been added. Instead, everything had been carved straight from the limestone. Subtle amber lighting bounced off the marble walls, staining the dazzling blaze of color and decoration in a warm glow. Nearly five hundred years of constant pampering had resulted in a masterpiece. Some called it the most beautiful church in the world, and they might be right.

"I'll leave you alone," the curator said.

Pollux raised a halting hand.

"Please don't. We need your help."

COTTON HAD VISITED ST. PETER'S BASILICA IN ROME, THE CHURCH of the Savior on the Spilled Blood in St. Petersburg, and Westminster in London. None were even in this place's league. So much assaulted the eyes from every direction it was nearly overpowering—a combination of pomp, art, religion, and symbolism in a clash of period styles that somehow mixed seamlessly.

He asked about its origins.

"For the first hundred years, the interior was modest," the curator said. "Then, in the 1660s, the grand masters ordered a massive redecoration, one to rival the churches of Rome. Mattia Preti was placed in charge and spent half his life creating nearly all of what you now see."

That was the name Gallo had mentioned on the plane ride.

"This is perhaps the greatest expression of baroque in the world," the curator added. "Thankfully, it survived the bombing in World War II."

"We have something to show you," Pollux Gallo told the curator, and he handed over the typed sheet.

Where oil meets stone, death is the end of a dark prison. Pride crowned, another shielded. Three blushes bloomed to ranks and file. H Z P D R S Q X

"A puzzle for sure," the curator said. "One part is clear, though. The first four words."

And the man pointed upward.

Cotton stared up at Preti's masterpiece. Six defined ceiling bays, each divided into three sections, made for eighteen episodes. The painted figures looked more like three-dimensional statues than flat images, all forming a single, smooth narrative from the life of St. John the Baptist, transforming what was surely once a plain barrel vault into something extraordinary.

"It's all oil painted on stone."

As the curator continued to discuss the ceiling and the lines from the puzzle, Cotton turned his attention to the floor.

Another one-of-a-kind.

There were hundreds of tombs, each unique, composed of finely colored inlaid marble words and images, lined in perfect columns front-to-back, left-to-right, wall-to-wall. Every inch of the floor was covered, forming a stunning visual display. A few rows of wooden chairs stood toward the far end, near the altar, surely for people who came for prayer.

The rest was all exposed.

He noticed the lively iconography, the colorful mosaic arrangements depicting triumph, fame, and death. Skeletons and skulls seemed popular. He knew why. One represented the end of a physical being, the other the beginning of eternal life. There were also plenty of angels, either blowing trumpets or holding laurel wreaths, along with coats of arms, weapons, and battle scenes, surely a testament to the deceased's chivalry. A turbulent tone and character dominated, which he assumed was reflective of the times in which the men had lived. Most of the epitaphs seemed grandiose and wordy, mainly in Latin or the deceased's native tongue. He spotted French, Spanish, Italian, and German. Commonality abounded in style, but so did individuality. No two were exactly alike, yet they all seemed similar.

"There is also a connection," the curator said, "with the next words of your message. *Death is the end of a dark prison.* Let me show you."

The older man stepped across the floor, searching for one of the tombs. "Here."

They all moved toward the center of the nave, where the curator stood before a particularly ornate memorial, centered with a shrouded skeleton before a wall of iron bars. Two columned pilasters supported an arch above the bars, the whole image flat, but animated in a three-dimensional trompe l'oeil effect. Cotton read the epitaph and learned it was the grave of a knight named Felice de Lando, who died March 3, 1726. Above the skeletal figure Italian words appeared in the arch.

LA MORTE E FIN D UNA PRIGIONE OSCURA.

Death is the end of a dark prison.

Coincidence?

Hardly.

KASTOR HAD ALWAYS LOVED THE CATHEDRAL FLOOR. NOTHING like it existed anywhere else in the world. And the tombs were not cenotaphs. Instead they were actual graves with bones beneath them—the more important the knight, the closer to the altar. All burials stopped, though, in 1798 when the French invaded. Important knights after that were buried beyond the city in far less elegant locations. Not until the British took the island in 1815 had they resumed, but then they ended forever in 1869. He knew all about them thanks to the nuns. The kids from the orphanage had routinely worked in the cathedral, himself and Pollux no exception. He'd explored every part of the building, finding the floor particularly intriguing. A mosaic of memory, ripe with words of consolation, instruction, and praise. Some exaggerations for sure, but memories needed "things" to prolong themselves, otherwise they never lasted.

The Roman Catholic Church was a perfect example.

As was his life.

His own parents died with nothing more than a simple funeral attended by a few friends. There was not even a stone marker over their graves. Nothing tangible remained of their existence, save for twin boys.

One of whom might soon be pope.

So far, two lines of the message had been deciphered.

One thing seemed clear.

They were in the right place.

COTTON TRIED TO THINK LIKE THAT CATHEDRAL PRIOR WHO, knowing the harbor was filled with French warships and an army was about to invade, still managed to get his job done.

Talk about pressure.

He said, "I'm assuming that since the *Secreti* existed in 1798, and all of the knights were housed here on Malta, any hiding places the *Secreti* may have used before the French came were on the island?"

Pollux nodded. "That is a reasonable assumption. The knights tried to confine things to this island. Their domain."

"So Malta falls," he said. "Knights start to flee, even the grand master leaves. To be safe, before the French take the island, the cathedral prior gathers up the *Nostra Trinità* from wherever it had been hidden and stashes it in a new place, one only he knows about. Then he creates a way to find it with clues the grand master can decipher, and instructs that the message be delivered to him. It never makes it that far, though, and ends up somewhere that Mussolini was able to locate it. Maybe the prior's grave? Who knows?"

He could see Pollux did not disagree with his logic.

He pointed down. "It has to be these mosaics. He specifically used an epitaph from this memorial, preceded by the words *where oil meets stone*." He motioned to the ceiling. "*Where oil meets stone, death is the end of a dark prison.* That's right here. There was no time for being ingenious. The prior was the caretaker of this building, so he adapted what he knew best."

"*Pride crowned, another shielded. Three blushes bloomed to ranks and file,*" Laura Price said. "Those words relate to this floor?"

He nodded, looking around at the many different images depicted on the memorials. "Yep. They're here. Somewhere."

"Any clues as to what *pride crowned* means?" Cardinal Gallo asked.

His mind was working on just that.

"Before we get too deep into this, I'm concerned about outside," Laura said. "We have no idea what's happening out there."

She was right.

Cotton faced Luke. "How about you two take a look. Make sure we don't have any unwanted visitors. We are a bit exposed here."

Luke nodded. "We'll take care of it."

He watched as they hustled back toward the entrance. He felt better knowing his flank was being guarded by Luke. He recalled Gallo's warning from the plane that the *Secreti* would know of the cathedral's possible importance and of the lieutenant ad interim's presence on the island. Solving this puzzle could take a little time, and whoever was out there might be waiting for that to happen before making their move.

Or the threat could already be here.

Inside the cathedral.

Watching right now.

THE KNIGHT WAS BACK ON MALTA.

It had been a while since his last visit.

Thanks to James Grant, he'd kept pace with the Americans. First at the obelisk, now here inside the co-cathedral. Right place, right time, and he was able to listen to everything Cotton Malone said.

He agreed.

The answer was in the floor.

And fitting, as each tomb told a story of men who gave their fortunes, lives, and reputations to God and Church. Men who fought at the Siege of Ascalon, the Battle of Arsuf, the Invasion of Gozo, the storming of Tripoli, and the Great Siege of Malta itself. Their graves stood side by side, linked together in a continuous smooth surface, a proper metaphor for the knights themselves. Too bad the remains of that brave prior who'd defied Napoleon never made it here. He would have earned a place of prominence near the altar. Instead his remains had been consigned to a run-down churchyard, his grave violated by a vile dictator. Sacrilege. Nothing less.

That wrong would have to be righted.

Mussolini had been shot like an animal, then his corpse hung upside down on a meat hook and pelted with vegetables, spat on, peed on, shot, and kicked. All fitting. Finally, he was buried in a Milan cemetery. Years later, to placate the conservative far right, his body was moved to the family crypt in Predappio, placed in a stone sarcophagus decorated with fascist symbols, and adorned by a marble bust. Flowers and wreaths remained a constant adornment. A hundred thousand people came each year on pilgrimage. April 28, the day he died, was still celebrated with neo-fascist rallies and a march through the town to the cemetery.

He'd even gone once himself.

To spit on the grave.

That abomination would end.

He'd personally see to that.

Nobody remembered the three knights Mussolini tortured and killed to get what he wanted. Nobody knew a thing about the cathedral prior who kept his oath and died at the hands of Napoleon.

Men with honor trying to protect—

What may now finally be revealed.

CHAPTER FORTY-ONE

COTTON PLAYED THE PRIOR'S MESSAGE OVER AND OVER THROUGH HIS mind, focusing on the last two lines. *Pride crowned, another shielded. Three blushes bloomed to ranks and file.* He walked the floor, eyes down, taking in the collage of images.

"There are over four hundred tombs," the curator said. "Even I'm not familiar with aspects of them all."

He noticed something toward the front of the nave, just before the steps up to the main altar. "There are two here identical. One to the left of the steps, the other there, to the right."

"Two knights," the curator said, "both named Francesco Carafa, both from Naples. One died in 1632, the other in 1679. For some reason, which remains unknown, the latter Carafa chose to have his tomb identical to the former."

A curiosity, for sure, but not relevant to the present dilemma.

He ambled away from the twin tombs and continued to study the memorials. The others did the same. Each trying to find some connection between the words and the floor. Something caught his attention.

Three lion heads on a shield.

Crowned.

Then it hit him.

He'd been thinking in the wrong direction.

Pride crowned.

He'd thought *pride* an emotion or a reaction of some sort. Instead it was something much more tangible. A group of lions. Their social unit.

A pride.

He smiled.

That prior had been clever with words.

"It's here," he called out. "The grave of François de Mores Ventavon."

He read out loud more of the Latin on the tomb as the others headed his way. *"He was granted by his Religion the Commandery of Marseilles, the Priorship of the Venerable Tonge of Provence and, his last office, the Priory of Saint-Gilles. Three titles."* He pointed at the marble memorial. "Three lions crowned. Pride crowned."

"You could be right," Pollux Gallo said.

He thought of the next two words and said, "We need to find a lion on a shield."

KASTOR HAD NEVER BEEN FOND OF PUZZLES, MUCH LESS ONE OVER two hundred years old. But he knew the *Secreti.* They'd not kept the *Nostra Trinità* safe for centuries by acting stupid. The threat from Napoleon would have been the greatest danger they'd ever faced. That damn Frenchman changed everything.

The knights were never the same after 1798.

While serving as head of the ecclesiastical court, he'd first heard the stories of Constantine's Gift. The keeper of the Vatican archives had told him of how the 3rd century was a time of chaos. Plague ravaged towns, civil wars raged, corruption ran rampant, twenty-five different men sat on the Roman throne within fifty years. Finally, in 324, Constantine eliminated all contenders and assumed absolute control. Trying to change, or even influence, entrenched religious beliefs proved impossible, even for an emperor. So Constantine cultivated his own religion, one named for a Jew who'd supposedly died on a cross and left behind a group of disciples to spread a message of love and hope.

Christians.

He issued imperial decrees that allowed them to finally worship without oppression. He supported them financially, building basilicas, granting tax exemptions to clergy, and promoting Christians to high public office. He returned confiscated property, then built the Church of the Holy Sepulcher in Jerusalem and the first St. Peter's Basilica in Rome. To this day Constantine the Great held a special place within the Roman Catholic Church.

One he hoped to emulate as pope.

"Over here."

They all hustled to where Malone stood, his finger pointed down at another of the marble tombs.

"Another lion shielded," Malone said.

Kastor nearly smiled.

They were close.

CHAPTER
FORTY-TWO

LUKE STEPPED OUTSIDE, LAURA RIGHT BESIDE HIM, AND GLANCED AT his watch. 2:48 A.M. He should be somewhere in Eastern Europe, working his previous assignment. Instead he was on a rock in the Mediterranean doing God knows what. He still wore the shirt, shorts, and shoes from this morning, which didn't make him look out of place, though he'd felt a little odd being inside the cathedral dressed that way. They stood in what was noted on a placard as St. John's Square, maybe fifty people milling about beneath the glow of overhead lighting. The cathedral itself, lit to the night, was surrounded by streets on all sides. Plenty of opportunities for unfriendlies to make a move.

"Let's check the perimeter," he said. "All the way around."

His Beretta was tucked at his waist beneath his shirt. Laura was likewise armed, having acquired a weapon from her people while they'd waited for Malone to arrive. He was actually glad to be outside. Malone was onto something and that was Pappy's problem to solve. He had his own to deal with, and she was standing right beside him.

"I'll go this way," he said. "You take the opposite and we'll meet on the far side of the building."

She nodded and hustled off.

He walked through the cobbled square, but stopped beneath a stand of trees, using one of the trunks for cover. A quick glance back and he saw

Laura heading for the building's corner where she would shortly be out of sight, around to the other side.

His mind drifted back to when he was eleven years old. He, his father, and his three brothers were in the last few hours of the last day of his first hunting trip outside Tennessee. To Nebraska. In bone-chilling cold. They'd been at it for three days, chasing deer across the breaks just above the Republican River Valley. They'd sat in blinds for two mornings and an evening, and not a single deer had wandered by. His father and brothers had already taken their limit. Still nothing, though, for him. Frustrating since it was the first hunting trip where he could legally carry a gun and shoot on his own.

Just one chance, that's all he wanted.

So his father decided to do what any self-respecting Tennessee hunter would do.

He took them into the hills for some stalking.

They chased deer for two more days, pushing them from one draw to the next. But no matter how clever his father seemed to be, the deer always stayed one step ahead. Eventually, his father began to understand how, when, and where the deer were moving.

And he got ahead of them.

Two shots came from the far ridge.

His father checked the wind and noted that it was still blowing straight down the draw. Perfect.

"Other hunters just pushed 'em," his father had said. *"In just a minute or so, those deer are going to come right down this draw. It's your turn, son."*

He smiled recalling that first opportunity, bestowed upon him by the man he admired most in the world.

All five Daniels made their way toward the cedars at the edge of the draw. His father hiked uphill about twenty yards for a better view and gave them five fingers, representing the number of animals, and pointed from where they were coming. He could still feel his grip on the .30-30 Winchester 94 rifle. Tight. Almost a stranglehold. His brother Mark had shook his head and motioned for him to loosen up.

"Hold it like a baby."

Laura rounded the corner, out of sight. He fled the cover of the trees and headed off in the direction she'd gone, lingering long enough to give her a head start.

More memories of that hunt flooded his mind.

The deer approached through dried leaves and leftover snow.

Their breathing, puffs of clouds with each exhale, strong and steady. The lack of their awareness as to the danger that awaited them. How they stopped just above the narrow draw, twenty yards away. The cocking of the rifle. Slow. Quiet. The stock nestled to his shoulder. Him sliding out from behind the cedar, trying to get a clear shot through the trees, fighting the cold that ate away at his face.

Then pulling the trigger.

The bang and retort.

Stronger than he imagined, tossing him back on his heels.

Two does and a yearling scattered, but his shot found the buck's front shoulder, clipping the spine, dropping the big deer in its tracks.

Everything about that day had stuck in his mind.

His first kill.

Made even better by his father and brothers being with him.

And the lessons learned from that trip.

Lessons he never forgot.

Asking a dumb question is far better than doing something dumb. Watch and learn from other people. And never use everything offered to you. Instead, make that knowledge work for you, in your own way.

Good advice then, and now.

He found the corner of the cathedral and peeked around, seeing Laura about thirty yards ahead, halfway to the next corner. He watched, hoping he was wrong and she would turn right and continue her patrol of the perimeter, supposedly catching up to him. But she hooked left, doubling back toward him, just on the opposite side of the street.

He shook his head, both pleased and disappointed that his instincts had been right. He quickly retreated to the line of trees so he could use the shadows for cover, watching as she hustled down the sidewalk, past the church and the square, negotiating an intersection, then entering, through a side door off an alley, one of the many shops lining Republic Street, all closed for the night.

Interesting that she possessed a key to the door.

Like those deer, she'd been flushed back. But not by some other hunter's shots. This was done solely on her own. Thankfully, he was waiting, downwind. And like those deer, she had no idea what awaited her.

He reached back and palmed his Beretta.

Holding it gently.

Like a baby.

CHAPTER FORTY-THREE

COTTON GLANCED UP FROM THE TOMB WITH THE SHIELDED LION, staring across the nave, back toward the altar where the other memorial, the one with the crowned pride, waited sixty feet away. The line between the two ran diagonally across the nave.

He turned his attention to the last few words of the puzzle.

Three blushes bloomed to ranks and file.

Another reference to something here on the floor.

In 1798 its obtuse wording may have been a deterrent, but in the 21st century it might not be much of a problem. He reached into his pocket and found his smartphone, noticing he had a solid connection to a local carrier. Technology was a great thing, so why not use it.

He accessed a search engine and typed in BLUSHES.

The expected came up first. Makeup. All sorts of blush for sale from various vendors.

"What are you doing?" Cardinal Gallo asked.

"My job."

He scrolled down and noticed an entry toward the bottom of the first page of hits. A definition site. The Free Dictionary. *To become red in the face. To feel embarrassed or ashamed. A red or rosy color. A glance, look, or view. Makeup used on the cheekbones to give a rosy tint. Middle English blushen, from Old English referring to roses.*

Flowers.

He'd seen a lot of those on the memorials.

He glanced up from the screen. "Search for roses."

The two Gallos and the curator fanned out.

He typed in RANKS AND FILE.

"Over here," the curator called out, from near the altar.

They all hurried that way and he saw three roses on a shield, above a Maltese cross. The first memorial, the one with the three crowned lions, was only twenty feet away, toward the other side of the nave.

"There are two markers at this end," he said. "The one with the shielded lion is at the other end. There has to be one more down there, in its vicinity."

He glanced at the smartphone's screen to see what came up for RANKS AND FILE. *A military term realting to horizontal "ranks" (rows) and "files" (columns). Enlisted troops, noncommissioned officers. People who form the major part of a group. A row on a chessboard (rank). A column on a chessboard (file).*

Several possibilities.

A lot of officers and knights lay beneath the cathedral's floor. Too many of each for any reference to the military being the correct answer.

It had to be the chessboard.

"Look for a checkerboard of some sort," he said. "Let's do it together."

They knew exactly what he had in mind, lining up in a row, each taking about a quarter of the floor, ten feet separating them. Slowly, they walked in unison from the altar at one end toward the huge set of double doors at the opposite side of the nave that served as the cathedral's main entrance. Eleven vertical columns of tombs stretched across, running the long side of the nave's rectangle. He'd counted six horizontal rows across the short side and they were just coming to the center. Another six or seven rows spanned ahead toward the main doors.

So far, no ranks and files.

They kept going, slow and steady, their heads down studying the myriad marble images.

At the thirteenth and final row, Pollux Gallo said, "Here it is."

Cotton stepped over and examined the tomb, a particularly macabre scene with a trumpeting angel, a pointing, accusatory skeleton, and a curious baby, all atop a checkerboard floor.

"This has to be it," Cotton said. "Ranks and files. What the rows and columns on a chessboard are called."

Four points on the floor.

Two toward the altar, the other two opposite.

Coordinates.

"We need to flag the four memorials."

The Gallo brothers walked back across the nave, Pollux heading left toward the lion pride, the cardinal finding the memorial with the shielded animal. The curator stood on the three roses. Cotton stayed with the checkerboard. Their positions formed a warped X, one line longer than the other, but an X nonetheless.

This had to be the solution.

"Keep your eyes on the man diagonally opposite and walk slowly in a straight line toward him. Try and meet at the center point of your line. We can adjust that once we're closer together."

They started walking, he toward Cardinal Gallo, the curator closing in on Pollux. He and the cardinal were on the longer line of the X, so Pollux and the curator met first. He and the cardinal kept approaching each other and met at a point a little off from where the other two had joined, which meant they hadn't found the center of their lines. So they adjusted to a spot where all four men stood together at the joining of the oblong X.

One tomb lay beneath their feet.

CHAPTER
FORTY-FOUR

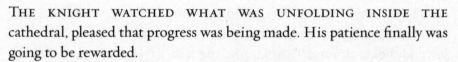

THE KNIGHT WATCHED WHAT WAS UNFOLDING INSIDE THE cathedral, pleased that progress was being made. His patience finally was going to be rewarded.

The words of the *Pie Postulatio Voluntatis,* Most Pius Request, one third of the *Nostra Trinità,* written in 1113, had suddenly taken on a new meaning. Every member of the *Secreti* memorized that sacred document. When Pope Paschal II established the Knights Hospitallers he wrote in the *Voluntatis* that *it shall be unlawful for any man whatsoever rashly to disturb, or to carry off any of the order's property, or if carried off to retain possession of it, or to diminish anything from its revenues, or to harass it with audacious annoyances. But let all its property remain intact, for the sole use and enjoyment of those for whose maintenance and support it has been granted.*

That directive had been violated.

The Turks tried and failed, but Napoleon stole everything he could. Hitler bombed and wreaked havoc, but it was Mussolini who killed to find what he wanted. The *Voluntatis* dealt with the consequences of such actions.

If, therefore, at a future time, any person, whether ecclesiastical or secular, knowing this paragraph of our constitution, shall attempt to oppose its provisions, and he shall not make a suitable satisfaction and restitution, let him be deprived of all his dignities and honors, and let him know that he stands exposed to the judgment of God, for the iniquity he has perpetrated, and let him be deprived of the Sacraments of the Body and Blood of Christ, and of the benefits of the redemption of our Lord, and at the last judgment let him meet with the severest vengeance.

How much clearer did things have to be?

All was prepared outside. His men were ready to act.

The *severest vengeance* had arrived.

KASTOR STARED DOWN AT THE TOMB OF BARTOLOMEO TOMMASI DI Cortona and read its Latin epitaph. *Bailiff, son of Nicolao of the house of Cortona, a nobleman of his city is wasting away. Admitted to the Sacred Militia of the Jerusalemite Knights, from the year 1708 onward he was dedicated to its service, fulfilling, as long as he lived, his duties on land and sea with the utmost faith. He lived for 79 years, 6 months, 18 days.*

The inscription at its top seemed prophetic.

MORS ULTRA NON DOMINABITUR.

Death will not reign beyond.

Three symbols appeared above the epitaph.

α ☧ Ω

Alpha. Omega. The first and last. The Chi Rho in between, formed by superimposing the first two letters of the Greek word for "Christ." It was not used much today, but in Roman times things had been different.

He knew the connection.

On the eve of a decisive battle to decide the future of the Roman Empire, Constantine had a vision. A cross in the sky with the words *IN HOC SIGNO VINCES*. In this sign thou shalt conquer. Unsure of the meaning, that night he had a dream in which Christ himself explained that he should use the sign against his enemies. Of course, nobody had a clue if that tale of a vision was true. So many versions of it existed that it was impossible to know which one to believe. But it was a fact that Constantine directed the creation of a new labarum, superimposing the first two letters of the Greek word for Christ.

The Chi Rho sign.

He then ordered that symbol inscribed on his soldiers' shields, and with his new military standard leading the way he drove his rival into the Tiber River. Eventually, he defeated all challengers and unified the Roman Empire under his rule. He came to honor the sign of his salvation as a safeguard against every adverse and hostile power, and decreed that it be carried at the head of all his armies.

Kastor smiled.

That prior had chosen his clues with clarity.

COTTON TRANSLATED AS MUCH OF THE LATIN FROM THE TOMB AS he could understand, which was most of it.

"This is significant," Cardinal Gallo said. "That symbol there, in the center, is the cipher of Christ. The Chi Rho. Constantine the Great created it."

"I agree," Pollux noted. "This was intentional on the prior's part. He led us straight here."

Which was all fine and good, Cotton thought, but it didn't solve the riddle. He studied the imagery on the memorial. A skeleton, shield, crown, staff, skulls and crossbones, anchors, and a table with a broken clock, on a plinth, beneath an arch.

"It's the clock," the curator said. "It exists, here, in the cathedral."

Cardinal Gallo pointed downward. "He's telling us to open that clock."

"Where is it?" Cotton asked.

"In the oratory."

They followed the curator to one of the massive gilded arches that led into a side nave and a magnificent doorway adorned with four marble columns topped by a white marble dove and lamb. The room beyond spanned a long, tall rectangle encased by more gilded walls, the floor dotted by more marble tombs. At the far end, through another gilded arch, past an altar, hung a huge oil painting depicting St. John the Baptist's gruesome murder.

"Caravaggio's *Beheading of St. John*," the curator said, pointing to the painting. "Our greatest treasure."

Cotton gave the image only a passing glance, then focused on the room.

Maltese crosses were everywhere, the ceiling another grandiose baroque expression in gilt. A few pieces of furniture were pressed against the walls, one a paneled sideboard that supported a marble clock. About thirty inches tall, it was identical to the one depicted in the memorial back in the main nave. Except this one was intact.

He walked over and tried to lift it. Way too heavy.

"We've not moved it in years," the curator said.

He examined the exterior, gently running his fingers across the marble.

"That's a valuable piece of history," the curator said, in a tone that advised caution.

"I don't have a good track record with those." He'd already noticed that this clock had a glass front across the face that opened, exposing the hands—a way to wind it and surely to access the inner workings. The face was set to twenty minutes before two.

"Does this thing work?" he asked.

"Not to my knowledge. It's sat here since the 18th century."

Why was he not surprised. "You don't change a lot of things, do you?"

"It's important that the building remain as it was. History matters, Mr. Malone."

That it did.

Something occurred to him. "I thought Napoleon looted everything?"

"I doubt a heavy marble clock that doesn't work would have interested him. There's nothing special about it, beside the fact that it's old. It survived, as did a lot of other artifacts, because it carried no obvious value."

No way to determine if there was anything rattling around inside, but he assumed if that had been obvious somebody over the course of the past two hundred years would have noticed. Within his eidetic memory he visualized the targeted memorial.

"On the cracked-open clock out in the nave," he said, "if you close the hinge the time would read twenty minutes before two. Just like here. This one is also identical in size, shape, and color."

"It was not uncommon for items in the cathedral to become part of the tombs," the curator said. "Either the knight himself would fashion the memorial, or a relative or a friend would do it in honor of him. It all depended on the ego and resources of the knight."

The cardinal examined the clock. "What we want is inside this thing?"

"It certainly seems that way," Cotton said.

Though the sides and base were marble, the ornate, pointy top was fashioned of ceramic, cemented to the stone by a mortar joint.

Cotton examined the seam.

Solid and old.

"We're going to need a hammer and chisel," he said.

CHAPTER FORTY-FIVE

LUKE STUDIED THE BUILDINGS FACING REPUBLIC STREET. ALL WERE dark and quiet, most of their windows shielded by metal accordion screens. Few people milled about on the sidewalks. Valletta had finally settled down for the night. But Laura Price had not. What was she doing in that shop? She'd clearly wanted to get there, as it had been her idea back inside the cathedral to check outside. He'd been suspicious of her ever since the safe house. He could not isolate one particular thing that had tripped his suspicion button, but something about her simply had not rung right.

He kept the gun at his side, close to his thigh, the barrel pointed down as he left the square, crossed the street, and approached the door she'd entered. It sat ten feet past Republic, in a darker narrow alley that ran on forever to another distant street. He tested the knob. It turned.

The door was open?

Nothing about that was good.

Why would she use a key to gain entrance, then leave it unlocked? Was she expecting someone else who didn't have a key? Or was this a trap laid just for him? Being the deer in the hunt was never fun. But like those cagey animals back in frigid Nebraska twenty years ago, he wasn't stupid. He pushed open the door, entered, then closed it, leaving it unlocked.

Why not?

Just in case there *were* others invited to the party.

He stood inside a small foyer. A doorway to the right opened into what appeared to be a souvenir shop. A stone stairway directly in front of him led up at a steep angle. Since all was quiet in the shop, Laura had to have gone up. He brought the gun out before him and climbed the narrow risers. Not a sound betrayed his presence. The stairway was nearly pitch-dark, only scant residual light leaking in from the shop windows below. He seemed vulnerable, as those deer should have felt when they were flushed back to the draw.

He came to the top.

A short hall led past two more open doorways.

He approached the first, pressed his right shoulder to the wall, and stole a quick glance inside. The minuscule room was filled with chairs, stacked one onto another, and collapsed folding tables propped to one wall, its single window faintly lit from the street below. At the next doorway the room was of similar size, but empty except for a small table set before another window, with a rifle lying on it. He noticed a nightscope and the caliber. Heavy duty. Meant for power and range. He stepped over and gazed out the window. The vantage point offered a perfect view of St. John's Square and the side entrance into the cathedral. In the dim light he saw a sound suppressor attached to barrel's end. Somebody was ready to do some serious hunting.

He heard the distinctive click of a gun hammer snapping into place.

"Nice and slow," Laura said. "Turn around. But first, let your gun hit the floor."

"You really want to go there?'

"I really do."

Okay. He released his grip and allowed the weapon to drop.

Then he turned.

"Kick the gun this way," she said. "Real slow."

He did as she requested.

"What gave me away?" she asked.

"Just a feeling."

"Not the dumb country boy you want people to think you are."

"I'll take that as a compliment. Let me guess. You've been working for Spagna from the beginning."

"Guilty as charged. When you showed up, he put me on you."

"I kind of got that impression when your boss appeared at the safe house and I wasn't part of the conversation. The cops on us, and Spagna taking you, that was all a dog-and-pony show?"

"Sort of. He needed to make contact, but not in a way that matched us together. He also needed you to stay in the dark. But you came to my rescue, as he predicted. So he decided to bring you on the team."

"That was the first moment I had my doubts. Those two local cops took you down way too easy. But when Spagna died, that cinched it for me. Everything was way too nicely wrapped with a pretty bow. Too many coincidences usually add up to a plan. The guys who tried to kill me. Entity people?"

She stepped into the room, gun still aimed, standing six feet away, just out of strike range. "That's the rub, Luke. They weren't Spagna's."

He was intrigued.

"There's so much more happening here," she said. "Things you know nothing about."

"Enlighten me."

She chuckled. "This is a solo job now."

He motioned to the rifle. "You planning on killing somebody? Is that what Spagna meant when he said to do what he told you?"

"That's exactly what he meant."

"I'm hurt. He only told me to find the cardinal."

"The archbishop always looked after the church and, right now, the church is being threatened."

"By Cardinal Gallo?"

"By what's happening inside that cathedral. I can't allow them to find the *Nostra Trinità*. It needs to stay gone."

"How can you be so sure they'll find it?"

"Spagna was aware of everything that happened in Italy with Malone and Pollux Gallo. He knew they were coming this way, to the cathedral, so he arranged for this perch. He, of course, had no way of knowing when the opportunity would present itself. But that's where I came in. I could see Malone was making progress. He's a smart fellow, or at least that's what Spagna said about him. It won't be long before Malone and the Gallos come out those doors."

"Is Malone on your hit list?"

"The *Nostra Trinità* must stay gone."

Not an answer, but close enough. "Who killed Spagna?"

"The same people who wanted you dead. The same ones who want Malone dead."

He waited.

"The *Secreti*."

"You still haven't answered my question," he said. "Is Malone on your hit list?"

Movement behind her caught his attention.

A man stepped into the doorway.

Short, stocky, of indeterminate age.

"No, Mr. Daniels," a deep voice said. "We have no grievance with America."

CHAPTER FORTY-SIX

COTTON ACCEPTED THE HAMMER AND CHISEL THAT THE CURATOR had located. While they'd waited he'd examined every inch of the clock's exterior and determined there were no other seams, except at the corners, no visible way in, no hidden switches or levers. Whatever had been secreted away must have been sealed inside from the top. With the hammer, he gently tapped the exterior, the metal resonating off the stone with a dull uniform sound.

"It doesn't appear to be hollow," he said.

The others watched him with clear curiosity, the curator with a concerned look on his face. There seemed little choice except to delicately bust the mortared seam between the top and the rest of the clock.

"How old is this thing?" he asked.

"Four hundred years," the curator noted. "It dates to a grand master in the early 17th century."

But before he used any force, he opened the circular glass door on the front. The clock face was mounted by three screws that held it in place and surely allowed access to the workings beyond.

"We need to be sure," he said.

The curator handed him a flat-head screwdriver, which he used to loosen all three. Behind the face was nothing but the gears and springs that would have powered the hands. He could see no access into the main part of the clock.

"Do it," Pollux Gallo said, seemingly reading his diminishing hesitation.

He pressed the chisel's metal tip to the mortar and started tapping. He took his time, careful that the lid would not be damaged and could be easily replaced. The mortar was hard and it took several blows at the same spot to produce results. Whether they were through-and-through fissures remained to be seen.

"Mr. Malone," Cardinal Gallo said.

He stopped chiseling.

"I think I've noticed something. May I hold the hammer a moment."

He was open to any better idea, so he handed over the tool. The cardinal studied the clock, then swung hard, slamming the metal end directly into the ceramic lid.

The curator gasped.

The lid shattered into several pieces, but those nearest the mortar joint remained in place.

He had to admit. *That'll work, too.*

"We don't have time for niceties," the cardinal said. "I have to be back in Rome in seven hours."

Pollux Gallo had remained silent, but nothing in his countenance or demeanor suggested he disagreed with the desecration.

"May I?" Cotton asked, wanting the hammer back.

Gallo handed it over, and he used it to tap away more of the ceramic, exposing enough of the lid so he could reach inside.

"Bring that chair over here," he told the curator.

One sat near the oratory's entrance, most likely for the docent to utilize during the day when visitors roamed. The curator retrieved the chair, which Cotton used to gain height on the exposed lid, allowing him to see down inside.

"It's filled with material," he said, carefully fingering the top layer, catching a glistening in the light. "You'd think it's sand. But it's broken glass, pounded to grains, packed tight."

"A defense and preservation mechanism," Pollux said. "Used by us in centuries past. I've seen other repositories with that packed inside."

He certainly could not stick his hand in and see what was there. The glass was packed tight, wall-to-wall, which explained the lack of any hollow sound when he'd probed earlier.

"You're going to have to be careful with any removal," Pollux said. "The glass could destroy whatever is inside. That's another security measure we've been known to use."

"The *Nostra Trinità*," the cardinal said, "would most likely be ancient parchments. They could sustain that kind of abuse."

Pollux shook his head. "It's not in there. The two papal bulls wouldn't fit inside that chamber. We've both seen the copies in the Vatican. They're much taller."

"And you're just now mentioning this," Cotton said.

"The *Constitutum Constantini* could be smaller," the cardinal said. "We don't know what form it took."

Pollux shook his head. "They would have never broken the Trinity. It's all or nothing. My guess is, what's inside this clock is a way to find the path to the *Nostra Trinità*."

Cotton had no idea who was right, but he did have a thought as to how to settle the debate.

He faced the curator. "Do you have a shop vac?"

KASTOR KEPT HIS FRUSTRATION IN CHECK. THIS WAS DRAGGING on forever and time was not on his side. It would take at least three hours to travel back to Rome, counting the time to and from both airports. He could slice that time in half if he could make a few calls. There were people in the private sector he knew, friends, who had access to jets. Perhaps one of those could be dispatched while the situation here played itself out.

"I need a phone," he said.

"In my office," the curator said. "You can make your call while I find the shop vac. We have several that we use to deal with water spills."

He followed the curator from the oratory, leaving Malone and Pollux with the clock. The office sat just beyond the cathedral's gift shop, on the back side of the building. The curator left him alone and he used the landline to make a call to Rome, waking up a longtime corporate ally, who agreed to send his corporate jet to Malta to wait for him, ready to go. Good to know that not everyone hated him. He'd actually amassed quite a roster of friends across a broad spectrum of government, banking, and industry. Men and women who believed, like him, that the Catholic Church had gone too far left. They were anxious for change, but smart enough to bide their time. What was the saying? *Good things come to those who wait.* Really? His experience had been that little to nothing came to those who wait.

Thankfully, his wait might soon be over.

He hung up the phone, his mind racing.

Normally, the power of a group soundly defeated that of an individual. And that, more than anything else, described a conclave. He'd planned to harness the power of that group through a select few individuals. The idea was both simple and time-honored. Infiltrate the adversary, learn everything possible, then turn that knowledge against them.

Which reminded him of the flash drive in his pocket.

He found it and studied the desktop computer that adorned the curator's desk. Why not? He was desperate to know if this was his salvation. He heard no footsteps or voices beyond the office door so he slid the drive into the USB portal. The display called for a password, so he typed KASTOR I.

A menu appeared that indicated only one file.

Titled PROOF.

A good sign.

He opened it and the screen displayed a copy of the summary he'd read earlier, laid out in the same order, with the same verbiage, only this time there was additional text, in red, listing the names of the offending cardinals along with links to an appendix. He clicked on a few and saw scans of financial records, contracts, investigatory notes, and other incriminating documents. Three held embedded recordings of phone calls between cardinals discussing incriminating details. He recognized all of the voices. More than enough proof to use as blackmail. He closed the disk, then ejected it and cradled it in his clenched fist.

Spagna was gone.

But thank heaven his work lived on.

COTTON FOUND HIS CELL PHONE AND CALLED STEPHANIE, SUR-prised at the signal strength from inside the cathedral. He'd excused him-self from the oratory, leaving Pollux Gallo alone with the clock, stepping back into the main nave but maintaining a clear line of sight to make sure everything remained inviolate. He watched through the open doorway as Gallo found a cell phone and made a call himself, stepping toward the altar and the Caravaggio painting at the far end. He explained to Stephanie what they'd found.

"We should know more in about an hour," he said. "Emptying that clock has to be done slowly."

"Where is Laura Price?"

"Outside with Luke."

"There's a problem with her. I was just told by Maltese security that they no longer sanction what she's doing. She's supposedly working with the Entity now. With Spagna dead, they decided to advise me of the situ-ation."

"Mighty generous of them."

"I agree. I'm pissed, too. In the beginning, I thought she might be help-ful. But Spagna played me. Maltese security played me. I have no idea what the hell is going on there. I need to get this info to Luke, but he has no cell phone. Spagna destroyed it."

"I'll deal with it, just as soon as I'm finished here."

"The Vatican is in an uproar over Spagna's death. There are a lot of nervous cardinals concerned about what's going on. Thankfully it's the Vatican, so they can keep a lid on things."

He kept watching Gallo, who stood a hundred feet away, at the far end of the oratory. "I've got a set of identical twins who clearly don't like each other. It's a little freaky at times. It's like the Roadrunner and Wile E. Coyote. One's a fish on a hot dock, no telling what he'll do. The other is semiconscious, on antidepressants, flat as Florida. Neither cares for the other, so there's no telling where this will go if we find anything."

"The Vatican tells me that whatever you find is a private matter. They want us to bow out at that point and let them resolve it among themselves. I have no problem with that. I just need you to make sure that whatever there is to find is found."

He knew the correct response. "Yes, ma'am."

"And get all that intel to Luke."

Across the nave he saw Cardinal Gallo returning with the curator, a shop vac with an extension cord in his hand.

"Gotta go," he told her.

CHAPTER FORTY-SEVEN

THE KNIGHT TRIED TO CONTAIN HIMSELF.

The story was one of long standing.

On October 13, 1307, the Knights Templar were rounded up en masse and arrested. They were tortured and many were killed, including their grand master, Jacques de Molay, who died a horrific death. Five years later the order was officially dissolved and most of its assets turned over to the Knights Hospitallers by the pope. No one ever questioned that move. No one ever challenged, or wondered, how that had been possible. Why would the pope do such a thing?

Simple.

Two hundred years earlier, sometime in the 12th century, during a raid in southern Turkey, a group of Hospitallers came across a cache of ancient documents. Mainly parchments. Religious texts. Most irrelevant and unimportant. One, though, seemed different.

The *Constitutum Constantini.*

Constantine's Gift.

A one-of-a-kind document that survived to the Middle Ages, staying with the Hospitallers during their time in the Holy Land, then with them on Cyprus, Rhodes, and Malta. Popes were eventually made aware of its existence. One in particular, Clement V, who sat on the throne of St. Peter in 1312 and knew of the document, proclaimed his *Ad Providam* granting all of the Templar assets to the Hospitallers. Proof positive of its apparent force. Occasionally, through the centuries, popes had required further persuasion and always Constantine's Gift would do its job.

Keeping the knights relevant.

But it ended in 1798.

Now, on this night, all that might change.

COTTON STOOD ON THE CHAIR AND MANEUVERED THE SHOP VAC'S nozzle across the layers of pulverized glass that filled the clock, slowly extracting them. The chamber measured about ten inches square and eighteen inches deep. He could not rush the removal as he had no idea what, if anything, had been left inside. He understood the advantage of glass as a packing material. It came with no mess, no dust. It also was dense, which made the clock extra heavy, further dissuading looters from carting it away. The shop vac was working perfectly, the granulations steadily rattling their way through the nozzle. He was concerned about Luke, but there was no way this task could be delegated to one of the men watching him intently.

He kept vacuuming. The top of something came into view. He maneuvered around the object and kept extracting. The outline of a bottle began to take shape. Wide mouth. Tall. Standing upright at about the halfway point. Sealed with wax. He kept going until over half of the container was visible.

"Shut it off," he said.

The curator killed the motor.

He laid down the nozzle.

"What's there?" the cardinal asked, impatient as ever.

He reached inside and gently wiggled the bottle free. Grains of glass rained off. He shook more away and held the container up for them to see. The opaque bottle carried a foggy, greenish hue. He saw the blurred image of something that filled the inside.

He stepped from the chair. "Any thoughts?"

Pollux examined the exterior. "Another message."

He agreed and grabbed the chisel from the table, working on the wax seal. The dark crimson scraped away in dry, bitter chunks. The wax filled the entire mouth, and he angled the bottle downward, careful not to allow anything to damage what was inside. A pile of two-hundred-plus-year-old wax, melted by a desperate prior trying to preserve the last bits of heritage to a dying organization, collected on the tabletop. He used the chisel to scrape away the remaining bits of the seal. He tipped the bottle and a piece of rolled parchment, stained the color of tea, slid out.

He set the bottle down.

"It can be unrolled," the curator said, seemingly reading his mind. "But carefully."

"Do it," the cardinal said.

Cotton laid the roll, about five inches tall, on the table. The curator used his index finger and thumb to hold down one edge. Cotton spread the roll out, slow and careful, the parchment's natural resilience still there after two centuries. He held his end flat and they all studied the image, the black ink bloated by time.

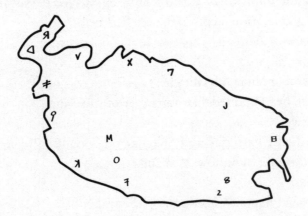

"It's Malta," the curator said.

Cotton agreed. A crude drawing of its shores, but the shape was unmistakable. Letters and symbols ringed the shoreline, a few more inland.

"That's the Latin alphabet," Pollux said. "The square with a line through it on the far right is the letter *H*. The two circles, joined, that looks like an *8* is the letter *F*."

"And their positions on the map could be watchtowers," the curator said. "There were thirteen encircling the island. There are thirteen letters close to the coast. The M could be Mdina, the backward F is roughly where the old Inquisitor's Palace lays. The O is near the Verdala palace."

It all made sense. The prior had made the clues difficult, yet not insurmountable, provided the person studying them knew the lay of the land. He'd wondered what the letters in the message found in the obelisk had referred to. H Z P D R S Q X. Now he knew.

"Do you know the whole Latin alphabet?" he asked.

Pollux nodded.

Perfect.

"We need to make a copy of this parchment. I need one I can write on."

LUKE TOOK IN BOTH THE DARK FORM OF THE MAN AND THE ANSWER he'd supplied about Malone not being in danger, then asked, "Who are you?"

"Monsignor John Roy. I was Archbishop Spagna's assistant. I'm now in temporary operational command of the Entity."

"You sound American."

"I am."

"The *Secreti* are here, on Malta?"

The black head nodded. "In a manner of speaking."

Odd answer.

"They killed Chatterjee and Spagna and tried to kill you," Roy said. "They're out there, right now. Waiting."

"For what?"

"To see what happens inside the cathedral."

Luke pointed at the rifle on the table before the window. "And who are you going to kill?"

"Don't tell me you haven't pulled the trigger before?" Roy asked.

"I'm not an assassin."

"Neither am I," Laura said. "But I do my job."

"I'm not going to allow either of you to kill anybody."

"This doesn't concern the United States," Roy said. "It's a Vatican problem, which the Vatican wants to handle itself."

"By killing people?"

"Washington interjected itself into this matter," Roy noted. "The Entity did not ask for your assistance. I'm asking you, as one professional to another, to walk away. I assure you, nothing will happen to Mr. Malone. At least not from us. The *Secreti*? That's another matter. You and Malone will have to deal with that problem. They're the enemy. Not me."

"They're after what Malone is locating right now? Inside the cathedral?"

"That's correct. And they're not going to stop until they get it. Archbishop Spagna was here to retrieve whatever might be found. He failed. Ms. Price and I will now finish that mission. You and Mr. Malone can go home."

Which actually sounded appealing.

As a boy he and his brothers had tended the cows his parents owned. Lazy animals. They loved nothing more than to loiter in the pasture all day, chewing cud. The horseflies were relentless. Nasty little creatures that left whelps with their bites. Some of the cows would run to get away from them. But most just stood there, chewing grass, using their tails to swat the flies away. Oblivious to any assault. Those cows that didn't run were bold suckers.

Like him.

"I can't leave, and you know it."

CHAPTER FORTY-EIGHT

COTTON HELD THE PARCHMENT FLAT AS THE BRIGHT LIGHT SCANNED the image and produced a copy. They'd fled the oratory and returned to the curator's office. The two Gallo brothers had stayed quiet, watching as he studied the prior's puzzle. He rolled up the original and set it aside, then laid the copy on the curator's desk, grabbed a pen, and wrote H Z P D R S Q X on a pad.

"Give me the Latin alphabet letters for those."

Pollux took the pen and wrote the corresponding Latin letters. Cotton immediately saw that he was right. All eight appeared on the drawing, scattered at intervals around the island.

$$H - \boxminus \qquad R - O$$
$$Z - \ddagger \qquad S - Z$$
$$P - 7 \qquad Q - 9$$
$$D - Я \qquad X - X$$

He circled them on the map copy.

"They're markers. Reference points," he said.

But they were useless unless read together. So he studied them, arbitrarily deciding the ones closest together along the coast had to be connected by short lines.

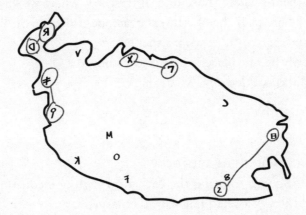

"You don't know that's right," the cardinal said.

"No. I don't. It's a guess, but it seems reasonable. We can try other combinations if this doesn't work."

Common sense demanded that the map had to lead to a single point on the island, and the only way that could be accomplished was by intersecting lines. In his mind he drew those lines, connecting differing points of the eight circles. Only one combination seemed to provide what he was after, the rest mere noise to confuse the searcher.

"It's like the X out there on the floor," he said. "You connect them diagonally across the grid."

He took a ruler the curator supplied and drew the lines.

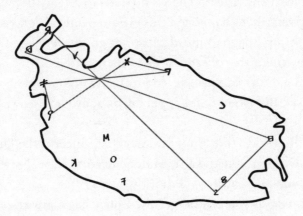

"It's a rough Maltese cross," the cardinal said. "A bit stretched, but one nonetheless."

"Which means where those lines intersect is where we have to go," he said. "Somewhere near the northwest coast, not far from St. Paul's Bay, if I'm not mistaken. Any idea what's there?"

"It can only be one place," the curator said.

Pollux Gallo nodded. "St. Magyar's."

LUKE GLANCED OUT THE WINDOW.

St. John's Square fronting the cathedral still loomed dim and quiet. Malone and the Gallos had not, as yet, emerged.

He still had time.

"Mr. Daniels, the church is facing a direct threat," Roy said, the voice resonant, controlled, logical. "This threat is made even more dangerous by the coming conclave. Once the cardinals are locked away inside the Sistine, we'll lose all control. It has to be dealt with right now. Archbishop Spagna discovered the threat and was working, in his own way, to eliminate it. He came here, personally, to deal with the situation. He planned to enlist both you and Ms. Price with his efforts. Unfortunately, the threat found him first."

"What threat?"

"I can't say. But I assure you, it's real."

"You have one of the best intelligence agencies in the world at your disposal. Deal with any threat. There's no need to kill anybody."

"Sadly, given what's happened this evening, only violence will end this now. Archbishop Spagna's murder cannot go unavenged. These people have to know there are consequences to their actions."

Something didn't add up. He said to Laura, "You said Spagna set this kill up for you. But when that happened, nobody had died yet. So what is this? A hit?"

"Again," Roy said, "this is not a matter that concerns the United States. Please, Mr. Daniels, you and Mr. Malone need to leave. Now."

"And let you kill Cardinal Gallo?"

"Mr. Daniels, as you just noted, the Entity has many resources. It has

existed for centuries. We've survived by always doing what has to be done."
Roy paused. "Killing is not unfamiliar to us. Never have we been afraid
to do what was necessary. In centuries past, if the Holy Father ordered
the elimination of someone in defense of the faith, we carried out that order. He is God's voice and we are his hand."

"This isn't the Middle Ages, and the pope is dead."

"Yet a threat remains." Roy shook his head. "But killing a prince of the
Church is not part of our agenda here."

He'd assumed with the mention of the conclave that Cardinal Gallo
was the target. That had been the entire reason for Stephanie Nelle in-
volving him in the first place.

"His brother is our problem," Roy said. "Archbishop Spagna dealt extensively with Pollux Gallo. Too much, in my opinion. But the archbishop
was not a man who accepted much in the way of . . . counseling. Sadly, my
personal suspicions regarding Pollux Gallo have proven true."

Which Luke would love to know more about.

But that wasn't going to happen.

"Leave this to us," Laura said.

"I wish it were—"

Two pops broke the silence.

Like hands clapping.

Roy lurched forward, grabbing his chest, then collapsed to the floor,
his face slamming the planks hard. Nothing had come through the window, so the attack had to be from outside in the hallway. Laura reacted by
whirling around and aiming her weapon at the darkened doorway. Luke
used the moment to drop to the floor and grab the rifle off the table on
the way down, flattening himself out, becoming the smallest target possible. Before he could warn Laura to do the same, he heard another pop
and her head snapped back as a bullet smashed through her face, up
through the brain, and out the back of the skull.

Her body dropped to the floor beside the monsignor.

He sent three sound-suppressed rifle rounds into the blackness beyond
the doorway.

Footsteps rushed away.

He sprang to his feet, pressing his body to the wall adjacent to the exit.
Beyond, the corridor was much darker. But he neither saw nor sensed

anyone. He switched the rifle for his pistol, which he grabbed from the floor. Then took a moment and checked for a pulse in Roy. None. Laura was clearly dead. Dammit. She hadn't deserved that.

He made his way to the stairs, then down. The door leading out to the alley was partially open.

Careful. Trouble could be outside.

He used the building's stone wall for protection and, with his right foot, kicked the door open. A few quick glances past the jamb and he still saw no one. He stepped outside. To his right, at the far end of the alley, a hundred feet away, where it merged with another street, he caught the image of a dark figure.

Running away.

He raced after it.

CHAPTER FORTY-NINE

COTTON COULD SEE THAT BOTH GALLOS AND THE CURATOR SEEMED certain of the location.

"What is St. Magyar's?" he asked.

"It's one of the oldest chapels on the island," Pollux said. "It was built in the mid-16th century, not long after the knights arrived."

He listened as Pollux told him about the church. According to legend, in the 12th century a local maiden had been working the fields when she saw a number of Turks running her way. She fled, with the invaders in hot pursuit. Out of breath, she found refuge in a cave whose entrance was blocked by a mass of cobwebs. Inside, she dropped to her knees and prayed to the Madonna for help. The corsairs kept looking for her, even finding the cave and peering inside, but on seeing the veil of cobwebs they moved on.

"It was the cobwebs re-forming themselves after she passed through them that was considered a miracle," Pollux said. "So a chapel was built in front of the cave, dedicated to the maiden, who became St. Louise Magyar."

"Every church here has a story like that," the curator said. "This island is littered with churches. Three hundred and fifty-nine at last count, a little over one per every square kilometer. Sixty-three different parishes.

St. Magyar's is one of the wayside chapels, off to itself, not open to the public."

"It's owned by the order," Pollux said.

That was interesting.

"The original stone church was rebuilt by the knights in the 16th century," Pollux said. "It stays sealed, but we maintain the site. I can call our representatives here on the island and have it opened, waiting for us."

"Do it," the cardinal said.

Clearly, Pollux did not appreciate being given an order by his brother, but no argument was offered and Pollux left the office to make a call.

Something was bothering Cotton.

"What is it about this church you're holding back?" he asked the curator and the cardinal.

"When Napoleon ravaged the island," the curator said, "he didn't plunder St. Magyar's. It's always been a simple place, with no ornamentation. There was nothing there to steal. So it's intact. Just as it was in the 16th century."

"It was also the *Secreti's* private chapel," the cardinal added.

Now we're talkin'.

Gallo explained that the *Secreti* had always maintained a certain distance from the rest of the knights. The whole idea of their select association was to be aloof. So after the order was gifted Malta, the *Secreti* constructed a chapel to be used only by members, the grounds declared off limits to all but those who wore the five-word palindrome that formed an anagram of *Pater Noster.* Our Father. The sign of Constantine.

"It was regularly used up to the time of Napoleon's invasion," the curator said. "Records show that French soldiers visited the site, but as I mentioned there was nothing there of value."

Apparently they were wrong. Cotton decided to shift tacks and faced Gallo. "You can go back to Rome now."

"I'll head there as soon as this is finished."

"Forgive me, Eminence, but what interest would a cardinal of the church have in all this? As I understand it, whatever there is to find belongs to the Knights of Malta."

"That's a matter of debate. And I'm the papal representative to that order. It's my duty to see this through."

"We can report our findings to you. Why does it require your *personal* involvement?"

He could see that scarlet feathers had been bristled by his directness. But he was pressing for a reason.

"I don't have to explain myself to you," Gallo said.

"No, you don't. But by your own statement there are men on this island trying to kill you. A conclave starts in just a few hours. Yet you insist on staying around. Some might call that reckless." He paused. "Or perhaps deliberate."

Like a cold mist, anger rose in Gallo's eyes.

"I'm a prince of the Roman Catholic Church, Mr. Malone, who customarily is shown respect. Even by those not of the church."

"Even when you lie?"

Before the cardinal could reply Pollux reentered the office, breaking the moment. "A representative will meet us at St. Magyar's with a key to the doors. The building has electricity. They will also bring some tools, as we have no idea what there is to find, or how to get to it." Pollux paused. "Mr. Malone, we can handle this ourselves from this point forward."

"I agree," the cardinal quickly added. "Go home."

Now a double team.

Interesting.

"My orders are to see this through to the end. We're not at the end."

"You've helped tremendously," Pollux said. "Your solving of the prior's message was masterful. But I have to concur with my brother, which is rare for me. This is an ecclesiastical matter, one we can now handle internally."

"The head of the Entity is dead. This is far more than a religious matter."

"I understand, and we'll address the *Secreti*," Pollux said. "All those responsible for any acts of violence will be dealt with. But the *Nostra Trinità* is a sensitive, internal issue, one we would prefer to keep to ourselves."

"How about this," he said. "Let's go have a look and see what's there. After that, I'm out of here. That would be the end, as far as I'm concerned."

"We don't need you," the cardinal said, with finality.

But Pollux nodded. "That seems reasonable."

CHAPTER
FIFTY

LUKE RAN THROUGH THE DARKENED ALLEY.

The guy ahead of him had a huge head start. But so had Buddy Barnes back at Ranger school. A twelve-mile tactical march with full gear, the last test over two days of intense physical fitness training. Don't finish the march in under three hours and you're out. The failure rate hovered at a constant 60 percent. But he'd not only finished, he'd caught Buddy, making up a hundred yards over the last two miles to cross the end line first. The winner received the honor of buying the first round of drinks during the next leave. No matter it would cost a couple of hundred dollars, everyone wanted to win that march. Problem was, when the time came he didn't have a couple of hundred dollars. So Buddy had loaned it to him until the next payday. That was what Rangers did for one another. He missed Buddy. A roadside bomb in Afghanistan killed his friend, and he'd helped carry the flag-draped coffin to the grave at Arlington.

He kept running, stepping up the pace, careful with the damp cobblestones. This wasn't a flat dirt trail at Fort Benning. It was a rolling city by the sea full of hostiles and friendlies, and it was sometimes hard to know which was which.

He thought of Laura Price.

She'd been a little of both.

But she'd been careless and that sloppiness cost her big time.

His target disappeared around a corner about half a football field ahead. He felt a familiar pulse of adrenaline. He was in the prime of his life, ready for all challenges. But he told himself to be smart. Always be smart. He wasn't sure if the guy was even aware he had a pursuer, as the man's pace had not changed. He found the same corner and whirled around, not losing a step. He stared ahead and saw that his target was no longer running. Instead, the man was down in the middle of the street, in a firing stance, arms extended, gun aimed.

Damn.

He launched himself into the air, leaping to the right, catapulting his body onto the hood of a parked car and slamming into the windshield.

Two shots came his way.

He rolled to the sidewalk, gun still in his grasp, and lay on his stomach, his chin to the street, poking his head around a bumper.

Another round whined off the side panel.

He reeled back into a crouch and tightened his grip on the gun, then aimed and squeezed the trigger, sending a bullet of his own toward the target.

A quick peek and he saw the guy was gone.

He came to his feet and rushed ahead.

Another alley opened to the right of where the shooter had taken a stand. He stopped at the intersection and saw the man running near the bottom of a long, inclined path. Beyond he caught the glimmer of water. They were headed toward the harbor, which actually wasn't far away at any point within the city. He kept going, hustling down to the alley's end where he stopped and surveyed the scene. A marina dominated the concrete wharf. Boats bobbed on mooring lines inside a high-density basin. His gaze scanned the many finger docks. No one was around. But he caught the drone of an engine to his left.

He ran down the concrete walk that fronted the water and saw a Zodiac, out on the water, motoring away, heading into the Grand Harbor. Two figures stood inside the inflatable.

One of them tossed a taunting wave back at him.

Asshole.

He needed a boat.

Now.

He bolted back to the marina. Many of the boats he could see were sizable, twenty-plus-footers with all the bells and whistles. Impractical for this pursuit. Toward the end of one dock he spotted a small, fifteen-foot V-hull with a solitary outboard. Of course, he didn't have a key to trip the engine but that shouldn't be a problem. As a kid, he'd learned how to hot-wire an outboard. He and his brothers would just take a screwdriver and spark the leads beneath the ignition pad, which always did the trick. He didn't have any tools, but he shouldn't need any. He untied the mooring lines and, as the boat drifted from the dock, bent down beneath the key panel and yanked the two wires loose. He got lucky. They came free, leaving some of their copper exposed. He sparked them together and the engine coughed to life.

The revs steadied and he quickly twisted the wires together. He then hooked the wheel left and goosed the throttle. The prop bit water and lunged the hull forward toward the harbor. The Zodiac had a big lead, and his newly acquired pleasure craft did not have much more horsepower. The best he could do was keep up and see where they headed. What exactly he was going to do once he learned that information remained to be seen. But he was tired of being one step behind. Laura, Malone, the *Secreti*, Spagna. All of them had been ahead of him from the start.

He passed Fort St. Angelo and the harbor mole at the tip of Valletta's jutting peninsula. The Zodiac was about a quarter mile ahead, a black smudge skirting across black water.

Beyond it, out in open water, he spotted lights.

Another craft at anchor.

Which had to be their destination.

CHAPTER
FIFTY-ONE

THE KNIGHT WAS PLEASED TO SEE HIS TARGETS LEAVE THE CO-cathedral and head for a car parked in a small lot across the street, toward the rear of the building. His men had already taken out Spagna and his minion, and they'd surely dealt with Laura Price by now. He'd severely underestimated the Lord's Own, not grasping the full extent of Spagna's passion and desires. But that problem was now solved.

The Americans, though, remained.

Killing both agents currently on the ground seemed the simplest solution, but that would only bring more inquiry. The Knights of Malta and the Roman Catholic Church were two huge, impersonal, monolithic objects, one unstoppable, the other unmovable. But the United States was something altogether different. He'd not expected their involvement and remained unsure exactly how to move them off the scent. Harold Earl "Cotton" Malone seemed highly capable, and the younger Luke Daniels had clearly held his own. But killing one or both of them seemed unwise, especially at this critical juncture. An ordered universe was always the goal. Everything to a certain arrangement according to set rules, all focused on a single goal. The route to that goal was fully prescribed within his mind. He'd been thinking about what was coming for a long time. Visualizing. Planning. Hoping.

Now he could see the end.

Not exactly how he'd envisioned it a few days ago.

But the end nonetheless.

KASTOR RODE IN BACK OF THE CAR. MALONE DROVE WITH POLLUX occupying the front passenger seat. It was the same vehicle they'd used to drive from the airport to the cathedral. They were minus two others, though, as Luke Daniels and Laura Price had disappeared.

Good riddance.

The less involved the better.

They were headed out of Valletta along the north coast highway. Soon they would pass the Madliena Tower, where all of this had started yesterday. His right hand felt the flash drive through his trousers where it rested safely in his pocket. He'd been considering how best to use it. He probably would not make it back to Rome until just before the 10:00 A.M. reporting deadline. There would not be time to do much more than shower and change into his scarlet cassock before the cardinals assembled in St. Peter's for mass. No privacy or meaningful opportunity to speak to anyone would be available. Then they would all gather in the Pauline Chapel before walking in a televised procession to the Sistine while collectively singing the Litany of the Saints. All part of the required tradition adhered to at every modern conclave.

Then the hypocrisy would start.

Beginning after the doors to the Sistine were sealed, when they would each take an oath to observe the Apostolic Constitution, maintain secrecy, never allowing anything to influence their voting save the Holy Spirit, and, if elected, to defend the Holy See. Some of that was going to be a stretch for a few of them, though none of the guilty parties knew that as yet.

Then the cardinal dean would ask if any questions relating to the procedures remained. After the clarification of any doubts, the first scrutiny, the first vote, would commence. Ordinarily a few of the minor rules that rarely came into play would be unimportant. But not here. An ill cardinal was allowed to leave the conclave and could be readmitted later. A cardinal who left for any reason other than illness could not return. No attendants accompanied the cardinals, except a nurse for one in ill health. Priests were available to hear confessions. Two doctors were also there, along with a strictly limited number of staff for housekeeping and preparing meals. All potential problems once the pressure started to be applied.

Just three cardinals were permitted to communicate with the outside world, and only under the gravest of circumstances. The major penitentiary. The cardinal vicar for the Diocese of Rome. And the vicar general for the Vatican City State. None of whom were on his hit list.

Thank God.

But he had to make sure not a one of the dirty cardinals tried to seek help or feign illness. Everything had to stay contained within the conclave.

The first scrutiny always came quickly.

And was meaningless.

Few ever achieved election then. Most cardinals voted for either themselves or a close friend. A few would collate and cast their ballots for their favorite candidate, sending an early message. Generally, the votes were scattered across a wide spectrum and not until the second scrutiny would patterns begin to emerge.

The rules stated that if a scrutiny took place on the afternoon of the first day and no one was elected, a maximum of four ballots were held on each successive day. Two in the morning, two each afternoon. If no result came after three days of balloting—twelve votes—the process was suspended for one day of prayer. After seven further scrutinies, the process again would be suspended. If after another seven no result was achieved, a third suspension came for another day. After a final seven and no election, a day of prayer, reflection, and dialogue occurred. For any voting thereafter, only the two names who received the most votes in the last scrutiny were eligible in a runoff.

In modern times the voting had never even approached such lengths. But nothing about this conclave would be normal.

The critical moment?

After the first scrutiny, when the conclave recessed for the day and the cardinals headed back to their rooms, there would be a few hours between dinner and when everyone had settled down for the night when he could make the rounds and have a private talk with the ones who mattered. By then there would be a lot of chatter happening. That was the whole idea of the conclave. For the cardinals to be sequestered alone, where they could make up their minds among themselves. He was just going to provide some added incentive. Each offender would be told what he knew, what he could prove, and what would happen if he did not hear his name announced as having achieved a two-thirds majority.

He also didn't care how it was done.

Just that it happened.

And fast.

CHAPTER FIFTY-TWO

Luke kept the wheel straight and the bow pointed out to sea. The inflatable ahead continued to speed through the water with little noise, the engine barely audible thanks to the half-mile distance between them. Its destination seemed to be a glossy, light-colored hull with a clean, slick outline. A main cabin projected above the gunwale extending maybe fifty feet. Lights illuminated the hull, cabin area, and aft deck, where a shadow could be seen walking around.

The inflatable eased up to the stern and stopped. Two men hopped from the Zodiac and cinched the craft tight to an aft swim step. Luke glanced back and saw he was five hundred yards offshore, due north of Fort St. Angelo, which was lit in its full golden glory to the night. He had a tough decision to make, one with enormous ramifications if he was wrong. The men on that boat had killed four people, that he knew of, tonight. They'd even tried to make him the fifth. Laura had wanted them stopped, and though her methods were questionable she hadn't deserved to die. Shooting it out with these guys seemed nonsensical. This wasn't a Bond movie. There were far more of them than there was of him, and they certainly could see him coming as he was a mere quarter mile away and closing.

Three figures now stood on the aft deck.

He saw bursts of muzzle fire and realized they were shooting his way.

Volleys of automatic weapons rounds kicked up the water around him like giant raindrops. He ducked low enough for cover, but still high enough that he could see beyond the windscreen. The closer he got the easier a target he would make. The smart play was to take these guys out and find out who they were after they were in the water, either dead or rescued.

His best weapon roared beneath his feet.

The boat itself.

His target rested at anchor.

He aimed the bow straight for the yacht's midsection, the throttle full out. He knifed across the calm surface, cutting a path straight for the darkened hull. He'd have to time his move perfectly as he could not risk the rudder not staying straight.

New gunfire came his way.

Rounds thudded into the fiberglass hull.

One hundred yards.

He needed to be closer.

More *rat, tat, tat* from automatic fire.

One last look.

On course.

People liked to say he was sometimes two fries short of a Happy Meal, but what had his father liked to say? *Your strings have to all be in tune for folks to pick on you.*

Hell yeah.

He leaped from the boat, hitting the water with his right shoulder, his forward momentum skipping him across the surface before he sank. He stayed down, beneath the surface, but gazed upward as the pewter-black night transformed into a blinding light.

COTTON STEPPED FROM THE CAR AND STARED AT ST. MAGYAR'S. The squatty church seemed scooped out of the bow of the hill, tucked away under a rocky outcrop, hidden by both nature and the night. He didn't have to see to know that the ancient stone walls were likely twisted and discolored by centuries of bakery heat.

He was still concerned about Luke, who'd been nowhere to be found when they'd left the cathedral. He understood Stephanie's urgency at dealing with Laura Price, but he had problems of his own. Surely Luke would head back inside the cathedral, where the curator had been told to direct him this way. He'd commandeered the car they'd used to travel from the airport to the cathedral. The curator had said that he would make his personal vehicle available to Luke when he showed up.

Another set of headlights pierced the night, and a small SUV approached the church and parked. A younger man climbed out, whom Pollux identified as one of his colleagues from Fort St. Angelo. The newcomer opened the vehicle's hatch where there were two shovels, a pick, a sledgehammer, and some rope.

"I wasn't sure what to expect," Pollux said. "So I told him to bring what they had."

Cotton grabbed the shovels, Pollux the sledgehammer and pick. The cardinal brought the coil of rope.

"Wait outside," Pollux told his man. "I'll call you in if needed."

The younger man nodded and handed over a key to the front door.

The terrain around them was hilly, fading down into a valley that stretched farther south. Scattered lights indicated people. The church sat on the knob of one of the steeper hills with a graveled path serving as a driveway. There were two barred windows and a small bell cot. The main door was an arched oval, unusually low. Above it, an encircled eight-pointed Maltese cross was carved into the stone. The dial of Cotton's luminous watch read 4:40 A.M.

Another all-nighter.

Thankfully, he'd grabbed an hour's nap on the flight from Rome.

Pollux used the key and opened the oak door. He heard a click and lights came on inside. Not many, and not all that bright, which allowed his eyes to adjust easily. The interior was rectangular with a circular apse at the far end. Simple and bare, with stone benches lining the exterior walls, the floor a mixture of flagstones and beaten earth. Only faint remnants of wall frescoes remained. Empty niches accommodated no statues. Everything a bland, sandy gray.

"The main reason there are so many churches on Malta," Pollux said, "is isolation. Roads were few and terrible, so every town and village wanted its own church. Incredibly, the vast majority of those buildings have survived. This one, though, was built for a select few. The locals were forbidden to come anywhere near it, on pain of imprisonment."

Cotton noticed the plain stone altar at the apse end, another Maltese cross carved into its front. The lack of any pews seemed curious. "Did they stand to worship?"

"There was no worship here," Cardinal Gallo said.

He'd suspected as much. There had to be more to this place.

Pollux stepped beyond the altar into the apse. Three stone panels formed the curved walls, separated by moldings, with limestone benches wrapping the semicircle. Cotton watched as Pollux laid the pick down and knelt, reaching beneath one of the stone benches and pressing something.

The center panel released inward a few inches.

"Centuries ago there was a manual winch," Pollux said. "But today we're a bit more modern."

"Napoleon never found the door?" he asked.

Pollux shook his head. "The French were in a hurry and not all that smart. They came, saw nothing, and left. We installed the electric lock about five years ago. The stone is balanced at its center of gravity, on a lubricated center post. You can push it open with one hand."

The cardinal stepped forward and did just that, exposing two blackened rectangles, about two feet wide, centered by the short side of the stone wall.

They stepped through and Pollux activated another light switch.

A tunnel stretched ahead.

Tall. Wide. Spacious.

"Where does it lead?" he asked.

"To a wondrous place," Pollux whispered.

DURING THE CAR TRIP KASTOR HAD ADMIRED THE PWALES VALLEY, a picturesque region of timeless wetlands that dominated Malta's northern corner. The land undulated with hillocks of lichens and foul-smelling mushrooms. It stayed carpeted with cape sorrel, crow daisies, borage, and spurge. Unusual for Malta, which was not all that hospitable to plants.

Some of the most stunning views on the island could be seen here, though darkness prevented him from enjoying any of them now.

People had lived on the land for over five thousand years and there were cave paintings in the nearby ridges to prove it. Its many bays had long made it prone to outside attack. The knights had fortified the whole area against Muslim corsairs with coastal towers and garrison batteries. The British manned a fort nearby during, and after, World War II. As a kid he'd visited it several times. The nuns would buy them sweets and sodas. They'd also taken swimming lessons in the nearby harbor.

Those nuns.

They'd at least tried to make things bearable, which was hard to do given all of their children were orphans. Few ever left until they were old enough to walk out as adults. He'd always wondered how many ever ventured back for a visit. He never had.

He knew all about the Church of St. Magyar's, which was actually two chapels in one. The outer portion had served as an overt wayside chapel and gathering place for the *Secreti*. But it was the inner portion—the Church of St. John—that had held a special place.

But not John the Baptist.

John of Nepomuk, the patron saint of Bohemia, drowned in 1393 in the Vltava River at the behest of King Wenceslaus for refusing to divulge the secrets of the confessional. He was often depicted in statues with a finger to his lips, indicating silence, keeping a secret. The Jesuits spread the story of his martyrdom that eventually elevated him to sainthood. A cult devoted to his worship flourished on Malta in the 16th century, so it was easy to see why the *Secreti* would have named their chapel for him.

Kastor had never visited St. Magyar's, nor, he assumed, had 99 percent of the knights' membership. As with its patron saint, the secrets within this place had stayed secret. Why Pollux had chosen to reveal this sacred location to an outsider remained a mystery.

They carried the tools and walked down the lit tunnel.

"This is a man-made extension of the original natural cave," Pollux said. "The exterior sanctuary was built to conceal the true chapel of the *Secreti*."

The path was lit by a series of incandescent fixtures attached to the ceiling, connected by an exposed electrical cable. The floor was flat, hard-packed earth, dry as a desert. The air was noticeably cooler the farther inside they walked. The tunnel ended at a set of arched, oak double doors hung on heavy iron hinges. No locks, just two iron rings that Pollux used to push open both panels. Not a sound betrayed the hinges. Obviously, things around here were dutifully cared for.

Beyond was a towering space that stretched in three directions, two lateral vaults off a central core. Arches and pillars supported the rock overhead. Statues dominated every nook and cranny. Not separate additions, either—as in the co-cathedral, each had been carved from the surrounding stone. He saw Madonnas, saints, Christ, animals. Most were freestanding. A few stood alone in niches, while others emerged from the walls in three-dimensional façades. Carefully placed floor and ceiling lights illuminated everything, casting the stone in varying hues of brown and gray, all combining for a hauntingly ominous atmosphere.

"All right," Kastor said to Malone. "What now?"

CHAPTER FIFTY-THREE

COTTON HAD NEVER SEEN ANYTHING LIKE THE MACABRE UNDER-ground chapel, which, thanks to all of the life-sized images, made him feel like he was standing in a crowd. Thankfully, no disturbing feelings of claustrophobia had grabbed hold of him as the room, though cluttered, loomed airy and spacious.

"Is there climate control?" he asked, noticing the lack of humidity and the breeze.

"We have dehumidifiers," Pollux said. "We installed them when we changed out the door mechanism. The air-conditioning is natural. We've learned that you have to be careful with something like this. Touching with bare fingertips leaves oil that degrades the limestone. Artificial lights encourage bacterial growth. Lots of warm bodies exhaling carbon dioxide change the airflow, temperature, and humidity. It's important this place survives, so we took measures to ensure that it did."

"Is this where the *Secreti* worshiped?" Cotton asked.

Pollux nodded. "This is also where new members were inducted. The *Secreti* were quite peculiar about who they asked to join their ranks. They kept no written records, so it's impossible to know who was a member. Unless you wore the ring."

"I guess there were no jewelry stores copying them back then," he said with a touch of sarcasm.

Pollux seemed perplexed.

He told them what the fake Pollux Gallo had explained.

"There actually is truth to the statement," Pollux said. "I've seen a few of those copies over the years—"

"But since the *Secreti* are gone, what did it matter?"

He couldn't resist.

"Something like that," Pollux said.

Cotton had been thinking about the answer to the cardinal's question of *what now.* There'd been nothing in the outer chapel to draw his interest, which was surely the whole idea of keeping things simple there. Here, though, there were a multitude of potential hiding places represented by the numerous figures carved in stone. He turned to Pollux. "How far are you willing to go to find what you're looking for?"

"If you mean defacing any of this, that depends," Pollux said. "Let's see how certain you are of a result once when we reach that point."

His mind sorted through the possibilities. So far the dead prior's actions had been wholly practical. But nothing in any of the clues pointed to anything inside this statuary. Only to the chapel in general. Both Pollux and the curator had made it clear back at the cathedral that there were no other chapels or sacred sites near where the lines on the map had intersected.

So this had to be the place.

"No telling what godforsaken things happened here," the cardinal said.

"The *Secreti* were only a danger to those who threatened the knights."

"And today? Now? What's threatening the knights? Why are the *Secreti* killing people?"

Pollux faced his brother. "No one says they are."

"You did," Cotton said. "The urgency to get here was because the *Secreti* were on the move. Three men died at that villa. Two more here on Malta. You said the likely suspect in all five killings is the *Secreti.*"

"It seems logical," Pollux said. "But I will deal with that possibility after we locate the *Nostra Trinità.*"

Cotton's gaze had been raking the room and he'd settled on the only spot that made sense. At the far end, up three short steps, an altar had been carved from the wall. It jutted out and faced away from the worshipers, as would have been common five hundred years ago. Above it was a Madonna and child etched from the stone. Two winged angels flanked either side. But it was the altar's base that drew his attention. Five words that could be read the same from any direction. The palindrome from the ring.

The sign of Constantine.

SATOR
AREPO
TENET
OPERA
ROTAS

He pointed. "It has to be there."

They approached the altar.

"Constantine's sign was carved there when the church was built," Pollux said. "It's always been here."

Cotton set the shovels on the floor and knelt down to inspect the altar. The letters sprang from a recessed panel at the altar's center, right where a priest would have stood while saying mass. Four fluted columns carved from the limestone flanked left and right. With his finger he traced a mortar joint in the recessed panel—dry, brittle, and gray, like everything else.

"I say we bust this open."

He gave Pollux a moment to consider the ramifications. This wasn't a broken clock. It was a piece of something that had survived five hundred years. Something men had dedicated their lives to preserve. Thousands of knights and Maltese had died fighting to keep all of this inviolate.

And they'd succeeded.

Only to have it destroyed now by an outsider, with permission from one of their own.

Pollux handed over the sledgehammer, signaling his assent. Cotton gripped the wooden handle and decided there was no delicate way to do it, so he gave the center of the panel, right above the word TENET, a hard rap with the business end. The stone held, but there was a noticeable give, as at the obelisk.

"It's hollow behind it," he said.

He swung again.

Two more times and the stone broke into pieces, exposing a cavity beyond.

The two brothers watched as he cleared away the fragments, holding in his hand bits and pieces of the palindrome. He removed enough to see an object inside the chamber beyond. A horizontal glass cylinder resting on golden legs with animal paws as feet. About twenty-four inches long and eight inches high. Both ends were enclosed by gold mounts sealed with wax. Through the thick glass he could see the out-of-focus images of three scrolls, each loosely rolled.

Pollux made the sign of the cross and whispered, "Our Trinity."

Cotton reached in and lifted out the reliquary.

Heavy.

The three parchments appeared intact and in reasonably good shape. He laid the container on the altar where they could examine every aspect of it.

"This is where I must insist we part ways," Pollux said. "We've located the *Nostra Trinità*. It belongs to the Knights of Malta—"

"Or the Roman Catholic Church," the cardinal said.

"Precisely," Pollux finished. "This is a dispute we have to resolve among ourselves. It does not involve the American government in any way. We apologize for all that you've endured and appreciate your efforts. But the mystery is now solved and *we* have to deal with what happens next." Pollux paused. "Kastor and I. We have much to discuss."

Of that Cotton had no doubt.

"A lot of damage has occurred over the past day," Pollux said. "People have been hurt and killed. My brother and I have to deal with that. Patron of the Holy See to lieutenant ad interim. It's our problem. Not yours."

He was used to the rough-and-tumble of the intelligence business, willing to be banged up. God knows he'd had his share of injuries.

But the brush-off?

That kind of hurt.

But he'd done all Stephanie had asked of him. And though he would love to know what was inside the reliquary, Pollux Gallo was right. It really was none of his, or Washington's, business.

"All right," he said. "I'm out of here. But you feel this is a safe place for you to linger?"

"We're perfectly fine here," Pollux said, extending a hand to shake.

He accepted the offer.

"Thank you, Mr. Malone, for all your assistance. I never asked, but are you Catholic?"

"I was baptized that way, but religion is not my thing."

"A shame. You would have made a good knight."

Cardinal Gallo offered no hand to shake and his dour expression never changed. He shook his head and glanced back toward Pollux.

"Good luck."

And he left.

CHAPTER
FIFTY-FOUR

THE KNIGHT WATCHED AS COTTON MALONE LEFT THE CHURCH OF St. Magyar's. Finally, the last problem eliminated. The Americans were gone. Fitting that it would all end here at this sacred place, where the special ones formerly gathered. Their numbers had been small and closely held, each bound by a common purpose, their fate sealed by a secret French decree issued April 12, 1798. How ironic, he'd often thought. After centuries of fighting it wasn't the Turks, nor any corsair or Muslim enemy, but the French who defeated them. And not by violence nor invasion. Simply through the stroke of a pen. An edict issued to Napoleon, as the general in command of the army of the East, that he was to *take possession of the island of Malta for which purpose he will immediately proceed against it with all the naval and military forces under his command.*

And it had been easy.

Barely a fight.

Napoleon dispatched his orders and claimed the island for France. And though only a general at the time, he had his sights set on bigger things. Eighteen months after taking Malta he would be proclaimed first consul of France, in total command of the nation. Twelve years of nearly constant war followed. Napoleon wanted an empire. Like Alexander, Genghis Khan, Charlemagne, and Constantine before him. He also wanted control over that empire and knew that one tool could be used with absolute effectiveness.

Religion.

How better to keep the masses in line than through a fear for their immortal soul. It was self-working, self-regulating, and required little more than consistency to maintain itself. Occasionally, some displays of force were required—the Crusades and Inquisition two notable examples— but, by and large, religion sustained itself. In fact, if dished out correctly, the people would crave its effects like a drug. Demanding more and more.

Napoleon came to Malta to find the *Nostra Trinità,* thinking it might supply him the means to either control or eliminate the Roman Catholic Church. At the time it was the largest, most organized, most entrenched religion in the world. He'd learned how the Knights of Malta had always been shown great deference and privilege. How they skillfully escaped per- secution and elimination, surviving for centuries.

They had to have had some help.

But ultimately Napoleon was defeated and banished to St. Helena. Mussolini tried the same bullying tactics, and died a violent death. Now, finally, after over two hundred years, the Trinity had been found.

He stared at the reliquary.

Then turned to his brother and said, "We did it."

KASTOR SMILED. "YES, WE DID."

And he embraced Pollux for the first time in a long while.

A feeling of triumph hovered between them.

They stood inside the inner chapel, safe within a thick layer of rock, protected by time and the ages. The knight who'd brought the tools stood guard outside, but he'd just informed them that Malone had driven away and that they were now alone.

"You're to be pope," Pollux said, smiling. "We now have everything to make that happen."

Kastor stared at the reliquary, still perched on the altar. They'd not opened it, as yet.

"And the *Secreti?*" he asked Pollux.

"I said nothing with Malone here, but we have them under control. I told you I could deal with them. I've been told that their leaders have been identified and are now in our custody back in Italy. We were fairly sure of the traitors within our ranks. They're being held at the palazzi in Rome, on the knights' sovereign territory, subject to our jurisdiction. I'll deal with them. They are no longer a concern for you."

He was glad to hear that.

Pollux always took care of things. He'd been so glad to hear his brother's voice on the call earlier in the car with Chatterjee, assuring him that all was going well in Italy. He'd been able to stay brave in that cavern when Chatterjee died knowing that Pollux had his back.

He reached into his pocket and found the flash drive. "This is a gold mine. I've looked it over. There's more than enough here to extort the key cardinals. I can make them do whatever I want. Spagna did a good job. It was almost like he knew what we had planned."

"Spagna was an opportunist. I realized that from the first moment he and I spoke. But he told me nothing of any secret investigation. I suspect he was planning on shutting me out and making a deal only with you, thinking us enemies."

He motioned with the drive. "It's protected. The bastard used KASTOR I as the password."

"Nobody ever said Spagna was stupid. He had good instincts."

But not good enough. They'd done an excellent job faking a sibling rivalry. The entire internal attack on the knights and the forcing of the grand master from office had simply been part of that ruse.

"Was it the *Secreti* who killed Chatterjee and Spagna?" he asked.

Pollux nodded. "No doubt. But there's nothing to indicate that they knew anything about that flash drive. The ones we have in custody have been questioned but, so far, they've admitted nothing."

Which made sense. No attempt to retrieve the drive had happened in that grotto. They'd simply shot Chatterjee and left.

"Why didn't they shoot me?"

"You're their patron. A cardinal of the church. They abided by their oath to not harm a Christian. Chatterjee was a different matter. I'm not entirely sure of their plan at this point, but I'll find out while the conclave happens." Pollux stepped closer to the reliquary. "It's time."

"Open it."

Pollux found a knife in his pocket and worked the wax at one end of the glass cylinder, freeing the end cap and allowing the first exposure of fresh air to rush across the parchments. He then reached inside and slowly extracted the three rolls, laying them gently on the altar.

Kastor reached for one and slowly unrolled it. The parchment crackled, but the fibers held strong. The *Pie Postulatio Voluntatis*. The Most Pious Request. The papal bull from 1113 that recognized the Hospitallers' independence and sovereignty. He'd seen the other original housed in the Vatican archives.

Pollux unraveled a second parchment.

The *Ad Providam*. From 1312, when Pope Clement V handed over all of the Templars' property to the Hospitallers. He'd seen that other original, too.

They both stared at the final parchment, which was a little longer than the others, and thicker.

"It has to be," he said.

"It's two sheets rolled together," Pollux said, lifting the parchment and unrolling.

Faded black ink in tight lines, with narrow margins, filled the top sheet, which measured about forty-five centimeters long and a little less than that wide.

"It's Latin," Pollux said.

He'd already noticed. Latin had been Constantine's main language, so much that he'd required Greek translators in order to communicate with many parts of his empire. This document being drafted in Latin was a good sign toward authenticity, as were the parchment and ink, which would surely survive scientific scrutiny and be dated to the 4th century. But it was the signatures at the bottom of the second sheet that would prove the point. He counted the names, signed one after the other.

Seventy-three.

Some he recognized from historical reading.

Eustathius of Antioch. Paphnutius of Thebes. Potamon of Heraclea.

Paul of Neocaesarea. Nicholas of Myra. Macarius of Jerusalem. Aristaces of Armenia. Leontius of Caesarea. Jacob of Nisibis. Hypatius of Gangra. Protogenes of Sardica. Melitius of Sebastopolis. Achillius of Larissa. Spyridon of Trimythous. John, bishop of Persia and India. Marcus of Calabria. Caecilian of Carthage. Hosius of Córdoba. Nicasius from Gaul. Domnus from the province of the Danube.

Then there was Eusebius of Caesarea, the purported first church historian, who provided the only written account of what happened at Nicaea.

But the mark at the bottom cinched the deal.

Five rows. Five words.

The letters in the Latin alphabet.

A palindrome.

SATOR
AREPO
TENET
OPERA
ROTAS

The sign of Constantine.

"The emperor and the bishops all signed it," he said. "It's exactly as it should be."

"Yes, it is, brother."

And at the top of the first sheet were the two most important words.

Constitutum Constantini.

CHAPTER
FIFTY-FIVE

POLLUX STARED AT THE PARCHMENTS.

Everything pointed to their authenticity. Including where they'd been found. Here, inside the sacred chapel, at the end of a trail created by the *Secreti*.

"There's no time right now to study this," he said. "We can deal with that between now and this afternoon. I'll photograph and translate it myself and have an English and Italian version provided to you before you head into the Sistine Chapel." He allowed the parchment to recede back into a roll. "You'll take the original in with you."

"It'll be good to have it," Kastor said. "Cardinals have a natural affinity for the past. But the flash drive. That's what will win the day."

"It is that good?"

Kastor nodded. "Even better."

They'd planned so carefully. Years in the making, it all started when the pope fired Kastor from his post as prefect of the Apostolic Signatura. Where Kastor had seen that as a rebuke, a setback, possibly even the end, Pollux had realized the possibilities and insisted that Kastor seek out the position of patron of the Sovereign Military Order of Malta. Kastor, being Kastor, had thought the idea insane.

Until he explained.

Kastor never had been able to see the grand picture. Time had been a friend Pollux had willingly embraced, but never surrendered to, always being able to restrain his impatience. Kastor was a different story.

The elimination of the grand master had been a necessity. No way they could have enjoyed any freedom of movement with that man in charge. Too many of the order's officers were loyal to him.

Better to just eliminate the problem.

In any other situation a bullet would have solved things with haste. But killing the leader of 13,000 knights, 25,000 employees, and 80,000 volunteers would have drawn far too much attention. Shame had seemed a better weapon. Especially once the careless distribution of condoms had been discovered. It happened in Myanmar. Thousands were handed out by one of the knights' charitable arms. How it happened no one knew, since the church banned the use of contraception in any form. The program was stopped but Kastor, as patron, the pope's emissary to the Hospitallers, conducted an investigation and laid the blame at the top, forcing the grand master to resign.

Then out of nowhere the pope died.

Like a godsend.

In the chaos it had been easy to secure Pollux's temporary appointment as lieutenant ad interim. Many of the order's officers had been wanting to appease Kastor, fearing his growing influence. It helped that the late pope had stayed out of the fight and allowed Kastor to handle things, perhaps hoping for another misstep, but things had played out perfectly. Added to the charade was their supposed sibling rivalry and personal dislike, which comforted those knights who had supported the disgraced grand master. After that, Pollux's unassuming mask had misled everyone, Cotton Malone and Stephanie Nelle the latest to fall for his performance. "He was there only temporarily." "Until a new pope was chosen." "He had no interest in being grand master."

All true.

Only the Entity had seen through things.

"Spagna never told me about having that level of incriminating information," Pollux said.

"You sent me here," Kastor said. "I came and met that man Chatterjee at the Madliena Tower, exactly as you told me to do. He took me straight to Spagna, who was anxious to make a deal. You knew nothing of that?"

He shook his head. "Spagna was only supposed to make a deal with you to find the Trinity. That was what he and I agreed upon. I told him you knew things that no one else did."

Which was true.

But when he'd spoken to Kastor earlier by phone and told him about what had happened at Como and in Rome, he learned for the first time about the flash drive. Something Spagna had held close. His men were already on the way to that clockmaker's shop, so he'd told them to flush the targets out on the water where Chatterjee could be eliminated. But he'd specifically told them not to take the drive. He knew Kastor, being the thief that he was, would do that for them and bring it straight to him.

Which was exactly what had happened.

"It's time for you to head to Rome," he said.

"And the Americans?"

He shrugged. "Malone seemed perfectly satisfied. I dealt directly with him and his superior. They were of great assistance, and now they're done. Nothing draws them back our way. It's just you and me now."

Exactly the way he wanted it. Ending up here, alone and underground, in a controlled environment was another fortuitous occurrence. This was the perfect place to end one part and begin another.

But first—

"Did you bring an overnight bag?"

Kastor nodded. "It's at the rectory in Mdina. I'll pick it up on the way to the airport. I have a private plane waiting to take me back to Rome. A favor from a friend."

Good to know.

He glanced at his watch. 5:40 A.M.

Less than five hours left to get back to Italy.

"My aide has prepared my belongings," Kastor said. "Clothes, toiletries, papers, everything needed for the conclave. He texted me earlier to say it's all at the Domus Sanctae Marthae, in my room. I'll go straight there from the airport."

"I'll head to the Palazzo di Malta and deal with the *Secreti*. They've caused enough trouble. I'll also translate the parchments."

"We need the *Secreti* gone."

"They will be. You just concentrate on the conclave and achieving the ultimate goal. Nothing matters unless you become pope."

Pollux slipped the parchments back into the reliquary and replaced the end cap. That seemed the safest place for them. Earlier, when the knight arrived with the keys and tools, he'd also had the man bring one other item.

A short length of thin rope.

About a meter long.

Which he'd slipped into his pocket.

"Let's get the tools and go," he said.

Kastor headed for the shovels. Pollux used the moment to find the rope and secure both ends within his clenched fists.

"I'm still puzzled why the *Secreti* did not kill me in that cavern," Kastor said.

He advanced and, as his brother crouched to retrieve the shovels, he draped the taut rope over Kastor's head, looping it tight, stretching his arms outward and cutting off the windpipe. Kastor reached up with both hands and tried to free the stranglehold, but he tightened it even more. Kastor's legs began to flail. Arms came up behind his head, trying to grab his attacker. Pollux angled back, out of reach, but he kept the rope firmly in place, pulling it ever tighter. Kastor gagged, struggling to breathe. His hands groped for the garrote, the grip weakening, the choking becoming more intense.

Pollux had long wondered what this moment would feel like.

For so many years he'd languished in the shadow of his arrogant twin. Many knew the name Kastor Gallo, but almost no one, outside of the Hospitallers, knew of Pollux Gallo. His brother had chosen the priesthood and risen to a level of respect and authority. Then he'd thrown it all away with reckless nonsense. All that he could have accomplished tossed to the wind so he could simply run his mouth. He'd tried to tell him to keep quiet but Kastor, being Kastor, chose his own path.

Now Pollux had finally done the same thing.

Chosen.

All movement stopped.

He kept the rope in place a few more seconds to be sure, then relaxed his grip. Kastor's body went limp, the arms draped at the side, the legs rolled outward, the neck no longer supporting the head. He unwrapped the rope and allowed his brother to fold to the floor.

"They didn't kill you," he whispered, "because I wanted to."

Interesting that for all his smarts, his brother never even imagined that he was being manipulated. Probably because he thought himself superior, the dominant one in their sibling relationship. Their entire life it had always been Kastor and Pollux. Never the other way around.

But no more.

Pollux Gallo just died.

Kastor Gallo would be reborn.

CHAPTER FIFTY-SIX

COTTON DROVE MINDLESSLY, HIS WORLD SHRUNK TO A RIBBON OF AS-phalt and the occasional headlight of an approaching car. Dawn was not far away, but some sleep would be welcome. Given the late hour, he'd deci-ded to find a hotel room and head home in the afternoon. The past couple of days had been interesting, to say the least, and he was a hundred thousand euros richer, but, contrary to what he might have led James Grant to think, it had never been about money.

Not that he had anything against money.

Federal agents weren't the best-compensated of public servants. About sixty-five thousand a year at the end of his time with the Justice Depart-ment. But no one worked that job for the pay. You worked it because it had to be done. Because you chose to do it. Because you were good at it. No glory, as few ever knew what you did. Which came in handy at screwup time. Nope. The satisfaction came from simply getting the job done.

He rounded a sharp curve in the highway and kept heading south, a swath of black landscape on one side and the Med on the other. Thoughts rummaged through his orderly mind, trying to seek a permanent residence. During his career at Justice he'd learned that the worst picture was al-ways what the brain fabricated. Never mind reality. A fiction could seem far more immediate. So he'd come to rely on his subconscious to know if something was out of order, didn't belong.

And something was out of place here.

But it wasn't his problem.

He'd done what Stephanie wanted and everything to be found was back in the hands of the Knights of Malta and the Catholic Church. The brothers Gallo and the Vatican powers that be would now sort it out. The cardinal would head for the conclave and do what cardinals did, and Pollux Gallo would dissolve back into his cloistered world. And the *Secreti*? Who knew? Did they even exist? If so, were they still a threat? Regardless, they were the problem of the authorities in Italy and Malta, where all of the crimes had occurred.

So he told himself to let it go.

He kept driving, paralleling the north shore. He'd visited Malta a few times and loved the island. Always he'd stayed outside of Valletta in the suburb of St. Julian's, at the Dragonara. Spacious rooms, good food, balconies that overlooked the Med. A lovely upscale seaside resort with all of the amenities, which he'd never had a chance to enjoy. But maybe he'd remedy that before he left later today, depending on the flight schedules. A few minutes by the pool. That'd be different.

He slowed and navigated through the narrow streets of St. Julian's, arriving at the hotel a little before 6:00 A.M. He valet-parked the car and headed for the front desk, where he was pleased to learn a room was available.

"Did you see the explosion?" the clerk asked. "Quite the excitement tonight."

That was true, but he was sure this guy had no idea how exciting his past few hours had been. So he asked, "What do you mean?"

"Big explosion out on the water a couple of hours ago. The boat burned for half an hour before sinking. We don't see that here often."

"Any idea what happened?"

The clerk shook his head. "I'm sure the morning *Independent* will let us know."

He accepted the room key and drifted from the front desk. Before going to bed he needed to make a report. He found his phone, connected to Stephanie, and explained what had happened at the cathedral and the chapel.

She told him, "Luke took down a yacht outside the Valletta harbor. He drove his boat right into it. Four men are dead. Luke's in custody. The harbor police are holding him. Unfortunately, none of the bodies carried any identification, but we're working on that now through fingerprints. And there's more."

He was listening.

"Luke says Laura Price switched teams and was working with the Entity. She was ready to take a rifle shot when you and the Gallo brothers exited the cathedral, a shot that Spagna himself arranged. The *Secreti* interrupted, killing her and the temporary head of the Entity, who'd come to Malta to oversee the hit."

"Who was the target? Me or the cardinal?"

"Neither one."

And there it was.

One of those wandering thoughts just found a home. "The Entity was taking out Pollux Gallo?"

"That's right. Which raises a whole host of questions."

More thoughts dropped into place. The subterfuge and organized attack at the Hospitaller archive by the so-called *Secreti*. The sudden appearance of the real Pollux Gallo. His gracious cooperation. The lack of any outside interference at the obelisk, though the *Secreti* had been on the move at Lake Como and in that villa. Then the curious lack of concern at St. Magyar's chapel. Isolated and out in the middle of nowhere, with plenty of vulnerabilities, Pollux Gallo had seemed totally at ease.

Why would a mere lieutenant ad interim of a benign charitable organization be a greater threat than a cardinal who had, at least on paper, a chance to be pope?

"Where is Luke now?" he asked.

"In Valletta. I'm dealing with it."

"Get him out." He told her the chapel's name and where St. Magyar's was located, indicating that the curator at the co-cathedral could provide exact directions. "When he's free, send Luke my way."

"What are you going to do?"

"Head back there. I may have misjudged the wrong Gallo."

CHAPTER
FIFTY-SEVEN

POLLUX WAITED FOR HIS MEN FROM OUTSIDE TO MAKE THEIR WAY
through the outer chapel and into the inner sanctuary, their movements
calculated but quick. He'd delayed a few minutes before telling them to
enter.

A little time alone with his departed brother seemed in order.

Their relationship had always been an illusion. Kastor had thought
himself the better of the two, superior, a touch above. It had been that
way their entire lives, even more so after their parents died and they moved
to the orphanage. Kastor the talker, thinker, scholar—while he was the
athlete and soldier. He doubted anyone at that orphanage even remembered he existed. But Kastor? No one would forget him. They couldn't.
He made a lasting impression, sucking every drop of oxygen from every
room he ever entered.

But none of that would have been possible without his help.

When Kastor had first come and said he wanted to be pope, Pollux
had thought the idea ridiculous. Especially considering the mess made of
his ecclesiastical career. Sure, there were people who agreed with him in
their heart, but none were going to openly challenge the pope. He'd re-
viewed the dirt Kastor had amassed on some of the cardinals. Not bad.
There was some clearly incriminating material. But not near enough to
change a conclave. And with Kastor's loss of position and access, the

prospects of acquiring more information seemed remote. That's when Kastor focused on the *Nostra Trinità*.

Thinking it might be enough.

He, too, had been intrigued by the Trinity, especially the *Constitutum Constantini,* which had certainly proved useful in centuries past. Kastor had discovered quite a bit of useful information from the Vatican archives. He'd supplemented that with annals the knights had long kept under lock and key. Together they'd made progress. The call from the greedy Italian at Lake Como had been one of those fortuitous events that sometimes made one think that there actually might be a God directing things in some sort of divine plan. He'd known for some time the British had information on Mussolini and the Trinity. There'd just not been anything to bargain with. So he'd headed to Como. Which had been fruitful since it led to Sir James Grant, which had sent him to the obelisk, then on to the cathedral in Valletta, and finally to here.

All had dropped right into place.

And while the pope's body had lain on view inside St Peter's Basilica and hundreds of thousands filed by, Spagna had appeared at the Palazzo di Malta with an intriguing offer.

A way to make Kastor pope.

The Lord's Own had become aware of Kastor's private investigations and his interest in the Trinity. But Spagna was several steps ahead, though he'd refused to share the details. Cardinals had long been bribed and coerced. Nothing new there. Before the 20th century the college had been small enough that it was easy to alter its course with just a few moves. Modern conclaves were different. 100 to 150 cardinals participated, which added mathematical challenges. But cardinals were men and men were flawed. So while the pope was buried beneath St. Peter's, he and Spagna had schemed. It had been Spagna who insisted Kastor be sent to Malta. He wanted to make a deal face-to-face, and he wanted Kastor out of Rome so he could not do anything stupid to ruin things.

And he'd made that happen.

Then, once the greedy Italian at Como had contacted the knights and wanted to sell the letters, a path opened to the Trinity. So he'd improvised and used the opportunity to finally bring the Brits to the table by acquiring the Churchill letters. James Grant had been easy to manipulate.

The Americans, too. But Kastor the easiest of them all. *Whoever exalts himself will be humbled, and whoever humbles himself will be exalted.*

The Bible was right.

Kastor never learned humility.

Neither had Spagna, which was why he had to die, along with his minion Chatterjee and Roy, his second in command. Spagna wanted the *Constitutum Constantini* destroyed. The Entity considered it a direct threat to the church, one that should be eliminated. Whether it was destroyed or not mattered little to him. But that flash drive.

It mattered the most.

So he'd allowed Spagna to play his hand. The fool had apparently wanted to be the pope-maker. And what better way than by providing a cardinal, with little to no moral structure, the ammunition needed to blackmail his way to the papacy. One who'd owe him big time.

What better way, indeed.

The only unexpected occurrence had been the Americans. But Spagna had assured him he had them under control.

He smiled at the dead spy's naïveté.

Sadly, the Lord's Own had never realized that the greatest danger he faced would come from within. Pollux's men had taken out Spagna, Chatterjee, Laura Price, and John Roy with each death blamed on the *Secreti*.

Which, of course, no longer existed.

It had all been a ruse. His creation.

"What a fool you were," he whispered to his brother.

Then he pocketed the flash drive, lifting it off the hard earth where it had fallen from Kastor's grip. He supposed he should feel some regret, but he harbored not a speck of remorse. Unlike the knight at the villa by Como. That death he'd regretted. Killing a fellow Christian had always been forbidden for the Hospitallers. It was part of their oath to protect Christians. But the murder had been unavoidable. He could not allow Malone to take that man into custody. Everything would have been placed in peril.

And killing Kastor?

He was a lot of things, but a Christian his brother was not. Just an opportunist who used the church to further his own ambitions.

Two men entered the inner chapel. One was the man who'd escorted

Malone from Rome to Rapallo, the other the man who'd impersonated him once Malone arrived and tried to eliminate the ex-agent at the archives. That had not turned out according to plan. He'd only made the attempt because James Grant had insisted. But once the effort failed, he'd adapted and decided to personally intervene, working the Americans himself. It had also allowed him to be on the inside and learn what Spagna and Stephanie Nelle were doing.

Just another of the many differences between him and Kastor. He possessed an ability to disregard what was not working and immediately change to something that would. It had been easy to ingratiate himself with both the British and the Americans. Easy to enlist their help to solve the obelisk and the puzzle at the cathedral.

The problems had come from Spagna.

A true maverick.

Impossible to control.

But not anymore.

He slipped the flash drive into his pocket.

"Grab him," he told his two men.

They grasped Kastor's ankles and wrists, lifting the body and following him deeper into the inner chapel. Another oak door waited at the end of a short apse. He opened its iron latch and switched on another series of lights. A spiral staircase led down, and he followed the corkscrewed path deeper into the earth. His two men, with Kastor, followed him down. His brother's bulk made the going slow.

At the bottom he navigated another corridor hewn from the rock to a small chamber. A doorway led out on the far side. The entire underground network of alcoves and corridors had been fashioned sometime in the 17th century. Most had served as gunpowder and ammunition depots. The hole in the ground before him had been dug long ago, too. About three meters wide, five meters deep, its walls bell-shaped, tapering outward the farther down they stretched.

A *guva*.

He motioned and they laid Kastor down on the parched ground. His men knew exactly what to do. All six of his trusted associates were now on Malta, three here for the past few days on the boat offshore, the other three standing ready at Fort St. Angelo, waiting for his call, which he'd made from the cathedral once Malone had solved the riddle. There was no way he could accomplish anything alone. That was why the *Secreti* had been reactivated. Of course it was all mainly for appearance's sake, but he'd bound them all together with the ring and a promise of good things to come.

His two men undressed Kastor.

One reason strangulation had been chosen was the preservation of the clothing. He needed it all intact.

"I'll help finish this," he said, then motioned to one of his acolytes. "Get the shovels and rope."

The man left while he and the other finished removing Kastor's clothes. His brother's body was not nearly as fit as his own, but the size and shape were reasonably similar. He carefully folded the clothes and set them to the side, along with the shoes.

The other man returned.

To the right of the *guva* an oak post protruded from the ground. To it, one of his men tied the end of the thick hemp rope they'd brought in earlier. There had to be a way in and out of the pit, and a rope was the most practical choice, the post having been there for centuries. The coil was thrown into the black yawn. He nodded and his men tossed the shovels down then used the rope to descend into the *guva*. Burying his brother at the bottom of the pit seemed the perfect place as no one was allowed inside St. Magyar's without express permission of the grand master. Since there wasn't one at the moment, control of this locale fell to him as temporary head of command. But even after a new leader was chosen, no one would venture into this *guva*.

There'd be no reason.

And by then all traces of this night would be gone.

"Bury him deep," he called out.

He listened as they dug.

This was not just the closing of a chapter in his life. More like an entire part. Nothing would be the same after tonight. But he was ready. The Hospitallers had provided him the perfect refuge. He'd managed to learn things, build relationships, establish loyalties, all in anticipation of what was about to happen. Two days ago he'd been unsure if any of this was possible, but now he was much more confident.

His men stopped digging.

They both climbed back up using the rope. They were about to toss Kastor into the *guva* when he recalled something. He found his phone and snapped a picture of his brother's face and hair.

Then he removed the ring from the right hand.

Each newly elected cardinal was presented with a gold ring by the pope. Kissing that ring was a sign of respect.

He slipped it onto his own finger.

Then nodded.

And they dropped Kastor's naked body over the edge, the corpse finding the bottom with a thud.

His men climbed back down to finish the burial.

Not the end his brother imagined. Surely Kastor had thought his mortal remains would rest forever beneath St. Peter's along with so many other popes.

Not going to happen, he mouthed.

Or at least, not exactly.

CHAPTER FIFTY-EIGHT

LUKE SAT IN THE HOLDING CELL.

Familiar territory.

How many had he graced over the years?

His clothes were still wet from his second dip in the Med. His boat had sunk the yacht, killing all the men aboard. The harbor patrol had responded to the explosion and fished the bodies and him from the water, though he'd tried to avoid them in the dark.

Damn night-vision goggles.

It would have been so much easier to just swim back to shore unnoticed. The locals were rarely helpful. Most times they were a giant pain in the ass. And this time was no exception. He'd deflected all of their questions, practicing the ol' Sergeant Schultz of *I see nothing, hear nothing, know nothing.* He'd loved *Hogan's Heroes.* The only thing he had said was United States Justice Department and Stephanie Nelle, coupled with a request to make a call.

Which they'd allowed.

He'd explained his current dilemma to Stephanie, keeping his story short, and she'd told him to sit tight.

No problem there.

But over an hour had passed since then in silence.

Which had given him time to think.

The steel door beyond the cell clattered open and a man entered the holding area. He recognized the face from the safe house. Kevin Hahn, head of Maltese security, and he did not look happy.

"I've spoken with Ms. Nelle," Hahn said. "She told me about what happened with Laura. We found her body, and that of the Entity's second in command, just where you said." He pointed. "You killed four men, Mr. Daniels. This isn't the United States. Murders are rare here. Yet we've had seven in the past twelve hours."

He stood and faced the idiot through the bars. He wasn't in the mood for lectures. Like Malone taught him. *Never take crap from the locals.* "I'm an agent for the United States government, on assignment, doing my job. Now get me out of here."

"You're a pain in the ass."

"I've been called worse."

Over the past hour a lot had raced through his mind. Especially what Laura had told him when they first talked outside the *guva.* When he'd asked who'd told her he was on the island.

My boss. He gave me an order. I do what he tells me.

"How did you know I was headed into trouble?"

"Same answer. My boss told me."

"How did you know that I'd been sent here?" he asked Hahn.

"Who says I did?"

"Your dead agent. What were you doing with Spagna at that safe house?"

"You don't really expect me to answer either question."

"Actually, I do."

"We need to go."

"That's not an answer."

"It's all you're going to get."

But he didn't need one. He'd already concluded that there was one constant across his entire encounter with Laura Price and that was this man, her boss. He was actually planning on looking this roly-poly up just as soon as he was sprung. Stephanie had just saved him the trouble.

"You were working with Spagna," he said.

And he suddenly saw regret in the man's eyes.

"I made a mistake. There's more going on here than I realized." Hahn paused. "Much more. Spagna asked for help. He made a good case, so I went along."

"Apparently Spagna and you underestimated the opposition. Whoever the opposition is."

"We're still working to identify the men from the boat."

"Laura and the guy from the Vatican said they were *Secreti*."

"That would be amazing, if true. That group was disbanded two centuries ago."

"They both seemed real sure that it was still around. And some of them tried to toss me through a window."

"Your Ms. Nelle was sparse on information when she called to tell me about you. Care to tell me what's going on?"

"I know about as much as you do."

Which wasn't far from the truth. But if Stephanie had stayed silent, so would he.

"She asked me to secure your release," Hahn said. "I've done that."

"I appreciate it. I also need a car."

"That can be arranged. Where are you headed?"

This guy was a bit of a Nosy Nellie, as his mother liked to say. So he gave him the standard reply.

"To do my job."

POLLUX STEPPED OUTSIDE INTO THE NIGHT. HE AND HIS MEN HAD come back to ground level to retrieve what they needed to finish. The clock was now ticking and there was a lot to be done.

Thankfully, he was ready.

He heard the buzz of a phone and one of his men drifted away and answered the call. He watched as the conversation ensued, then ended.

"We've just learned there's a problem. Our boat offshore was attacked and sunk. All of the brothers are dead."

He kept the shock to himself and calmly asked, "How?"

"The American, Daniels. He escaped during the kill on Laura Price and Bishop Roy and found his way to our boat."

Disturbing news, no doubt. But not game changing. And there it was again. That ability to shift directions at a moment's notice. To turn a problem into an opportunity. "Where is Daniels now?"

"In custody."

Perfect.

His personal motto came from the Book of James. *And let steadfastness have its full effect, that you may be perfect and complete, lacking in nothing.*

His life had been a series of hurdles. He'd dutifully served in the military, then was hired by the Hospitallers to work abroad in their medical missions. He eventually professed his allegiance and took the oaths of poverty, chastity, and obedience. Then he'd languished in unimportant jobs. Playing second to one knight after another. He eventually rose to grand commander, charged with spreading the faith, supervising priories, and compiling reports to the Holy See, becoming one of the order's top four officers.

Then came Kastor's chaos.

And he was made temporary head.

Time for another promotion.

"We keep going. As planned."

He headed back inside, then down to the *guva* chamber. His men followed, one carrying a folding chair and a duffel bag. He passed the hole in the ground and exited from the second door into another corridor that led to the next chamber. He'd chosen this spot for not only its privacy but also its lighting, which was much brighter.

"Set the chair up there," he said pointing. Then he pointed at the other brother. "Keep a watch outside. Though I doubt we'll be disturbed."

The man left.

He faced the remaining brother.

"Shall we start?"

COTTON ROUNDED A CURVE AND REALIZED THAT THE CHAPEL WAS not far ahead. His senses were on full alert. The situation had shifted from curious to serious. One or both Gallos could be in trouble.

He doused the headlights and stopped on the side of the road.

In the distance he saw the chapel on the ridge. A car remained parked out front. Were the two brothers still there?

How many times had he been in this exact situation?

Too many to count.

He thought of Cassiopeia. Where was she? Surely asleep, at home in France. He hadn't heard from her in a few days. Good thing, too. If she knew he was deep into a mess, she'd be on a plane headed his way. He didn't like placing her in danger, though she was more than capable of handling herself. She was an extraordinary woman who'd dropped into his life out of nowhere. Initially, neither of them had cared for the other, but time and circumstances had changed everything. What would she say now? *Figure it out. Finish it.* He smiled. Good advice.

He spotted a splash of light in the dark. The chapel's door had opened and a man stepped out into the night.

Alone.

He watched as the solitary figure stood for a moment, then eased away from the door, leaving it partially open. He waited to see if the figure was leaving. No. The car remained dark and still.

A guard?

Maybe.

He switched off the car's interior light, then eased open the door and slipped out, pocketing the key remote. The chapel was about three hundred yards away. He hustled in that direction, using the dark and a mass of low scrub and the few trees as cover. He approached from the western side and kept low, not catching sight of the man he knew was outside. It wasn't until he came close to the building that he spotted the figure about fifty yards away, back to him, surveying the valley that stretched to the south. A dull glow had begun to rise on the eastern horizon. Dawn was coming. He needed the guard distracted and had decided on the hike over that the car might prove the best mechanism. He pressed his body against the chapel wall and aimed the remote control back toward where he'd come from, hoping its range was sufficient.

Then he hesitated.

Pressing the button would set off the horn, accompanied by the head-lights flashing, and the element of surprise would be gone. He decided instead to be patient and glanced back again around the corner at the solitary figure. Darkness remained thick across the valley. The man casually turned to his right and moved farther away from the chapel, finding a cell phone and making a call. He crouched and used the shadows for cover, darting toward the open front door. He slipped in, keeping his eyes on the guard, who'd noticed nothing.

Inside was empty and quiet, the same lights from earlier still burning. He hustled toward the far apse and through the concealed panel, which also remained opened.

The inner chapel was likewise empty. This was as far as he'd gone earlier. The reliquary remained on the altar. He noticed chucks of red wax lying beside it and realized one end had been opened, but the parchments were still safe inside. He scanned the interior and noticed that the chapel extended farther into the limestone ridge. He followed its path and spotted another oak door, half open. Beyond, a spiral staircase wound down. He descended to a narrow, lit corridor. Immediately he was uncomfortable with the tight, enclosed space.

Not his favorite.

He sucked a deep breath and walked ahead to where he found a more spacious chamber with a black hole in the earthen floor. Everything was illuminated by honey-colored light, as thick and sickly sweet as the confined air around him. He glanced down into the hole and saw only blackness. A rope snaked a path from a wooden pillar embedded into the ground down into the void. He wondered how deep the thing was and its purpose.

He heard voices.

Coming from beyond a half-open door at the other end, about fifty feet away.

He crept toward the sound.

CHAPTER
FIFTY-NINE

POLLUX SAT IN THE METAL CHAIR.

His man found a pair of shears in the duffel bag and began to trim his hair. To help, he held up the image of Kastor, taken a few minutes ago on his cell phone, and they took care to make sure his new cut mimicked that look. He'd not worn his hair so short since his teenage years.

His man finished the trim and he admired the work on his phone screen, the camera switched to selfie mode. He nodded and a bowl was removed from the bag, which he filled with water from a jug. He handed over the cell phone, then lathered his chin with shaving cream. He found a razor and carefully began to shear the monk's beard away, again using the phone as a mirror. No nicks. No cuts. It had to be a clean shave. He focused on the sound of blade to whisker, keeping the strokes short and light. He also constantly rinsed the blade in the water so the metal remained moist. When he was finished, he grabbed a towel from the bag and swiped away the last remaining bits of lather.

His man nodded.

He agreed.

Not since they were teenagers had he looked so much like Kastor. They were born identical and remained identical until they left the orphanage. Nearly forty years had passed. Now they were identical again.

He stood, undressed, and donned his brother's clothes, shoes and underwear included. He found the flash drive in his old clothes, then cleaned out Kastor's pockets, retrieving a wallet and cell phone, but no passport. It must be with the overnight bag in Mdina. Then he slipped on a pair of eyeglasses, identical to what his brother had worn, only with the lenses clear.

Kastor Cardinal Gallo lived again.

He felt free, untethered, in rhythm, doing what God and nature had surely intended. He was also rested, healthy, and finally worry-free. Danger lurked, for sure. But he was fully immersed in the moment, each second precious, fulfilling, and ordained.

His time had come.

He motioned and his man emptied the bowl to the floor, replaced all of the supplies inside the bag, along with his clothes, then refolded the chair.

"We can go," he said.

COTTON HEARD THE WORDS.

We can go.

Pollux Gallo's voice.

No question.

He hadn't been able to get close enough to see what was happening, and precious little had been said. He retreated to the room with the open pit, intent on leaving through the other exit and heading back up to ground level. But as he approached the door he caught sight of another man in the narrow tunnel beyond, headed his way.

He was trapped.

Danger on both sides.

He could simply reveal himself, but something told him that was not the smart play. Not yet. There seemed only one choice. He stepped to the pit, grabbed hold of the rope, and eased himself over the edge. Hand over hand he descended and found the bottom, about fifteen feet down.

POLLUX REENTERED THE *GUVA* CHAMBER WITH HIS MINION.

His second acolyte joined them.

"All is quiet outside," the man reported. "I also loaded the reliquary and one of the shovels into the car."

The other rested against the wall where he'd asked it to be placed.

"What of our brothers who died on the boat?"

"I checked. Their bodies are with the authorities. They'll surely be identified soon."

He'd already considered that possibility. But any trail would lead to the Knights of Malta. Which was no longer a problem for him, since Pollux Gallo would not exist after tonight.

"We'll deal with that once it happens," he said. "There's little that can be done about the situation now."

"The jet the cardinal mentioned is waiting at the airport," one of his men told him.

Excellent. He'd head there and fly on to Rome. Kastor had already told him that an aide had delivered what would be needed in the way of personal belongings to the Domus Sanctae Marthae. His room was ready, simply waiting on an occupant. His first test would come with convincing that aide as to his authenticity, but he'd practiced being Kastor for a long time.

"Did you bring the laptop?" he asked.

The brother nodded and found the device in the duffel bag. He'd need it on the trip to Rome. He wanted to study, firsthand, the flash drive.

"And the other item?" he asked.

His man produced a Glock from the bag.

He accepted the weapon.

Everything had come down to this moment. Initially he'd intended on keeping his faux *Secreti* intact as a personal police force. Those men would come in handy, working outside the Entity, providing him with an immediate way to deal with problems.

And the concept was not without precedent.

In the 16th century Julian II maneuvered his way into the papacy, then safeguarded his hold against rival cardinals by raising his own armed regiment of 150 Swiss mercenaries. The best fighters in the world at that time, they'd served popes ever since as the Swiss Guard. But five of his eight men were dead. Recruiting more could prove problematic, and on reflection he'd decided they might not be necessary.

"Let us kneel," he said. "We should give thanks."

He laid the laptop and gun on the ground and dropped to his knees, as did his two brothers.

"Centuries ago the founding bishops of our faith proclaimed what we should believe. The great Council of Nicaea settled all debate as to what was holy and sacred, and the Emperor Constantine, in thanks, bestowed upon us a great gift. Tonight, through the grace of God, we have retrieved that sacred gift. It finally, once again, is safe in our hands. Let us give thanks by reaffirming that great Nicaean Creed.

"We believe in one God the Father Almighty, Maker of heaven and earth, and of all things visible and invisible. And in one Lord Jesus Christ, the only-begotten Son of God, begotten of the Father before all worlds, God of God, Light of Light, Very God of Very God, begotten, not made, being of one substance with the Father by whom all things were made.

"Who for us men, and for our salvation, came down from heaven, and was incarnate by the Holy Spirit of the Virgin Mary, and was made man, and was crucified also for us under Pontius Pilate. He suffered and was buried, and the third day he rose again according to the Scriptures, and ascended into heaven, and sitteth at the right hand of the Father. And he shall come again with glory to judge both the quick and the dead, whose kingdom shall have no end.

"And we believe in the Holy Spirit, the Lord and Giver of Life, who proceedeth from the Father and the Son, who with the Father and the Son together is worshiped and glorified, who spoke by the prophets. And we believe one holy catholic and apostolic Church. We acknowledge one baptism for the remission of sins. And we look for the resurrection of the dead, and the life of the world to come.

"Amen."

His men had repeated every word. He nodded and stood, the lust inside him breaking free of the decorum he'd always felt obliged to show.

He bent down and regripped the Glock.

Then fired twice.

One bullet pierced the forehead of each of the brothers, collapsing them instantly in death.

The trail had to be painted cold.

True, the cathedral curator remained, but the new Kastor Cardinal

Gallo would deal with him, nothing there to arouse any suspicion. Eventually, a letter would come, in his hand, writing as Pollux, explaining his resignation from the knights and his retreat from the world. He doubted anyone would miss either his men or Pollux Gallo.

Sad.

But true.

He laid the Glock down and dragged both bodies to the pit.

He crouched down and cleaned out their pockets, finding the key for the chapel's front door and the car outside.

Then he rolled each over the edge.

They would need to be buried, eliminating any trace of foul play. This place itself might prove problematic but, to his knowledge, only a handful of people within the knights knew of the secret panel, and the inner chapel was almost never visited. Kastor was buried deep in the ground, gone for the ages. These two corpses required a similar fate.

Which was why he'd had a shovel left behind.

He stepped over, grabbed it, then tossed it into the pit.

He had to return to Rome.

Thank goodness there was one final knight still around to clean up the mess.

Cotton heard Gallo's voice as he gave thanks, then said the Nicaean Creed. Two sharp barks signaled gunfire, followed by what sounded like dragging across parched ground. He'd already determined that the pit was bell-shaped, its walls flaring out the farther down they went, with the lower circumference much wider than the top. He'd also noticed that the pit's floor was not hard, like the ground above. Instead, it had the consistency of freshly turned earth.

He looked up.

An arm hung over the top edge.

He eased himself to one side using the pit's flanged shape to his advantage. A body fell down from above and smacked the ground.

Followed by another.

He recalled that the bottom had not been visible from above. Too much darkness. So he ventured a glance upward and saw not Pollux, but Kastor Gallo staring down, a gun in his right hand.

Revealing himself seemed like suicide. He'd just wait for the man to leave then use the rope and climb out.

Gallo vanished above.

He stared at the two corpses. Too much darkness existed to see their faces.

Something fell from above and embedded in the soft floor.

A shovel.

The rope began to head upward.

And disappeared.

The lights extinguished.

He stood in total blackness.

CHAPTER SIXTY

LUKE DROVE DOWN THE COASTAL HIGHWAY, SPEEDING NORTH toward a place called the Church of St. Magyar's. Once he was out of jail, he'd contacted Stephanie, who told him where Malone had gone. She'd contacted the cathedral curator, who'd provided directions. He'd declined Hahn's offer of assistance, deciding to keep the locals out of the loop. Better to hold everything close from this point forward, as there were too many unknowns in this free-for-all.

How many times had he sped down a black highway in the middle of the night? After dates. High school football games. Nights out with the guys. The terrain around him was nothing like the mountains of east Tennessee. Not much in the world compared to that sacred ground. He'd spent the first eighteen years of his life there and tried to go back whenever he could. Which wasn't all that often. Those hills were rampant with high tales. Lots of myths, legends, and ghosts. His father had loved to tell the stories.

Like Old Skinned Tom.

A charming, handsome man who won over nearly every girl he came across, one day he set his sights on a beautiful married gal named Eleanor. They began seeing each other in secret, frequenting the local lovers' lane. Of course, Eleanor's husband found out and skinned Tom alive. Everyone believed that Tom's bloody skeleton still roamed lovers' lane, clutching a hunting knife, waiting to catch a cheating couple so he could teach them a lesson. Which seemed incredibly unfair of him, given the circumstances of his own death.

The apparition even had a song.

Have you see the ghost of Skinned Tom?
Bloody red bones with the skin all gone.
Wouldn't it be chilly with no skin on.

That it would. He felt a little bare-skinned and exposed at the moment, too. Running on empty, but at full throttle.

He turned off the coastal highway and headed inland, following the directions Stephanie had provided into a darkened valley. Ridges rose in the distance on both sides with few lights. He kept going on the straight stretch of blacktop. Ahead, off the shoulder, among a scattered stand of short trees, he spotted a parked car.

One he recognized.

He brought his vehicle to a stop and saw that he was right. Same car he'd used earlier. The same one Malone had apparently taken from the cathedral. He doused the headlights, shut off the engine, and stepped out into the night.

Malone was here and seemed to have decided on a stealth approach. He decided to take the same option. He started off on foot down the road, keeping a watch out for vehicles in both directions. Cicadas chirped their earsplitting trill into the darkness. He was tired and could use some sleep, but he'd learned how to run on autopilot. He was actually good in that mode. Being barely thirty, a bit anxious, ambitious, and well trained certainly helped, too.

A couple of hundred yards away he saw the outline of a building up on a ridge and another car parked out front.

Had to be the chapel.

Its main door suddenly opened, revealing a splash of light and a person. The dark form walked to the car toting a bag and what looked like a folding chair, which was deposited inside. The form returned to the building's door and the lights extinguished, as if a switch had been thrown.

The car then drove off and did not head his way. Instead it turned in the opposite direction and disappeared down the highway, deeper into the valley, to the west.

His instincts smelled trouble.

He trotted to the building and approached the door. He tested the latch and discovered it was locked.

And no conventional lock.

Big. Heavy. Iron. Taking a friggin' skeleton key.

He tested the oak panels.

Thick and solid.

No way he could force it open, and there were no windows. He had only one choice. So he ran back to the car and fired up the engine. He sped up the incline to the ridge and focused the headlights on the front door. He came close and stopped, nestling the front bumper to the oak.

Stephanie had told them that this building had been around for centuries. Malone was noted for his effect on historic spots, especially World Heritage Sites. It looked like he was about to join the club. He pumped the accelerator and drove the front end into the door, splintering it inward.

That was easier than he'd thought it would be.

He backed the car away, then shut off the engine and climbed out. Beyond the doorway he saw more black. With his hand he examined the wall just inside and spotted a switch, which he flipped activating a few scattered lights that threw off long streams of radiance illuminating a bare chapel with a gritty stone floor.

His eyes began a brisk, energetic scan of the interior.

Not a sound broke the silence.

The floor stretched maybe fifty feet ahead. He noticed a clear path in the grit leading from the doorway to an altar, then beyond. He stepped in and followed the path, which led to the opposite side and a circular apse.

Where it stopped.

Abruptly.

At the wall.

Before him rose a stone half circle. Three panels, separated by moldings, limestone benches wrapping the semicircle along with a cornice at the top and a line of chiseled molding breaking the center. Had someone walked to here and sat on the bench? Possible. But not likely. The floor was relatively undisturbed except for the footpath to the main door.

He faced the curved wall and tapped it at places with his fist.

Solid.

Whatever there was to find had to be at the center panel. He traced the groove on either side with his fingertips.

Nothing unusual.

The cornice at the top was out of reach, the center molding possessed of no indentations. It was all one piece, carved from the stone. He sat on the bench and stared at the floor. Why not? He dropped to his knees and looked underneath. Nothing there, the stone bench supported by two corbels at either end.

Come on. This can't be that hard.

He studied the corbels and noticed that they were curvy, extending from the wall to the end of the bench, supporting its weight. A notch existed from the corbel's end to the stone wall. Maybe an inch. Not much more. He stuck his finger into the space on the right. Nothing. Then the left. And felt an indentation. Circular. With something in it. A button. He pushed. The entire panel shifted inward.

He stood, sucking in the whole Indiana Jones vibe.

He pushed the heavy panel, surprised at its balancing act. It took little effort to move a lot of rock. Blackness loomed beyond. He found another switch and activated more lights. A corridor led to another chapel, this one a bit creepy with a ton of statues and images. Like a visit to a stone Madame Tussauds. He noticed the altar, which had been desecrated with a hole in its lower center.

That seemed like Malone's signature.

So he kept going, finding another door that led to spiral steps, leading down. He descended to the bottom and saw another light switch, which he activated. More lights sprang to life. He followed a narrow corridor into a room with a hole in the floor.

Which he'd seen before.

In Valletta.

A *guva.*

What had Laura said?

They were once all over the island. Now only two remained.

Make that three.

He stepped over and gazed down into the blackness, the bottom not visible.

"About damn time," a voice said from below.

CHAPTER
SIXTY-ONE

POLLUX LEFT THE PWALES VALLEY. HE'D JUST KILLED THREE MEN. Add in the villa owner and James Grant, that made five murders. All regrettable, but necessary.

He'd made a call as soon as he left the chapel, using one of the phones he'd removed from the dead knights, telling the person on the other end to meet him at the Lippija Tower. It sat about ten minutes away from the chapel, a short, squat building from the 17th century, with two floors and a parapet roof facing Gnejna Bay on the northwest coast. He assumed the tower would be deserted at this hour and saw he was right as he drove close and switched off the car.

He reached over to the passenger seat and grabbed the laptop. It had been bought for him a few weeks ago and had sat dormant ever since, waiting. He could not bring his own laptop, or anything else, from his former life. Pollux Gallo would have left all that behind when he retreated from the world. There could be nothing that linked him with his own past. The transformation had to be complete in every way.

He slid the flash drive in and typed the password KASTOR I.

He opened the one file and began to read, closer at some parts, scanning others, but amazed at the wealth of incredibly damaging information. More than he could have ever imagined. For years he'd studied the cardinals, learning all of their pertinent biographical information. He'd even been privy to Kastor's private investigations and the bits and pieces that stumbled their way. But the information Spagna had amassed was so much more.

Kastor had been right.

It was a gold mine.

A car approached from behind, its headlights filling the rearview mirror. He had little time, but this matter had to be resolved before he left the island. He set the laptop aside and exited.

From the other vehicle, Kevin Hahn emerged and said, "Daniels is out of custody."

He waved off the concern. "The Americans should no longer be a problem."

"Except that Daniels killed four of our men."

"Which is a terrible tragedy. But that'll only lead to the knights, so we'll let them have that problem."

He and Hahn had been friends a long time. They'd met just out of their teens and served in the military together, then both joined the order. Hahn was not professed, but he was a knight. Over the years, it had been Hahn who'd kept him informed about all that happened on Malta. He was his eyes and ears on the ground, rising steadily to the position of head of Malta's internal security. When he'd formed the team that would make up his temporarily reconstituted *Secreti,* Hahn had been there from the start. Thanks to Hahn he'd become aware of the Americans on the island and all of what Spagna had been doing. With Hahn's help he'd learned of Laura Price's duplicity, her alignment with Spagna, and the attempt that would have been made on his life. Proverbs was right. *A friend loves at all times, and a brother is born for adversity.*

Hahn was more like a brother than Kastor had ever been.

"You look just like him," Hahn said.

And sounded like him, too. He'd been practicing for months. Not all that hard, as Kastor's pitch and tone were nearly identical to his own. Just a few variations, which he was concentrating on adjusting. The diction and syntax seemed the most difficult part. Everyone had their pet words, their own way of saying things, himself included. But he was no longer himself.

"Do you have any idea what Daniels might do?"

Hahn shook his head. "He told me little. He just left."

Surely Daniels would reconnect with Malone, who would report that the Trinity had been found and returned to the knights and the church, who would sort things out. Of course the incident with the boat would need resolution. Men were dead. But again, nothing led to Rome.

"What do you want me to do?" Hahn asked. "The Americans have asked for my help in identifying the men from the boat."

"Help them. It doesn't matter. Be cooperative. Let them investigate the boat and the four men. That will lead to the Knights of Malta, not to Kastor Gallo or you."

He could see that his friend agreed.

"Are you ready?" Hahn asked.

"I am." He reached out and shook Hahn's hand. "You've been a great help. But there's a problem at the chapel. Two of our brothers became greedy. They wanted more. I had to deal with them."

"I hate to hear that."

"They left me no choice. I need you to return there and bury them with Kastor. He's at the bottom of the *guva*, as are they. There's a rope and shovel there, too. Use them to clean things up. We can't risk anything being found. So far everything has gone perfectly and nothing leads back to the chapel. So let's finish this."

He knew his old comrade would not protest. Hahn was coming with him to the Vatican, eventually becoming the operational head of the Entity. Another reason why Danjel Spagna'd had to be eliminated. Having his man in charge of the world's oldest intelligence agency would be nothing but a plus. Though he would have preferred to do this alone, Proverbs again was instructional. *Iron sharpens iron, and one man sharpens another.*

"I'll get it done," Hahn said. "You go become pope."

"I have all of Spagna's information. It should be more than enough to convince the right votes."

He walked back to his car.

Pleased.

All that remained was to read the third part of the trinity.

Constantine's Gift.

CHAPTER
SIXTY-TWO

A new consciousness of personal human dignity has emerged across our empire. Men feel the infinite value and responsibility of a new life. But within their realm of imposed happiness a strange thing is happening. As naturally as they have rejected the former political structure, men have begun to seek a religion of a more personal and intimate nature.

It is admitted that when in recent times the appearance of our Savior Jesus Christ had become known to all men, there immediately made its appearance a new religion, not small, and not dwelling in some corner of the earth, but indestructible and unconquerable, because it has assistance directly from God. This religion, thus suddenly appearing at the time appointed by the inscrutable counsel of God, is the one that has been honored by all with the name of Christ.

It is true that religion and civilization advance together. But it is equally true that religious creeds and practices can often lag behind civilization. We find that situation at present with the lingering of the pagan gods and the emergence of a new Christian faith. We find a further example of this with the new Christian faith fighting within itself, so many varied views as to what should or should not be believed. So many different ideas as to who and what is God and who and what is our Savior.

Any religion must reflect the pure ideals of the society in which it exists. Its practices and sacrifices can only be as the general sentiment allows. No new religion can easily claim the soil where other gods have long been worshiped. To survive, a religion must have structure, rules, order, and, most important, consistency. The following mandates are offered as a means to protect that which we have created:

Always remember that an Angry vengeful God is preferable to a benign, loving entity. We must Proclaim that Obedience and compliance with God's directives is the only way to obtain eternal peace in heaven, while disobedience leads to everlasting suffering. The fear of that perpetual suffering should be used to keep the faithful under our control. The faithful can never forget that the only salvation from their fear comes from the Christian faith, its Doctrine and practices never open to question, their obedience absolute.

Sin is the mechanism whereby control will be enforced. For the Hebrew nation the Ten Commandments, which Moses first delivered, have long stood as their basic tenets. But we need more. A list of Sins should be created, a list that adapts with the times, each sin designed to instill fear. There must be a clear belief that a failure to obtain forgiveness of sin places the immortal soul in the gravest of danger, with forgiveness obtained only through the Christian faith. This concept should begin at birth with a belief that all men are born into the world with sin. Never will they dwell with God unless there is absolution for this original sin through the Christian faith.

Many of the prior religions fostered a belief that when one lifetime ends another begins, the cycle never ending. This spiritual immortality, this reincarnation, is surely comforting, but the Christian faith will offer only one physical life and One opportunity at eternal salvation. When that life ends the soul moves to either heaven or hell, both of which we must not only create but define.

Never can the failings of man be blamed on any lacking or deficiency in the Christian faith. Instead an adversary must be created. A diabolos, a spirit, a devil, who constantly poses challenges along the path to salvation. All of man's sins and shortcomings must be blamed on this devil, who is always present, always tempting, never relenting, with the only path to resistance coming from Christian doctrine.

No spiritual abilities can ever be tolerated. Those who profess visions or an ability to speak with God are a danger. As treason is punishable by death, heretical thinking and acts must likewise know the wrath of God. Heretics can never be tolerated, their deaths a righteous calling, a warning to others that actions and thoughts contrary to the Christian faith come with dire consequences. Killing in the name of God is not a sin. Defending the faith with the spilling of blood is a duty we must never abandon.

Religion expresses itself in terms of the knowledge of the world in which it exists. If that be defective then religion likewise is defective. Never be afraid to change. It is the only way to survive. But never be anxious to do so, either.

Sacred objects are those things that man must not use or touch because they belong only to God. Creating these, whether they be churches, places, people, words, or things, is essential to rooting our Christian faith. Keeping them sacred through rules and punishment is equally important.

Priests shall become a special class unto themselves. I am the natural choice to ultimately lead those priests, as religion is a vital part of politics. The first duty of the state is to stay right with God and keep God on good terms with the people. The priests' duty is to keep the people on good terms with me.

Above all, good bishops, the Essence of Christianity must be in loving God and following him in faith, but it must also include upholding the authority of the Priests and believing in Christian doctrine without question. On this objective we must unite as the conduct of public affairs will be considerably eased if we take this step. The state of your individual lives will likewise be altered. Each of you will become far more in many varied ways. That which once divided us seems now quite trifling and unworthy of such fierce contest. Let us rejoice in unity.

CHAPTER SIXTY-THREE

POLLUX STOPPED READING THE PARCHMENTS.

The Latin appeared on both pages in thin straight lines with minimal margins. The black ink was heavy, but mostly faded to gray thanks to seventeen centuries. He sat in the plush cabin of a private jet, flying north toward Rome. After leaving Kevin Hahn at the tower, he'd made it to the airport on Malta without incident, tossing the contents of the duffel bag away in three different dumpsters he'd passed along the way. The Glock was thrown into the ocean from a cliff. All of the evidence was now gone. He'd also stopped in Mdina and retrieved Kastor's overnight bag, including his Vatican passport. His mind was tired from months of worrying, scheming, and dreaming. But in a few hours he'd be inside the Sistine Chapel. And not as an obscure knight in a nine-hundred-year-old brotherhood. But as a *sanctae Romanae Ecclesiae cardinalis,* a cardinal of the Holy Roman Church.

For years he'd studied Latin and Greek, reading one text after another on Christianity and the Catholic Church, especially the time between its founding with Christ and the end of the third century. The formative years. Like when puberty shaped a child.

Then A.D. 325 came and everything changed.

Constantine the Great summoned the Christian bishops to Nicaea, bringing all of the players to one place for the first time, his terms simple.

Agree on a universal—a catholic—church, and the Crown would drape the new religion with great political advantage. Fail to do so and the persecutions would continue. Nobody knew for sure how many clerics heeded the call, but enough that they were able to forge a statement of their beliefs, one that to this day defined what it meant to be Catholic. They transformed the philosophy of a man who'd preached poverty, forgiveness, and nonviolence into a government ideology of power, one Constantine used for cohesiveness. Earlier, before sending his two acolytes to meet their God, Pollux had thought it appropriate that those ancient words—the famed Nicaean Creed—be uttered.

The history books loved to tell of how Constantine saw a vision in the sky, then won a great battle, crediting Christ with his victory. In gratitude, he supposedly converted and proclaimed Christianity as the official religion of the empire. But that was merely half right. Constantine only converted on his deathbed, though even that is open to debate. He spent his life hedging his bets, worshiping the old gods but using the new. The whole conversion story was but a way to make the new faith more acceptable in the eyes of the people. If it was good enough for the emperor, it was good enough for them. He did not create Christianity, but he did mold it in his image. And wisely, he never tried to defeat Christ, but he certainly wanted to define him.

And what Pollux had just read confirmed that conclusion.

Constantine wanted his own religion.

And why not?

Faith was the death of reason. Faith relied on blind allegiance, without thought, only an unquestioned belief. Irrationality seemed the nature of faith, and to institutionalize faith man created religion, which remained one of the oldest and strongest conspiracies ever formed. Look at what they fought about at Nicaea.

The nature of Christ.

The Old Testament was simple. God was singular and indivisible. That's what the Jews believed. The new religion had a trinity. Father, Son, Holy Spirit. Of course, that had been created by man as part of the new religion. But exactly what was Christ? Different from the Father since he'd been human? Or merely the same, immortal and eternal, despite being human? It all sounded so trivial, but the debate threatened to tear

Christianity apart. Even Constantine had thought the argument silly, *worthy of inexperienced children, not of priests and prelates and reasonable men.* He ended the division, proclaiming that Christ was *begotten, not made, being of one substance with the Father by whom all things were made.*

Religion had always been a tool. Its power came from capturing something dear, then offering a spiritual reality, with benefits, to all those who chose to follow. Didn't matter whether that was Christianity, Islam, Judaism, Hinduism, or even paganism. All of them created their own peculiar truths, then constantly misconstrued them to their advantage.

But all good things come to an end.

For the Catholic Church the end came in 1522 when Martin Luther translated the New Testament from Latin to German. For the first time the people could read God's word and they saw no mention of the church, indulgences, sins, cardinals, or popes. They could read the Gospel of Luke where it clearly said that *the kingdom of God is within you,* or Romans, which said *the spirit of God dwells in you,* both with no mention of any other place where God supposedly resided. Before Luther the scriptures were only for priests to read and the church to interpret, both providing a clear measure of control.

Exactly what Constantine had advised.

Priests shall become a special class unto themselves. I am the natural choice to ultimately lead those priests, as religion is a vital part of politics. The first duty of the state is to stay right with God and keep God on good terms with the people. The priests' duty is to keep the people on good terms with me.

Constantine wanted the bishops unified. He wanted his new religion to become a constant. Fitting, as his own name meant "steadfast." He realized that consistency bred confidence, and once the people acquired confidence they would unquestionably believe.

He made that clear at the end of his gift.

And indeed unto Abraham, who was a justified man, there was given by God a prophecy in regard to those who, in coming ages, should be justified in the same way as he. The prophecy was in the following words: And in you shall all the tribes of the earth be blessed. And again, He shall become a nation great and numerous; and in him shall all the nations of the earth be blessed.

What then should prevent those who are of Christ to practice one and the same mode of life, and have one and the same religion, as those divinely favored men of old? It is evident that the perfect religion committed to us by the teaching of Christ is a gift. But if the truth must be spoken, it should be spoken in one voice as the true religion. It is my hope that these directives will guide us all to that result.

The deal had been simple. Stay unified, follow his commands, and Christianity would flourish. Divide and disobey and imperial protection would end. Christians would find themselves back where they'd been before Nicaea. Ostracized and persecuted.

Not much of a choice.

In the beginning churches were started by planters, apostolic workers who moved from town to town, creating congregations. Each one of those became a religion unto itself, isolated and closely held. Eventually, elders emerged within those congregations, not special or set above the flock, merely serving within, chosen by seniority with no special powers or permanancy. But Constantine seemed to realize the political opportunities those elders presented. He saw an opportunity to cultivate an army of local supporters, men who did not wield a sword but instead could affect the hearts and minds of the people.

Smart.

Pollux knew his church history.

Constantine elevated the clergy. He granted them a fixed annual salary and exempted them from taxation. They were not required to serve in the army or perform any mandatory civil service. They truly became a *special class,* not subject to secular law or imperial courts. They dressed differently and groomed differently. They became the supposed guardians of orthodoxy, more powerful than local governors. A spiritual elite of holy men, supposedly vested with gifts and graces others did not possess. No surprise that so many men experienced a sudden call to the ministry.

Yet despite all of those privileges, the church languished for nearly five hundred years. After Constantine died his heirs made a mess of the empire. It split, the eastern portion becoming Byzantine, the western remaining Roman. Christianity likewise split. And though bishops were scattered across Europe, Africa, and Asia, the one in Rome began to assert himself over the western portion, rising above the others, claiming a lineage back to St. Peter and taking a pagan title. *Pontifex maximus.* Supreme pontiff.

By Christmas Day A.D. 800 the church was ready to expand.

It happened in Rome while the Emperor Charlemagne knelt in prayer. Pope Leo III placed the imperial crown on the king's head, then anointed the feet of the new emperor. History liked to say that the entire event had been spontaneous. Not in the slightest. It had all been planned. A Christian ruler could not be a god. That smacked of paganism. But he could be *chosen* by God, becoming the nexus from heaven to earth. In one masterful stroke, the king of the Franks became the first Holy Roman Emperor and the church became the means through which any claim to that throne acquired legitimacy.

A classic win–win.

Which changed the world.

All but a tiny portion of Europe eventually came under Rome's thumb. The Catholic Church became the dominant force in the world for the next eight hundred years. It systematically erased and replaced all competing spiritual beliefs, destroying every competing religion. It deadened the search for knowledge, persecuting mystics and heretics, and forced the mass conversion of anyone and everyone. At the same time it deprived its members of beliefs in prophecy, dreams, apparitions, visions, reincarnation, meditation, and healing. It assumed control of everyday life by claiming a divine authority to rule, then dominated every moment of the faithful's life.

A virtual stranglehold.

To keep its army of clerics special the church conceived the sacrament of ordination, modeled after the Roman custom of appointing men to high civil office. No one ever questioned that the New Testament made no mention of selective preaching and that baptizing new souls was to be limited only to the ordained. The Bible's personal access to God was replaced with the church's rigid rules.

And now Pollux knew where it all started.

Constantine's Gift.

No wonder the church never wanted the document public. What faster way to lose control than by exposing it all as an illusion. For the masses to learn that none of the so-called church doctrine was divine, that all of it instead had been created by man for the benefit of man, would have been a public relations disaster. All fear would have dissipated. All wonder quelled. Irrationality would have been replaced with reason.

He stared at the two parchments.

The past had come back to the present.

What would the modern world think of Constantine's Gift?

An excellent question.

In ancient times the church relied on ignorance and fear. Modernity demanded much more. Education was no longer a rarity. Television, radio, and the internet all captured people's thoughts. What would the modern world think once it knew that a Roman emperor, from seventeen hundred years ago, laid out a framework for a new religion that ultimately prelates in the Middle Ages implemented to ensure obedience of the faithful and promulgate its own importance. No divine intervention. No heavenly influences. No conduit to God. Just a bunch of men who liked living high and wielding power.

He imagined that revelation would not be welcomed.

But was it fatal?

Hard to say.

No doubt, in a world where religion was waning and faith in authority disappearing, where people were leaving the church far faster than coming toward it, proof that the whole thing had been concocted would not be good. Kastor had thought it enough to pressure key cardinals into supporting his candidacy. The threat worked in the Middle Ages with many different popes, most of them immoral and corrupt. It worked in the 1930s with two more named Pius, who faced an uncertain world that ultimately went to war. Would it work again today? Maybe. Maybe not.

It certainly would not help things.

Thank goodness he now had Spagna's flash drive loaded with incriminating information on important cardinals.

That would definitely work.

The jet began its descent.

He leaned back in the leather seat, made a steeple out of his fingers, and rested his chin on the point, trying to check the anxiety that threatened to swallow him. His eyes burned. His nerves screamed. There was always a possibility of failure. That element of chance. The threat of error. Which would be catastrophic considering the sins he'd committed. Thankfully, he was a man of precautions.

Always had been.

Outside, the sun had crested on the eastern horizon.

Daylight had arrived.

If all went according to plan—

By tomorrow evening, or the next day at the latest, he should be pope.

CHAPTER SIXTY-FOUR

COTTON STARED UP AT LUKE DANIELS.

Who smiled.

Which he knew was coming.

"Got yourself into a bit of a pickle?" Luke asked.

"You could say that. Self-inflicted, but a wound nonetheless."

He'd already surveyed the pit's bottom, using his cell phone for light. There was zero signal out. No surprise considering the amount of rock around him. The two corpses lay across each other, the shovel off to one side. As he'd suspected, an area of the floor had recently been disturbed, its color and texture different. But he'd yet to investigate further.

"How did you know I'd come?" Luke asked from above.

"I didn't. But I assumed at some point you'd talk with either Stephanie or the cathedral curator, and one or the other would tell you where I went. Stephanie told me about Laura Price and what you did."

"The Entity wanted Pollux Gallo dead. Any idea why?"

"Actually, I do have a few thoughts on that matter. Did you see anyone leave here?"

"One man," Luke said. "Carrying a bag and a folding chair. But I was too far away to see who."

"I imagine he's headed to the airport, then on to Rome."

"The cardinal, then?"

He stared around at the macabre scene before him, masked by the darkness. Then he reached for the shovel.

"There should be a rope up there," he said. "Use it to climb down."

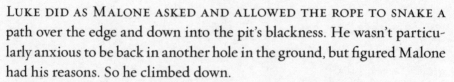

LUKE DID AS MALONE ASKED AND ALLOWED THE ROPE TO SNAKE A path over the edge and down into the pit's blackness. He wasn't particularly anxious to be back in another hole in the ground, but figured Malone had his reasons. So he climbed down.

"A little crowded, wouldn't you say," he said at the bottom, seeing the two corpses.

"Let's move them to the side. We need to get beneath them."

They heaved the bodies to one side.

Malone found his cell phone and activated the flashlight. Luke could see that the ground had been disturbed recently.

"Somebody's been diggin'?" he asked.

"It seems that way."

Malone knelt down and worked the soil with the shovel.

"What do you think is there?"

"Not what. Who."

"What's going on, Pappy?"

Malone kept digging. "When I was a kid, one night a bunch of us camped out in the woods. I was the youngest, about nine or ten, it was actually my first time sleeping under the stars. After we set up camp and ate dinner, the others took me out to a dark field and gave me a pillowcase. They told me there were snipes out in the field. Dark, furry creatures who prowl around at night looking for food. They made a great meal, like chicken or turkey. They wanted to catch one and roast it, so they taught me the animal's call. A ridiculous sound. They told me to keep a lookout and make the call over and over. When a snipe came running, I was to nab it with the pillowcase. Then they left me alone, in the dark, saying they were going to drive the snipes my way to make it easier. I believed every word, so I stood there, making those ridiculous sounds, waiting for a snipe, while they all laughed their asses off watching me from the trees."

He chuckled. "Sounds like somethin' I'd get myself into. How many did you catch?"

"You know the answer. It was a fool's errand. That's what I've been on. A damn snipe hunt."

Malone stopped digging. "I hit something."

He came over close and together they started clearing away the soil.

"The man who left here was Pollux Gallo," Malone said. "He shot those men in cold blood, after praying with them. He had no idea I was down here. If he had, he would have shot me, too. But I wisely kept my mouth shut."

Their excavations revealed skin.

A chest.

They cleared more of the gray dirt away to see a face.

Kastor Gallo.

"The only thing that makes sense," Malone said, "is that Pollux is going to make a play for the papacy. As his brother, Kastor. I saw him. He physically changed himself. Cut his hair. Shaved the beard. He's now a cardinal."

"Pretty damn bold. You have to give him that."

"I heard you've had a bold night, too. Sinking a boat. Taking out everyone aboard." Malone paused.

He could see Malone was gnawing on something. "What is it?"

"Gallo has no idea we're onto him. You saw him leave. Did he seem in a hurry?"

"Not at all."

"That means we have the upper hand. He thinks he has an open-field run with no need for blockers. We're now invisible."

Malone began shoveling the dirt back into the hole. "We need this covered over, so no one will know we're onto them."

He pointed, remembering other times. "You like being a corpse."

"It does offer a great advantage."

POLLUX STARED OUT THE WINDOW.

The sun had risen over southern Italy as the jet descended toward the airport. After he'd read through the two parchments, converting the words to a rough translation in his mind, he'd perused the flash drive in more detail, committing to memory many of the cardinal's sordid details. He would start at the first moment possible to use the information. Unlike Kastor, he knew none of the men personally, though he would have to act as if he did.

In the distance, through the morning sun, amid the clutter of Rome, he caught sight of St. Peter's dome. Impressive even from miles away, rightly bearing the label as the most renowned work of Renaissance architecture. And while neither a mother church nor a cathedral, it carried the distinction as the greatest of all sanctuaries in Christendom.

The same might one day be said of Kastor Pollux.

An obscure cardinal who rose to be a great pope.

He found it ironic that even with his transformation he was still dependent on Kastor for success. But at least he was now in total control. What kind of pope would he be? Hard to say. He possessed no faith and cared nothing for religion except for how to use it to his advantage. Thankfully, he'd studied the church in detail and had listened carefully to Kastor's countless rants. He was ready to lead. And that he would. Being pragmatic and purposeful.

The *Constitutum Constantini* had proven eye opening.

A literal blueprint for religion.

First, establish a consistent doctrine called the New Testament with select gospels that speak to a universal belief, which was precisely what the bishops had done at Nicaea. Then decree that all other beliefs are heretical, unworthy of consideration, and all who don't believe will be excommunicated. To further enforce dogma, create the notion of sin, adding that if it's not forgiven, the soul will be sent to eternal damnation in flames. Never mind that the Old Testament mentioned nothing of any such place. Just create one in your New Testament, then use it to cement loyalty and obedience.

The fastest way to ensure a constant laity is to proclaim that every person is born with the sins inherited as punishment for Adam's fall from grace. To purge that *original sin* a person must submit to baptism, performed only by a priest ordained by the church. A failure to rid that sin damns the soul to hell. To keep people dependent on the church for their entire lifetime, create more sacraments. Holy communion for children. Confirmation at puberty. Marriage for adults. Last rites on the dead. A womb-to-grave influence over every aspect of a person's life, each milestone dependent solely on adherence to church doctrine. Along the way the sacrament of confession allows a chance to purge oneself of sin and temporarily avoid hell—that forgiveness, of course, coming only from one source.

The church.

If an individual, or a group, or a nation, or anyone rises in opposition, root that dissent out and deal with it in the harshest of ways, including torture, execution, and genocide.

If the times require a change, do it. Adapt all teachings, as necessary. Which the church had done. Many times. Starting with Nicaea and continuing through other ecumenical councils and countless papal decrees. Change was good—just not too quickly, as Constantine had warned.

To ensure the outcome of any debate, declare that in all things spiritual the pope is infallible, incapable of error.

He really liked that part.

And even if a mistake is made, blame it all on the devil. Another New Testament creation. A fictitious nemesis upon which all bad things can be laid. The faithful have to believe that listening to the devil was the surest way to get a ticket to hell.

What a perfect, self-perpetuating concept.

And not a soul, until Martin Luther in the 16th century, effectively questioned any of it.

Even the first words of the so-called Lord's Prayer were pure hypocrisy.

Our Father who art in heaven . . .

What heaven? The Old Testament made no mention of any such place. It existed only because the early church fathers wanted to distinguish themselves from the Jews. So their God dwelled in heaven. And besides, if they'd told people that the kingdom of God dwelled solely within them, as the Bible said, it would not have been long before even the illiterate understood that there was no need for a church.

What a terrific concept. Done so effectively that few today, centuries later, had any clue as to how it all started.

Which would make the *Constitutum Constantini* pure poison.

He'd seen the numbers. Roman Catholic membership was dropping

by double-digit percentage points annually. Of the Catholics that remained, less than 20 percent worldwide attended church regularly. Even
more shocking, of the 20 percent that did participate, a recent survey
showed that nearly 80 percent of them believed that people should arrive
at their own spiritual beliefs, outside of organized religion. Imagine if they
knew that a Roman emperor had suggested most of what they believed to
be divine.

Yes, imagine.

Thankfully, they'd never know.

Once the conclave was over, and he was pope, Constantine's Gift would
be burned. Nothing, and no one, would exist to threaten his papacy.

But he'd hold on to it until then.

Just in case.

CHAPTER
SIXTY-FIVE

COTTON STOOD ON THE TARMAC AT MALTA'S INTERNATIONAL AIR-port. He and Luke had driven their vehicles here from the chapel and de-termined that a private jet had left the island three hours earlier and had already landed in Rome. On board had been Kastor Cardinal Gallo. He used his phone to call Stephanie, whom he placed on speaker. They stood outside in the morning light.

"Gallo is now inside the Vatican," Stephanie said.

"At least we know exactly where he is," Cotton noted.

"Any idea on the guys I took out?" Luke asked.

"We're still searching for names. Nothing pinged on their prints."

"Surely they were hired help Pollux Gallo convinced to go along with him," Cotton said. "Men who thought they'd be working for the next pope. Gallo has no money, so they had to be in it for other reasons. Unfortu-nately, their severance package is a bit permeant."

He checked his watch.

8:45 A.M.

"The DOJ jet is still there in Malta," Stephanie said. "I can have it fired up, ready to go in less than an hour."

"Do it," he said.

"And the cardinal?" Luke asked.

"Give him a long leash. Do nothing to spook him. We have to be sure before we do a thing." Cotton paused. "Absolutely sure."

"Then we split you two up," she said. "Luke, go back and get Gallo's body, and the other two, from that pit. Cotton, head to Rome. By the time you get here, we'll be sure."

POLLUX STEPPED FROM THE CAR AND STOOD OUTSIDE THE DOMUS Sanctae Marthae. The five-story pale-yellow building sat in the shadow of St. Peter's Basilica and normally served as a guesthouse for visiting clergy. Pope Francis had actually lived inside, preferring its bustle and austerity to the isolation and luxury of the papal apartments. During a conclave it served as the residence for the participating cardinals. A total of 128 rooms, run by the Daughters of Charity of St. Vincent, complete with a dining hall and two chapels. Nothing luxurious, by any means. Just a place to eat, sleep, and pray. Far preferable to stretching out on cots in spaces divided by hanging sheets, as previous conclaves had endured.

Its many rows of windows were all shuttered. He knew that internet and phone services would be switched off and blocked, all designed to keep the cardinals in isolation, as conclave rules required. Two Swiss Guards in colorful ruffs and capes and knee breeches stood guard on either side of the entrance. He was now inside the Vatican proper, beyond the gates and the crowds of St. Peter's Square. Thousands of people had already congregated for the beginning of the conclave. They would stay there day and night, waiting for the white smoke to escape from the chimney above the Sistine Chapel, signaling the election of a pope.

He steadied himself and marched toward the entrance.

Kastor's aide waited outside the glass doors.

His first test.

"Eminence," the priest said, offering a slight bow. "Welcome. Your room is ready. I'll show you the way."

He nodded in gratitude and followed the young man inside.

LUKE DROVE BACK TOWARD THE CHURCH OF ST. MAGYAR'S. HARD to get lost on this island, the whole place smaller than back home in Blount County, Tennessee.

He wondered what his mother was doing. She lived a solitary life, his father gone to his reward a long time ago. Two of his brothers lived nearby and kept an eye on her. She lived off Social Security and his father's retirement, but Luke made sure she never wanted for money. Not that such oversight was easy. She was one proud woman, who never wanted to be a burden to anyone. But he'd worked out an arrangement with her bank where he could transfer money into her account with a phone call. And she could not transfer it back out.

Not that she hadn't tried.

He slowed the car as he entered a town. Farmland and vineyards surrounded its shops and businesses, which all seemed gauged to agriculture.

Finally, he was focused.

On track.

He stopped at an intersection, then turned the car toward the Pwales Valley.

POLLUX ADMIRED THE VESTMENTS LAID OUT ON THE BED. A FULL-length cassock, mozzetta, zucchetto, and biretta, all in scarlet red to symbolize the blood a cardinal supposedly was willing to shed for his faith. The rochet was a traditional white, Kastor's a simple embroidered lace signifying his lack of jurisdiction over any post or diocese. Others wore more elaborate designs presented to them by their congregations. But always white. He already wore the cardinal ring, but a gold chain with a crucifix lay on the bed, ready to be donned. Kastor's aide, a priest he'd dealt with before as Pollux, had never hesitated, assuming that the cardinal himself had arrived.

"Is all in order?" the priest asked in Italian.

He looked away from the bed. "Yes. Perfect."

The bedroom was a reflection of simplicity. Just the bed and a night-stand with a plain crucifix on a cream-colored wall. A silent butler filled one corner, there for hanging his clothes, the floor a polished parquet with no rug. The sitting room beyond was equally austere with a table, three chairs, and a buffet against one wall. Nothing adorned its walls. Nothing covered the parquet on the floor, either. Both rooms emitted a musty, lived-in waft with a trace of masculine musk.

"You should change quickly," his aide said. "The schedule is tight. Mass inside St. Peter's begins in less than an hour. Then, contrary to usual, the cardinals will proceed directly to the Pauline Chapel, then start the procession to the Sistine Chapel."

He'd brought the four parchments, safely tucked inside the reliquary within the duffel bag, which had been delivered to the room. They would stay here. Constantine's Gift might be needed later, when they all returned here for the night. His laptop was also inside the bag, the flash drive safe within his pocket, where it would stay all day. That would definitely come into play later this evening.

"Leave me," he said.

The aide withdrew, closing the door behind him.

He stared at the scarlet robes.

A cardinal.

Once a title given to second sons and ministers of ambitious monarchs, most often now it went to those in the curia. The post was mentioned nowhere in the Bible or in the teachings of Christ. It had been totally created by the church. The name came from the Latin *cardo*. Hinge. Since the election of a pope hinged on their deliberations.

Like now.

He smiled.

Time to complete the transformation.

CHAPTER SIXTY-SIX

LUKE REENTERED THE *GUVA* CHAMBER. THE CHAPEL'S MAIN DOOR RE-
mained splintered into pieces, offering easy access. Malone had told him
the Knights of Malta owned the building and would be informed of the
entire situation once he was in Rome. Hopefully, they wouldn't send him
a bill for the damage.

It should bother him that Malone had assumed the lead, dispatched
to the Vatican while he was sent back to this hole in the ground with dead
bodies. But it didn't. He was a team player. Always had been. Stephanie
had sent him here and he would do what she wanted. Pappy would handle
things in Rome, and together they'd get the job done.

And that's what mattered.

He agreed with Harry Truman.

It's amazing what you can accomplish if you don't care who gets the credit.

He stood at the edge of the hole, gazing down at the black void. The rope
remained tied to the post, snaking a path downward. He grabbed hold and
planted his feet on the side wall, an easy matter to work his way down. His
eyes began to adjust to the darkness and he glanced toward the bottom.

No bodies.

No shovel.

He stopped.

Where the hell had they gone?

He'd seen no one and no other vehicles outside. But where he and Malone had dug earlier seemed disturbed, the area larger, nearly taking up the entire floor. Somebody had been here digging. Above, he caught the momentary flicker of a shadow in the light. Alarm bells rang in his head. He began to pull himself back up the rope, working his feet on the rough walls, hurrying. He came to the top, his head cresting the edge, his eyes seeing a man with his back to him, slicing the rope with a knife.

Damn.

The hemp snapped.

The fingers of his left hand swung up and dug into the hard earth, barely supporting his weight. He heard footsteps scrapping his way. He pulled himself up and saw Kevin Hahn, his right arm sweeping downward toward him in an arc, the knife coming straight for his hand.

Crap.

Pivoting, he swung out, his right hand finding the edge, which allowed him to yank the other away and continue to support his weight.

The blade pierced the hard ground. The fingers on his right hand ached. Hahn moved to withdraw the blade for another blow. Luke planted both hands and pushed up, one knee finding hard ground, his left hand grabbing hold of Hahn's ankle and yanking a leg out from under him.

He rolled out of the *guva*.

Hahn sprang to his feet, brandishing the knife.

Luke rose, too. "Are we seriously going to do this?"

"Let's see what you've got."

He gave the five-inch blade the respect it deserved, but he'd faced many a knife before. And what self-respecting east Tennessee redneck didn't like a good fight every now and then. Besides, he had a ton of questions for this bastard.

Hahn jabbed a couple of times, which he allowed, trying to gauge his opponent's potential. Which wasn't all that much. Surprising, given this guy's job. Maybe too many *ftira* and too long behind a desk.

"You bury those bodies?" he asked.

Hahn's answer was another swipe with the blade.

Enough. He dropped back a step and allowed Hahn to advance. He feigned left, then shifted in the opposite direction, swinging his right fist up hard, catching Hahn's jaw. The head whipped back and he followed with a left jab to the stomach. Hahn crumbled forward. He kicked the knife out of his grasp. Hahn tried to right himself, dazed from the two blows. But Luke grabbed two handfuls of shirt and wrenched him upright, swinging Hahn around and angling him out over the *guva*. Hahn's arms flailed as he tried to find some semblance of balance but the only thing keeping him from dropping below was Luke's two-fisted grip on his shirt.

"It's a long drop," he said.

He caught the fear in Hahn's eyes.

"I'm going to ask some questions. You're going to answer. If not, I let go. We have a deal?"

Hahn nodded.

"Let's start with the question you ignored. Did you bury those bodies?"

He nodded again.

"You're not going to make me ask, are you?"

"I was told to do it."

He shook his head and pushed Hahn farther out at a dangerous angle, which immediately got the guy's attention.

"Okay. Okay. Okay."

He pulled him back.

"Pollux Gallo. I did it for him."

"And the cardinal? What do you know?"

"He's dead."

Now they were getting somewhere. "Who killed him?"

"Gallo. Brother-to-brother. He's down there."

"I want to hear it all. And talk fast. My fingers are getting tired."

"Pollux and I go way back. He came to me with a plan and made me an offer. I went along with it."

"You sold out Spagna and the Entity to Gallo?"

Hahn nodded. "I hated Spagna. He deserved what he got."

This guy was a wealth of information. Stephanie and Malone both needed good intel, but to acquire it would take a little time.

He pulled Hahn back to solid ground.

The guy looked relieved.

But not for long.

Luke shoved him over the edge.

CHAPTER SIXTY-SEVEN

COTTON STEPPED FROM THE DOJ JET ONTO THE TARMAC AT ROME'S da Vinci–Fiumicino airport. The time was a little after noon and he was hungry. Some lunch would be great, but a white Vatican helicopter was waiting, its rotors turning. He hurried straight over and climbed inside.

The flight from Malta had been quick. He'd received no reports from either Stephanie or Luke. Obviously something was up, as Stephanie had managed to obtain the services of a Vatican chopper. Good thing, too. The drive from the airport to downtown would have taken a solid two hours. Rome traffic was some of the worst in the world, a cacophony of blaring horns, squealing brakes, and roaring engines.

And he had to admit.

Flying over it all was lovely.

LUKE LISTENED AS KEVIN HAHN DUG IN THE *GUVA* BELOW.

The moron had survived the fall and Luke decided Hahn would do the digging, retrieving the three bodies. He didn't much care about the two. It was the cardinal's that he needed exposed and fast. Hahn had been working for nearly ten minutes with steady swishes of blade to earth.

"You there yet?" he asked.

"Yeah. I have him," Hahn said.

About time.

He peered down into the dark hole. At the bottom he saw Hahn use his cell phone as a light, illuminating the grave in the pit's bottom. The light revealed pale-white flesh.

"It's a shoulder," Hahn said.

"I need a face."

The light extinguished and he heard work resuming. He sat down on the ground at the hole's edge, his feet dangling over the side.

"You ordered Laura killed, didn't you?" he said to the void.

"Gallo did that."

"You helped."

The digging stopped. "I went along."

It started again.

"She meant that little to you."

"She meant nothing."

Bastard. "What do you get out of this?"

"I was going to become head of the Entity."

"How does Pollux Gallo think he's going to be pope?"

"He has incriminating information on the cardinals. Stuff Spagna accumulated. We maneuvered Kastor Gallo to Malta to get that information from Spagna. What they didn't count on was you and Malone."

"We like to be underestimated."

"You leave a lot of bodies in your wake."

"Don't sell yourself short."

The digging stopped.

He peered down.

The light reappeared.

He saw a face in the ground.

"It's the cardinal," Hahn said.

"Did you know him?"

"Since we were kids. I never liked him."

He found his cell phone and opened it to the home screen. "Catch this." He dropped it down.

"Take a picture of the face." He watched as Hahn did as he asked. "Toss it back up."

Hahn hesitated.

"You don't want to piss me off," he said.

The phone came up through the dark.

Everything about this guy ate at his stomach. He was a turncoat, a traitor, a guy who put himself before his duty. Even to the point of selling out one of his own. No question, Laura Price had been pushy and overeager, but she never stood a chance. She'd been a pawn in a game that she never understood. And the guy in the pit below caused all of her problems.

The rope that had dropped down earlier, when Hahn cut it, came up out of the void in a coil and landed on the hard ground.

"Get me out of here," Hahn said. "I did what you wanted."

He needed to report in, but that could not be done from here. He had to return to ground level and get outside. Kevin Hahn was going to be the main witness in the prosecution of Pollux Gallo. And what better place to keep him on ice.

"Daniels. Get me out of here."

He turned to leave.

Hahn kept calling out.

He left the chamber and walked down the tunnel to the steps up. For added measure, he flicked the light switch off, plunging everything into darkness.

"Daniels," Hahn called out. "Daniels."

He climbed the stairs.

COTTON STARED OUT THE HELICOPTER'S WINDOW.

The triangular-shaped, walled citadel that was the Vatican came into view.

A little over a hundred acres with a population of a thousand. At its center rose the pillared façade of St. Peter's Basilica, capped by its majestic dome, which gleamed in the bright midday sun. Jutting off to one side were the long H-shaped galleries of the Vatican museums and the Vatican Library. Part of that complex included the Sistine Chapel, a simple rectangle at the southwest corner of the palace, where the cardinals would gather. Both religious and defensive in nature, as was evident from its austere exterior with battlements. The remaining pile of buildings, irregular in plan and clearly built at differing times without regard to any particular harmony, were all part of the administrative complex of the Catholic Church. The center of Christendom.

From his lofty perch he saw that over half of the enclosed space within the walls was consumed by the Vatican Gardens. A spectacular combination of poplars, maples, acacias, and oaks where popes once hunted for birds, deer, roebuck, and gazelles. The chopper swept in directly over the trees and he noticed a variety of medieval fortifications and monuments set among flowers, topiary, and grass. A rectangular slab of concrete at the far western corner, near the Leonine Wall, served as a helipad.

The chopper settled down on it.

He hopped out.

A priest at the far edge came forward and introduced himself, adding that Stephanie Nelle was waiting. He followed the younger man through the gardens, past Vatican Radio, the Ethiopian College, and the railway station, eventually entering St. Martha's Square. He'd never been into the closed areas of the Vatican before, though he'd visited the public portions. On the flight in he saw that St. Peter's Square, lined with the famed Bernini colonnade, was filled with people. The priest turned left and walked straight for the basilica and a side door that was being watched by a uniformed security guard.

Armed too.

Which was curious for a religious state.

But he assumed that the times were a-changing.

They entered the basilica.

No matter what a person's faith, or if they had no faith at all, it was hard not to be overwhelmed by the majesty that was St. Peter's Basilica. It had three claims to fame. A memorial to St. Peter. Coronation hall for popes and emperors. The foremost house of God in the world. Monuments and tombs were everywhere, adorning both the cavernous nave and the impressive side aisles. Every nook and cranny was dedicated to a pope or a saint. Beautiful marble empaneled the walls, the roof ornamented with sunken coffers richly gilded and stuccoed. Its immensity seemed disguised by the clear symmetry of its proportions. With few exceptions all of the wall images were mosaics, executed with such accuracy to scale and tint as to be almost surreal. The roster of artists boggled the mind. Raphael, Michelangelo, Peruzzi, Vignola, Ligorio, Fontana, Maderno. A perfect example of what five hundred years and unlimited resources could accomplish. Everything was made even more noteworthy by the fact that the building was empty.

Not a soul inside.

Making it possible to hear their footsteps echoing off the sheets of colored marble that formed the floor.

They passed the papal altar and its gilt bronze baldachin that kept watch on the stairs leading down to the tomb of St. Peter. It sat in the center of the Latin cross formed by the building itself. He glanced up into the main cupola that rose to the top of Michelangelo's dome. Mosaics filled its ribs, fading away toward the top as if dissolving into heaven.

The priest seemed unimpressed and just kept walking.

Off to the right he caught the bronze of a life-sized St. Peter, sitting as he gave a blessing while holding the keys to the kingdom of heaven. He knew it to be sixteen hundred years old. Intact, except for one part. For centuries pilgrims had kissed the right foot. Today people simply rubbed it. Each touch made little to no difference. But combined they had eroded the bronze, polishing the defined toes to smoothness. Surely there was a lesson in there somewhere.

They crossed to the far side of the nave and headed for an exit door, which was manned by another security guard. Probably a private firm contracted to assist during all of the commotion that came from a papal death and election. The exit door opened and Stephanie Nelle appeared, along with another man, dressed in black.

He stepped toward them.

"We have a big problem," she said.

CHAPTER
SIXTY-EIGHT

Pollux entered the Sistine Chapel, following in the procession with the other cardinals, two by two, all in their scarlet splendor, their hands folded in prayer. The chapel was forty meters long, thirty wide, and twenty tall, divided into two unequal parts by an elaborate marble screen, a loose interpretation of a Byzantium iconostasis. From the screen to the altar a raised dais had been built on each side to accommodate two tiers of cardinals sitting side by side in long rows. Each had a chair and desk space. All he needed now was a little luck, and the information on the flash drive, which rested safely in his trouser pocket beneath his cassock.

He'd visited the Sistine several times, but there was a special majesty about the chapel for a conclave. It owed its celebrity to the frescoes, where the great masters of the 15th century had left their most magnificent works. His eyes focused on the far wall and Michelangelo's *Last Judgment*. The largest painting in the world. At first glance it appeared confused and chaotic, but careful study allowed one to appreciate its mystic inspiration.

The singing stopped. The line dissolved.

He glanced up, past the arched windows on either side, at the flattened barrel-vaulted ceiling. He agreed with the critics. It may well be the most powerful piece of art ever created. When the despotic Julius II ordered the chapel redecorated, Michelangelo had rebelled. He was a sculptor, not a painter. But once inspired he'd entered into his commission with great enthusiasm. Four years he'd labored, creating a stupendous undertaking.

He studied the panels.

The Intoxication of Noah. The Great Flood. God Creates Eve. God Hovering Over the Waters. God Separates Light from Darkness. His gaze focused on one in particular. *The Brazen Serpent. And the Lord sent fiery serpents, and much people of Israel died, and Moses made a serpent of brass and those who beheld the serpent of brass lived.* He took comfort from Numbers 21. Some of the cardinals around him were about to behold a brazen serpent.

The presiding cardinal called out from the altar. "Please take a seat so that we may begin, brothers."

He found his assigned spot along the left wall, beneath Rosselli's *Passage of the Red Sea.* He settled into the chair, made comfortable by a red cushion and a pillow for the spine. So far his charade had worked perfectly. A few of the cardinals had approached him and made small talk. Some clearly were Kastor's friends, others not so much. He'd kept his comments short and vague, citing the distraction of all that was happening around him. Thankfully, the vast majority had ignored him.

The presiding cardinal, an Italian, the most senior in attendance, stood before the altar and told the assembled that they would now swear the oath, pledging to observe the norms prescribed by the various apostolic constitutions and rules laid down by previous popes. The process would take some time to complete as each cardinal, in order of seniority, would be required to step forward, place his hands on the gospels, and publicly swear.

He was going to enjoy watching that spectacle.

COTTON STOOD WITH STEPHANIE AND CHARLES CARDINAL STAMM, an Irishman, the man in charge of the Entity. He was thin, pinched in the cheeks, with a pockmarked face and a hooked nose. Just a trace of a scarlet bib showed below the white clerical collar above the top button of a plain black cassock. No signet ring. A simple brass pectoral cross was the only sign of his high office. Though Danjel Spagna had operational control, this man was the chair of the board, appointed too many popes ago to count. He was an older man, clearly past the age of eighty, which disqualified him from actively participating in the conclave.

"Luke called in," Stephanie said.

She showed him an image on her phone of the top half of a dead body.

"That's Cardinal Gallo," Cotton said. "Doubtful somebody killed Pollux Gallo, then cut his hair and shaved off the beard before dumping him in the ground. The guy inside the Sistine Chapel is an imposter."

They were huddled together inside the basilica, not a soul in sight. Both the uniformed guard and the priest who'd escorted him had retreated to the other side of the exit door.

"The head of Maltese security has confirmed to Luke that the Gallo brothers switched places," Stephanie said. "That man was also in league with Pollux Gallo. Now Gallo is inside the Sistine, pretending to be his brother."

"He must have a plan," Cotton said.

"He does."

And she explained about a damaging flash drive that Gallo had obtained from Spagna.

"Luke has been most persuasive in getting his prisoner to talk," she said. "He has him at the bottom of what he called a *guva*. He mentioned that you were familiar with the locale."

He chuckled. "I'll never hear the end of that one. But yes, I've visited the place."

"I'm aware of Archbishop Spagna's internal investigation," Stamm said. "It was done at the pope's specific request. But I was never privy to the results. Spagna falsely told me the investigation was still ongoing. Thankfully, I concluded he was lying. I suspect his plan was to use what he'd learned and have himself elevated to cardinal and replace me, taking both jobs for himself."

"Sounds like you didn't care for the guy," Cotton said. "Why keep him around?"

"Because he was extremely good at what he did. And the late pope liked him." Stamm shrugged. "This is not a democracy. There was nothing I could do. Except tolerate . . . and watch him."

"Cardinal Stamm is why the Magellan Billet is involved," Stephanie said.

"You knew Spagna was going rogue?"

"I strongly suspected. When some of my subordinates confirmed that he was on Malta, I knew there was a problem. But once I found out Cardinal Gallo was headed there, too, I decided to recruit some outside help."

"He quietly asked me to send an agent to keep an eye on the cardinal," Stephanie said. "Of course, we had no idea of the full extent of what was going to happen."

"To say the least," Stamm added. "I've lost my operational head and second in command."

"I'm glad you're here," Stephanie said to Cotton. "This is going to require care, skill, and experience."

"We need to get Gallo. Now," he said.

Stamm shook his head. "The sanctity of the conclave cannot be broken."

"The sanctity is already broken," Stephanie said. "The whole thing is a sham. It needs to end."

"We can simply wait until they break for the day, then move on Gallo," Stamm said.

But Cotton knew something about conclaves. "And what do you do if they elect him pope this afternoon? They'll take a vote today, won't they?"

Stamm went silent for a moment, then said, "Yes. They will. Probably sometime in the next hour."

"We have no idea what Gallo has done," Cotton said. "If the information he has is as bad as you say, he may have already applied pressure. He's been in Rome for several hours. This conclave has to end. I'm sorry if that's going to be a PR disaster, but the man is a murderer. Are the doors to the Sistine closed yet?"

"They are about to be."

"We need to move."

POLLUX WATCHED AS, ONE BY ONE, THE MEN IN SCARLET LINED UP and approached the lectern to take the oath. At his turn, he stood, laid his hand on the gospels, and swore to obey the Apostolic Constitution. Again, no one gave him a second look or even seemed to care.

But by tomorrow evening they would.

After the last man swore allegiance, the papal master of ceremonies uttered the classic words.

"*Extra Omnes.*"

Everybody out.

The public portion of the conclave had concluded and the functionaries at the back, beyond the marble screen—photographers recording the oath swearing, officials from the Vatican offices, along with various archbishops, priests, and monsignors who had helped prepare the event—left. Then the tall wooden doors were eased shut for the cameras beyond and latched from the inside. In centuries past it had been the opposite. That was when there were fewer cardinals, and such a small electorate magnified each vote and amplified the amount of corruption. Conclaves sometimes lasted months, even years. The bargaining among the participants anything but subtle. Finally, in 1274, Gregory X ordered that electors be locked in seclusion, their food severely rationed, until they came to a consensus. Needless to say, things began to happen faster.

This would be a short conclave, too.

Two days at best.

His election had to be viewed as one of divine inspiration, since Kastor's reputation was hardly *papabile*. The selection would be shocking to the world. He wondered if any of the offending cardinals would resist him. Maybe. But he'd make clear that they would end their tenure as princes of the church in disgrace, perhaps even in jail, with the world media knowing exactly what they'd done and the new pope forced to deal with their indiscretions. So why not have a friend on the throne of St. Peter. Albeit one who owned them. But nonetheless a friend.

Surely every one of them had realized the risks they were taking when they decided to break not only God's law but the laws of every civilized nation. The last thing they would want was to be exposed, but if that was their desire, he'd accommodate them. Instead of pope he would become God's Whistleblower. That should do wonders for the tarnished image of Kastor Cardinal Pollux.

But he doubted that would be the route they'd take.

Just a simple vote, in secret, one they could actually disavow later if they so desired, and all would remain as it was now.

If nothing else, cardinals were practical.

The doors to the Sistine were closed and locked. The conclave had begun. There would be another sermon, then the first vote would be taken. Before him on the clothed table were a few pencils, a scrutiny sheet where a count of any voting could be recorded, a copy of *Ordo Rituum,* the Order for Rites in the conclave, and a stack of ballot cards with the words ELIGO IN SUMMUM PONTIFICEM printed at the top.

I elect as Supreme Pontiff.

He planned to write his name on the first ballot. No one else would. And no one would think a thing of it, as many would vote either for themselves or for a friend, too. Never in modern times had a pope been chosen by two-thirds on the first vote. Supposedly that was to avoid the sin of pride.

But at least his name would enter the fray.

And by nightfall several of the men around him would fully understand that significance.

CHAPTER SIXTY-NINE

COTTON FOLLOWED CARDINAL STAMM AS THEY WALKED FROM THE basilica toward the Sistine Chapel. They entered a room labeled the Sala Regia, the Regal Room. A large audience hall where emperors and kings were once received, the walls were decorated with more massive frescoes. He caught some of the Latin captions beneath them. The return of Pope Gregory XI from Avignon. The Battle of Lepanto. The reconciliation of Pope Alexander III with Frederick Barbarossa. Each depicted an important point in the church's history.

Braggadocio, for sure.

These were glory walls.

Overhead, the ceiling was an elegant barrel vault that boasted ornate insignia of popes, together with biblical figures. Like everything else inside the Vatican, the color and style more attacked than soothed the senses. At the far side was the entrance to the famed Pauline Chapel. In the center of one of the long walls stood towering wooden doors, a Swiss Guard on either side, both in billowy costumes of blue, orange, and red stripes.

The entrance to the Sistine Chapel.

Closed.

The high vaulted roof above echoed the murmur of the fifty or so people who milled about on the marble floor. Some priests, some bishops, most men dressed in suits and ties. Several held cameras, with press credentials draped from their necks.

"We're too late," Stamm said. "Give me a moment."

The cardinal drifted away toward a knot of suits.

"We can't let this go on," he said to Stephanie.

"Unfortunately, it's a Vatican matter."

"Pollux Gallo tried to kill Luke. That's an American matter."

"That's a reach."

"But it could be enough."

She gestured across the hall. "Those two guards aren't going to be impressed by our jurisdiction, and I'm sure this whole palace is loaded with security, ready to deal with any intrusion."

He got the message. This was going to require diplomacy, rather than force.

Stamm walked back their way, his movements slow, his whole air casual, nothing to signify urgency. "The doors have been closed for less than ten minutes. They will be listening to a sermon for a short while. It's traditional before the first scrutiny is taken."

That meant they had time to think, and Cotton could see the cardinal was debating the next course. More conversations swept through the hall, amplified by the marble surrounding them.

"We need to clear this hall," Stamm said.

"You've decided?' Stephanie asked.

"I never cared for Cardinal Gallo. I considered him a blowhard who knew little to nothing about anything. I never cared much for Archbishop Spagna, either. But it was not my place to judge either man. And no one deserves to be murdered. It's my duty to keep the church protected, its priests and princes protected, and the process of selecting a new pope free of taint." Stamm paused. "You saw the knights' *Nostra Trinità*?"

Cotton nodded. "We found it."

"I checked," Stamm said. "Cardinal Gallo arrived at the Domus Sanctae Marthae with a large duffel bag. I had his room searched a few moments ago. There are four old parchments there, inside an ancient reliquary."

"With red wax seals on each end?" Cotton added. "One of which is broken?"

Stamm nodded.

"That's it," Cotton said. "Inside that reliquary is Constantine's Gift."

"I haven't had a chance to see if that's true. But if after seven hundred years it has found its way back to us, there could be a problem."

"It's that important?"

"If the rumors are to be believed."

Cotton smiled. This man knew how to play his cards close to his vest.

"Our imposter wants to be pope," Stamm said. "I would imagine that the last thing he desires is for the church to lose stature, in any way. Instead he plans to extort his way to the throne of St. Peter. Your point is a good one, Mr. Malone. We cannot allow that first scrutiny. We have no idea what Pollux Gallo has done. Whether we stop it now, or later, the public relations damage is the same. So I've decided to act."

POLLUX LISTENED TO THE SERMON, WHICH SEEMED ONLY TO BRING a sense of duty and long-windedness. As if any of the men in the room required a reminder of their responsibilities. This was his first experience at seeing how the cardinals functioned as a group and he'd watched the faces. Some were clearly interested, but most were trying to keep stoic, revealing nothing, holding their thoughts within. Surely some deals had already been made, preliminary alliances forged. Nobody here, other than fools, was waiting for the Holy Spirit to swoop down and inspire them.

Maybe *he* was the Holy Spirit?

Perhaps the flash drive had been meant to fall into his hands.

The German monsignor finally shut up and the presiding cardinal stood before the altar. The first scrutiny was about to begin. He listened as the prelate explained the procedure, grateful for the final instructions. He'd read all about the process, but any refresher was appreciated. On the card before them each cardinal would write a name. Then, in order of precedence, they would take their ballot to the altar and deposit it into a gold chalice. Before casting their ballot, each cardinal would swear another oath. In Latin. *I call as my witness Christ the Lord who will be my judge, that my vote is given to the one who before God I think should be elected.*

In former times a cardinal had to sign his name to each ballot, along with a small motif, a symbol unique to him. The ballot was then folded to cover the signature and motif, then sealed with wax to provide a measure of privacy. But the scrutineers, the ones who counted the ballots, all knew who voted for who. Pius XII ended that nonsense. This method was much better. Secret should be secret.

The presiding cardinal finished his explanations and invited the balloting to begin. Some of the men immediately reached for their pencils, while others bowed their heads in prayer. He decided to take a moment before scrolling his brother's name.

A banging broke the silence.

Which surprised everyone.

From the main doors.

More banging.

Incredible.

Someone was knocking.

He came alert and watched as the presiding cardinal stepped from the altar and paraded down the center aisle, his hands folded before him. All of the men focused on the massive double doors beyond the marble screen. A slight murmur of voices arose. A few of the cardinals stood and crept into the center aisle. He decided to do the same. More of the puzzled men joined him there.

The presiding cardinal approached the double doors, released the inner lock, and eased open one side enough that he could step outside. Suspicion brushed across his mind. Nothing about this seemed good. They'd already been told about the second way in and out of the chapel, through a small door behind the altar that led either up to Raphael's Stanze or down to Collection of Modern Religious Art in the Vatican Museums. The museums themselves were closed, their massive exhibit halls empty. Restrooms were provided on either floor for cardinals in need.

But the route could also prove a means of escape.

He drifted away from the cardinals, their combined attention fixated on the doors. He, too, kept his focus on the center opening in the marble screen, hoping this was a false alarm.

The double doors swung open.

Cotton Malone entered.

CHAPTER SEVENTY

Cotton had stood with Stamm and Stephanie as they spoke with the presiding cardinal.

He was not happy.

"Charles, do you have any idea what you have done?" the man whispered in English.

"Fully, my friend. But there's a problem with the conclave. One that requires it be halted."

They'd cleared the Sala Regia of the people who'd been milling about on the pretense of providing utter quiet to the men beyond the double doors. All of them had been ushered into an adjacent hall and the doors closed, leaving only the two Swiss Guards. Their boss had been informed of the situation and sworn to silence, he bowing to Stamm since, as the older man noted, no one inside the Vatican, save the pope, argued with the Entity. Cotton listened as Stamm explained the situation, the presiding cardinal's eyes alighting with each revelation.

"Are you certain?" the older man asked when Stamm finished.

"There's no doubt."

And Stephanie showed the cardinal the image of Kastor Gallo's dead face.

"We need to take the imposter into custody," Stamm said.

The other man, clearly flustered, nodded. "Of course. Absolutely."

Stamm motioned and Cotton pushed the doors open and stepped into the Sistine Chapel.

A sea of scarlet-and-white-clad men stood beyond an elaborate marble screen. He walked to an opening in the center, his eyes searching the faces. "Gentleman, I need Cardinal Gallo."

The men seemed puzzled at first, then a few pointed at the tables.

"That's his seat," one of them said.

Empty.

Stamm and Stephanie came up beside him.

"Slippery thing, isn't he," Stamm whispered.

"I assume there's another way out?"

"Behind the altar. Stairs up or down, both will lead you into the museums. They're entirely closed for the conclave, the exits are manned by armed security. I can alert them to move in."

"No. Let me go get him. Maybe we can contain this within the museums. Keep the guards on the exits so Gallo can't leave, but alert them. They have radios?"

Stamm nodded. "Cardinals are not supposed to leave the museums. They are under seal."

"I get it. So if he tries, have them detain him. How about the cameras in the museums?"

"Off during the conclave to preserve privacy. Which also helps keep this contained."

He got the message. Stamm would like to keep them off. "I'll find him."

"Do that. I would prefer not to issue an apprehend order for a cardinal of the church."

"He's not a cardinal."

"He's worse. I'm relying on your abilities and discretion here, Mr. Malone."

"Cotton can handle it," Stephanie said.

Stamm gestured and one of the uniformed Swiss Guards hurried over. Cotton watched as the guard removed a radio that had been attached inside the costume, along with a small mike and earpiece.

Stamm handed them over.

"Go get him."

POLLUX DESCENDED THE STAIRS TO A GALLERY FILLED WITH PAINT-ings, sculpture, and graphic art. All modern. Contemporary. Ugly. He kept moving, turning left and heading for an open doorway, entering the old Vatican library. He passed through three rooms then found the famed Sistine Hall, which stretched some sixty meters ahead. Seven pillars sheathed with frescoes divided the ancient space into two wide aisles. The walls and ceiling were all colorfully decorated and gilded, furnished more like a reliquary than a library. Mosaic tables filled the spaces between the pillars and supported an array of porcelain vases. More tables displayed other precious objects under glass, similar to the knights' archive at Rapallo.

He kept moving through the Sistine Hall, passing one pillar after another. He hated leaving the *Constitutum Constantini,* particularly after all he'd endured to find it. But there was no time to retrieve it from his room.

His freedom was now at stake.

He heard no one either behind or ahead of him. Malone would surely come in pursuit, but the American would have to decide if his quarry had gone up or down after leaving the Sistine.

He could only hope that Malone chose wrong.

COTTON FLED THE SISTINE AND HURRIED DOWN A LONG CORRIDOR that led into the Apostolic Palace and a staircase.

Two, actually.

One up. The other down.

Where to? Good question.

He chose up and hopped the stone risers two at a time, exiting into a room filled with biblical allegories on the ceiling and obligatory frescoes on the walls.

"I'm upstairs," he said into the mike clipped at his shoulder.

"Then you're in the Room of the Immaculate Conception," Stamm said in his ear.

A glass case stood in the center. He gave it a casual glance and noticed ornamented volumes dating to the 19th century dealing with, sure enough, the Immaculate Conception.

"Leaving there and entering a small room housing tapestries," he said.

"The Apartment of St. Pius V," Stamm added.

He passed through and entered the incredible Gallery of Maps. This place he knew about. Over 350 feet long, a straight, unobstructed line from one side of the palace to the other. The overhead vault was decorated with white and gold stuccos populated by people, coats of arms, allegories, and emblems. But the walls were its claim to fame. Enormous colorful panels alternated with the bright exterior windows. Forty maps all total, together depicting topographically the entire Italian peninsula of the 16th century. Eighty percent accurate. Remarkable given the state of cartography at the time.

"I'm in the map gallery," he said. "There's no one here."

He ran down the marble floor. Out the windows, to his left, he caught glimpses of the Vatican Gardens with fountains and trees rising toward the observatory. On the right was an inner courtyard, with an enormous splashing basin, empty of people. Cameras were everywhere. All off, according to Stamm. He was on the third floor, more galleries and halls beneath him and on the other side of the building, beyond the courtyard. Those electric eyes might be needed.

"The exits remain manned," Stamm said. "No one has reported anyone trying to leave."

"I'm at the end of the map gallery," he said into the radio. "There's no way to go from here across to the other loggia?"

"Not on the third floor. There is a way below on the second floor to cross," Stamm said. "Keep going. You can traverse over at the end, past the Room of Biga ahead. There's also a stairway down to ground level."

He entered the dome space of the Biga room. Four niches between pilasters and four arched bays formed the walls of a small rotunda. In the center stood a triumphal chariot. Definitely Roman. Complete with wheels, shaft, and horses. But no Gallo.

"I'm beginning to think I went the wrong way," he said.

POLLUX CAME TO AN INTERSECTION WHERE ANOTHER SHORTER loggia to his right led across to the other side of the palace. The library continued on there, as it did ahead, through a series of smaller collection rooms. His view through them was unobstructed. There had to be a way out at the end of those rooms, where the palace ended. Forward seemed the shorter and smarter play than heading for the other side. He could not afford to take any wrong turns. He needed to leave this building, and the Vatican, too.

Quickly and unnoticed.

The crowd out in St. Peter's Square would provide more than enough cover. Becoming lost within tens of thousands of people would be easy. But getting to them not so much. Every gate out would be manned. Surely soon the word would be passed by radio to be on the lookout for a wayward cardinal. He kept going, walking through a series of galleries with familiar names. Pauline. Alexandrine. Clementine. Beyond them he came to the entrance for the Vestibule of the Four Gates and a stairway that led down.

He started to descend.

On the landing he turned, but quickly halted.

At ground level he spotted a uniformed security guard manning the doors that led out. He assessed the situation and decided on his next move. Steeling himself, he continued down the wide marble staircase, his hands tucked into the roomy sleeves of his cassock. The guard had his back to him, staring out the glass doors, which made it easy to approach.

The man turned.

"Eminence—"

No hesitation. Move. Fast.

He removed his hands and grabbed the guard, wrapping his right arm around the man's neck. He clamped his left hand to his right wrist and tightened the vise into a choke hold, cutting off the man's breathing. The guard was younger but thirty pounds heavier and never anticipated a cardinal attacking him. Apparently, no arrest or detain order had yet been issued.

The man went limp.

He allowed the body to slump to the floor.

Immediately he removed his mozzetta and rochet, then unbuttoned the cassock. Beneath he wore an undershirt and trousers. They were dark, like the guard's. Blue, not black, but they would do. It was the shirt and cap he needed, along with the radio and gun. He slipped on the shirt, a little big, but a tuck of the tail into his pants handled the excess. He clipped the radio to his belt and popped in the ear fob. The microphone he stuffed into a pocket. He doubted he'd be making any transmissions. He buckled the holster to his waist. Grabbing hold of both arms he dragged the guard out of the vestibule and through an open doorway, leaving him stretched prone behind a statue that filled one corner of the nearest gallery. He rushed back and retrieved his robes, which he tossed over the guard's body.

He stepped back to the exit doors and smoothed his clothes.

Then he left the palace.

CHAPTER
SEVENTY-ONE

Cotton stood in the Room of Biga considering his options. The word meant "chariot" in Italian, pretty much the only name for this space considering the huge one that dominated it.

He took no comfort from the sacred, the prodigious, and the miraculous that engulfed him. He had a job to do.

And it wasn't going all that well.

He walked over to a large, twenty-paned window and gazed out at the sunny afternoon. Beyond was the dome of St. Peter's, the Vatican Gardens, and an assortment of other buildings set among the trees. Below stretched a street with little to no activity. Understandable given the conclave. A couple of vehicles moved about and a few people walked the concrete. The Vatican wasn't shut down. Far from it. Business went on. On the other side of the palace tens of thousands of people filled St. Peter's Square waiting for a new pope. Media outlets from around the world had also set up shop.

But here? No one was around.

It was odd standing in one of the largest, most visited museums in the world alone.

Something caught his eye below.

A man.

Moving away from the building.

One of the armed uniformed guards, like back in St. Peter's.

The guy stopped for a moment, looked around, then donned a cap.

He caught the face.

Gallo.

POLLUX PARALLELED THE BACK SIDE OF THE PALACE AND MARCHED toward the basilica. He wasn't sure where he was headed, but at least he was free of the building and his vestments. One was a prison, the other like a flashing sign. Until the body of the guard was found, the uniform he now wore should open a lot of doors.

But he had to move fast.

He passed beneath the Arch of Gregory and rounded an outbuilding that projected from the backside of the palace. He found himself in a piazza with another fountain—Santa Marta, if he recalled—and followed the street. The hulk of the basilica lay ahead. The day seemed wonderful, partly cloudy with lots of sunshine. Warm too. Malone suddenly appearing inside the Sistine signaled that things had not gone well in Malta. Kevin Hahn must have failed. He should have shot the idiot before leaving the island, but the bodies had to be buried. The last thing he needed was for those corpses to be found. So he'd had no choice but to keep Hahn alive. Also, having a friend as operational head of the Entity would have proven beneficial.

But none of that mattered now.

He'd been found out.

Which meant Malone knew about Kastor, too.

He had to disappear.

But first he had to flee the Vatican.

COTTON HUSTLED DOWN THE STAIRS AND STOPPED AT THE GLASS doors. Stamm had said all of the exits were manned. This one wasn't, and Gallo was wearing a uniform. He stepped over to the entrance of the first gallery and immediately saw a pile of red and white garments piled on a body lying in the corner. He rushed over and checked for a pulse on the shirtless man.

There. But weak.

Decision time.

Gallo was out of his robes and into a uniform that would provide a great freedom of movement. A definite problem. But Stamm had said the guards all carried radios, and there was no radio. That meant Gallo had ears, too. No gun was at the guard's waist. So Gallo was armed. The man lying before him needed medical attention but there was no time. He could not allow Gallo to dissolve into the woodwork, which was becoming easier by the second. Putting out an alert would require not only an explanation but a photo and description as well. He doubted any of the guards would recognize Kastor Gallo on sight. An open alert would also spook Gallo, who would hear.

That meant he was the only one who could get this done.

"I'm sorry," he whispered to the unconscious man.

He stood and headed for the exit doors. Beyond the glass, fifty yards away, he caught sight of Gallo as he rounded the end of a building and vanished from sight.

He ran out into the sun.

POLLUX WAS ON THE BACK SIDE OF THE BASILICA, THE GOVERNOR'S Palace off to his right. In order to get to St. Peter's Square he'd have to keep circling the basilica, but the closer he came to an exit gate the more people he'd encounter. No question that every inch of these surroundings was under video surveillance. But so far, there had been nothing to alert anyone. Only after the guard's body was found would things change.

But he'd be long gone by then.

COTTON RAN TOWARD WHERE HE'D LAST SEEN GALLO, THE PALACE on one side, grass and trees on the other.

His footsteps slapped the pavement.

Pigeons, shaken from their perch, squawked into the bright sky.

He made it to the building edge and stopped, glancing around and seeing his target past a piazza—

Just as Gallo vanished around the basilica's apse.

POLLUX KEPT WALKING.

Cool and calm.

A guard heading to his duty station.

Unfortunately, towering bastions surrounded the Vatican on all sides. No way out over those. He came to another square, this one more open than the others. Now he could see a whole array of 20th-century buildings. The Domus Sanctae Marthae and papal audience hall were both in view.

He stopped, hearing nothing but his own thoughts.

Be smart.

Use your advantage.

A hundred meters away he spotted salvation. A simple white marble building close to the outer wall.

The railway station.

To its immediate left was an opening in the Leonine Wall, wide enough to admit a train. The papal arms, carved in stone, hung above its center. Huge iron doors were retracted into the recesses of the bastion. The brown caterpillar of a train was parked on the other side of the station, most of it jutting out of the right side. The locomotive was running, steam billowing, its front end just short of the open gate. A worker busily unloaded large-wheeled plastic bins from the last railcar.

He studied the open gate.

Two guards dressed like him were on duty to make sure no one entered. Surely once the train left the big doors would be retracted, sealing off the portal.

But at the moment they offered a means of escape.

COTTON HAD PURSUED A LOT OF PEOPLE. SOME PROS, SOME NOT. Pollux Gallo seemed somewhere in between. Cunning, he'd give him that, and ballsy. He almost got away with the identity exchange. But like most psychopaths, he never thought that anyone might best him.

He came to the far end of the basilica and stopped, peering around and catching sight of Gallo headed for a white marble building with a train on the other side pointed toward an open gate in the wall.

Should he call it in?

No.

Somebody could get hurt.

Gallo was close to escape, desperate and armed.

He'd handle this himself.

CHAPTER SEVENTY-TWO

POLLUX AVOIDED THE INTERIOR OF THE RAILWAY STATION, HEADING around its right side and approaching the tracks. Five railcars were attached to the locomotive, their doors slid open, the spaces inside each of them empty. Several freight wagons were loaded with crates and boxes. A man stood off to the side, waving toward the locomotive.

He heard the powerful engine rev louder.

Finally, a break.

He pointed toward the worker and said in Italian, "I need to go out with this train for security."

The man did not argue.

He rushed forward and hopped into the second car behind the locomotive. The train began to move, heading toward the gate in the bastion wall.

He just might make it out.

Once beyond the Vatican he'd hop from the train and disappear into Rome. Where to go after that? He'd find somewhere.

He had no intention of spending the rest of his life in jail.

COTTON CHOSE TO GO LEFT, AS GALLO HAD GONE RIGHT. THE LEFT side of the station also offered more cover with a patch of grass with trees and bushes. A paved walk separated the grass from the building and led back to the tracks. The path also offered a way to get to the rear of the station without Gallo knowing.

He heard the diesel rev and the hiss of brakes releasing. The locomotive was no more than twenty feet from the open gate and would be outside the wall in less than thirty seconds. He counted five open railcars and saw a guy near a white van toward the end of the train. One of the tall bushes offered excellent shielding and, as the train passed, he caught sight of Gallo inside the second car.

The train gathered pace.

The third car passed.

The fourth.

He had no choice.

He sprang from the path and ran toward the final car. Most of the train was now beyond the wall, the front third rounding a bend in the tracks.

He leaped up into the empty car.

Someone yelled.

Had to be one of the guards at the gate, who suddenly vaulted into the car, too. He never gave the man a chance, stepping forward and planting a fist in the guy's right side. The man doubled over and he used the moment to shove the guard out the open door. The train was creeping along, yet to gain a full head of steam. The guard hit the ground and rolled away. He watched out the door as the train kept going and saw that the guard was okay, having landed on grass. The other guard who'd been watching the gate with him ran to the man's aid and helped him up. Surely they'd call in all the excitement, and Stamm would learn where he'd headed.

He decided to maintain his own radio silence.

He swung himself out of the doorway and grabbed hold of a steel ladder, which he used to climb to the top. Two cars were between him and Gallo, so he jumped to the next. The tops were flat but loaded with bumps and indentations made more treacherous by the constant vibrations from the tracks. He spread his feet against the roll and felt like a sailor on a rolling deck.

He leaped to the next car.

POLLUX BEGAN TO FEEL A MEASURE OF RELIEF.

He was away from the Vatican and only the one unsuspecting man at the train station had seen him. It was a shame that he'd not been able to complete the plan. He'd been devising it for many years and thought he'd anticipated all of the seemingly endless obstacles to a successful conclusion. His attempts to neutralize the Americans had apparently proven insufficient. But he still had the flash drive and it might be useful. Cardinals had resources that he could exploit, and taking the moral low road was nothing new for the Holy See.

The train kept moving, creating a constant groan from the warped wood and rusty metal. He'd wait a little longer before leaving.

Something thumped on the roof.

Footsteps moved from one side of the car to the other.

He reached for the gun at his waist.

COTTON SWUNG HIS BODY OUT AND ONTO THE STEEL LADDER attached to the side of the railcar. Down two rungs and he jumped into the open door, facing Gallo, who was reaching for a weapon. He lunged, pushing his weight against the other man and bracing his feet. He grabbed the gun and swung upward, wrenching the hand down, freeing the grip. The gun clattered away, then disappeared out the open doorway. Gallo rebounded, jerking away and jumping into the air, throwing a dive punch that crashed down on Cotton's shoulder, which he absorbed as he shifted away and whirled, coming back around with a heel kick to the sternum that lifted Gallo off the floor and sent him sliding. That had to have cracked some ribs but Gallo sprang to his feet, taking a swing that was easily sidestepped.

Cotton moved in and swung, his right fist connecting with the man's jaw.

Gallo blinked, then swung again, finding only air, the clenched knuckles swishing past without connecting.

Wheels racketed beneath his feet.

Gallo advanced.

Cotton swung again, crunching his fist into Gallo's face. He felt his nose give way. Gallo staggered back, dazed but showing no signs of surrendering. He could not allow him to leave the car.

Brakes hissed.

Wheels screeched on the tracks.

The train slowed.

Apparently Stamm had gotten the message.

Time to end this.

Gallo swung.

Cotton parried the blow and chopped at the neck, then pounded another fist into his solar plexus. He wrestled Gallo's arms behind his back and shoved the head and upper body into the wooden wall.

Once. Twice.

The body went limp.

He allowed Gallo to sink to the floor.

The train stopped.

He hadn't had a full fight like that in a while. Nice to know he still had it in him. Beyond the open doors he saw shadows approaching. Then he spotted Cardinal Stamm and Stephanie standing below. They stepped close to the open doors and saw Gallo lying still.

"Seems the rat finally found the trap," Stamm said.

Stephanie tossed him a grateful smile.

"Good job."

CHAPTER
SEVENTY-THREE

COTTON WAITED IN CARDINAL STAMM'S OFFICE, LOCATED IN ONE OF the many buildings that filled the Vatican, this one on the north side of the Apostolic Palace amid the post office, pharmacy, media outlets, grocery store, and barracks of the Swiss Guards. It was an odd location for the world's oldest intelligence agency. Reminiscent of the Magellan Billet, which was headquartered in a nondescript government building in Atlanta.

Stamm had ordered the train to reverse down the tracks, back to the Vatican station. The loading platform had been cleared of the white van and freight wagons, no one around except two men who, Stamm had explained, worked for him. Gallo was taken into custody, hustled to a waiting car, then driven away. The conclave had been halted with the story of a mechanical failure within the Sistine Chapel affecting the air-conditioning and electrical systems. It had been deemed a possible fire hazard so the extraordinary measure of interrupting the cardinals had been ordered. Luckily, nothing had, as yet, occurred relative to voting so it was decided that the conclave would reconvene tomorrow. The press was consumed with the story, but the cardinals were sequestered inside their rooms at the Domus Sanctae Marthae, unavailable for comment, including the presiding cardinal, whom Stamm had assured would never reveal a thing.

He and Stephanie had walked with Stamm back across the grounds. The injured guard had been located and taken to the hospital. He'd been partially asphyxiated but should be okay. Both he and his company had been sworn to secrecy. Cotton still felt bad that he hadn't been able to do something for the guy sooner, but if he'd delayed any longer he would have lost Gallo. Hopefully the guard would understand.

He was tired, his face deep in stubble and in need of a shave. Some sleep and a good meal would be great, too. Stamm's office seemed the picture of efficiency. Nothing fancy. Just what he needed to get the job done. Which seemed to fit the man. No nonsense, but fully capable. Cotton was glad this was over. Time to head to southern France and a few days with Cassiopeia. Strange that his thoughts now included another person. He'd been a loner a long time. But not anymore. A woman was again part of his life.

Which wasn't a bad thing.

Stephanie entered the office. "I really appreciate what you did."

"All part of the job, and I got paid."

"Speaking of that. James Grant's body was found in the Ligurian Sea, with a hole in his head."

"Gallo?"

"No doubt."

"Lot of dead people," he said.

"I agree. This one came with a cost."

"What about the Churchill letters?"

"Disappeared. But the Knights of Malta are cooperating and conducting searches of Gallo's rooms. He most likely has them hidden somewhere. They're appalled that all this has happened. But Gallo was working rogue. He recruited his *Secreti* on the promise of Vatican positions. Proof positive that you can hire anybody to do anything."

"I understand that concept fully," he said, adding a smile.

"I know you do."

Stamm reentered the office and walked behind his desk, sitting in a plain, high-backed wooden chair, which had to be uncomfortable. But the guy seemed right at home.

"The situation is control. The Vatican press office is dealing with the conclave interruption. The cardinals are tucked away. The two guards at the railway gate have been told that this was an internal matter and that you were working with us."

"The guy I tossed from the car okay?"

"He's fine." Stamm paused. "We were lucky today. An untenable situation has been resolved. Thanks to you, Mr. Malone."

"And a guy named Luke Daniels on Malta," Cotton added.

"I've already told him the same thing," Stephanie added. "Luke is on his way here with a prisoner. They landed a couple of hours ago."

He was perplexed. "Why here?"

"It was at my request," Stamm said.

Cotton realized the implications. He was sitting on sovereign soil. Stamm intended on treating both Gallo and Hahn as Vatican prisoners and dealing with them per canon law.

"For obvious reasons, we cannot allow the Italian, Maltese, British, or . . . Americans to deal with these crimes." Stamm stood. "Would you come with me?"

They left the office and walked to the elevator. Once inside the car, Stamm inserted a key into the control panel then pushed an unmarked button. The building had four floors and a basement. The button that lit up was below the one for the basement.

"This is an old building," Stamm said. "Built in the 1970s over a part of the grottoes."

They descended and came to a stop. The elevator doors opened. They were underground, a tall, well-lit corridor stretching ahead. All painted concrete with a tile floor.

"These subterranean chambers have proven useful," Stamm said.

The cardinal led the way and they followed him toward an iron door. Stamm approached and rapped twice. A lock was released from the other side and the panel swung inward. They stepped into a long room, one side lined with bars separated by stone pillars.

Cells.

Stamm dismissed the man who'd been stationed inside.

A table stood before one of the cells. The reliquary from the Church of St. Magyar's sat on it with parchments inside and another roll lying outside. Cotton walked over to see Pollux Gallo behind bars. The cardinal and Stephanie joined him.

"These cells have been used by us for a long time," Stamm said. "Mehmet Ali Ağca was held here for a time after he tried to kill John Paul II."

Cotton couldn't help but think of the infamous Lubyanka prison in Moscow beneath the old KGB headquarters building, where political dissidents, artists, writers, and reporters had been tortured. He wondered why the Roman Catholic Church would need underground cells with restricted access.

"Is that the *Constitutum Constantini*?" he asked, pointing to the parchment.

"It is," Stamm said.

"I don't suppose you'd tell me why it's so important?"

"It proves that all of this is a fraud," Gallo said, approaching the bars. "The Roman Catholic Church is fake. Tell him, Cardinal. Tell him the truth."

He waited for more.

"There's an African proverb. *Until the lions have their historians, tales of the hunt shall always glorify the hunters.* It's so true. In our case, the glory went to those who took the lead." Stamm paused. "Constantine the Great changed the world. He first united the Roman Empire, then divided it into two parts. Emperors ruled the eastern half. Popes eventually dominated the western. But not until they heeded his advice."

Stamm pointed at the parchments.

"It's a blueprint for a new religion," Gallo said. "Instructions on how to make Christianity important. How to involve it in every aspect of people's lives. How to use it to dominate followers. How even to kill them, if necessary, to preserve its existence."

Stamm seemed unfazed. "I've read it and he's right. Constantine wanted a religion of his own making, a mechanism whereby the people were kept away from revolt. All without them, of course, ever realizing they were being dominated. Unfortunately, that never happened during his life, or in the centuries after his death. Only bits and pieces of his ideas were implemented. No grand scheme. Not until his gift was rediscovered in the 9th century. Popes had, by then, become intoxicated with ambition. They were more than religious leaders. They were military and political leaders. By the 11th century the Catholic Church became the richest and most powerful institution in the world. All thanks to Constantine's Gift."

"Is this the only copy?" Stephanie asked.

"As far as we know. The Hospitallers obtained possession of it starting in the mid-13th century. Popes were terrified that it would be revealed, so they left the Hospitallers alone and the knights kept the secret."

"Is it authentic?" Stephanie asked.

"With only a preliminary look, my experts tell me the script is Constantine's. They compared it with verified originals we have in our archives. It's in the original Latin, which is rare for one of his surviving manuscripts. We can test the parchment by carbon dating, but I'm sure it will date to the 4th century. I'm also told the ink is consistent for that time. It appears to be absolutely authentic."

Cotton had no doubt.

"Napoleon tried to find it. Mussolini tried, too, and came the closest," Stamm said. "But it stayed with the knights until 1798, when it was hastily hidden away amid the French invasion of Malta."

"What do you think kings and emperors would have done after reading it?" Gallo asked, disgust in his voice. "Realizing that divine law was not God's law. It was all man-made for their own selfish purposes."

Stamm's face never flinched. Not a muscle quivered to reveal what he might be thinking.

"What would the faithful think of the church's original sin," Gallo said. "The price we all supposedly pay for the fall of Adam and Eve. The sin of disobedience for consuming the forbidden fruit. It had nothing to do with any of that. It was just a way to create recruits straight from the womb. No need to actually convince anyone to join your church. Just decree that you're born tainted, and forgiveness comes only from baptism, administered only by the church. Of course, if anyone declines that forgiveness they rot in hell, with the devil, for all eternity. But both of those were more of Constantine's creations. None of it's real. It's all there to create fear and ensure obedience. And what better way to control people than through irrational, unprovable fear."

Stamm stood quiet and still. Finally, the cardinal said, "My guess is that there would have been no church. Christians would have continued to fight among themselves, breaking into factions, accomplishing little to nothing. If left alone they never would have collated into anything meaningful. It all would have faded away, and kings and queens and emperors would have fought each other without reservation. Civilization, as we know it, would have been vastly different. The church, for all its failings, provided a measure of stability that kept the world from spiraling out of control. Without it, who knows how humanity would have fared."

"You keep telling yourself that," Gallo muttered.

"But the world is no longer composed of illiterates," Stamm said. "People now think of religion far more skeptically than did those of the 13th century. This revelation, made today, would have a huge impact."

"Which was precisely what my brother was counting on. Your fear allowing him to get what he wanted." Gallo glared at Cotton. "That parchment is eye opening. Don't let them suppress it."

Stamm reached into his cassock and withdrew something that he displayed. "Along with this?"

The flash drive.

"Archbishop Spagna was quite thorough," Stamm said. "He found the many failings that have long existed within these walls and identified the offenders. His problem was his own ego. And the underestimation of his supposed allies."

"Spagna was a fool," Gallo said.

"Perhaps," Stamm answered. "But he was my fool."

"What are you going to do with that flash drive?" Stephanie asked.

"All of the offenders will be dealt with. Contrary to what would have happened if Spagna, or our imposter here, had succeeded with their plans."

The iron door behind them clanged opened.

Luke entered with another man in tow. Fresh off a plane from Malta.

"Head of Maltese security," Stephanie whispered to him. "His name is Kevin Hahn."

Stamm led the newcomer to a cell and locked Hahn inside. Cotton took the opportunity to shake Luke's hand.

"The gang's all here. Good job," he told him. He noticed the same shirt, shorts, and tennis shoes from Malta. "Casual Fridays?"

"It's been a long day." Luke grinned. "I hear you're riding trains now like in some *Die Hard* movie. It's good to know that Pappy still has some life left in him."

"Thankfully, it wasn't moving all that fast."

Luke noticed Gallo in the cell. "Damn. He looks just like the cardinal. Nobody would have ever known."

"What are you going to do with the *Nostra Trinità*?" Gallo asked Stamm.

"The two parchments inside the reliquary will be returned to the knights as their property. But the *Constitutum Constantini* is church property."

"So it goes into the Vatican archives?" Stephanie asked.

Stamm stepped to the table and lifted the rolled parchment. His right hand slipped into his cassock and came out without the flash drive. Instead he held a lighter. He flicked the flame to life, then set it to the brittle scroll.

Which ignited.

Stamm dropped the burning scroll to the floor, which turned to charcoal in a matter seconds.

"The matter is now closed," Stamm said.

"We're still here," Gallo called out from his cell. "We know everything. This isn't over."

Charles Cardinal Stamm stood stoic as a statue. Burning the scroll was the most animation Cotton had seen from the man. But he also detected something else in the eyes as they'd watched the parchment destroy itself.

Relief.

"Archbishop Spagna, for all of his failings, always defended the church," Stamm said. "As do I."

Cotton imagined that men like Stamm had been making hard decisions for centuries. Each one thinking he was doing the right thing. Each one wrong. A piece of history had just been destroyed. A piece that could have shed a different light on things.

"What about the flash drive?" Stephanie asked.

"I'll deal with those offenders. In my own way."

He could only imagine what that would entail. Most likely lots of private meetings, then hasty resignations.

"I'll tell the world the truth," Gallo said. "You can't burn that away. This is not over, Cardinal. There'll be a trial. I'll see you, and all of the other hypocrites in scarlet, exposed for what you are. I'll make sure the world knows what was on that parchment."

Stamm said nothing.

But Cotton realized that without the document all Gallo had was talk.

Stamm stepped close to the bars. "You underestimate me. *Defending the faith with the spilling of blood is a duty we must never abandon.*"

He could see that Gallo caught the significance of the words.

"That's what Constantine wrote," Stamm said. "All part of his gift. The freedom to kill while *defending the faith.* The church truly took that one to heart. We've killed millions."

Gallo said nothing.

"What are you saying?" Hahn said from the other cell.

Stamm stepped back so both prisoners could see him. "Neither one of you will leave here alive. There will be atonement for your heinous crimes. Two more will die in defense of the faith."

"What did I do?" Hahn asked.

"You had Laura Price murdered," Luke said.

"Along with Monsignor Roy," Stamm added. "You are as complicit as your co-conspirator."

And Stamm pointed to Gallo.

Then he gestured that they all should walk away.

"Malone," Gallo hollered. "You can't let him do this."

Luke opened the iron door.

"Malone. For God's sake. You can't allow this. We're entitled to a trial. This is murder."

They all stepped out.

But not before he heard one last loud plea.

"Malone."

He kept walking, but something from the Bible flashed through his mind.

Romans 12:19.

Vengeance is mine.

I will repay, saith the Lord.

WRITER'S NOTE

The travel for this novel involved some of the best trips Elizabeth and I have ever taken. First, we visited Lake Como and all of the sites associated with Mussolini's failed escape attempt and ultimate execution. What a spectacular corner of the world. Next, we twice ventured to Malta, which is truly an amazing place. Rome and the Vatican were locales we've explored several times before.

Now it's time to separate fact from fiction.

Mussolini's escape from Milan, in an attempt to flee to Switzerland, as recounted in the prologue, happened. Claretta Petacci died with him, both of them executed by partisans (chapters 1 and 40). To this day no one knows for sure who pulled the trigger. Many have claimed the honor, though. Most of what Mussolini says in the prologue is taken from his actual words, uttered near the end of his life but not at the villa. The addition of a representative from the Knights of Malta was my invention. Mussolini brought with him gold, currency, and two satchels full of documents (chapter 3). Only a tiny amount of the gold was ever found in Lake Como by local fishermen. The vast majority of the cache (including the documents) has never been seen since. There was an Italian trial in the 1950s where several defendants were accused of theft, but it ended abruptly, without resolution, and no further investigation was ever undertaken (chapter 19). The connection of the judge in that trial with the villa owner in the prologue is fabricated.

This story spans a multitude of fascinating locales. Lake Como, the site of Mussolini's execution, and the Four Seasons in Milan are faithfully described. In Rome the Foro Mussolini (which became the Foro Itálico), the Hotel d'Inghilterra, the Palazzo di Malta, and the Villa del Priorato di Malta are there as described. I wanted this novel to showcase Malta, so a special effort was made to include as many locations as possible. Valletta, the co-cathedral, the grand master's palace, the Grand Harbor, the Madliena and Lippija Towers, Marsaskala, St. Paul's Bay, Mdina, the Pwales Valley, the grottoes along the south shore, the tunnels beneath Valletta built by the knights (chapter 17), and the Westin Dragonara are all real. Parasailing is a popular activity off Malta (chapter 4), one I (like Luke) enjoyed. Only the Church of St. Louise Magyar's (chapter 49) is fictional, but the maiden's legend I associated with it is accurate (chapter 32). Its inner chapel is modeled after the Church of Piedigrotta in Pizzo, Italy.

The fasces (chapter 3) is an ancient Roman symbol, and the Italian National Fascists took their name from it.

Mussolini did indeed leave a mark on Rome. Many of his building projects and grand roadways still exist (chapter 29). Inside the Foro Italico (once the Foro Mussolini) stands the obelisk described in the story. It's true that the *Codex Fori Mussolini* was sealed inside it in the 1930s, a manifesto to the greatness of fascism and its leader (chapters 28, 29, 34, and 36). We know this because its text was printed in Italian newspapers at the time. Unlike in this novel, though, the codex remains sealed inside. The medal commemorating the obelisk Luke examines in chapter 29 is real.

The tale about the croissant's origins (chapter 12) is one of those delightful fables nobody really knows is true. Charlemagne's symbol, as depicted in chapter 12, was his signature. I dealt with this extensively in *The Charlemagne Pursuit*. It's a fact that anyone can be elected pope (chapter 10), but the last time that happened was 1379. *Tal-lira* clocks are all over Malta (chapter 30), as are the colorful *dghajsa* boats (chapter 32). And the legend of Skinned Tom that Luke recalls in chapter 60 is popular in east Tennessee.

The Hospitallers, now known as the Sovereign Military Hospitallers Order of St. John of Jerusalem, of Rhodes, and of Malta, or more simply the Knights of Malta, have existed for nine hundred years. The eight-pointed Maltese cross (chapter 7) has long been their symbol. All of the history attributed to the knights (chapters 4, 12, and 16), and the laws quoted in chapter 44, are accurate. Today the knights are a highly success-ful humanitarian organization. The *Secreti* once existed within them. Whether the group still does today is unknown, since the inner workings of the order are closely guarded. My reconstituted *Secreti* are purely imag-inary.

The two villas in Rome—Palazzo di Malta and the Villa del Priorato di Malta—together form the smallest sovereign nation in the world (chap-ter 16). The Villa Pagana, at Rapallo, serves as the grand master's summer residence (chapter 19). A nearby archive (chapter 21) is my invention. *Gu-vas* once dotted Malta, the underground prisons unique to the knights (chapter 14). Now only one remains, at Fort St. Angelo in Valletta. I cre-ated two more. The keyhole on Aventine Hill, at the Villa del Priorato di Malta, does offer an amazing view of St. Peter's Basilica (chapter 28). Whether that was intentional, or merely fortuitous, is unknown.

The *Nostra Trinità* (chapter 26) is totally my creation, but two of its elements, the *Pie Postulatio Voluntatis* and the *Ad Providam,* are actual docu-ments. The *Constitutum Constantini* is all mine, as is its backstory (chapter 48), though the concepts it explores—that religion is a creation of man, and the Catholic Church formulated its core doctrine for survival—are real (chapters 62, 63, and 64). Religious historians have long explored that sub-ject in minute detail.

The co-cathedral in Valletta (chapter 40) is magnificent, especially the floor, which is consumed by over four hundred marble tombs. Each one is unique and magnificent. All of the ones used in the novel exist (chapters 41, 43, and 44), including the tomb of Bartolomeo Tommasi di Cortona (chapter 45) that contains three symbols, one of them the Chi Rho that is closely associated with Constantine. There's a clock depicted on that tomb, but a real manifestation of that clock inside the cathedral is my creation (chapter 46).

Malta was besieged in 1565 by the Turks (chapter 8), but the knights resisted the invasion. That victory did in fact halt a Turkish advance across the Mediterranean and save Europe. Afterward, the island was ringed by a series of thirteen watchtowers that still stand. All of the ones mentioned in the novel exist. It was fun to incorporate them into the treasure hunt, even more fortunate that eight of them, when joined, formed a cross (chapters 47 and 48). The Apostle Paul did in fact visit Malta, bringing Christianity to the island, his exploits expressly depicted in the Bible (chapter 13).

All of the Vatican locales are accurately portrayed, including the Sistine Chapel, Apostolic Palace, museums, the Domus Sanctae Marthae, Vatican Gardens, and train station (chapters 65, 67, 68, 69, 70, and 71). The position of prefect of the Apostolic Signatura (chapter 5), which Kastor Gallo holds, is one of long standing.

The legal and political distinction between the Vatican City State and the Holy See (chapter 13) came into existence thanks to the 1929 Lateran Treaty. The curia (chapter 15) manages both, with the pope in sole command. The problem of trying to contain the curia is one of long standing. Sadly, all of the corruption detailed from Spagna's flash drive (chapters 15 and 18) is taken from actual scandals that have rocked the Holy See for the past decade. A good discussion on this subject can be found in *Merchants in the Temple* and *Ratzinger Was Afraid,* both by Gianluigi Nuzzi. The Vatican continues to deny there are any scandals or internal problems, but Nuzzi makes a good case to the contrary.

The Entity is real. It dates back five hundred years and is the world's oldest intelligence agency. The Vatican has never acknowledged that the organization exists, but its history is long and storied (chapter 20). There is also a pope's spymaster whose identity is kept secret. My label of *Domino Suo* is fictional. A terrific history on this subject is *The Entity,* by Eric Frattini.

The Churchill–Mussolini letters described in the story are a matter of legend, rumored to exist, but never seen. Mussolini having them with him when he tried to flee Italy in 1945 is my addition to their story. The letters quoted in chapter 9 are my creations, but I drew heavily on Churchill and Mussolini's own words. Churchill's signature is real. Upon assuming the office of prime minister, Churchill wanted to use Malta as a bargaining chip to keep Italy from aligning with Germany. But the British War Cabinet rejected the notion. Ultimately, Malta became critical and held out a multiyear siege by Germany and Italy, the entire country earning the George's Cross (chapter 9).

Mussolini's supposed alliance with Popes Pius XI and XII (chapter 38) happened. Neither pope was progressive. In many ways they saw eye-to-eye with Mussolini's ultraconservatism. It's a fact that Il Duce managed to keep the Catholic Church at bay. Never once did the Vatican publicly strike out against fascism. By 1939 Pius XI was ready to shift gears and do just that, but he died before he could openly challenge the government. Pius XII never carried through on that move. The full extent of Pius XII's attitudes toward Germany, the Holocaust, Nazis, and Mussolini will probably never be known. For more on this subject, take a look at *The Pope and Mussolini,* by David Kertzer.

Napoleon invaded Malta in 1798 and took the island without much of a fight (chapters 11 and 15). The knights had, by then, deteriorated to nothing. At that point Napoleon had not achieved emperor status but he was definitely scheming. Part of his grandiose plan involved eliminating the influence of the Catholic Church and the establishment of his own religion, one with himself at its head (chapter 26). To further that end, he ultimately sacked and looted the Vatican, twice. He likewise pillaged Malta, taking all of his spoils with him to Egypt where they ended up at the bottom of the sea.

The Knights of Malta were immensely unpopular on the island (chapter 25). They ruled with cruelty and arrogance. But the French were hated even worse, forced to leave in 1800 after only two years of occupation, opening the way for the British to seize control in 1814. Malta remains under the British Commonwealth, but enjoys independent nation status.

The Sator Square has fascinated me for some time (chapter 12). It's been around since Roman times and does have a connection to Constantine, but not quite the one I invented. What the five-worded palindrome means is unclear, but there is a connection to early Christians, the anagram letters forming *Pater Noster,* Our Father, with four left over for alpha and omega (chapter 26). That cannot be a coincidence. The five words can be found carved in a variety of places across Europe, and rings with the words on it can be bought (chapter 19).

The main theme of this novel centers on the origins of Christianity.

The Council of Nicaea was the first great ecumenical gathering, called by Constantine the Great (chapters 27 and 63). Nothing but mystery surrounds its proceedings since there is only one account of what happened, which is minimal at best. Even the number of bishops who attended is in doubt, though the partial list of names in chapter 54 is accurate. What we do know is that several doctrinal disagreements were settled and a statement of belief was adopted, the Nicaean Creed, which is quoted exactly in chapter 59. That creed, with only slight modifications, remains today the Catholic Church's main statement of purpose.

Constantine is regarded with great affection by the Roman Catholic Church. By the 4th century Christianity firmly existed, though it was stalled in persecution and pandemonium. Once he'd taken it under his wing, the emperor made many contributions to the new religion. Those included official sanction, privileges, money, and buildings. Among the countless churches he constructed are the Church of the Holy Sepulcher in Jerusalem and the first St. Peter's Basilica in Rome.

It's a fact that a banquet was held at the end of the Council of Nicaea where the emperor bestowed gifts on the bishops for them to take back to their individual churches. As to a document he may have presented to them, which the bishops supposedly signed—my *Constitutum Constantini,* Constantine's Gift—that never happened. Religion is a concept created by humans and long used by humans for political advantage. That's historical fact. That the ideas of original sin, heaven, hell, and the devil were church creations is accurate. And before you reject that statement as fantasy, consider what Pope Francis said in March 2018. When asked about hell and what happens to a sinner's soul, the pope said, *They are not punished, those who repent obtain the forgiveness of God and enter the rank of souls who contemplate him, but those who do not repent and cannot therefore be forgiven disappear. There is no hell, there is the disappearance of sinful souls.*

Quite a statement from the head of over a billion Catholics. Shortly after those words were published in *La Repubblica,* a leading Italian newspaper, the Vatican issued a statement claiming the article was "not a faithful transcript" and that the meeting between Pope Francis and the writer was private and not a formal interview.

But there was no categorical denial that they were said.

What many consider sacred church dogma, with divine origins, has a much more concrete and practical basis. The problem is we know precious little about the early Catholic Church and what its founding fathers actually did. What we do know is primarily thanks to one man. Eusebius, who lived during Constantine's time. He wrote so many treatises that he's come to be called the father of church history. He was also a close adviser of the emperor, and many of Eusebius's works have survived. His *Ecclesiastical History* remains a vital source material on the early church. His *Life of Constantine* is regarded as an important work but is clearly skewed by his love for the emperor.

How much of his accounts are true?

Nobody knows.

Such doubts also apply to another quotation attributable to Pope Francis, as detailed in the book's epigraph and chapter 5. There are many different versions out there, understandable given their controversial nature. Some say the variations were created by the Vatican, after the original statement was uttered, in an attempt to defuse their obvious implications and add confusion to authenticity. Again, nobody knows. Still, the comments, in any form, are odd for a pope. In closing, consider them once again:

It is not necessary to believe in God to be a good person.
In a way, the traditional notion of God is outdated.
One can be spiritual, but not religious.
It is not necessary to go to church and give money.
For many, nature can be a church.
Some of the best people in history did not believe in God,
while some of the worst deeds were done in his name.